P9-BYU-743

The Last Voice They Hear

By Ramsey Campbell from Tom Doherty Associates, Inc.

Ancient Images
Cold Print
The Count of Eleven
Dark Companions
The Doll Who Ate His Mother
The Face That Must Die
Fine Frights (editor)
The Hungry Moon
Incarnate
Influence
The Last Voice They Hear
The Long Lost
Midnight Sun
The Nameless
Nazareth Hill
Obsession
The One Safe Place
The Parasite
Waking Nightmares

The Last Voice They Hear

Ramsey Campbell

A Tom Doherty Associates Book
New York

This is a work of fiction. All the characters and events portrayed in this novel are either fictitious or are used fictitiously.

THE LAST VOICE THEY HEAR

Copyright © 1998 by Ramsey Campbell

All rights reserved, including the right to reproduce this book, or portions thereof, in any form.

This book is printed on acid-free paper.

A Forge Book
Published by Tom Doherty Associates, Inc.
175 Fifth Avenue
New York, NY 10010

Forge® is a registered trademark of Tom Doherty Associates, Inc.

Library of Congress Cataloging-in-Publication Data

Campbell, Ramsey.
    The last voice they hear / Ramsey Campbell.—1st ed.
        p.   cm.
    ISBN 0-312-86611-9 (acid-free paper)
    I. Title.
  PR6053.A4855L3   1998
  823'.914—dc21   98-10256
                                                        CIP

First Edition: June 1998

Printed in the United States of America

0 9 8 7 6 5 4 3 2 1

for Maro and Caro, David and Jen—more red! more red!

Acknowledgments

Need I say that Jenny helped as always? Tam and Matt were on my side too. This is also the place for me to thank Petra Brandt for pediatric advice, Ned Porter for insight into police matters, and Brenda Neave for details of airport security.

The Last Voice They Hear

one

When the phone rang just after midnight he was sure it must be Gail. He threw a handful of cold water in his mouth to clear it of toothpaste and unhooked the receiver from the hotel bathroom wall. "Hi," he said, and then "Hello?"

He'd already heard a newsreader's voice. "Police have confirmed they believe there is a link between the murder of a Sussex couple," she said, and more that he covered up by repeating his hello. He was beginning to think he had a crossed line when he heard the close hollow sound of a face pressed against a receiver. Then the presence went away, and the broadcast voice came forward, reading another story. "This is Geoff Davenport," said Geoff, wanting to get to the end of rather too long a day. "If I'm who you're after—"

He was holding a dead lump of clammy plastic, which he returned to the wall. He switched off the anonymous glare of the bathroom and crossed the extensive panelled bedroom to the phone by the window. Beyond the parks on the far side of Princess Street, tiers of a dozen or more windows supported the gables of the tenements of old Edinburgh against the crags and a glowing stony sky. Very faintly through the double glazing he heard along one of the tracks gathered into Waverley Station a train shaking itself awake. He felt in need of doing so. He reached for the phone to ask the hotel operator if she could trace the call, and it rang.

"Geoff Davenport."

"That was worth waiting for," said Gail, her San Francisco voice hoarse yet sweet, invigorating as a cappuccino. "I hope it wasn't a playmate who stopped me getting through before."

"My only playmate's hundreds of miles away at the end of this line."

"Better had be. Sorry to call so late. The pride of the family's working on some new teeth."

"How is he now?"

"Quiet at last. Lifting weights in his sleep."

Geoff clearly saw younger than three-year-old Paul lying face up in his cot, fists half open above his head. "Will he have any new words to surprise me with when I come home?"

"He nearly said milk today if I'm not kidding myself."

"We knew he was fond of the containers."

"Takes after his dad. So who was that on the line before?"

"Must have been a wrong number. The kind that can't be bothered to say who they are."

"Not even any heavy breathing? Poor Geoff. Edinburgh's been looking after you better than that mostly, I hope."

"Plenty of books to autograph and questions to answer."

"Any awkward ones I could have helped with?"

"When's the next series of *The Goods* to be was the popular choice."

"To which the answer was . . ."

"As far as I'm concerned, not until my favourite researcher is ready to work on it. But then I'm only the front man who was lucky enough to be asked to write the book."

"Famous presenter and best-selling writer, you mean. Maybe the channel will have brought the crèche back by the time I'm needed. And if not you're the essential one, not me."

"Without you I wouldn't be where I am now."

"So long as you aren't at the weekend, or Paul will be starting to wonder what you look like."

"Show him a tape of *The Goods*. Help, no, don't. I've done enough trying to live up to how makeup and the camera make me look without having to at home as well."

"How you look at home is how we like it. Better head for bed now so you can look your best for Glasgow. Or are you in bed?"

"Wish I were, with you."

"Sleep well instead. Take the phone off the hook if you like."

"You know I won't."

"That'll help me sleep," said Gail, and then there was a silence, since neither of them liked saying goodbye. "We'll call you tomorrow," she told him instead, and was gone.

Having talked to her allowed Geoff to enjoy his tiredness, of which there was at least a day's worth. He slipped beneath the quilt, the underside of which was several degrees cooler than the room. He seemed hardly to have groped for the light-switch when he was nothing but asleep.

The phone wakened him. As he grappled the receiver off its cradle he saw twelve on the bedside clock reduce itself to one, and the minutes turn into the blank eyes of a double zero. "Hello?" he demanded, wobbling into a sideways crouch draped with the quilt. "Who is it? What's—"

The voice awaiting him might almost have been a recording one hour old. "Police have confirmed they believe there is a link between the murder of a Sussex couple and several similar crimes still under investigation . . ."

"Damned bloody—" Geoff snarled, then was sufficiently awake to control himself. "Whoever you are, you need help. I don't think it's my kind of help you need, but if you really want to talk to me I'd appreciate it if at least—"

He wasn't expecting the sudden violent breath in his ear. It seemed to focus the mugginess of the room on him, and made the caller feel uncomfortably close. "I can hear you," Geoff said, "and I'll tell you now—"

This time the breath was measured, and he knew the caller

meant to speak. The arm that held the phone was propped on the bedside table, and Geoff used it to hitch himself into a less cramped position. As the newsreader came to the end of the story Geoff's arm began to shiver. He was about to struggle out of the posture in which he'd trapped himself when a voice spoke so close that it felt like part of him. "You didn't stop it, Geoffrey."

two

As soon as Maureen stepped out of the terminal building at Heathrow the taxi driver caught her eye. She'd barely raised her eyebrows at him when he climbed out of the car. Despite his alertness, he looked sleepy-eyed. His mouth was framed by a moustache and chin-sized beard as black as his curly hair. She guessed him to be in his mid-thirties and trying to appear older. "Where to?" he said with a hint of an East End accent as he opened the passenger door.

"Not far from Windsor. I'll just wait for my husband," said Maureen, and saw Frank butt the automatic doors aside by aiming the baggage trolley at them. "You needn't have hurried, Frank."

"I'm fine now. In you get."

"I'll put your bags in for you, sir."

"Not this one," Frank said, hauling the plastic bag of bottles out of the trolley. Maureen saw him wobble on his weakened ankle as he let go of the support. He came towards her at a stumbling run that his expression couldn't quite deny was faster than he liked, and she gripped his elbow to ease him towards the taxi. "I'm fine," he repeated to convince himself.

"Just making sure you are, that's all. We don't want the grand-children having to visit you in hospital, now do we?"

He'd only almost fallen. He'd been adjusting the bottles in the bag when he'd stepped off the travelator one pace too late and wrenched the ankle that had never been much good. As he insisted on handing Maureen ahead of him into the taxi she gave a quick kiss to the face that was still the one she'd married, even if the cheeks had grown determined to increase their girth—still the same gleam in his deep brown eyes when they met hers, the same wry grin that said there was nothing she didn't know about him. "I'm not about to lose you after all these years," she said.

The driver closed the door behind Frank, cutting off a sudden wind colder than the sea had been last night in Portugal, when Maureen and Frank had walked along the moonlit beach at midnight. In seconds the cases were loaded and the driver was at the wheel. Having driven as far as the motorway approach, he glanced at his passengers in the mirror. "Holiday, was it, or business?"

"Anniversary," said Frank.

"Our forty-first."

"Is that special, is it?"

"Twelve months more special than ruby."

"Twelve more months of her having to put up with me."

"Not too much to put up with. Nothing that's not worth it," Maureen said, patting his more than ever knuckly hand.

The driver sped the vehicle onto the motorway and over-took a horse-box that responded with a whiff of manure. "You'll be celebrating, then," he suggested, nodding in the mirror at Frank's bag.

"These are going in the cellar for next year."

"A real cellar, is that?"

"Real enough for me to have to watch out for falling down the stairs."

"Bit of a connoisseur then, are you?"

"Not just an old soak, if that's what you mean. The children and their partners help us see the bottles off."

"That's our other treat," said Maureen, "dinner with them and the children."

"Only see them once a year, do you?"

"I should say not. Christmas and birthdays and quite a few times in between. In a couple of weeks," Maureen said, by now in the mood to display family photographs if that had been practicable, "we'll have the grandchildren to stay."

The taxi veered towards the middle lane although there was no traffic ahead of it for half a mile, and Maureen shivered. The next moment the driver had compensated for the chilly gust of wind. "That'll be another treat, will it?" he said.

"For them as well."

"Especially for them if she has her way, which I can tell you she knows how to get," said Frank.

Maureen felt a little more discussed than she liked to be with someone unfamiliar. "How about you?" she asked the driver. "Married? Children?"

"I should say so."

"Just the one?" Frank said.

"A lovely wife and two perfect children, what else? I bet you'd say the same."

"Most of the time," Frank admitted, and leaned away from Maureen's vengeful elbow. "Sorry, I should have told you to come off at this exit, not the Eton one."

In the few hundred yards that were left the driver ceased overtaking and found a space in the inside lane with an unruffled deftness Maureen decided was typical of him. Five minutes later they were passing through Datchet, and in less than another five they saw Windsor Castle across the fields, against an intensely blue sky cut to fit the sharp sandy outline of the tower and battlements. "Don't go too fast now or you'll miss us," Frank said as a line of trees beside the road put an end to the view. "Just on the left where the sign on the tree is."

An abrupt curve had brought the For Sale board in sight. Maureen wasn't expecting the pang of regret with which it affected her. Though this hadn't been their first house, it was their best, to which Hilary and Arthur had kept returning from their universities, more welcome and more civilised each time. It wasn't sold yet, she was glad to think as the taxi turned along the concealed drive.

Beyond the trees that screened it from the road the front of the house was as white as the teeth of its fence, except for the doors and windows, which were even redder than the roses arching over the gate. A wood pigeon strutted along the russet tiles of the steep roof before flapping down onto the garage, a simplified miniature of the shape of the house. The bird sailed cooing towards Windsor as the taxi halted on the square of gravel cornered by the garage and the fence. "You go in," the driver said. "I'll bring your bags."

"That's kind," said Maureen, and linked arms with Frank on the pieced-together stone path. She unlocked the front door and typed a message to the alarm while Frank stayed on the porch to pay the driver. "Thank you, Mr. Denton," he said.

"Thank *you*," said the driver, apparently unsurprised at having had his name remembered from the cab. When Frank stuck out a hand he shook it, having unstudded and peeled off one of his black leather gloves, which he drew on again as he made for the gate. He backed the taxi along the drive and waved to the watching couple as he was lost to view.

"Helpful sort of chap," Frank said, stooping to the suitcases, "but you'd have jumped if he'd touched you, his hands were so cold."

"Warm heart," Maureen responded. Then, though she couldn't have said why, she discarded the old notion. "On second thoughts, I don't think so. Not him."

three

Though Jess Bennett was ten minutes early for work, the moment she walked into the small stark office Harry Adrian stood up from the switchboard as if she was late. One look at her eyes, and he confined himself to a mumble of "How're they hanging?," the feminised version of his greeting to the drivers. At least there weren't any drowned stubs in the plastic cups she had to bin from the top of the switchboard and the low table in front of the faded creaky chairs where the drivers waited for calls; indeed, both Nikos and Muhammed were smoking on the pavement beyond the reception area with its flabby armchairs and its drinks machine. "Quiet so far," Harry complained to her, and was off to whichever of his pair of women was having him that night. That was women for you, Jess thought—long-suffering until they realised they'd suffered enough. That had certainly been her with Rex the Ex.

She spun the wobbly swivel chair up to give herself some leg room, and promised herself she was going to convince Harry to replace at least that piece of furniture before it showed the rest how to collapse. She took her crossword magazine and a ballpoint from her bag before perching on the chair. Her short clingy skirt rode up her long thighs, and she used her palms to draw it down an inch. She was dressing to please herself, but it made her wish she had never dressed, let alone the opposite, for Rex.

Maybe at twenty-eight, two years of which he'd had, she was no longer young enough for him, or maybe her legs weren't long enough. Maybe he'd meant her to see him in their very first restaurant, the one she would have proposed for their anniversary next week—see him sitting in the window with the receptionist from the car showrooms where he worked, as if to show the passing crowd how spectacular her legs were. One glimpse of the way they'd been holding hands across the table and gazing into each other's eyes had been all Jess could take, but she'd marched onward, laughing and pretending to her friends she hadn't seen, pretending once it became clear they had that it didn't matter because really she'd already known. Perhaps she had indeed known she was losing him when he'd realised her growing concern for her parents must leave her less time for him.

If that showed what a self-centred bastard he was, oughtn't she to have known sooner? Maybe she had only needed to admit it to herself. By now she'd passed beyond crying herself to sleep over him and imagining suitably horrible revenges for him to suffer, and had turned the glare of her examination on herself. By now he'd given up attempting to contact her, so that she stopped thinking of him as soon as the phone rang. "Twenty-four Hour Knights," she told the microphone in her best welcoming voice.

It was a call to one of the pubs where Harry had stuck up a card by the phone, probably pocketing another firm's card as he did so. Jess didn't much care for that trick, and wouldn't do it herself, though other firms did it to them. She had just located a taxi within half a mile of the pub and sent it when the street door opened and Pete Denton appeared, patting his curly hair down with both hands. "Borrow my comb if you need one," Jess told him.

While she wouldn't have said that to most people, she'd seen how fastidious he was, not to mention tidy. His gaze found hers and his neat mouth framed a smile. "Only making sure I was presentable to the fair sex."

"When I'm here I'm just one of the boys."

"I'm sure you could never be just anything." He didn't wait for a reaction. "How's your dad?" he said.

"Doesn't know what time it is any more, specially when it's time to sleep."

"Is your mother still on top of it?"

"She's moved into my old room, but she doesn't get much sleep for listening to him. Three o'clock this morning she had to stop him phoning me to ask if I'll be there for Sunday dinner, as if I'm not always. It's not his fault. Sometimes I don't think he even knows who he is."

"What about the drug you want to try on him?"

"All the family have been at him to accept some medication, all the aunts and uncles. He mostly won't admit there's anything wrong with him, and when he does he forgets he has."

"Do you—"

"Hold on," said Jess, and listened to the headphone she hadn't raised in order to talk to him. "Five minutes," she told the caller, and informed Pete "Two loads going to the West End."

"I'll tell the boys. They've been waiting longer." He made his quiet-footed way to the street door, leaving Jess to speculate whether his interest in her parents might be partly an attempt to win her affections, to reflect that given time she mightn't altogether mind if . . . She gave Nikos and Muhammed the address as Pete rejoined her in the staff area, where he sat on the least quavery chair and rested his heels against the table. "Do I what?" Jess said.

"Think the worst part is your dad not knowing how he is."

"It is for the family, but I wouldn't like to if it was me."

"Trust me, never you."

How positively was she supposed to take that? People didn't lose their minds in jobs like this, only wore themselves down to retirement if nothing better came along. She had to wonder what a person as intelligent as she sensed he was determined not to seem was doing in their line of business. "How about your parents?" she said.

"No complaints last time I checked. I'll be off to visit the old home when I get the chance."

"Sounds like you'd rather be there than here, wherever—"

"No need to fish," he said, and she blushed for the first time in years. At least he hadn't interrupted her; the switchboard had. She ducked towards it so that her hair concealed most of her face while she answered the call. Hair tickled her tingling cheeks when she raised her head and gave him the address. "I'm on my way," he said, but delayed long enough to present her with an uncomplicated wide-eyed smile that chased away her blush. Having achieved that, he strode out like a man with a mission, and Jess released a long breath that left her giddy as a fast glass of champagne. He was wasted, she thought; his charm was so long as he had nobody—no wife, not even a girlfriend, and not a boy either. There was more to him than he admitted, and she made up her mind to discover how much.

four

Almost within sight of Oxford the train stalled as though to give the party of American tourists in Geoff's carriage ample opportunity to enjoy an English landscape unspoiled all the way to the horizon. Even the protests of the Americans failed to stir the train, though they drew a series of apologies and explanations from the senior conductor, first in person and eventually from in hiding by way of the public address. By the time the train finished inching itself into the station it was ninety minutes late. The moment it decided that since it could absolutely crawl no farther it would have to let the doors work, Geoff was on the platform and dashing for the exit, his gaze searching the crowd for his name on a placard. When a student in an Oxford T-shirt and a minimum of skirt began to wave her hands alternately above her orange crew cut he thought she'd seen a friend, and her lurching into his path didn't stop him until she said "Geoff Davenport."

"Yes."

"We could run if you don't mind. I've left my car on the lines."

The Renault to which they panted had attracted the attention of a warden, and so Geoff barely glimpsed the sunlit spires bristling like impatience rendered into golden stone against a sky frowning with bars of dark cloud before the young woman unlocked the passenger door with one hand and ran the other down his spine to urge him in. "Amelie Perkins," she said, swinging the car out fast, and took her left hand off the wheel for him to shake.

"Good to know you," said Geoff, rather more convinced of it once she returned to steering two-handed. "What's left of my schedule?"

"We've moved your signing to after the broadcast. You'll just be in time for the last part of the show. I'll make sure you are. You watch."

On the whole Geoff would have preferred not to, and perhaps the publisher's representative sensed that he would appreciate being distracted from her succession of near misses in the traffic. "St. Mary the Virgin," she declared as a gargoyle that looked about to puke flew by, and "Balliol" and "St. Giles" and then "Keble." Geoff had just about grasped how her announcements related to the parade of amber buildings when the car screeched to a halt in front of a concrete bunker that his recent travels had taught him was the form most radio stations took. As she sprinted to the glass doors ahead of Geoff, a blonde rather older than Amelie and at least twice as dressed snatched them open. "You're on next. You're on now," she called to him, scooping with both hands at the air in front of herself.

As she turned Geoff ran after her, through a reception area where the blue carpet appeared to have crept thinly up the walls. A red light was glowing above the first door in a boxy white corridor. The blonde urged him under the light and immediately through a second door into a studio. The plump pink man with a greying pony-tail gathered as tight as his wide silk tie was loose could only be Rory Whetstone, who began to talk faster as he gestured Geoff to sit opposite him. "He's here at last, the man himself. Not his fault he's late, the train ran out of puff. Geoff Davenport, my friends, is the goods, and that's the name of Britain's most successful investigative television series, which is his baby. Now he's written a book to tell us everything there wasn't room for on the screen, and he'll be signing copies at Books &

Stuff here in Oxford when we've finished with him. Now I know we've callers going mad to speak to him, so just sling those earphones over your cranium, Geoff, and pull that mike a shade closer, and you'll hear Dave from Maidenhead."

Geoff put on the earphones. The sounds of his adjusting the microphone closed around his head, and then he heard a man's voice on both sides of him. "Is that the Mr. Davenport?"

"One of many. The one who's here."

"I was starting to wonder if you existed when I couldn't hear you."

"I'm not that much of a creation of the media."

"Aren't you?"

Rory Whetstone leaned towards his microphone. "Do you have a question, Dave?"

"About the children's home you got all the publicity for."

"Where we exposed one of the worst cases of institutionalised abuse in Britain," Geoff said gently, "that had been going on for years."

"You let it go on till you'd filmed enough for your show, didn't you?"

"Some of the things we filmed we couldn't show at all. We needed the evidence to close the place down, and everything we shot went to the police."

"Thank you for calling, Dave," Rory Whetstone said, but the caller interrupted. "What clues did you have to follow, Mr. Davenport?"

"Not clues so much as information from one of the staff. The one who wore the camera that filmed the evidence you saw, if you saw it."

"I saw enough, believe me, and I imagined a lot more. So what clues are you following now?"

"I obviously can't say what we're planning to investigate next. To be honest, I'm not quite sure what you—"

"Don't you know what I mean by clues?"

"Not in the context of anything I'm involved with."

"I'm sorry you said that, Geoffrey."

Geoff saw the presenter reach for a switch. "Hold—" he said, too late. "Thank you, Dave," said Whetstone as he broke the connection. "Next we've Mary from Aylesbury. He's all yours, Mary."

"Mr. Davenport? I hope that character from Maidenhead didn't put you off. Had a bit of a bee buzzing around upstairs, that's my opinion. Can I guess which of your investigations you're proudest of?"

"It would have to be the children's home. Only it's kind of you to give me so much credit, but I'm just the face you see. There are the people who get in touch with us, and there's the team that's made *The Goods* a success ever since it was an item on someone else's show . . ."

"Sad to say that's all we've time for," Rory Whetstone announced soon enough, and having passed the transmission to the news desk, rubbed his hands at Geoff. "Solid. Enjoyed it. Can you stay for some hospitality? You'd be my excuse. Ah no, I see the lady from your publishers wanting you back," he said, and waddled round his desk to open the door for Geoff. "Tell me. The first chap we had, did you know him?"

"Why should you think that?"

"The way he spoke to you, I suppose. Didn't he call you Geoffrey before I could get rid of him?"

"People who don't know me sometimes do. I haven't been called it since I was at school."

"I won't tell you what they called me."

When Geoff let that have all the smile it seemed entitled to the presenter opened the door. Amelie Perkins spun round and made for the exit as she saw Geoff. "I'll drop you outside the bookshop," she promised or warned, and only waited for him to begin to haul his seat-belt from its slot before the car raced off. He glimpsed a park adorned with outdoor sculptures that were students', and several dons shadowed by their robes trotting in wedge-shaped formation along a lane. Then the amber buildings closed in, spiny stalagmites of shadow climbing their westward walls, and the Renault scraped a tyre on the kerb beside a stone alcove fitted with a phone a young woman in a suit was using. "You're just round the corner," Amelie Perkins urged him.

He was unbending on the pavement when the suited woman

hurried away, still talking into her mobile phone. The alcove contained only a carved message Geoff hadn't the leisure to read as he dashed into a side street whose ground floors had admitted shops. The nearest on the left was displaying arrangements of *The Goods: The Inside Story*, together with an image of his face half as tall as himself. A good few dozen people were standing about inside the shop, and the sight of Geoff enlivened several, one of whom limped swiftly to meet him. "Geoff Davenport. Martin Hennessey. So glad."

The bookshop manager was younger than Geoff, but appeared to have lost some hair in staying that way. "If you'd like to sit with your books I'll bring a drink," he said, then detoured to the cash desk. "Nearly forgot. We were asked to give you this."

It was a sealed envelope that might have contained a greeting card. Geoff had to squint at it to convince himself the handwriting on the front said "Mr. Davenport." As the crowd in the shop began to form itself into a queue at the table loaded with his book he slit the flap with a paper-knife the assistant at the cash desk handed him. The envelope contained a photograph. "Who left this, do you know?"

"Do you recall, Simon? I know it was weeks ago."

"Some bearded guy who was in and out like that," the assistant said. "Sorry for the scribble on the front, Mr. Davenport. Everybody says I ought to be a doctor."

"Maybe he's said who he is inside," Geoff said, having seen the last letter of a word inked on the back of the photograph. When he extracted the square of cardboard, however, he saw a solitary word in capitals so stiffly formed he was sure they had been written wrong-handed. The noises of the bookshop sounded as though they were reaching him through headphones, and he didn't know how long he stood there before turning over the photograph.

five

Maureen and Frank had finished gardening and were lying on the patio when the doorbell rang. The noise probed Maureen out of a snooze composed of the afternoon sunlight, the scents of flowers and dug earth, the electric buzz of a bee that kept sounding as though contact with a blossom had fused it, the intermittent clatter of trains on the line through Windsor. Frank only groaned, and neglected to disagree when she said "I'd better see who it is." She pushed herself carefully off the recliner, a twinge in her right leg threatening to turn into a spasm that would kick over the remains of her gin and tonic, and groped her way into the kitchen.

Entering the shade of the house was a little too much like starting to go blind. She rested a hand on a cool stone surface and sent herself into the hall. A dozen increasingly confident steps took her to the front door. She was expecting the milkman, but the man on the path was nobody she knew. "I'm sorry to trouble you," he said.

"You aren't yet," said Maureen, wondering if he was a door-to-door evangelist—he had the wide-eyed direct gaze, the scrubbed fresh face. "What can we do for you?"

"I saw your sign, and I was wondering if I could make an appointment for my wife and myself to view the house. Or if I need to make it with your agent, could you tell me where their office is?"

"They're friends. They don't mind if we arrange things direct. Whereabouts have you come from, Mr. . . . ?"

"Norton. My name, that is. We live in Cambridge at present, me and my wife."

"Quite a long way to come."

"I'm here for an auction. I'm sure the journey will have been worth my while."

"We've friends who have picked up some bargains. What I was meaning, though, it's a long way for you to come back with your wife."

"It won't be if it's the kind of house she'd like."

His gaze flickered past her as she heard Frank stumble into the kitchen. As she saw Norton welcoming the knowledge that she wasn't on her own she said "Would you like to come in for a look? Then you won't have had a wasted journey if it turns out not to be the kind of thing you're looking for."

"I'm already sure it will be."

"Frank, this is Mr. Norton. He's scouting houses for his wife, and I said he could have a prowl now."

"Always glad to see a friendly face. Mr. Norton, will you have a drink to take with you on the tour?"

"Thanks, but maybe later."

"Whatever appeals. Where are you parked? Do you want to come up the drive?"

"I'm better off leaving it. I'm well out of the way."

"You'd have to get used to our drive if you lived here. She won't admit it, but Maureen's always worried we'll be killed one day coming out on that bend."

"Let's hope I'll be saving you from that."

"Well, here's where the best meals of my life have come from," Frank said, and waited in the kitchen while their visitor, having closed the door, followed Maureen along the hall. "Mostly fitted, so it'll be staying, but I don't suppose it's your territory, is it? The son keeps telling me I should learn to cook. Too old to change, that's my excuse."

"You haven't heard me proposing to trade you in," said Maureen, and gave his cheek as lingering a stroke as seemed polite in company. "Now here's the dining-room with a hatch through from the kitchen for whoever does the cooking, Mr. Norton."

"It's seen a good few birthdays and Christmas dinners, that table has. All the furniture will be leaving with us, you understand."

"I imagined that would be your plan. The house is all I need."

"And here's where we while away our evenings," Maureen said. "The television's that big because of my eyes."

"She reads a lot, and I try to beat that board at chess. You'd think I'd be able to see further ahead than a computer chip, wouldn't you, Mr. Norton? Do you play?"

"You should see me."

"Maybe we'll have a challenge later."

"I expect Mr. Norton may be wanting to hurry home to his wife, Frank."

"I always leave myself time to spare," said their visitor. "I'm in the mood for a game."

Having concluded that didn't mean an immediate session at the chessboard, Frank led the way up the stripped pine stairs. "Four bedrooms. More than we need these days, sad to say."

Maureen hung back while the men sidetracked into the guest rooms which had been Hilary's and Arthur's bedrooms. However many words a picture was supposed to be worth, a room could be worth that many times a picture, and you couldn't take rooms with you. Before she and Frank moved, and before the rooms were left bare of the beds and the rest of the items that were part of the children's growing up, she was going to sit in each room for as long as it took her to remember all they meant to her. She caught up with Frank in their bedroom, where he was stretching an almost steady hand towards the distant view of Windsor Castle. "Looks like the neighbours are out. If you're lucky you may see the Queen to wave to."

"Or her old mum," said Maureen. "Mr. Norton, have you any relatives round here?"

"Do you think I should have?"

"I'm sure I don't know. It's just that you remind me of someone, and I can't think who."

"It'll come to you. But no, I haven't any relatives unless I can call you two some."

"I've always thought it would be exciting to find you'd a relative you didn't know you had," Maureen said, feeling obscurely sorry for him. Once the bathroom and fourth bedroom had been viewed she followed the visitor downstairs. He was flexing his fingers as if for balance, and his light tread put Frank's and her heavy descent supported by the banister to shame. Behind his right ear she noticed a single curl that had eluded a determined brushing of his sleeked-back hair. That was threatening to arouse her maternal instinct for tidying such details when Frank said "Any children, Mr. Norton?"

"What about them?"

"I was wondering if you had any, that was all."

"Why should you do that?"

Maureen would have decided her curiosity was unwelcome, but Frank ploughed on. "With you looking for a house this size it struck me you must be thinking of children."

"They're what I'm thinking of all right."

That silenced Frank until he reached the hall. "Do go in and sit, Mr. Norton. You didn't say no to a drink."

"Perhaps he will now he's driving, Frank."

"Don't let me intrude if you're expecting visitors."

"We aren't, are we?" The milkman wasn't worth mentioning. "I just want to be sure you get home safe," Maureen said.

"I always do," said Norton, seating himself in one of the massive leather armchairs, and nodded at the photographs that occupied the shelves of the Welsh dresser. "Are all these yours?"

"All except the top shelf are our son and daughter. The top shelf are their children, but we like to think those two are ours as well."

"I know exactly what you mean."

"So was there a drink you would like?" Frank said.

"I don't suppose there might be any wine."

"You're in the right house, my friend. Red or white?"

"Red's my colour."

"My feeling too. White's for the ladies, especially the German stuff," Frank said, and performed an exaggerated flinch, though Maureen was yards away. "Let me find something to impress you with. Oh, would you like to see?"

Norton didn't move or blink. "See what, grandfather?"

"We ought to have included it in the tour. I don't know what use you would have for it, but we've a cellar."

"I'd like to see that, certainly. Shall I come down with you?"

"Do."

"I may as well join you," said Maureen, anxious to be there in case Frank lost his footing on the steps. She moved between him and their visitor, giving him an apologetic pursed smile to which he responded by widening his eyes, the opposite of a wink. They stayed widened while Frank muttered at his pockets until he located his keys to unlock the door in the side of the staircase.

The door swung into a wedge of darkness that put on its whitewash as Frank flicked the light-switch, and Maureen remembered the day ten-year-old Hilary had tumbled all the way down the steps after the children had been forbidden to use the cellar in their games of hide-and-seek. She remembered eight-year-old Arthur in tears at the thought of having killed or at least permanently injured his sister; Hilary opening her eyes as though she'd lost the knack, so that when the doctor had diagnosed only mild concussion Maureen had had to remind herself how to breathe; the family dinner after the recriminations, when the four of them had simultaneously fallen silent with relief at still having one another; her and Frank making love that night, a passionate restatement of their life together . . . Life moved on, and now she was trying unobtrusively to watch out for Frank. She did without a sigh as he set foot on the stony floor.

The wine-racks, rather less than half full, occupied the walls opposite the steps and to the right of them. Beneath the steps, and cut off from most of the glare of the unshaded bulb, the gas and electricity meters whispered and clicked to themselves. Norton halted on the bottom step, his fingertips splayed on his thighs. "I don't see how this could be improved upon," he said.

"I take it you're serious about your wine, then. Come and see what you'd like me to open."

"I'm serious," said their visitor, but had made no move when, adding the resonance of the floorboards above their heads to itself, the doorbell rang.

"Excuse me, Mr. Norton. You'll have to come down to let me up."

"Who's that going to be?" Frank complained.

"The milkman, I should think."

Norton moved aside at once, and rested his fingers on her elbow to help her on her way. His hand felt not much warmer than she knew the stone floor to be. "Hurry back, grandmother," he said. "We'll be waiting."

She didn't altogether care for his familiarity, and she had the impression he didn't want it to be liked. Perhaps it was his way of protesting at having been reminded of whatever children meant to him—some problem with conceiving them, she guessed. She was steadying her climb with one hand on the banister when Frank said "So what are you going to be up to in Windsor, Mr. Norton?"

"He was here for an auction, Frank."

"What kind was that?"

"A car auction," their visitor said.

"I didn't know we had those," Frank admitted, and Maureen had to agree with him. She supposed they were new, and somewhere outside Windsor. She climbed out of the cellar and fetched her handbag from the front room before tramping to the front door.

The slow stocky placid milkman was indeed there, poking change about in the palm of his hand. His van was parked opposite the drive, hardly the safest place. "Was there a car in your way?" she said.

"When was that?"

"It doesn't matter. I just thought . . ." If she went on she would seem critical of his parking, and besides, she wanted to get back to Frank and their visitor. "Don't let it bother you. An old lady's prattling. Thanks, and see you next week."

"That you will," he said, and having handed Maureen her

change, used the hand to scratch his head. He continued to attempt to enliven his brain that way while he completed his deliberate progress to the gate in the rosy arch. "Bye," Maureen called as he slammed the gate with a firmness she was always intending to ask him to moderate. She closed the door and hurried to toss her bag onto the nearest armchair.

The men had ceased speaking, no doubt rather than shout over her footsteps. "Everything all right down there?" she called.

"It will be once you join us," Norton said.

Presumably the selection of a bottle was preoccupying Frank. Maureen started down, only to realise she couldn't see him. Their visitor was facing her from the corner formed by the wine-racks, his hands behind his back, his eyes unblinkingly wide. "Where is he?" she demanded, intending her briskness for Frank to answer.

Norton nodded at the area beneath her—his whole body seemed to unstiffen itself towards it. "Just there."

She grasped the banister with both hands and leaned over, and saw an unopened bottle of Cotes de Roussillon standing by the rack opposite the meters. "Frank, what are you playing at?" she demanded, a glance beneath her feet having shown him crouched under the steps. "Save playing hide-and-seek for when the grandchildren come, and not down here either."

She heard movement below her—the restlessness of the meters. At the limit of her hearing the milk-van receded into inaudibility. She held onto the banister and clattered down the steps, hoping that gave Frank a headache. "You're all right, aren't you?" she demanded, knowing that he must be, because otherwise their visitor would have gone to him. "Really, sometimes you're worse than the grandchildren. What must Mr. Norton think of you?"

Norton brought one hand from behind his back and took hold of his mouth and chin, miming pensiveness. The chill of the stone floor insinuated itself through Maureen's shoes as she hauled herself around the end of the banister and saw Frank.

He wasn't crouching in front of the meters; he was collapsed against them, his right cheek flattened by the electricity dial. A stripe of light through the gap between two steps bandaged his closed eyes and displayed a zero clicking into sight beside his face.

The rest of him was dark as the space beneath the steps—extinguished. Part of the darkness was moving, worming over the section of the meter between his head and right shoulder. It was a trickle of liquid from the concealed side of his head.

Maureen's hands went out helplessly to him, then found themselves slapping the edge of the steps as faintness raced through her from the top of her head, parching her mouth and unstringing her body. She swallowed and struggled to be capable of ducking under the steps. Then Norton started to hum to himself, and she twisted her head round to him.

He was still in his corner. He'd stretched his forefinger along his upper lip and was covering his chin with the remainder of his fist, framing an eager expectant smile. As their eyes met, he drooped his eyelids. At once she knew where she had previously seen him, and that he was wearing a glove and humming "Here Comes the Bride." He saw her recognise him, and brought his other gloved hand into view as he strode very fast across the cellar. He was holding a stained bottle-opener—not just an opener, a knife fat with blades and tools. He closed it deftly and slid it into a pocket of his jacket, producing a rustle of plastic. He was within reach of her now, and she tried to make a claw of her right hand, to defend herself or attack him for whatever he'd done to Frank. But he uncovered his face and darted past too swiftly for her wild swipe to make contact, though it nearly overbalanced her. "Time to put your lipstick on, grandmother," he said, and clubbed her with the bottle he'd snatched from the floor.

six

The train out of Portsmouth was only two carriages long. Geoff shared his table with an elderly couple and his seat with their granddaughter, a little girl in a green velvet dress, who mightn't have fidgeted so much if they hadn't kept telling her what to do. "Read your book now," she was told as the suburbs thinned out, and not much later "Play your game" and "Draw on your pad" and eventually "Look out of the window." Geoff was closer to it—to houses shuttling past, fields that took longer and dragged more of the sky encrusted with white clouds as they went, bridges that pierced the train with the shrill rush of itself—but saw nothing to distract him from his thoughts. "Would you like to sit by the window?" he said.

"That's kind of the gentleman, isn't it, Jeanette?" said her grandmother. "What do you say?"

The little girl would have been entitled to point out that she already had while she was being told to, but repeated "Thank you."

"That's our girl. Would you like to do as the gentleman says?"

"Climb over me if you want," said Geoff, a suggestion that earned him a wary look from both oldsters and the little girl a preemptive rebuke from her grandfather. "We know we don't put even feet as pretty as ours on the seats, don't we."

Once she was swaying in the aisle with her grandfather holding her hand like a dance partner too weary to stand up, Geoff made way for her. As the train flung him onto the section of seat she'd vacated, he felt the end of its arm catch the contents of his jacket pocket. He disengaged it while the little girl cleared the table in front of him as though inviting him to lay it there. He couldn't help feeling discovered as he looked up to find the old lady watching him. "Thank you," she mouthed, and said aloud "We're going up to London while our em you em and dee ay dee—"

"While mum and dad what, gran?"

"Look out of the window now like a good girl." The old lady twirled one hand in a circle above her own scalp, wriggling the fingers, and Geoff was close to deciding she was miming some form of insanity when he grasped that she was picturing a party hat. "While they get my party ready," the little girl cried.

"I hope you're as clever as that at school," her grandfather said. "Let's all look out of the window. I spy with my little eye something beginning with I."

Since presumably Geoff wasn't expected to play, he risked slipping the envelope out of his pocket. He was inserting a finger and thumb into the paper slit when the little girl said "Ivy and an ice cream van. May I see?"

There surely couldn't be two correct answers, thought Geoff, but any hope that the grandfather might say so was misplaced: the old couple had joined their granddaughter in gazing at the envelope. "I expect someone sent the gentleman a card," the old lady said.

"Is it your birthday too?"

"No, it isn't that." Geoff was willing someone to tell her to stop bothering him, but the pleasantness with which he felt bound to respond appeared to be all too convincing. "It's a photograph," he said.

"What of?"

He didn't have to show her or even to answer; he could shove the thing back in his pocket and let them all think him as rude as they liked. The prospect of being trapped for several hours in the midst of that opinion of him was more than he could take, however. He pulled the photograph out of the envelope and slapped it face up on the table. "You tell me," he said.

The little girl leaned over and put one finger almost to a nostril before recalling that she was in company, then giggled and shook her head. "What's it meant to be?"

Her grandparents had been narrowing their eyes at it, and craned in unison over the table, only for a lurch of the train to throw them back. "May we?" the grandmother said, stretching out a bony hand until Geoff turned the photograph towards her. Her frown and her husband's stayed in place, expressing bewilderment now. "I can't make it out," the old man said.

The little girl reclaimed it and turned its edges to her one after another. "It's just a bit of a room."

"That's all," said Geoff, sliding it into the envelope and the envelope into his pocket.

"But what's it for?"

"Your turn to spy," her grandfather said firmly, so that Geoff wondered if it was meant to divert her from further contact with him. Perhaps his haste had betrayed that more was wrong than he was pretending. "I spy with my little eye something beginning with X," the little girl said, her last few words and the pauses between them extending themselves in order to creep up and pounce on the letter, and Geoff was tempted to join in, because the game was altogether less daunting than the one occupying his thoughts—but he had no time for distractions now. Before he reached home he had to decide how much of the truth he could bear to tell Gail.

seven

Five minutes after Gail had flown him back into the playpen Paul, having thoroughly twirled the dial of the activity board clamped to the bars, threw his picture book across the dining area and clambered in pursuit. "Out," he declared.

"You sure are. I can't imagine anybody giving you an argument. Don't forget there's In as well. How about practising that to give your father even more to be impressed with and the chef a chance to fix tomorrow's dinner?"

Paul was supporting himself on the rail of the playpen as though rehearsing how to lean against a different kind of bar, and favouring her soliloquy with a bemused grin. Apparently her conversation wasn't to his taste, because he toddled at a speed that more than compensated for any unsteadiness to his Fisher-Price garage and plucked a car off the roof. "Now where might that be racing off to?" said Gail, and "No" in the tone of a question as he veered towards the television. When he dropped to his knees in front of the empty mouth of the video recorder she repeated the word in her best voice from the skies, which sent him fleeing back to her. "I think you can go in your chair with a biscuit," she said, "and work on chewing yourself another tooth."

"Kit," he agreed with enthusiasm.

"Biss-cuit," Gail pronounced, earning herself a seven-toothed grin but no other response. She sailed him through the air to the dining-table, where she strapped him into his high chair before ceremoniously unwrapping him a rusk. As he set about gnawing she returned to the kitchen and her much-requested Chinese marinade, and was adding more wine from the box in the towering refrigerator when the phone trilled.

"Fo."

"Bet if that's MetV they aren't saying they've brought the crèche back so you can come to work with me, and if they aren't, screw them."

"Skoo."

"Yes, well, I don't think we need to work on that. You didn't hear me say it, all right? What's that in your hand and all over your fat little messy chin? It's a . . ."

"Skoo."

She gave up trying to conceal her amusement in the midst of her attempts to look reproving. Just in time to beat the answering machine, she went to the knee-high bookshelf between the dining area and the rest of the pale expansive room that seemed to have stored the light now the sun had moved behind the bridge over the Thames. "Hello," she said into the white sliver of a receiver.

She heard an enormous hollow voice saying it was sorry, and then Geoff. "I'm at Waterloo at last. Hello."

"Do you want to say that to someone else who'd love to speak with you, or shan't I say who you are?"

"Best wait. Spent nearly all my change in the buffet while we were nowhere for an hour."

"How about we pick you up at Hammersmith?"

"That would be—" At this point the phone decided he'd had what he'd paid for and turned him into a monotonous two-note chord, but she'd heard his enthusiasm. "We'll fetch your father and dine out tonight," she said.

She called to book a table, then she dabbed at Paul's generously decorated protests and demonstrations of how well he could say no, and managed to trap his feet in socks and shoes before releasing him from his chair. "Now I think Mr. Diaperless had better prepare himself for the road," she said, and carried him upstairs to save time, his chubby bare arms warm around her neck, pressing against her cheek his face that smelled like milk. Once she'd unbuttoned his overalls in the bathroom on the middle floor he yanked them down and demonstrated how improved his aim was since last month. "Enty," he announced.

He was doing well, she told herself. Even if some of his friends had more to say, not all of them were out of diapers at less than three years old or even off the breast. She helped him to button himself up and walked downstairs ahead of him, his breaths soft and warm on the back of her neck.

She set the alarm and held his rebellious hand while she locked the front door. As she raised him to his lookout on her shoulders a bus stuffed with children bound for Mortlake cruised by like a condensation of the imminent rush hour. Paul objected and twisted his head round when, having passed under the railway bridge, she turned away from the Thames, up the side street where the retired myopic teacher let the Rover have her parking space. At the sight of his personal seat in the back, however, Paul almost squirmed out of her hands around his waist with eagerness to be off.

Two minutes' driving took her through Barnes, past the pond on the green and Paul's favourite street with its abundance of lions, sprouting on the gateposts and the roofs among stone eggs and buds. None of this provoked a word, nor the drive along Castelnau past the reservoirs to Hammersmith Bridge, which had been painted bright as any of his toys. As she drove beneath the flyover beyond it, the reason for their journey must have struck him. "Daddy," he said, clearer than she'd ever heard.

"You got it."

In another minute they saw Geoff outside the station entrance, one foot on his suitcase, one hand massaging the back of his neck while he closed his eyes and opened them again. Gail had pulled up where only taxis were supposed to before he noticed her.

"Sorry," he said, and dealt his wide forehead a slap that almost connected. "Far away."

"So long as you're back with us."

He slung the case into the trunk and sat beside her. "No risk there," he said, and leaned over from tugging out his seat-belt to kiss as much of her mouth as he could reach.

Gail sent the car around the square of roads that returned it to the bridge. As the Thames shimmered on both sides of the Rover she said "Was it harder than you figured, being shown off?"

"Not as hard as your week, says a fiver."

"Exhausting isn't hard, it's just exhausting. One good night's sleep would fix that. Ten says you've had a week of those."

He turned away to dig in his hip pocket. "I won't argue. Do you want it now?"

"I'll take it in trade," said Gail, and then "Anything we should discuss?"

He widened his eyes, which were almost as luminously dark as Paul's. "What makes you ask that?"

"Don't turn on your eyes at me while I'm driving. I was wondering how it feels not to come home just to me any more."

"That's what kept me going all my lonely week."

"Poor solitary Geoff. We're so glad to have you back that we thought we'd eat out to celebrate."

"You've booked somewhere."

"The Italian by the river. Don't you want to?"

"It'll be fine. Portable Davenport will have a fuss made of him. When I've dumped the luggage why don't we go along to the pub," Geoff said, and it was clear to Gail he was trying to find somewhere that would help him talk.

She halted the car at their front door to let him dump his case out, then she drove the Rover to its space. At the main road she met Geoff and the stroller, into which they managed to persuade Paul with the promise of a fizzy drink. While Geoff bought the round she sped Paul to a table by the river, along the far margin of which a heron was skimming parallel with the wake of a rowing team. "Welcome home," she said as Geoff sat on the bench opposite her and clinked his glass of wine with hers, "only that's where you're going back next week, right?"

"You can't actually go back, can you? Things change, except up here." He rested his chilly glass of white wine against his forehead. "Maybe there as well, particularly if you want them to."

"Why would you want to change—"

"Dink."

"That's right, babe, drink," said Gail, and refilled the lidded cup. "What are you saying you've changed, Geoff?" she said as Paul set about sucking and chewing the toothmarked mouthpiece.

"What's your impression of my childhood?"

"That you were spoiled like only children tend to be. Maybe more than someone sitting not too far away from us, since your parents were way older than the average, only I'm not saying spoiled in a bad way. I remember wishing I could have met them to thank them for making you."

Geoff was rolling his cold glass across his forehead. He brought the glass down to swig from before he raised his eyes to her. "Was I wrong?" she said.

"Not exactly. In a way we can even thank them for my career. But . . ."

"Why do I get the feeling that's suddenly such a big word?"

"I've never lied to you—at least, I hope you won't think so. I wanted to forget, and being able to help people was one way of forgetting." He frowned at Paul as if to reassure himself he wasn't being overheard, but the toddler was watching ducks march past in the mud at the edge of the river. "Not lying isn't the same as telling the truth," Geoff said.

He put down his glass in order to take Gail's hand, a gesture that would have made her feel closer to him if his eyes hadn't grown distant. "There was something I never told you I had," he said.

eight

When the first pub off the motorway came into view Becky started to tug at her seat-belt. "Can't I go in there, daddy?"

"You can wait for ten more minutes. We're nearly at grandma and granddad's," Melanie said, but as the Volvo reached the entrance to the pub car park Arthur steered it in. "You may as well see if they'll let her," he said to his wife. "I'll wait here."

"Come along then, young lady. Just don't be asking for a drink to replace the one you're bursting to get rid of."

She was pretending that nothing was wrong for Becky's sake, thought Arthur. Perhaps nothing much was. Just because his parents hadn't answered when he'd phoned last night to confirm they were ready for Becky to stay—just because there had been no response when he'd called this morning . . . He wished he knew if Hilary had spoken to them, but she would have left near dawn to bring his little nephew up from Devon. Arthur was beginning to regret not having made his two-hour journey by himself. When Melanie and Becky reappeared, the five-year-old skipping to demonstrate her relief, he said "Do you want to come in while I give the phone another go?"

"We can't very well without buying, do you think? Which wouldn't do much for my credibility after my stern warning."

"I thought if I can't get through you could both stay here while I go and see."

"They did something like this once before, remember? They were so busy shopping for treats for the children they forget to be in to be called."

"Yes, and I remember how upset they were at having worried us. Could they do it twice?"

"They are a couple of years older."

"There is that." He didn't want Becky distressed, that was all, but why should she be? "Let's see if Hilary and her lot have arrived," he said, and drove onto the road to Windsor.

Though the trees beside the road did their best to catch the sun, they couldn't prevent it from finding his eyes. As he reached the curve off which his parents lived, light flooded his vision and he had to brake, harder when a woman in a sports car and dark glasses swerved impatiently around him. At first he didn't understand why Becky said "It's gone."

"They won't have yet, Beck," said her mother.

Arthur narrowed his eyes and saw, as he braked again in preparation for the sharp turn into the drive, that the For Sale sign had been removed from the tree, leaving a pair of metal bands wrapped around the trunk. As the Volvo swung into the drive it found the shadows of the trees, and the shade let him see the house. The ground-floor curtains were drawn.

His parents could have overslept, perhaps after seeing off one bottle too many. A prolonged crunch of gravel under rubber was grinding its way into his ears when Melanie touched his arm. "Look, there's a note."

A gleam like light on a knife-blade—the sun flaring in a milk bottle on the doorstep—helped draw his attention to the piece of paper behind it. As he halted the car on the broad square of gravel in front of the garage Melanie sprang her seat-belt and ran along the garden path. She stooped to the note, then shaded her eyes to see that Becky was still in the car. "Beck, I'm sorry, but it looks as if they aren't here. It says no milk until further notice."

"Stay there a moment, Becky," Arthur said, and only that until he was well on the path. "That isn't like them, Mel, shooting off without calling Hilary or me."

"You see what you make of it, then."

She sounded less sure of herself than she had before. As she handed him the note her eyes wavered. Perhaps she was troubled by the unsteadiness of the handwriting, but he saw at once that more was wrong. "Neither of them wrote this."

"I was starting to wonder. What do you think we'd better . . ."

Her gaze had strayed to the vertical strip of frosted glass beside the front door. She stepped aside so quickly he thought she was flinching from the sight beyond the glass, but she was unblocking his view. All he could distinguish were several blurred objects, their shapes as regular and similar as their sizes were various, lined up along the floor of the hall. He dropped to his haunches and dug his thumbs into the letter-slot low on the door. The metal flap squealed inwards, and the spectacle beyond it pinned him in his crouch for too many seconds before he managed to stand up.

He saw himself reaching for the doorbell as though the hand had very little to do with him or his thoughts. The hairs on the backs of his fingers glared like wire, like the electricity of his nerves made visible. He heard the shrill note of the bell penetrate the house and eventually, when he let his hand fall, die away. Then the house was silent as a block of stone. "Can you keep Becky in the car?" he said. "I'm going to see if there's any way in at the back."

"You think . . ."

"I don't want to think," Arthur said, hurrying around the side of the house. The grass between it and the garage looked shaggier than usual, and had been invaded by a solitary dandelion on which he trod before it could produce seeds. He shuddered at the squelch beneath his heel as he ran to the kitchen window.

The room looked dusty with the angle of light on the window. The only sign of life beyond the glass was a torpid wasp crawling along the white-tiled windowsill. The back door was locked and doubly bolted. He stepped back and peered up at the uncurtained window of his parents' bedroom. "Mother. Dad," he shouted, feeling unexpectedly young and vulnerable, not having called them

anything since he couldn't remember when. There was no response, and he tramped past the garage again, staring about for any
item he could use to break into the house.

A chunk of the crazy-paved path was loose. He dug his fingers
under it, soil gritting beneath his nails. He showed a palm to Becky
and her mother, to reassure them if possible and to keep them in
the car, and tried to use his body to conceal what he was about to
do. As he smashed the frosted glass, however, and enlarged the
hole so as to reach the latch, he heard Becky's dismayed voice and
Melanie doing her best to calm her. As soon as the door was edged
open he withdrew his hand and stepped through the smallest gap
that would admit him, and pulled the door shut.

He had to step over the For Sale sign that lay on its face just inside. Beyond it six pictures, three of Becky and the others of his
nephew, had been dropped face up. The glass on every one of
them was smashed—trampled, he somehow knew. The line of
them led to the door to the cellar. It was partly the fear that Becky
might run to the house to discover what had happened to her
grandparents that sent him to the cellar door.

It wasn't locked. The knob wobbled in its socket as he pushed
the door inwards. The highest of the steps creaked as he trod on
it and groped for the light-switch. His fingers closed around a
dangling wire and jerked back. The switch had been wrenched off
the wall—was no longer even attached to the wire. He clutched
the rough banister and peered down into the blackness. Something large was lying on the floor beside the steps. By narrowing
his eyes until his cheeks ached he was able to identify a body—no,
two bodies huddled together.

A stench that combined shame and terror rose from the dark,
and he recoiled into the hall. Did his parents keep a flashlight in
the house? He had no idea where, and searching would only delay
him. He sprinted out of the house, leaving the door just ajar, to the
Volvo. As he flung the glove compartment open and grabbed the
flashlight Becky, seated on her mother's knee and clinging to her,
shot him a pleading look, but it was Melanie who spoke. "Are—"

"I can't say," Arthur blurted, trying to apologise with his eyes
for his abruptness before he fled to the house. He dug his thumb

into the rubber switch of the flashlight as he came abreast of the yawning entrance to the cellar. The beam swooped over the white-washed wall and down the steps, and picked out fragments of the light-switch strewn across the floor. Closing both hands around the flashlight to keep it steady, he pointed it over the banister.

His parents were huddled on the bare stone, his mother on top, their faces pressed together. He couldn't help growing hot with an embarrassment he found inappropriate even before he re-alised they were fully clothed. His first confused thought was that they had at least been able to embrace, and then he saw how his mother's hands were thrusting at his father's shoulders, her nails digging into them. From where he stood he couldn't see the faces. He took a step down, and another. He was halfway down when he began to understand what had been done to them, and the flash-light almost slipped from his hand as the darkness seemed to im-plode into his skull.

nine

Rain."

"A train, sure enough, and an upside-down one under the bridge." As the train and its reflection made for London, Gail found Paul's small warm hand and hid it in hers. Above them the pub was filling up with late-afternoon drinkers, but the Davenports still had the tables by the river to themselves. Soon Geoff carried another trayful of drinks down the steps, and returned the tray to the bar before resuming his seat opposite Gail. His eyes were asking her to give him some idea how she felt, but the best she could do just now was to ask for more information. "You haven't told me his name."

"Ben. That's what he liked to be called, but they always called him Benjamin."

"You mean that was another way they got at him."

"One of the hundreds, like telling him he wasn't my brother."

"He wasn't quite, was he? You didn't have the same father. But your parents saying that, it must have affected him and you as well."

"I knew it wasn't fair as far back as I can remember." Geoff risked a smile at her and laid his hands palms upwards on the table. "I do appreciate how you're taking this, I hope you realise. I know it must be a shock."

"I'm not shocked. Maybe a bit disappointed that you didn't tell me sooner, but I see it upset you. I know the person you are now, that's what counts. It can't change that, can it?"

"You'd hope not."

"So carry on."

"What do you want to hear?"

"Everything, what else? Now you've started I want to end up knowing there's nothing you've kept from me. Tell me the single worst thing."

Geoff glanced at Paul, who was busy gnawing the mouthpiece of his cup, and looked down at his hands on the table before turning them over. "For him it must have been when they sent him away."

"Because they split the two of you up, you mean?"

"Because of where they sent him."

"Boarding school? Not a home."

"My mother's parents."

"Couldn't his father . . ."

"She was always telling him his father hadn't wanted him. When I got older I wondered if her having custody of Ben was a way of scoring off his father. I wouldn't be surprised if she'd told him Ben didn't want to see him. Ben told me they hadn't been divorced a year when his father went off to New Zealand to live with another woman and raise a family, but even before that mother was forever finding ways to stop Ben spending a day with his father. And once they'd gone Ben never even saw a card from him. It didn't occur to me at the time, and I don't know if it did to Ben, but chances are she would have destroyed anything he sent. Do you want me to stop?"

"Of course not, Geoff. She just sounds so unlike the mother I thought you had."

"I'm sorry," he said, several apologies in one. "That's because I only talked about how she and my father were to me."

"I'm not blaming you. So your grandparents . . ."

"If it's possible, they thought less of him than my parents did."

"Poor Ben," Gail said, not that it seemed adequate. "So really he only had you."

"I'm not so sure he felt he did."

"I'm sure you helped him all you could. How old were you then?"

"Eight, and he was eleven. I'll tell you one thing he did that shows how he felt. While he was away he made up a family for himself."

"Made how?"

"Convinced all his friends at school he was an only child with a mother and father who hadn't much money but couldn't do enough for him."

"I can imagine how he might have wanted to do away with everyone but you. So then was he sent home?"

"Eventually, if you could call that his home. They still wanted him out of the way, so they sent him to boarding school. Left when he was sixteen, and my father put him to work for the firm."

"He couldn't have been too intelligent, then. Not that I'm saying you can't be intelligent if you're a builder, but you'd think he would have done his best to stay away from working for your father."

"Ben was intelligent all right. That was one of the things they hated about him. Too clever for his own good, that was their refrain. I always thought he did badly at school so he could get on with earning some money and freedom, not realising my father could force him to work for him."

"He couldn't once Ben was eighteen, could he?"

"I wouldn't be surprised if he spent those two years thinking that. The day he turned eighteen they were actually going to take us out for dinner. It was a Sunday, so he didn't have to go to work. About the middle of the morning mother started shouting for him to come downstairs, and when he didn't she flounced up to his room. I remember her flinging his door open and shouting 'You creeping crawling reptile, after all we've done for you' and then just standing there. He must have sneaked away while everyone was asleep. And that was the last we ever saw of him."

"Or heard of him?"

"I've absolutely no idea where he is."

"Didn't anyone ever try to find out?"

"I did after they died. They had practically nothing to leave by then, but they left it all to me. I paid the solicitors to try and track him down, only it seemed he wanted to stay hidden. I thought he must have made himself a new life and he wanted to keep clear of the old."

"Maybe he'll get in touch when you aren't expecting it."

"Maybe."

She would have liked to know how he felt about the possibility, but a family composed largely and loudly of teenagers had arrived at the adjacent table. A boat mounted with the upper halves of five women glided by, the oars of four of them digging at the water. "Lift them up for me," shouted the cox. "Give me a long strong one." As the bare arms of the rowers darkened with the shadow of the bridge Gail was caught by an unexpected shiver. "It isn't cold, is it?" she said to Geoff.

Paul produced a sneeze that included a sample of his drink, and Geoff pulled out a handkerchief to dab the small startled face. "Must be getting colder."

"Let's hit the road, then." Gail took hold of the handles of the stroller, and could have wished the rubber grips to feel a little firmer. "So you've been remembering because you're going back where you came from."

"Yes," Geoff said at once.

ten

Before Geoff could question the receptionist he was swooped on by the hotel manager, a not outrageously young man stout enough to be a chef and displaying a sample of his ebony hair above his top lip. His smile widened beyond the professional as he extended Geoff a soft pudgy hand to shake. "Mr. Davenport, if there's anything that doesn't suit you, just let me know personally. We don't want anything to mar a celebrity's return home."

"Thanks, but you shouldn't treat me different from any other guest who isn't paying."

"Ha, ha." The manager swivelled the reservation form towards him to confirm Geoff's bill was taken care of by the publisher, then broadened his mouth to compensate for any offence. "It's you some of us are proudest of. We haven't missed a show since you were on local telly. We still remember you going for that dog breeder—bleeder, my wife calls him." He watched as Geoff withdrew a ballpoint from its gilded scabbard on the counter. "While you're having to write your name once, could you sign this book for her? I'll be sleeping with the German shepherd for a week if I take it home blank."

"Your marriage is safe in my hands," Geoff said, and to the receptionist "You won't have any messages for me."

"I was about to give it to you," she said with a reproachful blink at the manager. Geoff was inscribing the copy of *The Goods* "To Deanie," having managed to establish without sounding incredulous that this was the name of the dedicatee, when the receptionist handed him a long white envelope. He had to concentrate on tracing his usual flourish of a signature before he could turn his attention to the message. Having opened the flap, which came away reluctantly in several sections, he found that the sheet of paper set out tomorrow's media and signing schedule. "No calls?" he said.

"None yet, Mr. Davenport."

An open lift welcomed him with an image of Geoff Davenport, media personality and investigative reporter. Its expression once the door closed wouldn't have convinced the public he was much of either, and he turned his back on the mirror while he was lifted to his floor. The corridors were deserted except for a trolley heaped with a Before and After display of towels. Arrows underlining a progressively smaller range of numbers led him around five corners to his room. Another bed, he mused as he let himself into the boxy lobby and found the light-switch, another bathroom. The phone emitted a hint of a ring as he dropped his luggage near it, and he thought of Gail. He'd hardly even started to tell her the truth.

He hoped he'd told her enough to let her feel she understood however much of his uneasiness he failed to conceal. She had plenty to worry about with Paul, despite his being half Geoff's responsibility and a subject they could always discuss. Perhaps he should have allowed her to assume it was Paul who was making him edgy, or said as much, except how could he have used Paul that way, even to prevent Gail from being anxious for himself? Surely he'd succeeded in that. He sat on the bed and slipped the photograph out of the envelope.

It emerged back uppermost, showing him the word. The handwriting was so awkward he wondered if it could have been done in front of a mirror. The word was FIND, which lit up a memory he would rather stayed dark. So did the photograph of the corner of a room—a triangle of turfy carpet, two quadrilaterals of wallpaper not quite so green, an angle of the skirting-board. Neither the carpet nor the wallpaper was familiar, but he couldn't mistake the initial carved into the skirting—a B trying to pass itself off as a G.

He had to move his car. He dropped the photograph in the bedside drawer and left his key at Reception before hurrying out of the hotel. The Rover was parked around the corner, in a street that raised itself beside the station until it was higher than the iron and glass barrel of a roof. He cruised along a side street to the hotel garage, which was locked. He only had to ring the bell. Instead he drove past and uphill.

The university rose above him, brandishing its red-brick clock tower across Liverpool at the speared concrete doughnut of a disused restaurant. Ahead a motley assortment of buses was labouring up a slope. They led him to several minutes' worth of intermittent small shops that seemed recognisable in a generalised way. A patch of American territory—a McDonald's, a Deep Pan Pizza, a Kentucky Fried Chicken drive-through—Geoff tried to take as a promise that nothing would be too oppressively familiar. Then the road turned residential, and he could have thought it was the imminence of the motorway that caused the houses to draw themselves together.

An expanded crossroads called the Rocket bristled with a dozen traffic lights that helped it send up petrol fumes beneath a flyover. A few shops he remembered being sent to in his childhood endured in corners of the intersection. Immediately past the lights several students were holding up placards, demonstrating where they hoped to be driven. Geoff waved to indicate he wouldn't be using the motorway, and found himself wishing he could use one or more of them as an excuse to take it. In a minute it was arching away from him, and he was going down where he used to live.

The slip road that had once been a main road swung past Broadgreen station and divided. One half led into the rumbling gloom beneath the motorway, the other turned left under a railway bridge. The shadow of the bridge dragged itself through the car, and he imagined that he felt it catching on his face as he saw his old house.

It was the lowest on the hill up which its capacious neighbours supported their partners in pairs as far as the suffused blue sky. The house was as white as they were, but twice their size, and surrounded by its own plot of land. The front door and the woodwork of the four rotund front windows, which had been red, had turned green. A signboard stood on the concrete where the front garden had been and which was by no means fully occupied by two parked cars. HOME FROM HOME, the board said, and the names and phone number of the proprietors. It would be easier for Geoff to talk his way in now that the house was a hotel, but until that moment he hadn't known how difficult he would have preferred the task to be.

He halted the car and took slow deep breaths as he stepped onto the warm tarmac. Having eased the door shut, he climbed the three steps through the grass verge of the pavement opposite. Though the solitary house was by no means as enormous as it had appeared to his childhood self, he felt as though it was withholding its ability to spring that impression on him with every step he took. The wrought-iron gates were new, but closed themselves behind him with a clang much like the one he remembered. It made him glance back nervously. When he turned towards the house again he saw that a woman had opened the front door above him.

She was nothing like his mother. Only the eager closing of the gates, and the manner in which the motorway noise had risen to meet him as he approached the house, belonged to the past. She had cropped grey hair and a compact face like a pale fruit just starting to wizen, and wore a floral dress his mother would have considered several varieties too vulgar. "Bring your car up," she said. "I'll get them out of your way."

She meant the gates, Geoff realised. "I was just passing. I'm not looking for a room," he lied twice.

"Come and see anyway if you like. You aren't from round here, are you?"

"I keep being told I don't sound like it, but . . ."

"You're never, are you?" She lined up the edge of a hand with her straight fringe while she scrutinised him. "You are. From the box. We always have you on. What brings you to this part of town?"

"I used to live here."

"Whereabouts? You're not saying *here*." She hadn't finished beaming when she stamped a foot. "Isn't it the way when you want to share something. Even my husband's at the allotments. We always try to serve fresh. Can you stay for dinner?"

"That's kind, but I'm dining with some old friends."

"You've time to see what we've made of it, though."

"That would be—yes. Thank you."

"It's all yours," she said, and stepped back. "That'll have to be except for the couple of rooms we have guests in, you understand. Slack week."

Three paces took him over the threshold and into the hall. Its paper had turned almost the green of the new carpet, but it was unexpectedly as wide as he recalled, though brighter. Perhaps its darkness in his memory was emotional as well as physical. A faint scent of blossoms had ousted the smell of the fly killer that his mother would spray throughout the house once a week. A pay phone on the wall near the front door was an addition, together with a long shelf heaped with sightseeing brochures. Enough was unfamiliar, hence welcoming, that Geoff felt his forehead relax from within. A glint of cutlery drew his attention leftward, to a room set with eight tables draped in sunlit white. "You've moved the dining-room across," he said.

"We needed more space than the family we bought from."

"Have you done much with the bedrooms? If you've this many tables . . ."

"We've made eight rooms and a second toilet out of, you'll remember there were six, and put a shower in all the accommodations."

"I wonder what you've done to my room."

She couldn't know it wasn't his he had in mind, but she paused before asking "Which was it?"

"In the left-hand corner at the back."

"That's number four, most of it, anyway. We took a slice of your room for number five, but that's occupied."

"Could I see, do you think?"

"Number four, certainly. I'll get the key," she said, opening the door next to the dining-room.

So that was still an office. Geoff didn't quite brace himself to hear his father yell "Not now, I'm trying to work something out" and then more softly if it was Geoff "Give me half an hour, son" or redoubling his fury if it dared to be Ben. The house was quieter than Geoff remembered—perhaps quieter than his father and his obsession had led everyone to believe. The office produced a rattle of keys on a board and then one of them attached to a miniature club in the landlady's hand. "Ready?" she said.

He could have done without the echo of so many childhood games, but he said "Of course."

"You'll know your way, won't you? Be going up and let me take my time."

"I'll let myself in if you like."

"I'll do that. I want to see how the changes take you."

The stairs still hid themselves between the office and the room opposite the kitchen—the room that used to be the playroom, which Geoff's father seemed to have taken every opportunity to drive Ben out of. Geoff remembered the fist pounding on the office wall whenever there was reason to suspect it was Ben who was making a noise, and his father flinging Ben onto the stairs to indicate he should go to bed. Now, as Geoff climbed towards a new skylight displaying an intensified sample of blue, he felt as though the landlady's painstaking slowness was trying to drag him back into the memory that was only a sample of worse.

The stairs turned back on themselves under the square of sky before they gained the upper corridor. In the process of growing a fresh set of doors it had shortened itself. He was moving his head back and forth to ease the sudden tension in his neck when the landlady appeared with a triumphant flourish of her key. "Nothing like you remember?" she said.

"I'd have to say that," Geoff told her, and made for the door that was almost where Ben's had been. "Who's been staying in my room lately?"

"Only people who've liked it."

"I'm glad to hear that, of course," Geoff said, and risked another try. "Anyone recently? This isn't your high season, is it?"

"Once they know we're here they come back, if they want somewhere close to the motorway with the personal touch. The last chap was up for the sailing ships on the Mersey. That was a good week, not a bed empty, even if some of them hardly spoke English."

"Did he?"

"Like a charmer. Not that I'm saying any of them weren't a pleasure to have in the house."

Geoff could think of nothing more to ask that wouldn't sound suspect. She aimed the key at the door, then turned to him. "Close your eyes," she said.

Her playfulness was serious. If he didn't indulge her, mightn't she show him the room? He made his eyelids falter shut and concentrated on the vague pale glow within them. He heard the key engage the lock, and the muted turning of a doorknob, and imagined he felt a change in the air on his face, like a smell that was about to declare itself. "Now you can look," she said.

No sooner had his eyelids begun to venture open than they shut again, allowing him to glimpse the merest flicker—bed, curtains, sky so bright it monopolised most of his vision. He widened his eyes until they stung. "You've done wonders," he said.

"I'm glad you like it."

Geoff wished he could. The blue counterpane was unable to distract him from the part of the room he knew, the corner upon which the pale green walls and greener carpet—the entire room— seemed designed to focus. Surely the landlady could see the letter in the skirting-board. Before she could speak he blurted "Do you mind if I . . ."

"It's all yours, of course."

Geoff strode headlong into the room. The view from the back of the house expanded to meet him—the red-tiled roofs of Knotty Ash scaling the miles towards the green hills that had changed colour to record the passing of each year of his childhood—until he veered aside from it, to the corner that was cramped by a wardrobe, where he fell to his knees. "Are you all right?" the landlady called.

"Perfectly. I'm just . . ."

He was attempting to prise up the corner of the carpet before she came near enough to see, but the carpet was stuck to the floor. For a moment he thought he'd been the victim of a malicious joke, whatever that might imply. Then the carpet peeled back an inch, revealing that it had only been wedged in the angle of the skirting, and all Geoff could do was dig his fingers underneath.

They felt the rubbery underside, and a splinter that was lying in wait for him. He splayed the fingers and groped as far as they could reach without disturbing the carpet too obviously. A flat pointed object poked the tip of his index finger, which closed on it along with his thumb, more in desperation than triumph. He shoved himself to his feet, sliding the right one to press the carpet down, and slumped against the wall. "Mr. Davenport, you aren't all right," the landlady protested.

"I will be. Got up too fast." The room and the sunlit view had indeed appeared to blacken as he'd risen quickly with his prize, but he'd kept his back to her mostly so as to conceal the pocket-sized envelope. He turned as soon as he felt able, and found her just a pace away from him and peering at him, with concern rather than suspicion. "I really should apologise," he said.

"For what on earth?"

He moved so that she could see the carved initial, and the secret in his pocket nudged his ribs. "So long as you haven't been thinking it was any of your guests."

She rested her fingers on his arm and leaned forward. He might have thought she was noticing the damage for the first time until she said "We wouldn't have dreamed it was you."

"Well, here I am. The culprit found out at last."

"You must have been very young, were you? You weren't too good at your letters."

"I got better," Geoff said, and put the room behind him.

"You won't mind if we give away your wicked past, will you?"

she said, locking the door. "We won't if you'd rather we didn't, but it would be a little secret to share with our guests."

"Go ahead and tell them what I told you. I expect my reputation will survive."

"I should think so," she said with some force. "Have we anything else you'd like to revisit?"

"Nothing, thanks." He might have said that less hastily and more gratefully, and so he rigged himself an excuse. "If you'll forgive me, I ought to be leaving. The friends I'm meeting for dinner, we're starting with a few drinks."

"Have a lovely evening." She led the way downstairs and returned the key to the office. "Think of us whenever you're in the area," she said. "Think of this as still your home."

"I don't know when I'll be back," Geoff said, more of a wish than he hoped she could sense, "but thanks. You've very kind."

She ought to have children, he thought as she opened the front door. Perhaps she had. He stepped out of the house, into less of an uproar than he'd prepared himself for. Of course, over the decades the trees beside the motorway had grown and spread, screening much of the noise. He could imagine the ancient forested landscape was reclaiming all the land that wasn't built over. He gave the landlady a smile and held up a meaninglessly cupped hand as the gates fell shut behind him, but he'd hardly turned away when his smile failed. The past was closing in.

eleven

Geoff was in the playroom when the noise began. He'd managed to coax the white mouse out of her cage, and was watching her scurry from his hand to his hand to his hand. Just as he took pity on her—she must think she was going somewhere, she might even imagine she was making her escape—he heard a sound of chipping or digging upstairs. It was a noise he thought a mouse in a wall might make, or a prisoner tunnelling out of his cell, but he knew it came from Ben's room. He was willing it to stop before anyone else noticed when he heard the lounge door open, and a mass of deliberate footsteps that seemed to be treading the grownups' voices low. He cupped his hands to keep the mouse safe and tried to send Ben a mental warning. They were supposed to stay absolutely quiet whenever Geoff's father showed someone what was wrong with the house.

The caller wasn't just another of the increasingly reluctant council officials Geoff's father knew well enough to persuade them to visit. He was a lawyer and so, apparently, more important— Geoff had gathered this from his parents' conversation at dinner, and would have expected Ben to have before he'd been sent upstairs for eating in a way Geoff's father didn't like. But the noise from Ben's room didn't relent, and Geoff opened his hands for fear that he might crush the little palpitating ball of fur. He was carrying her back to her cage when the playroom door was thrown open with a violence that almost made her jump out of his hands. "What do you—" his father demanded, then moderated his voice. "What was the row? Was it in here?"

He was wearing one of the suits he donned to impress official visitors, and otherwise only for church or for the dinners he attended more frequently than his wife did. The weathered breeze block of his face, which often had Geoff wondering if the plaster dust his work spread everywhere could insinuate itself beneath the skin, was perched on the strangulated collar of his whitest shirt. His reddened eyes had given up narrowing themselves at the possibility of seeing Ben, but his undersized mouth was still trying to render itself smaller by drawing its corners in. "Was that doing it?" he said, pointing at Geoff's hands.

The mouse was in less danger than Ben, thought Geoff. "I took her out so she wouldn't."

"Put it away now before you get germs," said his mother, following his father into the room. Her perfume came first, and then her face around the door—her wide lips pinked, her eyebrows tweezed, her eyelids painted the blue of a sky with a milky skin of cloud. Her light quick purposeful step brought in the rest of her, a ruffled white silk blouse both softening and emphasising the thrust of her front, a kilt without a tartan swirling around her stockinged calves. "Put it away so the gentleman can see what a good boy we have," she said.

"She's a her, mum."

"Put it away regardless. You shouldn't be able to tell the difference at your age."

"I'd have to bang my hammer there, Jewel," Geoff's father said. "Can't know the difference too young is my belief, or you won't know what to use your barge pole for."

"I'll bow to that, but I haven't seen him putting what he was told to put. We don't want the gentleman thinking we've no boys we're proud of."

Geoff experienced the familiar tug-of-war of emotions: wanting to live up to his parents' estimation of him, wincing at the prospect of giving them yet another reason to compare Ben unfavourably with him. "I was just seeing she wasn't frightened," he said.

"Nobody here needs to be frightened if they don't deserve to be." She watched queasily as Geoff poured the mouse into the cage and fastened the gnawed wire. "Sit quietly now and let your father demonstrate for Mr. Marsh."

Geoff sat at once in a playroom chair that was slightly too small for him—Ben's old desk chair, into which he'd seen Ben cram himself as though to make himself less conspicuous—and watched his father raise a finger. Here came the rumble of a lorry, and before the sound had finished dragging itself through the ears of the listeners it was joined by the protracted muffled thunder of an even larger vehicle and the underlying vibration of a train. "See what I'm getting at?" Geoff's father said. "It's louder in than out. It's shut in."

"I'd have to have that monitored, Mr. Davenport," the lawyer said from the hall.

"You're saying that's worth it."

"Definitely, if you want something that has a chance of standing up in court."

"What I'm saying, you'll take the case."

"Just remind me now. You aren't satisfied with the compensation the council are offering."

"Not when they want to give us what the neighbours got for half the noise. I want the council sorted out, and the architect who said he'd cut the row down and it's like living in a hut under the flyover."

"You altered the interior to his design yourself, I think you said."

"That's me, bricks for brains. He's supposed to be the expert. I'm just the brickie that made good."

"Point taken, Mr. Davenport. I'm on your side, do believe me. And if the question were to be raised as to why you moved to this location when the proposals for the motorway were public knowledge . . ."

"It was Julie's aunt's that died. We were going to sell it, we still are, only we had to move in when a firm that owed me went bust and the bank said the solution was sell the house we had."

"Perhaps I could glance at the relevant correspondence."

There would be plenty of that, thought Geoff. His father often sat up after midnight in the office, drafting letters for Geoff's mother to correct and tone down and type. The adults made for the office, then all the footsteps shut themselves in the dining-room. Muffled voices were becoming part of the grumble of the house when Geoff heard the sound of chipping recommence up-stairs.

He levered himself out of the chair and dodged across the hall. The boxy staircase had trapped the smells of tonight's boiled veg-etables and of a recently smouldering saucepan, together with a lingering trace of the fly killer his mother seemed to believe could double as an air freshener. He tiptoed quickly up the stairs into the corridor decorated with paintings of rosy-cheeked curly-haired children, heavy-framed items his father had acquired while reno-vating somebody's grandmother's house. The sharp dogged noise hadn't relented when Geoff reached Ben's door. No sooner had he begun to inch the door open, however, than the noise ceased and Ben swung to face him.

Ben was crouched beside the window. Though the June evening wouldn't be dark for hours, the thick brown curtains were drawn. The light was uneconomically on, which wouldn't please Geoff's father. The room was almost as tidy as ever—so tidy that it looked as if it was begging for praise or at least acknowledge-ment—except for a sprinkling of wooden dust and fragments on the dark brown carpet in the angle of the skirting-board. Whatever expression Ben had produced as the door opened had vanished at the sight of Geoff, and now his narrow bony uncoloured face said he was ready for a game, his pale eyes wide, his lips parted in a grin that bared his moist top teeth. "What were you doing?" Geoff blurted. "They can hear you."

"Shut it then."

Geoff eased the door shut behind him. "They already heard."

"Can't be helped then." He sounded proud of himself, perhaps trying to judge what that felt like. "Look at my art," he said, springing to his feet.

He'd carved his first initial in the darkest corner of the room. It resembled a diagram of one squarish object pressed under another. "They'll see too," Geoff protested. "Don't you care?"

"It's my room. Anyway, they don't. Why should I?"

"I do," Geoff said, so awkwardly it emerged as a mumble he was too embarrassed to repeat, and cleared his throat of the taste of the air on the staircase. "I mean, don't you care what he'll do when he sees?"

"What's he going to do?" Ben let his gaze sink to the penknife in his hand, and reopened the blade with a thumbnail. As the metal glinted, his eyes did. "He won't do this."

"What are you—"

"Look," said Ben, and fixed Geoff's gaze. He placed his left forefinger just beneath his left eye and pulled his cheek down, exposing a strip of glistening pink skin and more eyeball than Geoff liked to think was in anybody's face. "He wouldn't dare," Ben said.

Ben wouldn't either, Geoff tried to convince himself. He was only playing with the knife, only lifting the blade level with his bulging eye, only aiming the point at it: that would be where he would have to stop playing. "I believe you," Geoff assured him, so hastily he left half the last word behind in his mouth. Ben lowered the point of the blade into the niche he'd made in his face, and rested it against his eyeball, and let go of his cheek.

"Don't," Geoff screamed, and slapped himself across the mouth at the thought of having made Ben move inadvertently, causing the knife to— The sharp edge of the blade was uppermost, he saw; only the dull edge was resting between the eyeball and the skin, and so long as Ben's hand didn't jerk or waver— "Sorry," he pleaded. "You're right, he'd never. He'd be too scared. Better stop now before they come."

"That's nothing. Watch this."

He was just saying that, Geoff did his best to think: there was nothing more he would risk doing to himself. Then, slowly and deliberately, Ben raised his left foot and planted it on his right knee. He swayed an inch to either side before steadying himself and widening his delighted eyes at Geoff. "That's amazing," Geoff said with at least as much control as Ben must be exerting. "Only stop now."

"Want a go?"

"No, I just don't want a one-eyed brother."

"Who said you had a brother?"

"I'll bet they said you had one."

"Maybe."

Geoff thought the idea had found a home until Ben threw out his free hand to ward it off, and had to sway in search of his balance, his fist tightening on the knife. "And then they let me know I hadn't," he said.

"Well, you have. I say you have. It's up to me to say." Geoff felt in danger of losing control of his words, which were making Ben widen his eyes again, pressing his left eye against the blade. Geoff's own eyes were stinging—he could almost feel cold hard sharp metal digging into the hidden parts of them. "You've got a brother," he said, nearly as desperate to stop repeating himself as to shift the knife away from Ben's face. "Give me that and I'll show you."

Without warning Ben overbalanced. The knuckles of his free hand collided with the wall behind him and saved him. His face winced, then pretended it had done no such thing, and he pressed his foot harder against his knee. "Show me what?"

Geoff hadn't thought beyond persuading him to give up the knife. An outbreak of noises downstairs let him look away. Footsteps and voices stopped at the front door, which closed gently. That seemed to be the last of the restraint Geoff's father could bear to exert, because he'd hardly started back along the hall before declaring "There goes another clever sod."

"He said he was in our corner, Alf, so shush."

"He'd better be, and I don't care if he can hear. It's when they think they're cleverer than you they take advantage if you give them half the chance. I hired one weasel to design the house, I'm not paying another. Maybe they think I'm not good enough to employ them."

"Of course you are. Your men know that, and so do we."

"Who's we? I can tell you one who doesn't think so in this house." His voice was at the stairs now. "I'm going to find out what that row was. It was never down here the second time."

"Don't go getting yourself in a stew so you can't sleep again."

Geoff turned, so carefully he felt crippled, to make sure his father's words had reached Ben. The other boy had lowered his foot but not the knife. "I'm not kidding. I wouldn't," Geoff pleaded, hearing his father set foot on the stairs with a thud like a blow from a lump hammer. "Give it me, quick, and I'll show them."

Ben cocked his head while keeping his attention on Geoff— keeping the blade against his rolling eyeball. He listened to five footsteps on the stairs before he eased the blade out from beneath his eyelid. "Let's see you then, Geoffrey."

Geoff closed his fist around the handle. He was expecting it to be warm, even clammy, so that its coldness came as a shock. A single minute tear of blood clung to the point. He hadn't time to let it affect him. He sank to his knees and began to gouge at the initial on the skirting-board.

He saw the drop of blood run off the metal and soak into the wood. He drove the point in deeper and prised out a splinter that almost doubled the length of the top bar of the B. He was starting to extend the middle bar when the footsteps rushed upstairs and along the corridor and, with scarcely a pause for the door to be thrown aside, into the room.

Geoff staggered to his feet and crammed his shoulders into the angle of the walls so that his father must see the knife and, framed by Geoff's ankles, the damage he'd done with it. But his father took a step at Ben that made the comb and brush and hair-cream jitter on the dwarfish dressing-table. "What's he doing in here?" he said through his teeth.

"Ask him."

"Don't get clever with me, Ben Jam In. I'm asking you and no sod else. What were you up to that needs the curtains shut?" He slapped the light off before shoving Ben aside and flinging the curtains apart, at which point he looked directly at Geoff. "What's he doing with a knife? Whose is it?"

"It's Ben's, dad, but I was—"

"Give it here," Geoff's father said, glaring at Ben, and stretched out a hand twice the size of his son's. Having closed the blade, Geoff placed it on the swollen white palm that looked ingrained with white dust. His father opened the knife with a cracked rough thumbnail and waved it in front of Ben's face. "Where'd you get it?"

"Someone in my class was selling it."

Geoff's father inverted his fist, pointing the knife downwards, and swooped it through the air. As his wife gasped in the doorway, her perfume flaring to fill Geoff's nostrils, he pressed the blade against his jacket over his heart. The veins in his wrist swelled like tubular bruises for a second before the blade snapped. He caught it in his free hand and thrust both pieces of the knife into a pocket of his trousers. "Now it's nobody's," he said, "and God help you if you mess up my house with anything else."

A tear leaked from the inner corner of Ben's left eye. He pinched the bridge of his nose at once, dismissing the moisture, but not before Geoff glimpsed a tinge of red. "I did some of it," he said, his voice shrill with the attempt to draw some of the anger to himself.

"I saw you, son, and there'll be no pocket money for you this week." His father looked at him, or rather between his legs. "But I know a B when I see one. Know a few of the things it can stand for, as well."

The boys' mother leaned forward from her pinched waist to peer at the damage, then recoiled. "If you ask me it looks like the kind of thing we'd have carved on a tree when we were in love, initials stuck together like that. I'd like to know whose idea it was."

"I don't reckon we need to ask."

"Dad, it was—"

"I said we don't want to hear." Geoff's father met his eyes, at the same time performing a jerk of the head. "Get in your room and stay till you're told. And listen to me," he said, throwing so much weight on the last word but one that it felt like a poke in Geoff's chest. "Don't you ever, that's never, understand, never ever come in this room again."

Geoff thought he had succeeded after all: he'd managed to divert some of the blame to himself, and so there would be less for Ben. He was easing the door shut, only to have his mother push him out with it, when he heard his father say "Not so clever this time, were we? Or maybe a bit too clever." The door slammed, blotting out the sight but not the memory of Ben's face. It was saying that Geoff had made the situation worse for him.

twelve

The staff behind the desk had changed when Geoff returned to the hotel from dinner at the Laughing Starfish in Chinatown with Trudy and Joe. A young woman in a jacket whose buttons set off their gleams one by one had to be told his room number. He was feeling relieved not to be detained by having been recognised when he saw she'd taken more than his key from its pigeon-hole. "Here's a message for you, Mr. Davenport."

Call from Mrs. Davenport, 9.38 P.M. Hope you're having a good time—we did at Gemma's party. Little one's asleep so grabbing early night. Talk tomorrow. Love.

"Thanks," Geoff said, though he didn't feel especially grateful. Until he'd read the note he hadn't realised how much he was looking forward to speaking to Gail—to being reminded that there was a part of his life to which he needn't fear returning. He supposed the message did that, but it wasn't the same as hearing her voice.

In his bathroom he unwrapped a glass and fed himself three increasingly cold glasses of water, all that he felt able to contain, and as an afterthought half of a fourth. More water went on his face, which he saw blinking at the impact. The bathroom felt insufficiently settled by his toiletries, and he was glad the light in the bedroom was less relentless. He stood at the bedroom window to watch thin young people thinly dressed swarm towards the nightclubs, and saw himself hovering above the nightlife. He let himself drop into the bedside chair and pulled out the envelope he'd found under the carpet of Ben's room.

The photograph inside it had been taken from a bus or a coach, and owed its pallor to the reflection of the camera's flash on the window. The view through the glass was slightly blurred, but altogether recognisable—a section of motorway wall sloping upwards, and beyond it a suburban street mounting a hill beyond a railway bridge. If it hadn't been for the bridge Geoff would have been able to see his old house.

"I'm not going up there," he muttered. "Never again. I've been back as far as I go. Find someone else to play." Nevertheless he was peering closely at the image when the phone rang. For a moment he felt overheard, and then he couldn't help hoping that Paul had wakened—that Gail had decided it wasn't too late to call. He sailed the photograph onto the bed and completed the gesture by scooping up the receiver. "Hello," he said.

Perhaps his tone of greeting them as if he could see them had taken the caller aback; the only sound the earpiece offered Geoff was the retreating howl of a police car. "Yes, hello," he tried saying with enthusiasm.

"You sound as if you were expecting me."

The response brought Geoff forward on his chair, closing him around the sudden ache at the centre of himself. The man's voice was light and quick as a disc-jockey's, and had no discernible accent. Geoff might never have heard it before, but he knew he had. "Wasn't that what you wanted?" he made his mouth say.

"You tell me what I want, Geoffrey, if you think you know."

"For me to play your game."

"You've started, haven't you? It gets better, you'll see. You can't imagine."

"I'll have to, because I've had enough of playing."

"Oh, Geoffrey, that's not you. You'd never give up while there's a chance of winning. Nothing could stop you trying to do me a favour." The voice had grown playful, close to prancing, but Geoff heard no mirth in it. Abruptly it calmed so totally it might have belonged to a different speaker. "Now this isn't right, is it? You're the one person I shouldn't be making fun of. How are you, Geoffrey? You've done well for yourself."

"For some other people too, I hope."

"Goz without saying with you, does that. Teks more than one thumping to change a lad, as granddad used to say." The Lancashire accent vanished as swiftly as it had appeared. "How are you, though, that's what I was after. Happy? Secure? Pleased with yourself?"

"I try not to be that too much. It's not as if I'm indispensable."

"You are to some people, Geoffrey, trust me. I can't believe you don't know that by now."

Geoff managed to sit back, away from the crushed pain. "So long as I've done more good than harm. That's the best any of us can expect to have said about us."

"Why, I never knew you were a philosopher. You ought to introduce your show with a thought for the week. How about, how about you won't know how close it came until it's too late?"

"How close what came, Ben?"

Geoff heard a breath as thin as a sniff, then silence. He was wondering whether he had inadvertently brought the conversation to an end when a breath much longer than the inhalation sighed into the earpiece. "That was an experience, I don't mind telling you. It's been a long time since anyone called me that."

"What name are you using, then?"

"Now, Geoffrey, you don't expect me just to tell you. It wouldn't be much of a game, would it? You must have to be cleverer than that in your job."

"Sometimes, but I don't see—I don't see why you've bothered to get in touch if you're going to be so mysterious."

"Maybe that's all there's left for me to be, will that do you?"

"Tell me something else, then. Tell me—"

"Careful. Too many questions I can't answer and I'll be off."

"Tell me why you've got in touch now."

"Don't you think I've been following your career?"

"I did wonder if you were ever watching."

"I wouldn't have missed it. I was betting myself how long you'd take."

"Take . . ."

"I knew you'd be bound to have another go at saving kids sooner or later. Only this time you managed, didn't you? Nothing like a bit of practice."

"You were Dave from Maidenhead, weren't you," Geoff blurted. "You phoned when I was on the air in Oxford. You asked about clues."

"I've been Dave, I'll let you have that. It won't get you anywhere."

"Don't you want me to find you? Because if you do—"

"Oh yes, I want that. You and only you." For those words Ben's playfulness wavered, then it regained its poise. "Don't say I've given you no help. I left you two pictures, and now there's another. You used to like that game, or you played it, anyway."

"We were children. We both did things because we knew no better."

"Clever, Geoffrey. Slick and professional. You're saying I ought to know better now like you do."

"I'm saying you're asking too much if you expect me to go up where this photograph was taken."

"Why, you've never forgotten the fun we used to have when we were living round there."

"I've tried to forget."

"Then it's a good job you've got me to remind you where the life you're living came from."

"And how about you, Ben? What have you made of yourself?"

"Don't hurt my feelings by pretending you don't know. I've got as much publicity as you now, haven't I? We'll see who's done best by the time you track me down."

"I don't want to compete with you. I'd just like—"

"To help. I know. That'll always be you." Ben's voice was

prancing again, with urgency or with delight. "But you won't tell me you haven't been following the news. Don't say you didn't hear they've found another couple dead near Windsor. If I were you I'd be wondering what he does, the character who deals with them— what he does that the police aren't saying."

Geoff became aware that his mouth and limbs had stiffened. "Sounds as if I'm about to be told," he said as evenly as he could.

"Oh, Geoffrey, don't be so impatient. A game's no fun if you play too fast. We'll save it till the next time we talk, after you've gone where I've shown you."

"I told you I won't go there."

"You aren't saying I have to do something else before you'll look for me. You don't want me to think up a different game."

"Why play games at all, Ben?"

"Because it has to be just you and me. I want it to be like the old days, don't you? Nobody except us knows about our game. Do they?" Ben said, his voice all at once cold and sharp.

"No, of course not. I'd forgotten it myself."

"You should be glad I reminded you, then. Don't deny your past, Geoffrey. How about your little boy and your wife?"

Geoff felt as though an icy weight had been dumped into his stomach. "I just told you I'd forgotten—"

"I heard that much. I'm asking if they've any idea what be-came of your brother that wasn't."

"How could my son have? He isn't even three, for God's sake."

"Maybe he takes in more than you think."

"Not about you. He couldn't have." Geoff drew a surreptitious breath to add force to the lie and said "I haven't even mentioned you since you started calling."

"See, Geoffrey, you were playing the game and you didn't know it. That's one of the rules. As far as your family's concerned I don't exist. You wouldn't want them to find out I do, so don't tell anyone about me. Not a single person. Not a word."

"What do you expect me to do all by myself? If this isn't just a game you're playing—"

"You're going to say I need help, Geoffrey, aren't you? I've got it. I've got you, my personal crusader, the knight in all his armour, the man who saves the young. I'm giving you another chance to stop it," Ben said, and was gone.

Geoff unbent himself from the posture in which the ache in his guts had skewered him, and dropped the receiver into its housing, only to retrieve it and phone the switchboard. The number from which the call had been made was blocked by the caller, of course. When the telephonist bade Geoff a good night he echoed her, though the words struck him as a joke at his expense. In the midst of the thoughts that were scurrying around the cage of his brain, he found one idea to hold onto: Ben could never contact him at home. It had to mean that home, and Gail and Paul, were safe.

thirteen

The first thing that came to find Jess was a whiff of cigarette smoke. From her position at the switchboard of Twenty-four Hour Knights she saw through the reception window a silhouette on the frosted glass that faced the street. The silhouette turned, and turned again, and each time redness flared before its face. There came a noiseless explosion of sparks that suggested the pacing figure had crushed the cigarette in its fist. The street door was pushed inwards, forcing its rheumatic metal arm to give, and revealed her disused boyfriend Rex.

He held up his parted fingers at the sight of her and risked an apologetic grin that was uncertain how far to raise itself. It made his face as emptily genial as a badge with a smile on it, and she couldn't believe she had once thought him cuddly enough to hug whenever she had the chance. He was wearing a Majorcan souvenir cap with its peak turned backwards to display where he'd come from. "I'll stay out of your bit, Jessy," he said.

"You can stay further out than that. Try the street and then don't stop."

"I'll sit here," he said, and dropped himself on one of the long-suffering chairs in front of the calf-high table on which magazines were turning up their corners like old bread. "This bit is for the punters, isn't it? You can let me sit here while I talk."

"You'll be talking to yourself." When the chair gave a belated groan she said "If you break that you can pay for it."

"I would, you know that. I'd never stick you with a bill."

"No, you were always good at paying. Buying people for as long as you want them."

He answered that with an extravagant flame that his petrol lighter shut off with a clunk. She'd laughed at the size of his fire when they'd first met, but now he could be signalling his distress for all she cared. As he emitted a mouthful of smoke she said "You can take that outside as well."

"There's an ashtray here with someone's ash in."

She felt as if he was daring to rebuke her for not cleaning up after a fare. "Couldn't you even stay off that?" she demanded.

"I only gave it up for you. Remember when you used to sniff my hair to see if I'd—"

"Pity you didn't do without a few more things while you were at it." That was too much like the kind of remark she might have made while they were together, and so she added "Not that I give a stub in the gutter either way."

"Whatever you say, Jessy. I just want you to know I didn't come here for myself."

"Who's the cab for, then?"

"No, I mean—I mean I didn't want you to feel more badly done to than you really were over, you know, that night."

"As far as you're concerned, mate, I don't feel anything at all."

"Well, that's . . ." He clearly didn't know what it was. So long as he couldn't sense it was growing less true by the moment, Jess told herself furiously as he said "There really wasn't anyone but you while we were together."

"I must have dreamed I saw you feeding some little secretary to get past her stomach."

"That's all you saw, us eating, me and her. That's all there was to see."

"That must have been a relief to the rest of the diners, not having Sexy Rex put them off their stroganoff." When the cigarette had the grace to droop in his fingers she said "Just hungry for company, were you?"

"No, all it was, and being a woman you'll know how it is, she was depressed. They'd put her brother out in the community, and he'd forgotten to take his medicine and gone for a dog in the street. All I did was buy her a drink after work to try and take her mind off."

Jess wasn't about to remind him how he'd started to find her concern for her father excessive—she wasn't going to recall how that had hurt. "Funny place to do that, a restaurant," she couldn't help responding.

"No, I mean we went to a pub. Only then she thought she hadn't better drive till she'd had something to eat, and she'd been meaning to try, you know, our restaurant." He gave the cigarette a suck while watching Jess's face and said "She wouldn't let me buy her dinner in case you thought I did. She even tried to pay for mine."

"Thanks for coming to tell me you weren't stuck with the whole bill."

"She saw you, I should tell you. She wouldn't say another word till I told her about us. She wanted me to go after you, but I thought you wouldn't want me to, not in front of your friends."

"No other time either. She must be as understanding as you're thoughtful."

"Tell you what, Jessy, if I didn't know you better . . ."

"You've no right to think you know me at all. Go on then, what?"

"I'd think you were glad of an excuse to get rid of me. I'd think there was another bloke."

"You'll never know, will you?" That was the last answer she was giving him. She hugged herself with her folded arms and raised her eyebrows above her indifferent eyes. He only laid his cigarette in a glass gutter of the ashtray so as to use his finger tanned with nicotine to poke the rear end of his cap higher on his forehead, and

she was about to ignore him when the door announced a new arrival with a creak of its untreated elbow. "Oh, Pete," she said. "I'm
glad you're back."

"What do you need me for, Jess?"

Just to be there, she told herself: just to embarrass Rex so that
he went away. But Rex shoved his cigarette in the corner of his
mouth, a spectacle he knew she didn't like, and used his fists to
shove him to his feet. "Is this him?"

"Could be."

That was Pete. Jess had been about to tell Rex he had no right
to ask, but Pete's playfulness was seductive. "Maybe," she said.

"You weren't so bare-faced last time I saw you," Rex said to
Pete, and the cigarette levered itself up, its tip reddening.

"I like him without the beard," Jess said. "Liked him with
it too."

"That's the trick, is it? That's how to hold their interest, keep
changing how you look."

"That's part of it," said Pete, and gazed invitingly at him.

"Let's have the rest, then. Who's going to tell?"

"Leave it out, Rex." Jess strode across the waiting area and
hauled the door open. "You've said what you came to say and all
you're going to."

"Haven't got what I want yet."

"Let me guess."

"Don't encourage him, Pete," said Jess as Rex barked "What
would I want in this hole? A cab."

"I'll call one."

"No need. Your friend's here."

"I'll—" Jess started to repeat, but this time it was Pete who interrupted. "Fair enough. I am."

"It's up to the two of you." Jess threw her hands wide, then
turned them up to show she had no hold on anyone. She watched
while Rex mashed his cigarette into a smouldering mass in the
ashtray and stood back with a laborious politeness to let Pete reach
the door first, only to have Pete open the door and bow him out.
The sliver of evening narrowed after them and pinched itself invisible, and she heard two car doors chop shut in unison. The

switchboard buzzed and she ran to it, leaving behind most of her thoughts. Rex had better be careful, she was thinking, not quite sure how that made her feel. Whatever happened, she sensed Pete could take care of himself.

fourteen

When Rex saw the curly-haired driver pull on his gloves he knew the man was a bit of a ponce. Rex planted his legs wide and sat forward to grind his thumbnail against the dashboard, finishing what someone else had started—scraping off the last trace of the word that had made all the difference in THANK YOU FOR   SMOKING. That accomplished, he jammed a fresh cigarette against his teeth and lit it, and shut the lighter with a satisfying bite of metal. Rex would have been more than happy for the driver to start an argument they could finish elsewhere, but the man only said "Where to, sir?"

Rex sent the fat end of a cone of smoke at him and sat back, bulging his crotch. "Where do you reckon we should go?"

"That's for you to say, sir. You're the fare."

It was impossible to tell from his eagerly intent expression whether he was making fun of Rex. "How about home?" Rex said.

"I don't know where that is, sir, do I?"

"I'd like to know where you're from. I'd like to know what you're doing round here." Rex was beginning to feel forced to trade words too soon. "Just drive till I find a place I want to find. Head off up there till I say different," he said.

The taxi moved away from the kerb as carefully as a hearse, past a couple stooping hand in hand for a closer look at a picture of a house in an estate agent's window. That might have been Jessy and him, Rex thought in a fury that whitened the tip of his cigarette with ash, and at once knew where would be ideal. "I want to go through the estate they're building."

"Looking for a house for yourself?"

The driver sounded so politely interested Rex had no doubt he was being mocked. "You'll see when we get there, mate."

"I'm looking forward to it." The driver paused at a set of traffic lights that were fishing for green with their amber. "Sir," he then said.

In less than a minute the car swung off the main road into a street of tall houses that had once been whiter. Most of them were tuned to several different sounds now that they were divided into flats like hi-fi stacks contriving to play all their components at once. At the end of the street a sky red with the last of the sunset was laid with elongated loaves of cloud. Against it the sketched new roofs looked charred, skeletons left by a fire. They and the ribbed trails of mud splaying out of the unsurfaced roads marked the edge of the estate.

The apartment-sized houses began to flap their temporary windows at the taxi as it cruised over the bare earth. Yellow tapes that might have been used to cordon off a crime scene lay on the stone-flagged pavements between the lightless unconnected street-lamps. Once the road curved, the only sound was the throaty purring of the taxi, and the only sign of life was a beaten-looking mongrel that darted in front of the vehicle with a bone in its mouth. The driver leaned on the horn as if to demonstrate how the wall-eyed houses swallowed up the noise. "Good place for it," he remarked as it died without an echo.

Rex did his best not to respond, but only felt stupid, hence even angrier. "For what?"

"To bury something, wouldn't you say? What do you think the loner's name is? Here, Romulus. Here, Ripper. What's another good name for a dog?" The driver seemed to lose interest as the animal fled into a side street leading to raw earth. "Are you planning to find yourself a place round here then, sir?"

Rex stuck his hand out of the open window to stub the cigarette on the roof, and felt sparks prick the back of his hand. "This'll do it. Stop here."

"Here, sir? You want me to leave you here?"

"Did I say that? Just stop."

"Whatever you ask for, sir. You're the one who'll be paying." The driver halted the car and dragged at the hand brake, grinding its teeth. "Have you seen something you want a closer look at?"

"You're not far wrong. Don't mind if I have another fag, do you? There won't be anyone else sitting in here for a while."

"I'll clean up if I have to, don't worry."

Rex fed his lungs some smoke and chunked the lighter shut. "So what do you think of her?"

"That's your lady friend, is it? She's a pleasure to be with."

"You've been with her, have you?" Rex demanded, and almost bit through the cork tip. "When was that, then? When did you start?"

"Why, I'm with her every time we're at the office."

Rex was beyond knowing which enraged him more: the notion that Jessy fancied the driver or the possibility that the man was playing at convincing him she did. He was reaching for the door handle, to take the discussion onto the street, when the driver said "You're jealous, aren't you, Rex?"

"Never mind calling me, Peter," Rex said, jabbing the hot end of the cigarette at the man's identity photograph on the dashboard. "You're Pete to her though, aren't you? And what else?"

"This is new. This is interesting. A side effect of love, is it? That stuff should come with a warning." The driver lounged sideways to confront Rex. "Let me put you out of your misery. I'm sure you've heard nothing about me from the lady who's mixed up with your brain."

"There's nothing wrong with my brain," Rex snarled, and thought of a better retort. "Don't be so sure what I could have heard about you."

"Make me sure," the driver said, and in one easy motion opened his door and slipped out of the car.

This was more like it, thought Rex. This was how men settled their differences, not poncing about with words that squirmed out of reach when you tried to counter them. All the same, he didn't make his move yet. "I hope you aren't expecting me to carry on paying, Peter or whatever you like to be called."

The driver switched off the meter and stepped back. He might have switched off his footsteps too, because there was no sound throughout the nameless streets until he said "What do you think I should be?"

"We'll stick to Peter, eh? Just keep it in your pants while you're round her, and a bit less of the clever chat as well."

The colourless eyes seemed to swallow the adjective. "You were going to tell me what was said."

"I could tell you what I might have that I didn't."

"I can't wait." The driver strolled to the opposite pavement, however, and halted on the corner of a street in search of an identity. "Stop my breath," he called.

Rex threw open the passenger door and left it open as he crossed the gouged roadway. The glow within the taxi made the empty streets beneath the extinguished sky seem darker. As Rex crossed the scribble of tape on the pavement the driver swung to face him, rubbing his gloved hands together. "It's killing, this suspense. There's nobody on earth now to hear you except me. Just us two boys playing."

"You'll find out how much I'm playing," Rex promised, and spat the remains of his cigarette into the road. The lighted tip vanished into a rut as though the earth had gulped it up. "Try this," he said. "You aren't what you want everyone to think."

The driver flexed his hands by his sides. "Go on. It's been a while since anybody told me what I am."

He wouldn't pose much of a problem, thought Rex—not when he wasn't even taking off his gloves. "What are you trying to look like, some killer in a film?"

"I don't need films." For a moment the driver's expression was almost pitying. "You've seen through me. Don't pretend, now. Tell me my secret and you'll get your reward."

Just his voice was playful—just his words. His face was telling the truth: that he cared about nothing, and so was capable of anything, and didn't care about that either. Once, when Rex was in his teens, he'd seen a schoolmate attacked with a wallpaper knife, only to grab the knife by the blade and send the attacker off to hospital for more stitches in his face than he'd needed in his own hand. He hadn't cared how badly injured he was so long as his opponent came off worse, but his determination was feeble compared to the indifference in the driver's eyes—a disinterest so profound it couldn't be bothered to threaten, so total it suggested that the driver's personality had been shut down while his body took care of the situation. The back of Rex's mouth grew dry as though smoke had lodged there. "Forget it," he said.

"That's one thing I never learned to do."

"Then don't. There's nothing to remember. All I meant . . ." Rex felt clammy and unmuscular, but he was ready to appear weaker if that would let him walk away. "I just meant you've been trying to make people think you're less than you are. You don't want to bother with the likes of Jessy and me, you can do better than her," he said, and in the midst of his panic thanked the stars overhead that she couldn't hear him. "Give someone else a chance."

"That's fascinating. That's really all that's on your mind still, is it?"

"Don't you think she's worth it?"

Eyes that seemed to sum up the growing darkness searched his face. He held his breath and kept his gaze steady and open, and clenched his throat to hold down a cough that would sound dangerously nervous. He even managed not to flinch as the driver moved. "Nobody is," the driver said, and turned towards the car. "Seen enough? Are we on our way?"

"How much do I owe you?" Rex said, and when a cough had finished catching up with him "I'll walk."

"No toll this time. It's enough if I'm sure we understand each other."

"If you say so," Rex called across the road. He was already walking past the taxi. The driver shut the passenger door, killing the light, before climbing in. The emptiness flattened Rex's footsteps as he walked, not so fast that he would appear to be fleeing but not as fast as he would have liked either, towards the lit and lively streets that would soon be within earshot, soon within sight. He hadn't walked a hundred yards when he heard the taxi swing around with a crunch of ribbed earth and follow him.

He didn't look when it crept up behind him. He kept his gaze on the fluttery windows ahead while the unlit headlamps insinuated themselves into the edge of his vision—even when the front wheels inched past him and the driver's face turned to him. Rex knew that if he met the man's eyes he would see they were dead as the headlamps. The taxi paced him for at least a hundred yards, and his own eyes began to ache from refusing to look. Suddenly the engine roared and the taxi sped around a curve, igniting its lights as it vanished.

It wasn't waiting farther on when Rex ventured around the curve. The light that poked its beam at him between the uncompleted houses once he'd run and walked and run again through fifteen minutes' worth of wilfully devious streets that caught at his throat with their dust wasn't a headlamp but a streetlamp. He stumbled across to the street piled with apartments and planted one hand on a low wall to support himself as he swallowed and swallowed and then swallowed air while a giggle of children far too young to be on the street after dark, never mind in charge of their younger siblings, pointed at him. Just now he was too busy breathing to react to them or even to light a cigarette. He was only glad, and surprised how unselfishly glad, that the driver could have no reason to see Jess as a threat to himself.

fifteen

Geoff phoned home from the hotel lobby, since he no longer had a room. He stood with his head in a plasterboard helmet like an item of a pantomime giant's armour and dialled, and waited for five rings to rouse Gail's recorded voice. But she answered after three, and not on tape. "Are you on your way?" she said.

"Not quite on it yet, no. More people showed up to do interviews than we were expecting. They like their local boys round here once they've made good. Why, are you anxious to have me back?"

"A bit."

"Anxious? Is something . . ."

"Just Paul. I don't think it's much."

"What about him, love?"

"A touch of a bug. Well, more than a touch. He didn't get to the can in time, and he's upset about that. There was quite a face for a while. Maybe that bottom lip is going to be his special weapon, like your big eyes."

"Like just about every inch of you. So is anyone else suffering?"

"I won't pretend I'm having the most fun of my life."

"I can hear that. I wish I could be there right now. I was really asking if any of his friends have been misbehaving internally."

"Half the pack. Seems last year's summer virus has mutated. Ginny who's going back into tropical diseases says the bugs are getting cleverer."

"Does that mean you can't do anything?"

"She's given me some of her three-year-old's medicine to hold Paul overnight, and I'll take him to morning surgery if he's no better, or you can. When are we expecting you?"

"I thought of eating here to let the traffic die down unless you'd rather I set off now."

"I can stand a few more hours by myself in bed if it keeps you safer."

"Maybe you'll find I've crept in when you weren't looking," said Geoff, and told himself there was no reason to regret his choice of words. "I'll see you soon. I'll see you very soon."

He wheeled his luggage up to the car park and paid to let the Rover out. He hadn't altogether lied to Gail; the city was expelling its herds of evening traffic. When he came in sight of the traffic lights that did their best to control the race for the motorway, there were tail-backs in every lane. The next dispensation of the lights moved him no farther than the entrance to a pub car park, and he gave in. He had a pint of ale that tasted increasingly metallic, a ham salad sandwich to tone down the effects, and a packet of crisps to render a second pint somewhat less immediate in its consequences. By now he wasn't sure if he was drinking to delay what he had to do or prepare himself for doing it. As he drained the second pint he saw that the traffic had died away, and he lingered only to visit the Gents with an orchestra under its roof before heading for the car.

Some of the vehicles that were stringing themselves into view down the motorway had switched on their headlamps. For the few moments Geoff would need concealment, the twilight ought to be enough. The traffic lights released him at the motorway, and he had travelled only a few hundred yards up the concrete slope when he parked the car on the hard shoulder.

The pale brow of the motorway, six lanes and a central ridge wide, stood above him against a sky that was turning to ash. The desertion made him feel vulnerable, and not only to being seen— to the memories that were poised to crowd into his mind. He turned on the hazard lights and ducked out of the car, only to find he'd miscalculated. He was at least a hundred yards short of the stretch of motorway that overlooked his old home.

It wasn't far enough to drive. He hurried uphill alongside the parapet lower than his waist and surmounted by a wide rail on stumpy metal posts. When the house came in sight through the railway bridge he turned to the wall. He was peering at it in search of a hiding-place when a glare of light flattened his shadow against the concrete. The headlamps of a police car had found him.

It was on the far side of the motorway, and it didn't stop— surely had no reason. Geoff was heading for the nearest motorway phone to have his car seen to, that was all. Once the police had vanished in the direction of the traffic lights he crouched by the wall. It was decorated with shallow rectangular grooves, and there was half an inch of overhang beneath the capstones, but no niche when he felt for it, only cold rough stone. He straightened up, re-sisting the impulse to clutch at the rail as the height fell away be-neath him, and was fishing out the envelope to check the angle from which the photograph of the wall had been taken when he heard a car approaching up the slope.

It pulled over behind his with an imperative squeal of brakes. He moved his hand away from his pocket and stood still as a car door creaked open. When it slammed he had to turn. The police car had come to find him. The driver was advancing on him at the pace of the hazard lights.

His body was trained for action, but his face had stayed almost plump. An expression that wasn't yet a warning took as much time to form as he spent in approaching within a few feet of Geoff. "Looking for help, sir?" he said.

"Not really for anything," Geoff heard himself blurt, and tried to intensify the neutral look that often helped him into places he needed to investigate. "Thanks for offering, though."

"What's the problem?"

"To be honest, there isn't any. I know we aren't supposed to stop here without one, civilians, I mean." He might have said less if the low sun hadn't been probing his eyes at the same time as blotting out the policeman's face. "Sorry, I'm babbling. The truth is I'm here revisiting my childhood."

"On foot on the motorway?"

Geoff could have said yes. He was scratching around in his mind for some response that would lead no further than itself when the policeman stepped forward and held out his hand. Geoff almost grasped it, having assumed that the man had belatedly recognised him, before he understood what was required. "My licence, yes, of course."

The ragged plastic sheath caught the flap of the envelope in his pocket, and he had to disengage it for fear of spilling in front of the policeman the photograph of where they were standing. "Bit tatty, I'm afraid. Here it is in all its glory, anyway. All present and correct, I think you'll find."

He'd pinched the torn sides of the flat sheath together, but it splayed itself so wide as the policeman's thumb closed over the far end that Geoff made a snatch at the documents in case they slipped out. "Just—" he began to explain, and held his hand back from covering his mouth or fingering the envelope in his pocket or betraying his sudden unsteadiness by clutching at the rail. There was more to fear than the policeman—there was being seen with him.

Eventually the policeman, having extracted the insurance certificate from within the fifteen-year-old licence whose folds were showing their age and subjected the papers to a scrutiny so prolonged it made Geoff feel interrogated, raised his shadowed eyes. "Quite a long way from home, aren't we?"

"How long do you think it should take?" Geoff's nervousness was loosening his words. "I mean, do you know if there's anything I should be looking out for?"

"Depends when you get started. Depends how long it takes to fix your car."

"There's nothing up with it. Sorry, I thought we'd established that."

The sun had edged behind the policeman until he moved to keep it in Geoff's face. "Were you waiting for somebody, sir?"

"Up here? I should say not. If I were involved in anything like that I'd be a fool to do it here, wouldn't you say?"

"What kind of thing is that, sir?"

"The kind of thing you might meet somebody somewhere out of the way for. The kind of thing I investigate sometimes, if my name there means anything to you."

"Should it?"

"Well, you know, *The Goods*, the television series. Or maybe you don't. I'm not suggesting for a moment that I'm in the same league as, I don't know, your favourite footballer."

If possible, that earned even less of a visible response than Geoff's name had. "All I was trying to say," Geoff insisted, "I was here in town signing the book of the series, here where I was born even if you wouldn't think so listening to me, and I'd just driven onto the motorway when I remembered being able to see my old house from here. Not *here*, not *up* here, you understand. The motorway wasn't built then."

He was babbling, he knew. The policeman's inexpressive gaze was trawling words out of him. He felt the taste of ale returning to his lips. He was going to burp, he was going to breathe alcohol into the policeman's face. He crammed a knuckle into his mouth, against his clenched teeth, and gulped until he felt safe to speak. "Sorry. I didn't know when I got out it was going to be this high."

"So you're saying that's your show."

"*The Goods?* Mine and a lot of other people's."

"I saw it once." The policeman paused long enough to be readying a criticism. "I don't remember him looking much like you."

"People never look the same on screen. Fatter, for one thing."

"Have you any other form of identification?"

"What, with a photo? Why would I—" He was going to be arrested not for having drunk too much, Geoff thought, but for claiming to be himself. He looked away from the policeman and the throbbing of the hazard lights and the sun that was continuing to lower itself, the better to drive his dried-up thoughts against the inside of his skull—and then he saw a chance. "There is something, someone, rather. They can identify me at the hotel down there. It was my old house."

The policeman looked down, but at the documents. He slid the insurance certificate inside the licence and closed the torn plastic on them, then he used them to point at Geoff's car. "We'll see about that, shall we? I'll be behind you."

"I'm not sure how to get there from here."

"Watch me in the mirror. I'll show you how to go."

Geoff could only climb into the Rover and start the engine and wait for the police car's headlamps to urge him out of his stasis. It wasn't just his failure to find whatever had been left for him that made him want to stay where he was. He mustn't invent reasons to be nervous, his situation was fraught enough, but he couldn't help feeling watched by not only the policeman. Surely there was no way Ben could learn that Geoff had been with the police—no possibility of his suspecting that Geoff had been talking about him.

sixteen

Though Geoff wasn't quite asleep, he believed he was alone until he felt breath on his face. Moist air found his uppermost ear and turned into words. "It's great now. Come and see. They're asleep."

"Don't. Tickles," Geoff mumbled, and didn't know which way he was turning as the doze into which he'd been sinking did its best to submerge him. Then he was facing the dark outline of Ben's head, which put him in mind of the faceless hole he'd once seen in a fairground sideshow, a hole through which people stuck their faces to make them belong to the cartoon body underneath. "We can't," he said, and was glad to be sufficiently awake to have realised. "How'd we get back in?"

Ben held up an object that borrowed light from somewhere with which to glint, and Geoff was afraid he meant to perform another trick with a knife until the object owned up to just enough of a rattle to identify it. "I've got her keys," Ben said. "Took them out of her bag."

"Suppose she finds out, Ben?"

"She won't want them till the morning, will she? The only way she'll know is if you wake her up, or him. I'm going, so you do what you want, only I thought you'd want to come. Don't if you don't want to play while they can't stop us."

Geoff pushed the edge of the quilt away so as to wipe the spittle of Ben's whisper from his cheek. "I said I would. Get off or I can't get up."

Ben moved at once, so quickly and soundlessly that he seemed to vanish before reappearing as a more compact shape halfway across the room. By the time Geoff had kicked off the bedclothes the boy was lifting a corner of the curtains to admit some of the orange glare from the motorway on the far side of the house. Apart from his shoes, Geoff was already dressed. He thrust his clammy feet into the nearest pair and fumbled to produce two dim sketches of knots and stood up, releasing a creak from the mattress. "I'm ready. Don't know about you," he whispered, using the flat of one hand to level the words at Ben—except that although the curtains hadn't finished swaying together, Ben was at the door.

Geoff had never been able to close it without provoking the mechanism of the knob to click, but as soon as both of them were in the corridor, Ben did. A smell of boiled cabbage rose from the boxed-in darkness of the stairs, and so did the snoring of Geoff's father. He wasn't in the big front bedroom—the room which, despite his insistence that it caught more of the noise and light of the motorway than anywhere else in the house, he insisted he and his wife still use, as if he was more concerned to gather evidence than sleep. He must be in the office.

Before Geoff had time to convey his doubts about trying to sneak past, Ben started down, and there seemed to be nothing left to do but follow, pressing his outstretched fingertips against the lumpy pattern of the wallpaper to steady himself. Just as he reached the hall, which was both carpeted and painted with an orange glow, the snoring faltered, and he had to choke down a giggle of panic that earned him an orange-eyed glance from Ben to ascertain whether he'd finished. When the snoring recommenced he ventured to the front door. Having listened to make sure he wouldn't be letting any sounds into the house, Ben opened the door just short of the point where the hinges would squeal and eased it shut as he came after Geoff.

The glare held the suburb as immobile as a photograph. The lamps along the motorway—inverted circular pans of light spiked on metal stalks—towered over the silenced railway tracks, the intimidated streets. A single car passed on the far side of the motorway with a whoosh like a wind in a tree, and then there was only the start of the squeak of the gate at the foot of the garden. As soon as the boys were through the gate Ben let go of it, and Geoff grabbed it barely in time to stop it from clanging shut behind them. "Hey," he protested, "you nearly—"

"Nearly," Ben agreed, and ran downhill under the railway bridge.

Its echoes exhibited Geoff's footsteps as he followed, then the watchtower lights of the motorway displayed him. Ben was halfway to the foot of the motorway slope. Now that home was out of sight Geoff risked raising his voice. "We won't go too far, will we?"

Ben didn't turn, but the bunch of his pale shadows pivoted around him. "We won't go any further than you're scared to go."

"I'm only scared for you. They won't do much to me if they find out."

Ben sent him a pitying look as he crossed the slip road to the end of the motorway. "I'm used to it," he said.

Geoff ran to join him on the narrow cobbled wedge. Above them the wall began, its concrete parapet no taller than Geoff's waist and not lent much more conviction by a metal rail as wide and half as high. Its lack of protectiveness might have been intended as an extra warning to pedestrians that only cars were allowed, but Geoff was able to believe it meant only children would be safe. He watched Ben step off the wedge and trot uphill along the strip where cars weren't supposed to drive, his knuckles extracting a series of gong-notes from the rail. "See, it's nothing like he says," Ben said. "I'm glad they built it, aren't you? Glad it got on top of him. Are you coming to watch the house?"

"Watch what, Ben?"

"Anything that happens. I bet you hope that's nothing."

"No I don't," Geoff retorted, as angry with himself as with Ben for being right, and stalked after him.

As Ben reached the top of the slope he swung round and stretched his arms wide. Geoff had never seen him hug or be hugged by anyone, and Ben wasn't proposing that now. He seemed to be taking credit for the view—the ranks of houses asleep beneath their turtle roofs, the light glaring off their windows so that it was impossible to judge if any were lit from within, the arch of the bridge pinning down a corner of the Davenport house and most of its garden. Then he leaned across the rail and thumped it with his forearms and began to shout. "Wake up, you dozy stupe. Here I am if you want to look."

"Ben, they'll hear you."

"Who says I don't want them to?" Ben raised his voice so that it echoed under the bridge. "Come and try and catch me. Maybe you'll fall off. Smash your head open so we can see if there's anything inside."

"You'll wake them, Ben."

"No I won't. I never do."

"You never . . ."

"I didn't wake her when I got her keys, did I? And I was in his office before that. I like watching them when they don't know. I like thinking what I could do. Maybe I'll show you when we get back," Ben said, and turned his head just enough for his eyes to find Geoff. "If you want."

Geoff wasn't sure. He was wondering how long Ben had watched him in his room before speaking to him. He might have asked if Ben hadn't pushed himself upright and said "I'm going over."

"Don't, Ben, it's too high," Geoff cried and trailed off, feeling foolish. Ben hadn't meant to climb over the wall; he'd stepped into the nearest motorway lane. "Are you coming?" he said.

"I will in a minute," Geoff said, but craned over the rail. For the moment the traffic lights at the crossroads were performing their act solely for their own benefit. Ben had strolled across the bare bright concrete to the central rail, where he teetered playfully on one leg before jumping over. He ambled to the far wall and leaned back against it, elbows on the rail—leaned back another inch, another. "Ben," Geoff pleaded.

"Come across if you want to stop me."

The brow of the motorway was just too high for Geoff to see if any traffic was approaching in the opposite direction, but he could hear nothing that sounded close. He dashed to the barrier and clambered over it, scraping his shin on a metal edge rougher than the flat glare made it appear. He staggered into the lane beyond it, and heard the sudden revving of a car engine somewhere near and speeding nearer. He sprinted towards Ben, who was watching him as he might have observed the subject of an experiment, and bruised his palms against the wall in time to see the car disappear beneath the motorway. "Thought I wouldn't, didn't you?" he gasped.

Ben leaned back farther on his elbows, gripping his hands together against his stomach. His knees rose and began to shake, his feet strained onto their toes, his face raised itself to the lights that were holding up the seared sky. Geoff saw his knuckly throat stretch. Then he was balanced only on his elbows, and Geoff was about to grab him when he unbent like a bow with such momentum that it took him halfway to the central barrier. "Thought I would, didn't you?" he said.

Geoff hurried after him, overtaking him in time to be first at the wall above the bridge and slap the rail, if timidly. "Maybe we should go home now," he said, "before—"

"Race me first. Let's see who's best."

"You are, Ben. I think you are."

"Let's find out," Ben said, and dropped to all fours, planting his hands on the nearest lane. "Ready?"

The sooner they did it, Geoff told himself, the sooner they could go home. He crouched down, pressing his knuckles against the prickly concrete. "Steady."

"Go," said Ben, and sprang as the word left his mouth.

Geoff was half a second slower. That was no bad thing if it meant Ben would win—and then he saw that Ben would hate him if he thought Geoff had deliberately lost on his behalf. He put on speed and vaulted over the central barrier just as Ben did. Both of them threw out their hands as they sprinted for the far side of the motorway, and slapped the rail so nearly simultaneously that Geoff's impact almost merged with Ben's. "Only just," Geoff panted.

"Bet it won't be this time," Ben said, and crouched again. "Ready."

"Steady," said Geoff, stooping over a breath that filled him with his pulse.

"Wait." Ben raised his head as though to listen, but Geoff heard only his own heartbeat. "Go," he saw Ben mouth.

For the moment nothing mattered except that Ben should have no reason to suspect him of throwing the race. In the second it took Geoff to reach the lane midway between the wall and the barrier, he hardly noticed that the light at the top of the slope had turned pale. Then the headlamp beams exploded over the brow, and two cars intent on their own race swooped down at him.

The beams glared brighter at the sight of him. They seemed to pierce him—to pin him like an insect. The double blare of horns only helped skewer him. Perhaps he was still running, but not fast enough—not when his legs were doing their best to trip him up as they fought to send him back to the wall, not when the cars appeared not even to have started braking. Their blinding light and klaxon chorus and hot oily stench filled his head, and he felt as though he'd already been struck. Then he saw a silhouette dart between him and the headlights, where he wouldn't have believed there was anything like enough space, and its speed conveyed itself to him. He felt a car at the back of his legs—felt sweat cold as metal break out behind his knees—and then the cars were past, still blaring, while he floundered to the barrier.

He almost fell over it, only just remembering to lift a leg. His running stumble took him to the wall above the bridge. His chest struck the rail with a dull bong, and he had to grab the wall so as not to stagger back onto the road. Ben leaned an elbow on the rail and watched him. "That was more like something," Ben said.

Geoff gulped down several breaths in order to be able to speak. "Did you know they were coming?"

"Didn't you?"

Ben sounded more playful than ever, but Geoff wasn't about to join in. "I'm going home."

"We needn't yet. They're still asleep."

"You don't know that. I'm going," Geoff insisted, and made his legs begin to wobble down the hard shoulder.

"That'll wake them, you trying to get in if I don't let you."

"So give me the keys if you're not coming home."

"Home," Ben said with an audible grimace. "All right, Geoffrey, don't shake yourself to bits. I'll come with you. I want to show you they're asleep."

When Geoff reached the cobbles at the foot of the slope his legs had steadied themselves enough for him to let go of the rail. As he headed for the pavement somewhat more rapidly than he planned to go he said "Why do you keep saying that? Mum could have found he's not in bed, or sitting could have woken him."

"He's asleep at his desk with his fists stuck out and she's on her back in bed with her mouth wide open. Looks like someone when you tell them to shut their eyes and open their mouth. I'll show you when we get in," Ben said.

Geoff caught up with him under the bridge. As they left the shadow of the arch Geoff felt as though the house had trained a security light on them. But the curtains stayed drawn, and the front door failed to burst open as they arrived at the gate, which Ben unlatched and held for Geoff before lowering it gently shut. He slipped the key into the front door, and Geoff pressed his arms against his sides to hush the scrape of metal.

Apart from the light of the motorway the hall was unlit, and it was empty of snoring. Every one of Geoff's movements sounded several times as loud as it had any right to be. The office door was shut and underlined by the edge of the glow of a desk lamp. He was tiptoeing towards the stairs—was within a few inches of them—when a hand grasped his sleeve.

It was Ben, who had made no noise at all in closing the front door and coming up behind him. He leaned his face close to Geoff's in the twilight of the hall. "Come and see," he mouthed.

He was reaching for the office doorknob with his other hand. If Geoff struggled or protested, that might waken his father. He allowed himself to be led to the door—to be held by his sleeve as Ben worked the doorknob. The glow beneath the door spread up the edge and extended itself along the top, and the widening gap showed him his father.

He was indeed sleeping at the desk with his fists thrust out before him and his back to the hall. His right cheek rested on his right arm, whose fist and its potential for violence were spotlighted by the inverted cone of the desk lamp. Perhaps that was how Ben had seen him earlier, but Geoff was more impressed and unnerved by Ben's perception than he'd expected. He nodded and let his mouth hang open and gazed admiringly at Ben, and restrained himself from trying to pull away in case Ben prevented him. It was impossible to judge Ben's thoughts from his eyes. A very long time seemed to pass—longer than Geoff would have thought his father could stay comfortable, even if asleep—before Ben released Geoff's sleeve. At that moment his father mumbled fiercely and raised his head.

Geoff froze and bit his lips together. His father's right arm stirred, relieved of its burden, and jerked up in a spasm. The fist clanged against the bell of the desk lamp, levering it vertical, shining it straight at the boys. "What the bloody—" he yelled, and sucked his knuckles. "Stupid bloody—"

Whether the latter was aimed at himself or at the lamp, which he'd seized by the neck, wasn't clear. He was making so much noise that Geoff didn't hear himself flee upstairs, nor Ben behind him. They were almost at the top when he heard his father's footsteps thud across the office. Praying that his father was unable to hear anything except himself, Geoff lunged at the door of his bedroom, swung it open with barely a moan of the hinges, darted in and pulled Ben after him, closing them in just as his mother opened the door of the parental bedroom. "Hide," he risked whispering, and retreated to the bed.

"Who opened this?" his father shouted. "Who's been in here?"

"Never mind it now. See in the morning." The boys' mother was doing her best to keep her voice soft while projecting it down the stairs. "You'll be waking Geoffrey. It wouldn't have been him. Maybe you've woken him. I'm going to see."

Geoff wriggled under the bedclothes and hitched himself to the edge of the mattress. "Get in quick, hide," he said in a whisper that bared his teeth.

He felt the mattress sink with the weight of a body before he realised the other boy was at the bed. He pushed his face into the pillow and squeezed his eyes shut so hard they began to leak. He heard the door inch out of its frame, and his mother hushing his father on the stairs. "Quietly now," she murmured, "he's—"

She fell silent. Geoff heard a board groan as she took a step into the room. He heard his father mount the stairs, having been beckoned, Geoff suddenly knew. He could only lie motionless and will his parents to be seeing nobody but him in the bed. Then the bedroom light seized his eyes through their lids, and footsteps marched to both sides of the bed. As the bedclothes were snatched off the mattress, he began to shiver as if he might never stop.

seventeen

"Leave him alone," Geoff heard himself protest, perhaps aloud, and stared at himself in the mirror. In the dawn over Brent he looked haggard with sleeplessness, not at all the ideal driver. A milk cart he overtook might have been enacting his sluggishness. He could barely remember the motorway on which he'd spent most of the last five hours; he'd been trying not to remember the consequences of having concealed Ben in his bed. Now he should be home in less than half an hour, and he wanted nothing to distract him.

At least the Liverpool policeman hadn't arrested him. "You're never going to lock him up for seeing where he was born," the landlady of the Home From Home had said. She'd done her best to entice the policeman with an offer of tea and home-made cakes, but he'd retired to his vehicle after cautioning Geoff for not having had a conventional reason to park on the hard shoulder. Nevertheless Geoff had hardly regained the motorway before repeating his offence. He'd located the envelope almost at once, in a niche that had been scraped beneath the capstone less than an arm's length from where he'd previously searched. He hadn't risked examining his find until he arrived at the motorway services ten miles up the road. One glance had shown him that the photograph recalled far too much.

It wasn't going to reach him now. He switched on the car radio and found a local station in time for the travel news. There was no warning about his route, and here was the news: a plane crash, a riot, a renewal of war, but no mention of the couple who had been murdered near Windsor. He suspected that the media were finished with them unless the police announced they had a lead, and he didn't know how much he was hoping the police would track their man down before Geoff had no option but to follow up the photograph—to dig deeper in himself.

Where the North Circular met Hanger Lane a dispatch rider overtook him with a spurt of fumes and sped into Ealing. On a pond in Gunnersbury Park a duck fanned its head high with its wings. Beyond Kew Bridge, beside the gardens, the alarms of a house and a parked car were calling to each other. The road swung away from the Thames, then back at Mortlake, and ten minutes later Geoff was home.

The bridge was counting the wagons of a goods train as prolonged as a dream. His overnight bag leaned over the shoulder it was strapped to as he unlocked the front door and typed the code on the keyboard of the alarm before it could declare him to be an intruder. Having deposited his bag on the couch nearest the door, he tiptoed upstairs.

At least he hadn't wakened Gail and Paul; he couldn't even hear their breathing. The shared spout of the bath taps loosed a drip as he brushed his much-travelled teeth and gave his face the wash it had been missing all night. He delivered himself of the contents of his bladder, more than a minute's worth, and leaned on the handle of the flush. He glanced into the guest room and the workroom, across which a blank computer screen and the glint of the river greeted him, before he padded to the top floor.

Sunlight was probing between the curtains of the window above the stairs that climbed into the bedroom. Light pierced Geoff's eyes as his head rose above the floor, and he blinked hard. He saw a pale rectangular blotch that was the window, and then the beds considered taking shape beyond a patch of blindness that moved wherever he looked. He made out the wooden cage of Paul's cot, the double bed between it and the stairs to which Gail had fixed a temporary gate, the contorted forms lying still in the cot and the bed. Geoff closed his eyes as he unlatched the gate, and then he could see. Bedclothes were tangled in the cot and on the bed, but there was no sign of Gail or Paul.

He stumbled to the window and snatched the curtains open. His family was nowhere on the road beside the river, and nobody was to be seen from the back window. Brittleness spread from his scalp through his body as he ran downstairs. Perhaps the phone might give him a clue—the number of the last person to have called, if they hadn't blocked their number. He was halfway down the last flight when he saw a note which must have been propped against the phone had slid down beside it. At that distance he could read just a single word: GONE.

His knuckles struck the telephone, clattering the receiver in its hollow, as he grabbed the scrap of paper. The handwriting was Gail's—became more like hers as it progressed. There wasn't much reassurance to be found in that when it suggested how close she must have been to panic, nor in her words. GONE TO HOSPITAL WITH PAUL was all they said.

eighteen

When the bars of Paul's cot rattled Gail thought the dawn had roused him. She felt as if she'd spent the night observing her thoughts. There was nothing like wanting to sleep to rob you of the ability, and just because she'd hoped to catch up on her rest she'd had a spell of reliving her life with Geoff. She'd been on vacation in London when a friend of hers had introduced them at a party as both working in television, and before the evening was over they'd established she was a researcher and his series had just lost one to another channel and a great deal more that had brought the two of them together. She was proud of having got the job all by herself—she'd always been grateful to her parents for employing her on their Bay Area channel, but she'd wanted to prove she could excel without their help. Only since Paul had been born she often wished her mother could be there to help with him.

Her parents would be visiting before the month was out, a thought that allowed her to doze until the bars rattled again. "Try and sleep a bit more, babe," she pleaded. Then the toddler began to wail in some kind of protest, and she floundered out from beneath her half of the quilt, knuckling her eyelids up as she trekked across the yard of carpet.

Paul was clutching the top bar, looking hot and rumpled and confused. "Mom's here now," she assured him and herself. "You aren't worse, are you, babe? We weren't going to risk the medicine Catriona's mommy gave us unless you got worse." She stroked his cheek, which was puffy and too warm. Perhaps he'd been lying on it, she thought, and laid her palm on his forehead. It was hot as the July day would be at noon.

"What a hot little head," Gail told him. She wasn't going to panic. She fetched the medicine from the night table and gave it a vigorous shake, coating the inside with thick pink liquid, and poured out just less than the contents of a teaspoon, which she slipped into Paul's mouth. "What a face," she said with a sympathetic grin, "it never tastes as bad when you're older," and carried him down to the bathroom to mop his face with a cold damp cloth. She popped all the studs of his sleepsuit and peeled it off him and flung the soggy wad of it into the laundry basket, and helped him wriggle into another night-time overall once he'd demonstrated his widdling skill. By the time she delivered him back to his cot his forehead was cooler, and he was half asleep.

She wasn't going to sleep until he did. She lay on the quilt and let her eyes close for a moment, not much more than that, and then again for not much longer. If she stopped watching him, she thought or perhaps dreamed, he might be taken from her and come back changed, if he came back. The fear jabbed her awake, and she heard Paul stirring. She peered towards the cot and saw standing at the bars a figure that, though it was wearing Paul's clothes, had the puffy red swollen-eyed face of a monster.

She jumped up so violently that he wobbled backwards and fell over. "It's all right," she said, at least as much for her own benefit. "It's going to be." His having acquired the sort of face mad scientists in old movies gave themselves by drinking potions had to mean he was allergic to some element of the medicine. She saw his face readying itself to wail, and picked him up, and heard him try-ing—only trying to voice his distress, because he could scarcely breathe. She hugged him to her and ran downstairs faster than she thought she had ever moved in her life.

She almost dialled 911 before she remembered the British equivalent. In not much time at all so far as the clock was concerned, an efficient female voice asked her what service she required. Gail managed to weather the pause before the voice of the ambulance service produced itself, and barely heard its questions for answering them. "He's nearly three. He's having trouble breathing. Swollen eyes and mouth. Very. An antibiotic. I'll have it here for you to see," and at last "How long do you think . . ."

She poked the top of her breast with the aerial to push the rod into the receiver, which she fumbled back into its stand before hurrying upstairs, Paul's clammy puffed-up cheek quivering against her lips. All she could hear was the wheezing of his attempts to breathe. She pulled on yesterday's clothes and grabbed the bottle with Catriona's name on it. "Sorry, babe," she whispered, "I only meant . . ." She made her way downstairs with both hands full and held Paul while she set about writing Geoff a note. Then the window to the river began throbbing with blue light, and she heard the sliding of two metal doors. She scribbled the quickest message she could think of before running to the ambulance.

One paramedic was built like a bouncer, squashed nose and all. He glanced at the label on the bottle she displayed, then stooped over Paul in her arms to peer at him, in the process caressing the back of her hand with a lock of hair that had been helping to conceal his baldness. "Reaction," he said. "Just hop in the back, love, and pull them down for me."

"I'm sorry?" said Gail, meaning the opposite.

"We'll need to give him a shot in his bum."

She sat on a padded bench inside the ambulance and stripped Paul as far as the top of his chubby muscular thighs, by which time the thinner paramedic was waiting with a hypodermic and an ominously regretful look. "Let's hope this makes you yell, son," he said.

Did he really have to jab the needle so deep into the muscle of Paul's buttock? The small body jerked in her arms, so violently she thought the contents of the syringe might have been too much for him. Then she felt his lungs suck in a heroic breath and hold it for a second before launching a bawl that brought tears to her eyes— tears mostly of relief. "That's it," the bouncer said.

She raised Paul's face to hers as she dressed him. His eyes were still swollen, but to some extent with tears, and he was squalling as if he'd just been born. "You won't be taking us in, you mean?" she said.

"Have to have him checked, love. We'll be off if you're set."

She hefted her howling bundle and stepped down from the ambulance. "You can leave him with us," the needle-wielder said.

"Thanks, but no." Gail programmed the alarm and locked the door, crooning to Paul. He began to gulp himself quieter as the ambulance sped through the village. "This is exciting, isn't it?" she said. "Everything has to stop for us." It almost seemed the world had, except for a woman trying to disentangle the leads of three Pekinese on the glittering common and a solitary golfer practising strokes on the course behind the Convent of the Sacred Heart. Then the ambulance swung into the grounds of the hospital, past the factory where they made artificial limbs, and she saw other vehicles unloading casualties, a man with a sodden crimson pad over one eye, a woman clutching to her head a reddened wig that Gail saw in dismay was her scalp, a teenage youth with the right leg of his jeans slashed up to the knee, exposing flesh and, if she wasn't as mistaken as she hoped she was, bone too. They made her feel guiltier than ever, especially when the bouncer ushered her past all of them and found a young doctor whose face looked starved of sleep, his eyes squeezed bright by their red rims. He listened to a description of the adrenaline shot before turning any attention to Paul and his mother. "What did you give him?" he asked her.

She held up the bottle and bent her thumb away from the name on it so hard her joints ached. The doctor took the bottle from her and frowned at it, then at Paul. "Catriona?"

"Rona," Paul declared with all the force of not having spoken for hours.

"You sound like a survivor," the doctor told him, and focused his tired eyes on Gail.

"She's a friend of mine's little girl. She's in medicine, my friend is. Catriona, shush a moment, Paul, Catriona had the same as him, the current bug. I wasn't going to give him any of her medicine, but then his temperature went stratospheric and it seemed the best idea to try a spoonful when the surgery wouldn't be open for hours. I know I shouldn't have."

"Has he suffered any kind of reaction like this before?"

"Never. Nothing like it. None at all."

"You'll need to show this to your doctor." As he passed her the medicine she saw his hand was trembling a little, no doubt with fatigue. He held onto the bottle and said "If you're worried about facing him, I'd say with no history of reaction he might have prescribed it himself."

She didn't want to be given excuses: she wanted someone other than herself to blame her on Paul's behalf. Perhaps old Dr. Chatterjee would when she owned up to her mistake. "We'll just take your details and then I think we can send you home. You look to me as if you'd come through worse than this," the young doctor told Paul, but she wouldn't use his strength as a reason to be soft with herself. When the paperwork was completed she had to struggle to remember the number of the taxi firm she and Geoff used. "Nigh," Paul echoed as she repeated the name aloud. He might have triggered something in her brain, because at once the number came to her, and she called Twenty-four Hour Knights to send a car.

nineteen

And I think you should definitely keep after the supermarket, Gail," said Angharad Bailey, producer of *The Goods*. "There's something big and nasty there hoping nobody will notice."

"Not just cheap and nasty like their stock," said Anna Wren, the editor.

"Don't say you've ever shopped there," director Bella Raymond protested with a shake of her small blonde thatched head.

Anna propped her heavy forearms on the long conference table and displayed her rueful face on top of her knuckles. "Once."

"I thought Fortnums was your style. I'd never have taken you for a Frugo customer."

"Neither would my cats, and believe me they let me know it. Frugo was the only place open at midnight when they started crying they were starving."

"Open all hours, but not to scrutiny," said Angharad, and patted herself on the head, flattening her cascade of red hair where it escaped beneath the arch of a tortoiseshell comb. "No overtime and no unions, and the customers can't afford to care."

"The guy I'd almost persuaded to tell his story has cried off," Gail said. "The way he was talking he wouldn't just have been out of a job. Seems like staff who try to go public find themselves in trouble with the police or their house broken into or their car stolen, stuff like that. I don't think we're in the business of destroying people's lives to get a story, are we? Don't worry, I'll find another way to it. I'm in a hunting mood now. I'm glad to be back, and amazed I was the reason MetV resurrected the crèche."

"You were just the last and best," Angharad told her. "We told upstairs we couldn't be sure of keeping up the standard without you, and they got the message there was one saving they better hadn't make."

"How about you, Geoff?" Bella said. "Glad your tour's over? You haven't been your usual fluent self."

"He does look a bit shattered," said Anna.

"Sorry if I was too eager to establish where we're heading," Angharad said, pushing her comb deeper into her hair.

"I'll be fine so long as nobody tries to persuade me I'm indispensable," Geoff told her.

"We won't, because you are."

"And not just to us," Gail added.

Geoff was searching for an appropriately self-deprecating response when the door opened with a knock just about preceding it, and Ruth from the financial news looked in. "Thought I'd better answer your phone when it didn't give up. Sounds as if it may be urgent, and they'll only speak to you, Geoff."

"Point proved," said Bella.

"The price of fame," Anna suggested.

"They're who?" Geoff asked the financial reporter, and when she responded with a polite smile "Did they say it had something to do with *The Goods?*"

"They said only you could deal with it."

"We'll talk about you until you get back," Angharad said.

Geoff always experienced a surge of anticipation whenever a new story seemed about to break, a new institution-sized stone to be turned over, and a hint of adrenaline made itself felt as he followed Ruth along the corridor to the office opposite hers. In the sunlight across Hyde Park the upturned white receiver on the grey expanse of his desk looked as though it had been carved from soap, the cord curling away from it like an unbroken shaving. As he picked it up he saw cars dart onto the Marble Arch roundabout, dragging segments of traffic along Bayswater Road after them. "Geoff Davenport," he said.

"That's the Mr. Davenport who investigates."

It was a man's voice, light and rapid and with an edge to its vowels. "I'm part of a team that does," Geoff said.

"You're the part most people see. Look up to, you might say."

"I'm afraid that's in the nature of the medium, having just me visible, I mean. Can I ask . . ."

"Of course. Pardon me. You must be expecting an interview."

"Not that I'm aware of. Why . . ."

"You must think I'm asking to interview you."

"I wouldn't assume that. It isn't generally why people ring us here."

"Assume if you want to, Mr. Davenport. It is a kind of interview. I'd like to discover what you feel able to say about a particular matter."

"If it's something we've broadcast, you ought to know we always pass a copy to the appropriate authorities, and not only of the material we broadcast. If it's anything we're in the process of investigating—"

"It would be more in that area."

"You'll need to speak to my producer, then. If you'd like to hold on while I fetch her—"

"That won't be necessary, Mr. Davenport, or advisable. The matter in question is being investigated, but not by your team."

"I—see." All at once Geoff found he had considerably fewer words at his disposal. "By you, you mean."

"Exactly." The caller paused and said "By the police."

"Which is you, you're saying."

"That saves time. Some aspects of law enforcement aren't public knowledge, if you follow me."

"I don't know if I do. To be frank, I'm not clear yet why you've called me."

"Now, Mr. Davenport." The reproof was sharp and disappointed. "I imagine we're both thinking of a person I've been led to believe is close to you."

"Go on."

"I think you must be clear now, Mr. Davenport. I think you must know what to do."

"You're asking me . . ."

"To help in any way you can."

"Perhaps you can tell me what you already know."

"More than you in some areas. Let me propose an exchange of information and begin by asking if you've been contacted."

"By . . ."

"Mr. Davenport."

Geoff couldn't tell if that was intended as a rebuke or a precise answer. Not only the sunlight in his face was making his throat feel parched. "Look," he said, "I don't know how much longer I'm likely to be alone in here. Somebody's bound to come looking, and then I won't be able to talk."

"What do you suggest?"

"I . . ." The fear that Ben might somehow learn he'd talked to the police had been waiting for this moment to revive it. "I ought to leave that up to you," he said.

"I take it you're implying we should meet."

"Isn't that what you've been leading up to?" When that was greeted by silence, or possibly a breath, Geoff said "Did you have somewhere in mind? How would I recognise you?"

This time a breath was definitely audible. Though it was short, it was split in half, and by its nasal shrillness he knew it for a snigger. Then the voice—no longer the same voice, but the same speaker— said "Well played, Geoffrey. Very close. You're learning."

"It's you." If he said that, or betrayed that reaction in any way, Geoff saw Ben would know he'd been tempted to inform on him: barely in time, Geoff saw. He swallowed to ease his shrunken throat, and closed his eyes to fend off the brightness that was flaring out of the contents of the office. "It *was* you," he said as lightly as he could.

"Don't tell me you weren't sure."

Geoff's lips twitched, and he almost overstated his loyalty. Before he could speak Ben said "When did you know?"

Geoff thought fast, but had to speak first. "Guess," he said.

"Don't play with me too much. We need to get serious."

"When you wouldn't say what you were, wouldn't even give me a name."

"That's our secret, isn't it? Who I am and what. That's my present to you for old times' sake. I was making sure it still means something to you now you're back at work."

"It means as much as it ever did, Ben. But listen, I'm not playing now. I meant it when I agreed to meet you, the real you."

"We've a long way to go before that, Geoffrey. How did you like the reminders I've left you so far?"

"I wasn't supposed to like them, was I? They brought too much back."

"That's our Geoffrey, always the sensitive one. Just think what you may have to remember before you come to the end of the trail."

"Look, Ben, I want to help. I'll meet you any time, anywhere you say. You must want that or you wouldn't be calling. But I can't keep making time to search. I can't go driving halfway up the country just to find a photograph when they need me here at work."

"Couldn't you wait to be back at it? Don't you care about anybody you can't put in front of the public?"

"You know bloody well I do, Ben. I should think if anyone does—"

"I'd have thought you would be more concerned about your little boy."

"What do you mean?" Threats were ready to crowd out of Geoff's mouth, every one of them helpless. "What are you saying about him?"

"I'm saying it about you, didn't you hear? You and your wife, going back to work and leaving him with someone as if you've no idea what can happen to a child then."

"We aren't leaving him. He's here with us."

"He'll be learning how to watch, will he? How to watch until you've got enough material before you stop it."

"It isn't just material, it's evidence. And I hope you won't say that when you and I were children—"

"There's plenty yet for you to see. If you don't go looking soon there'll be some more news for you to hear."

"If that means what you want me to think it means, Ben—if it does and you want to be stopped, why don't you stop it yourself?"

"You don't know what you're asking, Geoffrey. Why don't I stop?" Ben's voice had grown playful—it sounded as though it was dancing on an edge. "It's too much fun."

"I can't believe that, Ben. Not of you. I'm not sure I even believe you're the person who's been doing—whatever it is."

"You will."

Geoff's surroundings flared again: the desks occupied by papers, a gathering above Hyde Park of blinding clouds with contours sharp as tinfoil, the lines of traffic hitching themselves to Marble Arch and speeding away. It wasn't just Ben's words that had unsettled him; he'd heard Gail's voice along the corridor. "Ben, listen. If you don't want—"

"You know what I want, and I'll be checking to see you've done it. Now do you want me to keep my promise?"

"Which was that?" Geoff said, hearing footsteps start towards the room.

"Don't say you've forgotten. I said this time I'd give you an idea what I do."

"I remember." Geoff felt his mind preparing to protect itself. "Better tell me, then. We haven't much time."

"Eager Geoffrey. That's more like it. You'll be the only one who knows apart from me and the police and some people who can't talk any more. They couldn't for a while, however much I'll bet they tried." This time his snigger sounded not unlike a shiver. "I put their lipstick on so they can have a kiss," he said, and Gail came into the room.

It was impossible to tell whether Ben heard her footsteps. No sooner had he finished speaking than he'd gone, leaving the receiver to hum monotonously at Geoff. Replacing it allowed Geoff to turn away for long enough to think what to say to Gail. "It could be something. I'll tell you about it when I've had a chance to think. I may want to follow it up."

twenty

The train was ten minutes late at Waterloo. That surely wasn't long enough for Geoff to seem to have decided against meeting, but he sprinted out of the station onto the concrete walkway leading to the South Bank. Beneath the scoured pale sky the sunlight was so fierce it felt like a weight on his scalp and shoulders. As he hurried down the steps to the riverside a pennant of cloud lowered itself behind the clock tower of the Houses of Parliament across the river. Most of the benches sprouting from the tables outside the National Film Theatre were occupied, but no amount of peering at the drinkers there or in the bar crowded with voices showed him anyone he recognised. He was excusing his way out of the bar, and narrowing his eyes at the silhouettes of browsers in a second-hand book market on the promenade, when he realised he was being hailed. "Here, come and tell me if you know this face."

Geoff had to blink hard before he located Terry, leaning over a large book on the corner of a stall. He was leaner and several shades darker than the last time Geoff had seen him. His compacted face bore its default expression of readying itself for a surprise, the corners of its blue eyes crinkling, the thin lips slightly parted. He stuck out a hand well before Geoff was within range, and prolonged the handshake almost negligently while he tilted his head to indicate the book. "That's Ginger."

Geoff saw a line of young women with hair as white as their short dresses. Their arms were on one another's shoulders, their raised left legs stretched leftward. Not a face could have been smiling harder, yet all the eyes were blank. Somebody had scraped every one down to the white of the page. "She's well hidden if she is," Geoff said.

"Sixth from the right. Despite the mutilations, it's her. *Bouncing Blondes from Brooklyn*, are they? I'd better take the evidence with me." Terry squared the unglued pages before turning to the price on the flyleaf. "Bit steep for a crippled old library book that's been defaced as well."

"Out of print," the stallholder, whose curly hair doubled the outline of his cranium, informed him.

"What's this library sale price you couldn't quite rub out? Maths were never my subject, Geoff, you'll remember. He can't be asking a hundred times what he paid, can he?"

"I believe he is. Or maybe now he isn't."

"Could be in better nick," the stallholder admitted. "Call it five."

"Let's," Terry said, closing *Scenes You Never Saw*, and nodded at Geoff to send him towards the bar. "Solid performance," he murmured as he caught up with him. "I think he's convinced you're on the force too."

"He wasn't breaking any law though, was he?"

"He was guilty of something. Couldn't you tell?"

Geoff wondered how he himself might fare under that kind of scrutiny. "Still bitter?" he said.

"Make it a pint since I've finished for the day. I'll keep us a place out here."

Geoff reached the bar after a good deal of arrested sidling, and bought himself a glass of Merlot to clink with the tankard. Terry had made space opposite himself with the reopened book. "Here's to whatever," he said. "Our old school if they haven't set fire to it. The pool and whoever else climbs out."

"How long has it been, Terry?"

"Fifteen months since I came to the Yard. Most of a year since I said we should get together for a drink."

"Sorry about that. Blame work."

"Better too much than the other thing. I used to argue with my granddad about that, but he was right all right. Too many characters around with nothing to do except turn against the rest of us."

"Anyone particular in mind?"

Terry raised a fist with his tankard in it and took a drink as a preamble to saying "You aren't fishing for material, are you, Geoff?"

"That'd make me some kind of worm, wouldn't it? I hope you don't think I wanted us to get together for anything like that. We don't go for cases the police are investigating. Of course if there's ever anything you think it might be a help to you for me to know . . ."

"I'll keep you in mind." Terry sounded friendly rather than convinced. "There are things you're ace at sorting out, and things best left to my lot."

Geoff felt as though he'd talked himself into a dead end. "Still fond of your old films, I see."

"Those were the days, when the studio had control and most people had too."

"I can see why you wouldn't want to watch anything too real." That got Geoff nowhere, and he dipped his glass towards the blinded photograph. "Why do you think someone did that?"

"Either they thought nobody would know what they do when they're alone or they wanted someone to."

"You've more insight into cases like that than I would have."

"You aren't saying because I catch people you wouldn't want to meet I'm like them."

"Not a bit. Not at all. You've more idea of how they really are than I have, that's all I meant. And I'll be honest, I did want to ask you about something, purely off the record, no connection with my job."

Terry shut the cover on the loose pack of pages and gave Geoff all his attention, more than Geoff found he welcomed. "I thought we were getting to it. What's it going to be?"

"Let me tell you why I'm asking first. It may sound like over-reacting to you, though I'm sure you know how people can be. You like to put their minds at rest, especially if it's someone close to you, don't you?"

"Tell you what, Geoff, you don't need to crab around it so much. If you say it's not for your show I believe you. You can stop selling me."

"Good enough. It's just this. My wife's parents will be staying for a few days and then doing Britain for three weeks. The only problem is, and I can't say I blame her for being a bit anxious, my wife, it's no exaggeration to say she's been losing sleep. Actually that's more to do with the youngest member of the family, but while she's lying awake she keeps worrying about these old couples who've been found however they've been found."

"Usually by their families."

"That's what we thought. Something else that would prey on her mind, of course." Geoff was unhappily aware that however devious he was capable of being while investigating for *The Goods*, he was less skilled on his own behalf, and misrepresenting Gail as well. "Am I going to be able to reassure her, do you think?"

"How would you want to do that?"

"If we could tell her parents anything to look out for, the sort of place they shouldn't go, any situations to avoid . . ."

"Believe me, if we knew that we'd have released it to all you media people."

"Don't tell me what they are if you can't, but have you no leads at all?"

"Not one single. Just eight old couples dead in not many more years, two this year already, and what's left of eight families trying to live with it."

Until that moment Geoff hadn't known how much he was hoping the police were close to making an arrest. "You'll have had a psychologist construct a profile of him though, won't you?" he said. "I assume it's a him. I hear these, they mostly are."

"He's bloody clever, that's for sure. Maybe just for once he'll think he's cleverer than he is."

It was his father's voice Geoff heard, and the guilt it roused was so sharp he could only try to talk over it. "Why," he said, "why . . ."

"Why doesn't come into my job much. There's enough people think why's important without me having to. I know why I do the job, and that'll do me."

"You still might wonder why someone like that does what he does."

Terry observed him over the tankard before lowering it. "What do you think that is?"

"He kills them, doesn't he. If there's more, I'd hardly know."

"Your in-laws should be safe if they're visiting. He seems to like to get his victims in their homes." Terry pushed aside the tankard so as to lean across the table. "Just between us, not for broadcasting. When they're found they're always dead, but he only kills one."

"I don't . . ."

"I thought of a name for him," Terry murmured and stood up, his gaze trapping Geoff's. "The Kissing Bandit," he said out loud. "Same again?"

Geoff forced his mouth to work: to smile, to speak. "Please," he said, and watched Terry head for the bar, having relieved Geoff of his last hope. Deep in his mind Geoff had wanted to believe Ben was only playing a tasteless game, claiming responsibility for crimes with which he had no connection. He downed the last of his wine, which returned sourly to his throat as Terry reappeared. "So how's life otherwise?" Terry said, setting down the drinks. "What's the news on your brother?"

"My . . ." Geoff had to dislodge some words from his mouth before his silence or his clumsiness betrayed him. "You mean my . . ."

"You used to call him your brother even when your parents said he wasn't. Did you ever hear from him?"

Geoff shook his head and almost spilled the wine he was making to sip as the alternative to draining it. "Less and less likely as the years go by."

"Maybe he'll give you a surprise when you're least expecting it. Don't you ever wonder what he's up to?"

"I wonder that all right. Christ, yes."

"Thought so. Knew you hadn't changed that much. He's still your family, however far he's gone."

"I've someone younger to care for now," said Geoff, digging out his wallet to produce from among the plastic rectangles the shot of Paul in Gail's arms. "I'm making sure he grows up right," he said, and much more along those lines until he was certain even a policeman would take him to be just a father with no more worries than everyone should have about the world.

twenty-one

J ess never wore a hat except on holiday abroad, but that Sunday she wished she had. She felt as though the sun was targeting her scalp. The heat made her a little dizzy, and it shrank her thoughts like drops of water unable to meet so as to flow. She ought to feel better once she was inside Pete Denton's flat, not least for having found a reason to see where and how he lived.

The car wash on the corner of his road was holding up its insect legs of brushes to show how dry and dusty they were. A less than teenage boy on a mountain bike raced across the forecourt, guzzling Zingo from a plastic bottle he then flung under a car with two wheels on the pavement. Many of the tall white houses had spilled people dressed for the beach onto the front steps, but the occupants of Pete's house were represented only by a little girl sitting on the top step.

She wore the lower half of a minute green bikini and was solemnly dunking a doll wearing the whole of one in a jug of water. "You can swim," she was insisting. "It's the simplest. Just float." Jess gave her a smile she was too preoccupied with teaching to return, and read the name-tags by the doorbells. She was taking her finger away from her lips so as to reach for the bellpush, and rubbing a trace of lipstick from her fingertip with her thumb, when the little girl bumped her thin shoulder-blades against the front door, which swung inwards. "She can go in if she wants, can't she, Salmon?" she said to the doll. "We let ladies in. It'll be a good surprise."

"Who do you think I'm visiting?" Jess said.

"We'd like it if it was Mr. Denton, wouldn't we, Salmon? Nobody ever comes to see him."

"That's a bit sad. What does he do when he's home, then?"

"We don't know, do we? Nobody sees in his room. He doesn't stay in much."

"Is he in now, do you know? Maybe I'd better ring to check."

"He's up. Me and Salmon heard him before."

"Up. You mean . . ."

"He sleeps funny. Not like us," the little girl said, and dropped the doll head first into the jug. "You try properly now, Salmon. You can do it if you want to."

"So you don't think anyone will mind if I go up."

"Salmon and me don't, and there's nobody else in."

"Well, thank you. Thank you, Salmon," Jess added in the direction of the legs protruding from the jug, and felt it was polite to ask "Why's she called that?"

"It's her colour," the little girl said with several times her age's worth of ostentatious patience.

Only if the salmon came out of a tin, thought Jess, managing to look suitably corrected as she ventured into the house. The glossy white walls of the broad hall gleamed like ice and laid a chill on her. A wide staircase with banisters supported by arthritic posts bent itself double to reach the next floor, and Jess saw a trail of drops leading downstairs from the flat where the jug must belong. Somewhere in the house she heard a repeated fanfare, and as she turned past the middle floor the music proved to have announced a man's voice—a television's voice. "For most of us childhood is a place we had to leave," it said, "but for some it's a place they may never escape from . . ."

As Jess left the stairs, the banister rattled an upright. Another voice that sounded less professionally assured had taken up the tale, beyond the right-hand door at the top of the house. The door had been not too expertly stripped down to the scratched wood. It bore a brass doorknob that smelled of metal polish, and a brass number 6 that tallied with his name-tag downstairs, but no bell-push. A spyhole gleamed at her from beneath the polished number. She raised a hand to knock, and then she peered one-eyed through the lens.

She saw a miniature hallway drowning in green that had swollen the walls into curves. At the end of it, beyond an open door almost too small to be recognisable as one, a point of light flickered like an undersea lure. It must be the television, which she could hear describing a nightmarish childhood. She felt as though the microscopic view and the hesitant voice were shrinking her in readiness to draw her in, beginning with her eye. She rested a hand on the panel to push herself away, and the point of light went out. The voice was silenced in the middle of a word, and the door was snatched away from her so swiftly that she almost fell into Pete Denton's arms.

She didn't know what he would have done if she had. His eyes weren't saying, and his smile seemed meant exclusively for himself. As she regained her balance, she saw he was holding the remote control for the television. "Did you see me coming?" she demanded.

His eyes joined in the smile and lit it up. "Maybe in my dreams."

"Oh, very witty," Jess said. "So this is where you live."

"The place I call home."

"Are you likely to invite me in, do you think?"

She could have imagined the proposal was outside his experience. For some moments he only continued to smile, and then he said "What made you come?"

"Just to see how you were, Pete."

"And how might that be?"

"Fine by the look of you. Same as ever. You tell me. You know yourself best."

"Like nobody else."

Footsteps were coming upstairs, making so little impression on the emptiness of the lower floors they seemed rather to be demonstrating it, and Jess heard the little girl say "We'll get you some new water and see if you can float in that." Jess would have expected his expression to acknowledge his fellow tenant, but it didn't stir. "She told me I should come straight up," she said.

"She's the concierge today, is she?"

"There's nobody else in. Not much of a surprise on a day like this."

"Were you hoping for one?"

"I told you, all I wanted was to make sure you haven't had any trouble with my ex."

"Oh, that. Him. No trouble. I'm sure he'll tell you the same."

"He won't get the chance."

"Sent him away, have you?"

"Maybe it'll help him grow up."

"That's still how it's done, is it?" Pete said, and stepped back. "I'm being rude, aren't I? I'm supposed to ask you in."

"Not unless you want to."

"Why wouldn't I?"

She almost thought the question invited an answer. He watched her cross the threshold, and didn't turn until she'd closed the door behind her, shutting herself in the underwater glow that turned her hands green; then he strode along the corridor, rapping on doors with his knuckles. "Bedroom. Bathroom. Kitchen," he said, but opened none of them. "And here's where I mostly live."

"Did you move from a smaller place?"

The room contained the television and a video recorder that were faced by a chair with a footrest. That was all the furniture. Hanging behind the television was a single framed picture, an abstract as green as the carpet and the walls, which would have been of that colour even if the green curtains weren't drawn. She felt as though the self-absorbed colour was stifling her thoughts. She let herself sink into the chair as he upturned a hand at it. "Are you going to finish furnishing?" she persisted.

"It does for me."

The rectangle in the picture-frame wasn't an abstract painting but a mirror, placed so that the head and shoulders of anybody seated in the chair were visible above the screen. Her face looked rather too much like a cartoon of nausea, so that she met Pete's interested gaze instead. As if she'd given him a cue he said "Drink?"

"What are you having?"

"Nothing alcoholic."

"Don't you like to lose control?"

"Nobody's ever seen me do that."

Maybe he should let someone, she thought but refrained from saying. "Water would be fine on a day like this."

"I'll bring it to you."

As soon as he glided out of the room she realised all over again how empty it was. It seemed to have absolutely no smell. She heard the rumble of tap-water in a metal sink grow shrill and confined in a glass, and the surreptitious movement of the videotape. She glanced about for the remote control, then remembered that he'd slipped it into his pocket. At least she had time to identify the theme tune she'd heard on her way upstairs, and when Pete reappeared with a single glass she said triumphantly *The Goods.*

"Water."

"Yes. Thank you, Pete." She took a sip, which tasted more metallic than it should until she understood that she was smelling polish on her hand from the brass knob. "I just figured out what you were watching when I came up. The programme you'd taped."

At that moment she became fully aware that there was no other tape in the room, only the slipcase gaping at her with its long thin mouth on top of the video recorder. "I'm sorry," she said, feeling as though she'd trespassed somehow. "Was someone you know in there?"

He was standing against the light through the curtains, his face less defined than the room. "Where?" he said.

"A care home, I thought it was, the bit I heard. Was there someone?"

"Not for long."

"They got out, you mean?"

"They think so."

"Have they a family of their own now? That ought to help."

"They've one of those all right."

She closed both hands around the perspiring glass. It had struck her that she could be talking about Pete if he had later been adopted. "Have you been to see yours yet?" she said.

"I'm saving that."

"Saving it for . . ."

"For when I can take all the time I need."

She mustn't trespass further, not now—perhaps if there came a time when he felt more at ease with her. "You're owed a break," she said. "Have a word with Harry. Tell him why you need to go away."

"Maybe I will."

He sounded playful, which only made her feel awkward and intrusive, understanding far less than she presumed. She drained the glass and took hold of the arm of the chair. "I'll let you have your throne," she said.

She must have touched a lever. The chair fell away from behind her, and she sprawled backwards, dropping the glass with a dull hollow clunk. "Don't say I've broken it," she said, and "What an exit," holding out her hands for Pete to help her up.

He was standing over her before she'd finished speaking. "Did you find out what you wanted to know?" he said.

"Whether you were all right, yes."

"And am I?"

"I think so. I hope so, Pete."

"Who's going to hear?"

"Nobody at all." She didn't know why she felt threatened, pinned down, because what had she done? She wished that his face were clearer—that he were. "I won't be discussing you with anyone if you don't want me to," she said, a little too loudly. "I just wanted to find out for me. Now are you going to be the gentleman you've always been and give me a hand up?"

"Always? Nobody knows anyone that long."

He was somewhere in his past, she sensed; he seemed hardly to be seeing her. "As long as I've known you, then," she said, and took a wary hold of both arms of the chair, trying to avoid whatever mechanism would render it more treacherous. "I hope that'll be for a good while longer," she said.

At once he stooped to her as though her words had caught him. For all his closeness, she had a disconcerting impression of not being able to make out his face. He found the hidden lever with one hand and hauled the chair-back vertical with the other, and she felt he wasn't seeing a person below him, just a burden that needed to be shifted. Then their faces were scant inches apart, and as her eyes sought his she saw him come into them, bringing an instant smile, tolerant and amused, even playful. "Nearly," he said, and moved aside.

Jess ignored his remark as she stood up. "Thank you," she said, deliberately enough for it to be half a rebuke. "Thanks for cooling me down. I'll see you at work."

She was angry both with him and with herself. In the corridor she clenched her fists to prevent herself from flinging all the doors open as if they hid secret areas of him it was her duty to discover. She was at the door, in the dimmest of the green light, when it grew dimmer still. His shadow had caught up with her without her realising he'd followed her. He reached past her and grasped the latch beside her face, and a metallic smell surged into her nostrils before the stagnant introverted light gave way to the pale glow of the landing. When she reached the stairs she looked back. His door was about to close, but he was watching her. "Thank *you*," he said.

More confused than ever, Jess hurried down into the sunlight. The little girl had managed to persuade her doll to float by sticking its legs through a tyre from a toy car. "You be good now or I'll have to push your head under," she was saying. Jess gave them both a smile that went unnoticed and walked away, more than usually glad that she was going to her mother's for the inevitable Sunday roast and gossip. She wouldn't be mentioning Pete, though just now her thoughts were all of him—of his last words in particular. She would have thought he'd intended them as a joke, except that she had never heard him mean anything so much.

twenty-two

The Davenports and their guests were emerging from the tropical house at Kew, into a warm breeze laden with scents that made Gail's mother close her eyes and raise her chin high enough to erase all the wrinkles in her throat, when Gail's father said "I'm going to say this to your face now, Gail. We're glad you wouldn't stay and work for us."

His small mouth and perfect teeth stayed slightly parted, an expression that meant he was timing his punch line. It hardly needed his wife to say "Don't tease, Paul, or maybe she'll remind you what her slaps used to feel like."

The youngest member of the party wobbled round from wheeling his pushchair along the path. "All," he pronounced.

"Not you this time, little guy. The stern voice is for your grandaddy who gave you his name. Did you know from Gail he was like he is, Geoff? Never says anything straight out if he can get there by way of a joke? Can you imagine how long it took me to be sure he was asking me to marry him?"

Paul looked hurt, which could mean that he was. "Used to be that taking time was called romance, Bebe."

"Still can be when that's what it is. Come here and don't bring that doghouse face." She rubbed his cheeks quite roughly with her palms until his expression had to give in. "Don't you dare look that way any more or the children will think we aren't glad to visit."

"Do I at least get to tell her why we're pleased she isn't on our staff?"

"Because she wouldn't have made it half so successful if she'd stayed with a channel that's owned by her folks. She wouldn't have had to work so hard at getting where she has," Bebe said, and to compensate for having robbed him of his pay-off, added one he would have been embarrassed to produce. "And she wouldn't have met our favourite son-in-law."

"Our favourite and only."

"Proud to be," said Geoff. Having been referred to twice, he couldn't very well pretend he hadn't heard. He turned from peering over his shoulder at the shadowy jungle beyond the glass doors. "Don't forget your favourite grandson."

"We won't now we've seen him again." Perhaps that sounded to Bebe like a complaint she wasn't entitled to make, because she went on quickly "Was there something we didn't give you time to see? That's us tourists, always racing to the next experience. Just say the word if you want to go back."

Geoff shook his head, then nodded it at his son's back. "I told someone—" He shot out a hand to grab a fistful of air and sling it into his mouth. "He can see another time. There wasn't any movement I could spot. No unlucky flies."

Bebe responded with a grimace so tight-lipped it seemed she was imitating a carnivorous plant rather than repulsing the notion of one. At least Geoff could assume that nobody had noticed anything odd about his behaviour on the gallery overlooking the interior of the tropical house. Just because he'd managed to catch no more than a glimpse of a silhouette vanishing into the cover of a bunch of man-sized leaves attached to an obese corky tree trunk, he'd lost all awareness of the conversation around him. "Let's keep him oblivious," he said, meaning the toddler, who was trundling the buggy through the perfumed sunlight towards the car park.

Geoff couldn't spend his life retreating into paranoia, or he would lose all sense of when he needed to be on his guard. "So what's the plan now?" he said.

"We buy you dinner at your best restaurant," Paul told him, "and tomorrow we start our trek."

"Or if you're asking us to look way ahead," Bebe took the chance to say, "you two could have more kids for us to come and spoil."

"Or you could send them over to us special delivery if you wanted us to care for them like we cared for Gail."

"Better than that if you like to remind us of our mistakes, honey."

"I don't remember any. I really don't," Gail said. "But the little brother or sister have to wait till work gives me time to produce them. Sorry, kids, wherever you are."

"Maybe work that paid you more would help," said her father. "Just a thought, if I'm not too old to have one. Half of one really. The rest came out of a prettier head."

"I thought we were going to save this for dinner," Bebe said, and directed a series of blinks at him.

"The eyelashes, the eyelashes. All we wanted to say to you two was that if you might like the idea of a major change of scenery in say the next few months—"

"We've been feeling Bay TV could get a little more aggressive. We aren't all as laid back on the West Coast as the rest of the media like to portray us."

"We've been thinking we need a new voice with an edge."

"And according to our research when you put an English voice on air the ratings go up like a champagne cork."

"We really think it's past time you had your chance on screen as well if you want it, honey. Maybe a double act with Geoff."

"The only thing we wouldn't let you argue about is if you decided to make the move you'd be partners with us in owning the channel."

"Well, gee, mom, dad," Gail said, and nothing else for several seconds. "I mean, thanks. You'll appreciate this is unexpected. Great, but unexpected."

"Don't even think of giving us an answer now," her mother said. "You two talk about it when we're not here. If you find you've enough of a sense of what you might want to do to give us a hint before we leave for home . . ."

Gail flashed her a promissory smile before swooping after Paul, who was making to speed his pushchair into the car park. The previous owner of the name turned to Geoff, and didn't speak any more than Geoff was inclined to, then did. "If there's anything you think had better keep you here, don't let our offer get in the way."

Geoff was touched by the glimpse of his father-in-law at his most real, and he experienced a sudden revulsion at his absurd fear of being spied upon. "I don't believe there's anything I couldn't bear to leave behind except the two of them," he said as he followed Gail and protesting slowed-down Paul into the car park.

Bebe saw to loading the pushchair into the back of the Hundrai and the smaller of her Pauls into the child's seat with which she'd insisted on equipping the van. The other Paul saw everyone was comfortable, not that anybody had room not to be, before steering the vehicle between the dwarfed cars. As those were left behind Geoff took Gail's hand, the one that wasn't busy smoothing her son's windswept hair. "How would you like to get away for a few days?"

"Away from . . ."

"Join this tour, I mean. Go up with them as far as, I don't know, the Lakes."

"We could. Nobody needs us as far as I know for the rest of the week."

"We'd love that," Bebe said. "We can phone ahead and book you into our hotels or one near if they're full. Either way we'll pick up the tab."

"We'll argue about that later," said Gail, then looked askance at Geoff. "Only . . ."

"Only," he said, willing her not to have thought of any real objection, "yes?"

"The Lakes mean mountains, don't they, and I wonder how little legs would stand up to the sort of walking my phenomenally fit folks have in mind."

"That won't be a problem." Indeed, he felt guilty that it solved so much. He would be giving her more time alone with her parents, he told himself. As the Hundrai swung out of the car park towards Richmond he said "You three can walk like you used to, and if I can borrow the van"—for an instant his eyes burned, but he didn't let his voice falter—"I'll take Paul to the sea."

twenty-three

For the first time ever in their lives Geoff seemed to hear something like affection in the roughness with which his father addressed Ben. "If you've finished deciding what you can bear to be seen in then maybe you'll let us be off."

Ben was dressed in a school jumper and grey trousers too hot for the summer morning. "Mother packed all the things I'd wear."

"Just get on with taking the bags out, you two," she said, "while we see to the house."

Geoff took hold of the suitcase she'd packed, which was smaller and certainly lighter than Ben's. "We're really going to stay by the sea," he said.

She turned a mascara-framed stare on him. "Would you rather not?"

"Ben and me both want to. He's looking forward to it more than me."

If anything was capable of cancelling the holiday, he saw at once, this would. He was trying frantically to think of a comment that would displace its predecessor when his mother said "Your father told you what we're doing, didn't he? When you're older you'll know grownups can do with a break."

Geoff felt as if he'd started at that moment to grow older. At last he saw a reason for his parents' mysterious behaviour. All these weeks since they'd found Ben hiding in his bed he'd spent dreading what they might do, what their wordless stares at him and Ben that night had promised. The longer he'd waited, the worse and more unimaginably menacing the unfulfilled threat had seemed. When the pet mouse that was mostly his had died last week, he'd wanted to take that as the punishment; he'd even wondered if one of his parents could have poisoned the little creature's food, except that surely they would have wanted the boys to realise—to feel responsible. He hadn't dared hope his parents had forgotten or decided to forget their discovery in his room, but now that seemed much closer to the truth. They wanted to get away from all the complications and frustrations the house or his father was creating, even if their break involved giving him and Ben a treat. "Come on," he urged Ben out of the house.

His father had cleared the back of his builder's van. There was room enough for all the luggage and both boys, but Geoff's father insisted he sit in front next to his mother. The first belch of the engine brought Mrs. Slough and her trowel into view over the shared hedge. Geoff's mother sent her a neighbourly wave he couldn't help thinking pathetic, his father started muttering. "Stare all you want, missus, you aren't getting rid of us. You can tell all your pals that, the whole lot of you that think you're better than the rest of us. I'll bet I'd be welcome if your precious houses wanted fixing."

None of this had much to do with the situation as Geoff understood it. The lawyer had hired someone to check the noise level, which didn't register as high as Geoff's father believed it was. Once he'd calmed down, or rather as a means of doing so, Geoff's father had asked neighbours to have their houses monitored at his expense so that he could demonstrate his was worst affected. That the lawyer had predicted their refusal only made him as resentful of the lawyer as of them. At least, Geoff thought, there was something that wasn't Ben's fault for once.

The van emitted a defiant blackened belch that sent it under the railway bridge. Geoff remembered when his parents had owned a shiny Jaguar that would have been used for a journey like today's, but he wasn't going to let that spoil the occasion. He was so excited as the van headed for the intersection that he didn't think what he was saying. "Are we going on the motorway?" he hoped aloud.

His father gave him the stare he usually reserved for Ben. "I only meant it'd be quicker," Geoff stammered.

"We'll get where we're going, and that's a promise," his father said in the tone of a warning not to bother him, and Geoff saw his mother pressing her lips together until a corner she'd missed with her lipstick grew almost as pale as his father's skin.

Neither of the boys spoke again as the van sped out of town. Beyond Aintree, where Geoff's father and some of his men always went to the Grand National more rowdily than they returned from it, houses scattered themselves among fields that looked ironed out to the horizon by the metallic blue sky. More than once, to Geoff's eager eyes, the horizon seemed to glint with sea. Houses lined up beside the road at Maghull, and forced it to narrow itself to wriggle through Ormskirk, and then there was most of an hour's worth of intermittent villages as far north as Preston, where signs for Blackpool started to appear—signs for sand and games in the waves and rides on the Big Dipper and so much ordinarily forbidden food that you had to vow to yourself not to be sick.

Then Geoff's father took a firmer grip on the wheel and hauled it rightward, away from the direction of the signs, into a road closed in by ranks of small two-storey houses the colour of scabs. Some of them had shops in their front rooms, and all of them gave the impression of wanting to squeeze themselves smaller and darker. Geoff saw Ben sit forward and stare about, his eyes narrowing as if they were pulling the skin around them closer for protection. Geoff couldn't keep quiet now, not when he would be speaking for the other boy as well. "Dad, this isn't the way."

"It will be when we've dropped off at my parents," his mother said.

He ought to have remembered that was where the road led—to his least favourite place in the world. He felt as though a gloom that smelled of dogs had closed around him; worse, around Ben. Above the roofs the hills called fells had loomed into view, huge vague shapes like storm clouds fallen to earth. Then the sky closed down, and the rain over the fells closed in, and the houses turned the colour of both.

In just a few miles there were no more houses, only the road labouring to squirm clear of muddy fields, sodden unkempt hedges. A smell of wet manure seeped thickly into the van, overpowering even the scent Geoff's mother had sprayed on twice that morning. Geoff stood the smell as long as he could before releasing a sound half delighted with his disgust. He wanted Ben to share it, but the other boy's face wasn't letting him in. At that moment the windscreen wipers heaved the rain aside to reveal the sign by the road.

KENNELS, it said. The first time Geoff remembered having seen it, he'd thought it was the name of the house, as so many of the houses at home had names: The Arbours, Bella Vista, Hideyhome, Herewestay . . . Now he knew what the outburst of barking meant that greeted the van as it swung between the shaggy hedges taller than itself into the rutted squelching drive. He saw Ben's stare draw itself farther in, and his lips part for an instant over his tight teeth.

The wide squat two-storey house shouldered its way through the downpour to meet the van. Even when the sun was out here, which Geoff had the impression was seldom, the facade was as dark as rain beneath black clouds. Fifty yards or so to the left of it was a long low stone shed of the same colour, divided internally into six cells, from the far side of which six narrow wire pens stretched. As the van drew up before the house with a gritty squish, it seemed to Geoff that every pen was vibrating with dogs that snarled and leapt and yapped furiously. He saw Ben refuse to be made to flinch, just as their grandparents appeared at the front door.

They stepped into the rain as the van's engine died. Geoff saw rain twitch the ends of the moustache that was the one extravagance about his grandfather—that struck him as having used some of the old man's wizened face to create itself, to be pinching his mouth until it had hardly any lips. "You've all come, then," he said, no more unwelcomingly than usual.

Rain streamed down his wife's long blonde hair that put Geoff in mind of a sheepdog's coat. She lowered her weighty eyebrows to peer at Ben. In an accent as flat as her husband's, or as her broad face with its disappointed mouth, she roared "Have you not—"

Both Geoff's parents shook their heads. "Best way," his grandfather said.

Geoff understood none of this. As soon as he was clear of the van he could think only of taking refuge in the house. Once his grandfather threw open the back doors of the vehicle, Ben followed. The rain lashed the boys across the grey slab of a doorstep. "Feet," their grandmother shouted in her deaf voice, and barely gave the boys time to scrape their shoes on the grid in the vestibule before herding them into the glum hall too narrow for the house. "Lounge," she shouted over the barking that, for a moment of flinching on Ben's behalf, Geoff thought was coming from that room. "Don't be sitting while you're wet," she bellowed as he opened the door.

Neither boy would have, not when all the chairs hardly less dark than the back of the cold gaping fireplace—as dark as the walls and the rest of the hulking furniture illuminated only by the light the rain let in—were ready to attach to any sitter some of the dogs' hairs that seemed to be adhering even to the downcast shade of the overhead bulb on its hirsute flex. As she marched to the kitchen to fetch two high hard stools, Geoff heard through another outbreak of barking the slam of the front door, and a thud. The other grownups had come in, bringing some item with them. They crowded after Geoff's grandmother into the lounge and stood watching while the boys perched on the stools. "Had to come in too, did he?" their grandfather said.

Geoff looked away towards the barking in the next room. If his position made him feel like a child in disgrace in an old school story, how much worse must Ben feel to be talked about that way? Geoff assumed his grandmother had misunderstood his reaction, because she poked a finger at the noise. "Lady dog's been bad."

"Got herself some whelps," said his grandfather.

"If they don't find themselves a home they'll be going up the chimney."

"That's what happens to creatures nobody wants."

"Would you like to see them, Geoffrey?" his grandmother yelled.

"Yes," Geoff said, and made to climb down from the stool.

"Don't be wandering," his grandfather said, and stared so hard at both boys it seemed to squeeze a raindrop out of his left eyebrow. "We'll let them in."

Everyone knew Ben was afraid of dogs—ever since Lady had chased him the length of the drive and brought him down. "I can go and see," Geoff said, and managed to think of a reason. "Then she won't miss them."

"No," his father and his grandfather said as though they were sharing a voice.

His grandmother vanished out of the door, leaving the rest of the grownups in a line between the boys and the hall. He heard the next door open, and his grandmother emit a piercing whistle that brought a great deal of barking and a confused stampede into the hall. He saw Ben crouch forward on his stool and grip its legs as four Alsatians, each of them no bigger than Geoff's torso, piled through the doorway. "Look, Ben," Geoff said, unable to think of any other way to help. "They're sweet, aren't—"

He'd jumped down to stroke two of the puppies, all of which had the softness of stuffed toys and were as animated as the grownups were immobile, but that wasn't why his voice trailed off. Lady had followed her litter into the room. At the sight of her Ben either fell off his stool or put it between himself and the dog. Lady dropped into a crouch, chafing her nipples on the carpet, and skinned her teeth and gums until her lips could stretch no farther. A snarl that kept giving way to breaths like water dragging gravel forced its way between her teeth as Geoff's grandmother grabbed her collar. "Still the same and no mistake," she said of Ben as if she was shouting at him.

"He'd have been the first to turn tail in a battle," said her husband as loudly.

"Turn it for anyone who had a fancy for it too, I shouldn't wonder."

"If he hadn't run your guard dog wouldn't have gone after him," Geoff's father said.

"We wouldn't have had to break a stick on her," Geoff's grandmother yelled, glowering at Ben and patting Lady's head.

"We've trained worse," her husband shouted back.

"Their owners didn't know them when they came to fetch them."

"Leave anything with us and you'll get it back improved, that's our motto."

"That's fine with us," Geoff's mother said.

Ben was still gripping the stool like a circus performer about to defend himself. Geoff continued stroking the puppies, glancing at Ben in the hope of communicating some of his affection for the animals. Ben wasn't about to look away from the snarling dog as long as she was in the room, however. "Like them as a boy should, do you, Geoffrey?" his grandfather said.

"Yes," Geoff felt forced to admit.

"Take them through, then. Whistle them and they'll be after you."

Geoff stood up at once. If he enticed them out of the room, presumably Lady would follow. The noise his pursed lips emitted was so feeble, however, that his grandmother stared as though he'd made no sound at all. Nevertheless the puppies scampered after him as he sidled past Lady. They almost knocked him over as they tumbled like the contents of an opened package full of fur and muscle into the hall.

Because of the dimness, and his eagerness to lure them away from Ben, at first he didn't notice what was there. Before he could shepherd the puppies to their room, the grownups marched out of the lounge and shut the door behind them—behind the three of them.

Geoff's grandfather uttered a whistle as sharp as the teeth it penetrated, and the puppies dashed after him down the hall. "Come along, Geoffrey," said Geoff's mother as his father took his arm to steer him towards the front door, past Ben's suitcase. Geoff was too stunned to resist, and too small to make a difference. He wasn't just stunned by knowing that the grownups must have planned a trap for Ben. Much worse—so bad it shrank him almost to nothing—was the knowledge that they'd used Geoff to help carry out their plan.

twenty-four

All at once Geoff was overcome by a shudder, and gripped the wheel hard. "I never said a thing till we were back on the road. I ought to have made it harder for them."

Paul's only answer was a giggle at the blaring of a lorry. Geoff braked for his sake—he wouldn't have bothered on behalf of the self he was feeling like—and let the monolith on wheels swing in ahead of them. "You would have, wouldn't you?" he said. "You would when you get to be as old as I was then. No use saying I was too young. I could have made a difference."

"Din."

"I'll give you a drink just as soon as the motorway lets us stop. You don't know what I was talking about, do you, thank God. I hope you never will. I hope you never meet—I don't know what I hope. Where do you think we're going, Paul? Have you any idea?"

"Going sea."

"That's absolutely right," Geoff said, feeling ashamed of having expected any less. "I don't suppose you can read what that sign says, can you? Read, like looking at your books?"

Paul gave him the comfortable smile that seemed to mean he

was content with his own untroubled silence, which increasingly affected Geoff with so many emotions, anxiety disputing with resignation among them, that he suppressed them for the present. "It says a mile to the Blackpool exit," Geoff said.

"Backpoo."

"We're going there, I promise. There isn't a promise in the world I'm more likely to keep. I wonder if you'd mind if we make a detour first, though. It shouldn't take more than an hour or so, just to go to a house."

"How."

"Why aren't you this talkative when your mother can hear? It worries her, you know, though I keep telling her you're going to be fine. As fine as we can make you. I know, I can't talk about not talking to her."

In less than five minutes the road off the motorway raised a signboard, warning him that Blackpool was straight ahead. Paul didn't protest when the Hundrai veered away from it, down into the fields laid flat by the blazing sky, but his silence only made Geoff feel guiltier for using him. An hour's drive away Gail and her parents would be walking on a mountainside above a lake while Geoff's past dragged him down into itself and took Paul with him.

As the road sneaked under the motorway, Geoff found himself remembering the route. He'd come this way just once, returning from Blackpool. It had been a dark day even for the area, the sky hanging lower than the mountaintops, but now the twisting of the road between ragged sunlit hedges that kept taunting him with mountain views made him feel even more closed in, unless it was the imminence of memory that did. Here was a crossroads he remembered, the inscription on its milestone erased by moss. He turned left at it, up a steep road that felt to him like going downhill.

The thorny hedges must have grown, but as they towered over the van he could have imagined he was reverting to the size he'd been last time on this road. He remembered fearing that its deviousness would make him sick, a memory that threatened to revive itself. He glanced at Paul in case he was approaching the same condition, but Paul was grinning to himself. "Dog," he said.

In a moment Geoff heard barking. Could the kennels still be operating when his grandparents had been dead longer than his parents? At the next bend a gate showed him a flood of fuzzy white rushing away down a field—a flock of sheep herded by a sheepdog. "Good boy. Well done," he said belatedly to Paul, having overcome a ridiculous panic. "You've sharper ears than me." The bleating barking field sank behind them, the road bent in the opposite direction uphill, and as it straightened he saw poking out of a hedge part of the sign he would have hoped never to see again. It had been amended for his benefit. BEN, it said.

The Hundrai juddered to a halt outside the gateway as he thought to brake. He threw it into neutral and switched off the engine, and heard hot metal ticking like a timer. The letters on the surviving fragment of the sign, which had been wrenched half off the sodden mossy gatepost, said KEN after all; only a twig and the shadow of another had altered it. Geoff turned his head to stare up the drive so overgrown with brambles it was virtually indistinguishable from the abandoned garden, and saw there was no house.

A few dwarfish random jagged chunks of wall sketched its outline, within which a single blackened chimney-breast survived, complete with fireplace. It had belonged to the room where Lady and her litter had been kept—it was the fireplace in the photograph he'd found in the niche of the motorway wall. He had a wild urge to use the Hundrai to rip apart the brambles all the way to the ruin while Paul giggled with delight, but of course he wasn't going to return the hired vehicle to Gail's parents with the paintwork scratched. "Don't go anywhere," he said to Paul, not that Paul could do otherwise when he was strapped into his seat, and stepped down into the road.

He'd progressed no more than a few yards beyond the gateway when he gave in to swearing under his breath at the brambles he had to wrench aside with both hands wherever he couldn't trample them down. He thought Paul might be amused by his antics, but when he glanced back, sweating all over and running out of words to snarl, from halfway up as direct a path as he could force towards the ruin, a sprawl of the hedge was between him and Paul's seat. "Won't be long," he vowed, kicking at a creeper that had done its best to trip him.

It couldn't have taken him even five minutes to struggle to the ruin. He was aware of every second of his progress, that was all. It left little space in his mind for a sense of why he was there, but now the past was poised to settle on him. Suddenly his reluctance to stick his hand up a fireplace with weeds decorating its mantelpiece struck him as absurd. He tramped through the wet undergrowth where the room had been, and ducked to peer up the flue.

He stooped too quickly. The dark of the vanished house seemed to loom out of the fireplace, destroying the sunlight and shrinking his mind. Then the darkness drew into itself, and he could see up the sooty throat. Protruding from two bricks high on the chimney-back, and almost invisible with soot, was the corner of an envelope. He snatched it out and turned to make his way back to the van. At once he saw the sea.

It was no more than a glint on the horizon, like the edge of a concealed blade. How often must Ben have seen it? For a moment the thought seemed crucially important, and then it was driven out of his head. The bonnet of the Hundrai was visible around the hedge that overhung the gatepost. He'd had no reason to use the headlamps during his journey, but now they were switched on.

He shoved the envelope into his breast pocket and dashed between two fragments of the house. Beyond them so many of the brambles had replaced themselves across his path he might almost not have made it. "Paul," he shouted. "Paul, can you hear me? Say something. Anything will do." He could hear nothing from the van—no sounds anywhere except his own tread crashing through the undergrowth, and the creak and swish of the brambles he was hauling aside with hands that kept clenching into fists. Before he was halfway to the road his hands and forearms were bleeding. Now he could see the headlamps weren't switched on—only a trick of the sunlight had lit them—but that didn't explain the silence. "Paul," he yelled, "speak up when you're asked for once," and his shout turned into a savage curse at the creeper that had almost tripped him a second time. None of this brought him a response, and he found he couldn't talk as he disentangled brambles, kicked at them, ground them underfoot. When he staggered to the end of the drive at last he had no breath left for a word.

Paul was lolling as far sideways in his seat as the straps would let him, asleep in the sun. His mouth was open, his head was tilted back; he looked like utter peace made flesh. Only his right hand was upturned on the seat next to him as if it had been groping for a hand to hold. Geoff waited until he could draw a long breath and release it slowly and indulge in another. "I'm here now," he said to himself, "and we're going where I said we would." Then all the relief that the sight of Paul had brought him faded, because his words had released the memory that had been lying in wait for him. All at once he felt so cold and enclosed that he might have been back in his grandparents' house.

twenty-five

They were almost back at his grandparents' house when Geoff's mother said "So did you manage to have a good time with us?"

Geoff saw no point in trying to get at the truth. "Yes," he said with all the enthusiasm he was beginning to experience.

It was enthusiasm for seeing Ben after a week of wondering about him and his situation—enthusiasm that they were going to rescue him. Geoff's father gave him a searching sidelong glance, and his mother said "We didn't cramp your style too much, then."

"He did enough that boys like, I reckon. He did everything I'd have done when I was his age."

"I expect that's all right then, is it, Geoffrey? You being your father's son."

She wasn't asking if that was all right, Geoff realised. "Yes," he said, no less enthusiastically than before.

He was eager to tell Ben about his week in Blackpool. The part he couldn't tell was how he'd ended up feeling reluctantly grateful that his parents had tried to be adequate companions for him. Lying in deck chairs with handkerchiefs over their faces while he built forts at the edge of the lazy waves hadn't taxed them, but much else clearly had: his mother eating fish and chips out of a newspaper on the vulgar seafront instead of dining in the hotel, and sitting stiffly next to him in a Ghost Train car and fanning herself whenever she was made to gasp, and clinging to the neck of a horse beside his on a roundabout while each rise and fall of her steed put her shoes more in danger of flying off; his father accompanying him on rides she wouldn't even consider, the roller coasters and the headlong spinning rockets and the bucket seats that seemed determined to fling themselves off the spokes to which they felt none too securely attached—his father swaggering off each ride with the expression of a hero who had yet to find a challenge worthy of him, although Geoff knew that during the rides his father's face had looked as if the features yearned to retreat into his head. . . . "I loved it all," he said. "Thanks for taking me."

"That's what we like to hear," his mother said.

"Thanks for being with me all the time."

She blinked hard once and stared ahead. "Well, you've finished with just having us."

It must be the thought of Ben that caused her and Geoff's father to grow as heavily silent as statues, rocking with the swerves of the van on the bends of the deserted road—so deserted that he wondered whether Ben had seen anybody other than his grim hosts all week. Then the sign for the kennels poked out above the road, the lower corner of the board dripping like a nose with rain. The van swerved through the gateway, slewing the luggage about in Ben's section of the van, and the dogs in the pens began barking at once.

They weren't the same dogs as last week; they were considerably bigger. Wherever Ben was, he must be hearing them. Geoff tried to imagine being him in the house—hearing dogs on the other side of doors, smelling dogs in every room and finding traces of them on himself, knowing that they wanted nothing more than to chase him and bring him down, their claws digging into his back, their mouths on his neck. Rescue had arrived now, Geoff told himself. The van squelched to a halt as Geoff's grandfather came out of the house and stood like a warder on the step. "Are you all coming?" he demanded.

Geoff's father seemed taken aback by the uninviting tone. "If you'll have us."

"Suit yourselves. The door's not shut that I know of."

Geoff did what he could to improve the mood of the grownups. Once out of the van he called to the dogs, which barked louder and sprayed a mixture of rain and saliva through the jangling fences, and the moment he reached the vestibule he scraped his muddy shoes on the grid. "Good boy," said his mother, which at least earned a grunt from her father as the family trooped down the hall.

Geoff was last into the ponderous gloom of the lounge. He was hoping to see Ben, but only the grownups were there, his grandmother with one hand doubling her ear. He heard the puppies yapping and yipping in the next room, and would have liked to think Ben was playing with them. "Is Ben packing?" he said, more realistically. "Shall I go and help him?"

"He isn't that," said his grandfather.

His voice was blunt as a club. There was silence until Geoff's grandmother bellowed "Is he getting his surprise?"

"That's what we said," Geoff's father bawled.

"Are you coming to see?"

She was shouting at Geoff. "Yes," he said with as much confusion as enthusiasm.

"What's that? A piece of cod can make more noise than that. Pipe up or you'll have us thinking you're no better than the other lad. You like surprises, don't you?" she roared, and cupped both her ears.

Geoff felt as if he'd been enticed up on stage in a pantomime where everyone but him knew what was about to happen to him. "Yes," he nevertheless responded, twice as loud as before.

"Come and make friends, then."

Geoff assumed that would involve the ordeal of a sloppy kiss and a hug that smelled of dogs. Instead she tramped into the hall and opened the next door, and as the puppies did their utmost to sound as big as dogs he realised what she might have meant. "Are we having one of them?" he said at the top of his voice.

"You want one, don't you?"

He did—he would love one—but would Ben? He had to make sure he chose a puppy even Ben would like. "Yes," he said with all his breath.

"Get in and wait, then."

Was she going to fetch Ben? Perhaps Geoff ought to delay choosing until they both could. When she narrowed her eyes at his hesitation he thought it best to hasten into the small dingy almost unfurnished room. The four puppies scampered to meet him while their mother, having delivered herself of a token bark, watched from her wicker basket spread with old blankets. The puppies jumped up to lick his bare knees and hands and face, and he would have hugged and stroked them all except for realising that Ben wouldn't welcome such an onslaught, however affectionate. "Sit," he said. "Sit. Lie down, good dogs."

One did—the softest of them. Having lain down, he rolled over to have his stomach patted. If any dog could take away Ben's fear, Geoff thought, this one would. He picked up the puppy and hugged the soft warm wriggling body to his chest, and laughed as a hot wet tongue found his ear. He held onto his prize as he heard his grandmother in the hall, bringing Ben with her, he hoped; her tramp was certainly heavy enough to blot out the boy's unobtrusive tread. But she'd brought only a collar and lead. "That's your friend, is he?" she shouted.

"Please, gran. What's his name?"

"Whatever you've got for him."

"I'll—" Just in time Geoff thought it might be inadvisable to say he would wait for Ben, in case she hadn't meant the puppy as a present to them both. "I'll think," he said.

"Get him carted off before Lady wants him back."

Geoff was more than ever anxious for Ben to see their pet—to begin emerging from the nightmare Geoff had brought on him by hiding him in the bed. He could hear his father saying "How's the training?"

"He's done nothing we don't do. Cleaning out the pens."

"Can they get at him?" Geoff's mother sounded actually worried. "They're bigger than him, some of those dogs."

"They're locked in the cages while the inside's cleaned. He'll know they're there though, right enough."

"That's some of what he needs," Geoff's father said.

Geoff felt as though the gloom of the house was sticking to the inside of his head. He hugged his prize and went into the lounge. When the puppy gave a playful growl his mother turned from the cold cavern of a fireplace and smiled with both ends of her mouth. "That's yours now, is it?"

"He'll be ours."

"It's clean, is it?" she said to her mother. "It won't . . ."

"It's trained like all our dogs."

"Just the same, it can go in the back of the van."

"We both will, shall we?" said Geoff.

"I thought you would. There'll be plenty of room."

"Me and Ben, I mean. Will there be room with his luggage?"

The silence seemed to weigh more than all the grownups put together. He dragged his gaze from face to grim face, none of which was quite looking at him, and heard his father's exact words before they were spoken. "He's not coming."

"He's staying until he leaves school," his mother said. "They've always wanted another boy to bring up."

"Ever since her brother was killed in the war," his grandmother yelled, shoving her ears forward.

"We'll hear no crying over him," said her husband. "He was the sort we needed."

"He'd never back away from owt, our Jack."

"Benjamin knows that's how we'll have him before we're done."

"Let's get the leash on him."

Geoff's thoughts were so clogged with dismay that for a moment he imagined his grandmother was still referring to Ben. He yielded the puppy to her, and watched her yank a collar at least one notch tighter around its neck than he would have, extracting a yelp from the dog. "Be still," she shouted loud enough to make it cringe, and having clipped the lead to the collar, thrust the end at

Geoff. "You treat him like he understands and your parents won't have any reason to get rid of him."

Geoff gripped the lead and patted the dog to keep it from jumping up at him in defiance of her. "Good boy," he murmured. "Thanks, grandma, grandpa. Thanks, mum and dad."

"I should think so," said his mother. "Keep tight hold till it's in the van and we'll be off."

"Can't I see Ben first?"

The presence of the grownups turned itself into a barrier that didn't need to be physical. "Maybe you will as you go," his grandfather said.

Geoff didn't know what they suspected him of planning; he only wished he had some plan to rescue Ben. He found himself being virtually marched along the hall without their touching him, the women deafening him with a discussion over his head of the care of the puppy while the men maintained twice a silence behind him and his new friend tried to wrap the lead around Geoff's legs. As the puppy emerged from the house the dogs inside the wire started reminding it how to bark, and Geoff saw Ben in the enclosure closest to the drive.

It was the only cage empty of dogs. He was scraping turds with a shovel into a flat pan at the end of a pole. At first he seemed determined to ignore everyone, and then he looked at Geoff. Whatever expression might have revealed itself on his face vanished as he saw the puppy, and he grew expressionless as a piece of slate.

"Ben," Geoff pleaded, and took a step towards him. The dogs hurled themselves against the fences, but Ben's face didn't change, his eyes didn't waver. Why couldn't he have hidden in the van while he had the chance? thought Geoff. "He's stopping," his grandfather said in only just three syllables.

Ben let the shaft of the shovel fall against the wire in front of him. "I've stopped."

"Still too clever for his own good," said his mother.

It might have been a rebuke to her parents. "He won't be when we've done with him," her father said.

Geoff knew instantly that the old man was wrong. He tried to make Ben look at him, and perhaps Ben was doing so, but his gaze through the fence saw nothing Geoff wanted to think was himself. Then Geoff's father grasped his shoulder and steered him to the van. The back doors slammed, the puppy snuggled against him. Ben had already turned away with the shovel, yet Geoff saw his face, hard as a mask that was holding down more than Geoff could begin to imagine. Through the rear window he saw Ben prowl out of the cage into the stone building. The van pulled away with a crunch of mud, and in a very few seconds the hedges swallowed the house and the kennels and everything they contained as if to keep a secret best forgotten.

twenty-six

As Paul raised his glass of orange juice he was tempted to crack a joke, but saw it wouldn't be appropriate. "Here's to family," he said, "and damn the ocean that keeps it apart."

"Family," responded Geoff and Gail and Bebe, and looked at Paul's namesake while Bebe wiped his breakfasted face. "Family," she told him.

"Fammy," he said with the casualness of a master, and resumed demolishing the contents of his plastic dish.

"Give him a cigar," said Paul. "Just a miniature. I could see him chewing it too."

"He's talking more since we came over, don't you think?" Bebe said to Gail. "Can he say his address yet? Maybe you remember we made sure you did as soon as you could."

"We do keep telling him. It hasn't recorded yet, has it, Paul? Can you tell grandma where you live?"

"Twenty-eight the Terrace, Barnes by the Thames."

"Well done, Geoff, but we weren't asking you."

"I did wait. Just trying to help."

"Did you get it, Paul? Where's home?"

The toddler cocked his head to send Gail a glance that could have been meant to be teasing, and uttered a syllable along with half a mouthful of egg. "He was trying to say Thames, wasn't he?" said Bebe as she mopped him up.

"Sounded more like home to me," Geoff said.

"I thought he was asking for ham," said Paul.

Gail and her mother shared the kind of look with which women despaired of men, and kept repeating the Davenports' address while Geoff and his father-in-law finished their helpings from the buffet. When it became obvious that the toddler had lost interest the men lined up their utensils on their plates. "Well," Bebe said, "we'd better drive you to the station. You need to get back to work."

"We should really, mom."

"That's what I said."

Gail let her hand rest on her mother's and was rewarded with nearly all of a smile. It was what Bebe hadn't said that counted, Paul knew as well as their daughter did, but sometimes it was best to pretend you didn't know. He wondered if she might give him a hint when they kept the toddler in the lobby while his parents fetched their luggage, but his wondering aloud what was on her mind only made her nod at their grandson as a warning not to ask.

Ten minutes' drive took the party from the hotel by the lake to Windermere station, where a train was unburdening itself of hikers ridden by their packs. Once the Davenports were settled on the train, the flattened silence of the stationary carriage seemed to rob everyone of any conversation worth the breath. Then a guard began slamming the doors, and everyone made haste to shake hands and pat backs and hug and, man to man excepted, kiss. "Call us before you get home," Gail said to her mother. "If you decide to fly from London after all, stay another night with us."

"We'll do our best, honey. I feel we haven't really talked."

The guard dealt the door of their carriage a vehement slam whose finality sent Bebe flurrying to counteract it. There was time only for the women to touch each other's faces through the open window before the train moved off. Paul held Bebe's preoccupied hand as the train curled away towards the spiky stone horizon and vanished. "Was that it?" he said.

"Was what what?"

"Whatever's wrong. Was it not being able to talk enough to Gail?"

"That's part of it," she said, and searched his eyes with hers. "Only whatever's wrong is with them. There's something between them they aren't talking about."

"How do you know they aren't? Maybe it was just while we were around them."

"I don't believe so. Remember when he came back from his day out with Paul?"

"With his hands scratched up. I remember."

"And saying they got that way from lifting Paul out of a hedge."

"When he had to stop on the way back to let Paul go behind one. Seems likely enough to me."

"You don't think it's queer Paul didn't have a scratch on him."

"Not queer or gay either. Like Geoff said, his hands got that way from keeping thorns off Paul."

"You'd say that was the kind of hedge a person would put a child in."

"If the child was desperate, which Geoff said he was. I would have then myself."

"It must be how men handle things."

"You mean me, but Geoff's one too."

She gave up searching his eyes and let her hand sag in his. "I'd have liked to hear Paul's version of events."

"Not much chance of that for a year at least, I'd say. Do you really not believe Geoff?"

"I wish I could."

"What makes you not?"

"You didn't see him when he got back, did you? When he came in the bar to find us."

"Right, I was buying the drink you were panting for."

"And Gail was upstairs taking all the time she takes to have a shower."

"What are you saying we'd have seen?"

"Listen to this," Bebe said, and grasped his hand. "He came in looking as if everything was fine, he'd enjoyed his day by the sea as much as Paul had. And then I saw him realise he couldn't just say that. He looked at his hands and he realised. Then you saw him and asked what he was drinking, and by the time you bought that Gail came down. Only if you noticed, he didn't let her see his hands straight away, and by the time she asked what he'd done to himself he had that story waiting."

"It must have been pretty fast, what you say you saw."

"Not too fast for me."

"So what are you saying, he used Paul as an excuse to sneak off somewhere he doesn't want to talk about? You think someone scratched him up that way, or what?"

"I don't know, not yet. How can I?"

"Maybe all you saw was him not wanting you and Gail to fuss over a few scratches. Maybe he thought it would be bad for his public image. All right," Paul said as she pushed his hand away and turned towards the exit from the platform, "let's say you saw exactly what you think you did. It doesn't seem much of a reason to do whatever you're planning."

"What do you imagine that is?"

"To talk to Gail, I thought. To tell her what you think."

"I'm not about to go trampling into their marriage. If Gail says nothing I won't either."

"She did say she'd like us to stay with them again before we go home."

"Which means she wants to say things she hasn't had a chance to say," Bebe declared, and managed a rueful grin that she might have seen lying dormant in his eyes. "All right, which may mean that. At least I want her to know we're there to help whenever she needs us."

"I'm certain she does, Beebs. And maybe it mightn't be a bad idea, do you think, if he felt that way too?"

"We'll do our best."

He wasn't sure how much agreement that contained. She was making for the street, and he thought it best not to insist, especially since he couldn't judge how much the man who was the only other person on the platform might overhear—had overheard. Outside the station Paul slid the passenger door of the Hundrai open for her. "It might be good for him to know he's got family," he said.

twenty-seven

The sun was rusting in the Thames when the Davenports came home. A heron flew towards the sunset, its extended neck charring in the shadow of the bridge before emerging pink as an unextinguished ember. As the taxi drew up outside the house Gail raised a faint cheer that was half a sigh. Paul's wriggling and wails of protest had only recently subsided into grogginess, and Geoff had never been more aware why luggage was called luggage. By the time he'd paid the Greek driver and waved away his change Gail had unlocked the front door and quelled the alarm and carried Paul in. Geoff struggled with the folded buggy and the luggage into the house, and saw that the answering machine at the foot of the stairs had registered eight calls. At once he was anxious to hear the messages before Gail could. Though he felt grimy with exhaustion he said "Do you want the first shower?"

"I think someone else had better have the first one."

"You take care of him while I make us some coffee."

"I'll have mine upstairs. I might share a bath."

"I can take him out, and put him to bed by the look of him, when I bring your coffee."

"It was you I was thinking of sharing it with," Gail said, and gave him a look whose weariness he prayed was only the effect of all the day's travelling. He hurried to squeeze her free hand in both of his. "Sorry I'm so dull."

"Better dull than unreliable," Gail said, and after not much of a pause "You aren't either."

She hitched up a smile to leave with him while she bore Paul upstairs. Geoff set the coffee brewing in the kitchen, and ran to rewind the answering tape once he heard the drizzle of the shower become a downpour. A cartoon voice gabbled backwards and turned around to reveal itself as Angharad Bailey's. "Hello Gail and Geoff whenever you get home. Interesting developments on the Frugo front. I'll ring you in the morning. Oh, and Geoff, did anything come of the call you took during our last meeting?"

"Nothing for transmission," Geoff muttered as a bleep brought her message to an end. The tape produced an expectant silence and then another bleep. Somebody had failed to speak to the machine. Callers who didn't even bother to identify themselves frustrated Geoff, but now, as he heard only a series of bleeps that suggested a parody of censorship, he felt as though his nerves were tightening around his stomach. A seventh bleep cut off a silence that admitted to no presence, and he twisted the knob to rewind the tape. The machine was rearranging its innards with a good deal of busy clicking when the phone rang, and he grabbed the receiver. "Davenport," he said. "The real thing, in the flesh."

"Nice to hear you own up at last."

He crouched beside the stairs and pressed the mouthpiece against the corner of his lips. "What are you playing at now, Ben?" he whispered furiously.

"Just checking on my only person in the world. You tell me when it's safe to talk."

"It is now, but not for long. Look here, Ben—"

"I wish I could. I can see you when I shut my eyes. You'd be amazed what I see. You're telling me your family's safely out of the way, are you?"

"In the bathroom. If you've anything to say—"

"You know me. Unstoppable as ever, and all unrehearsed. You and the family were away being together, were you?"

"I won't apologise for that. It doesn't mean I don't also care—"

"You're saying quite a lot if you don't want us to be overheard, aren't you? I thought there wasn't meant to be much time."

Ben's voice seemed to be forcing itself to stay playful. If he was angry for some reason, that angered Geoff too—made his head feel like the inside of a rusty bell about to clang. "What did you mean I was owning up to?" he demanded.

"Why, being the real Davenport. Everybody always thought you were."

"Not everybody. I never did, and let me assure you, these days—"

"You will. I'm going to help you be real. I'm devoting myself to that now. I'm the devoted brother."

"If that's how you're feeling it's time we got together. Don't just keep sending me on—"

"That's still the way it's played, Geoffrey. You must remember."

"I don't want to remember you like that. You were only a boy when you did it. You'd never been given a chance to grow up, so you pretended you had to everyone but me. It was a dreadful thing you did, but you shouldn't keep reliving it. It doesn't have to mean—"

"You're wasting time, Geoffrey." There was no playfulness in Ben's voice now. "You found what I left you. Better follow it up. It isn't just my time you're wasting."

Geoff crouched lower over the scooped-out hollow his stomach felt like. The shower had fallen silent. "What do you mean?" he whispered, so close to the mouthpiece his teeth scraped the plastic.

"I know something you don't know."

"You've got my attention. You already had it. If time's so precious—"

"It is for some people, believe me. I'm looking at two of them now."

"Leave them alone, Ben. Don't harm them, whoever they are. If you promise not to touch them I give you my word—"

He almost bit his tongue. Gail had opened the bathroom door. "Geoff," she said, conversationally but loud. "Do you want to take him?"

"I'm just . . ." Geoff straightened up as though the dead receiver had hooked him like a fish. Gail couldn't see him, and might not have heard him on the phone. "Coming," he called, hoping that covered up the noise of replacing the receiver. He ran upstairs to be handed pink squirming Paul in a bath-towel, and was heading for the family bedroom when Gail said "Just what?"

"What?"

"You were just what before?"

The panic Ben's call had implanted in him flared up behind his eyes. He kept climbing so that she couldn't see his face. However it looked, it made Paul giggle. "I was on the phone," he said.

"I figured out that much. Who was it?"

Paul was giggling harder. "Hold on," said Geoff, and lowered him into the cot where his sleepsuit was waiting. "See if you can dress yourself as long as you've so much energy," he said, and went to the top of the stairs into the bedroom. "Remember the call I took last time we were at Metropolitan, during the meeting?"

"The one you said was something about children in danger, that you were so mysterious about. Yes?"

"That was all I told you because that was all I was told, and they took all that time to make that much clear. I said so then if you recall. Well, that was them again."

Gail stepped out of the bathroom to gaze up at him. She was wearing only a pair of black panties, and he couldn't help feeling watched by her dark nipples too. "They called here?" she said.

"That's—yes."

"How did they get our number?"

"There aren't many G. Davenports in the book."

"I could be happier if there was one less. There are things we mightn't want to come this close to home," Gail said, and folded her arms as though to protect her breasts. "What did he say this time? Was it the same guy?"

"He wants to meet me. I think I ought to give him the chance, do you?"

"Where?"

"In Liverpool. The thing is, he wants it to be tomorrow, only Angharad's called a meeting. You can go, can't you? Will you mind if I take the car?"

"I won't have to mind. Do you know any more about him?"

"I don't even know what he looks like, never mind what he calls himself. He'll have to make himself known to me," Geoff said, and tried to gaze the doubtfulness out of her face. "All I know is it may have to do with a child who's been mistreated. I wouldn't be going except he insists I can't tell anyone else."

"You just did."

"Involve them, I mean," Geoff said, more sharply than he meant to.

"Then you should go ahead."

"Go ahead with . . ."

"You should do what you told him you'd do. Just promise me you'll tell me what comes out of it, all right?"

"Of course I will," said Geoff, and leaned a smile on her before turning away, ashamed of having lied to her. What a professional, he thought, and then was struggling to speak. "Look," he called, and louder "Come and look."

Gail ran upstairs and halted close beside him. "Gee," she said. Paul was sitting on his mattress, both legs and one arm snug in his sleepsuit, his expression a mixture of pride and frustration as he attempted to capture the empty sleeve. "That's our boy," said Gail, and slipped an arm around Geoff's waist. He hugged her bare midriff and felt the envelope in his breast pocket intervening between them. As soon as he could he gave her a squeeze and went to guide Paul's hand into the sleeve. The envelope flexed itself secretly against his heart, and he told himself that once he went back where its contents led there surely could be nothing worse for him to find.

twenty-eight

When Paul came to a parking area beside the road he pulled the Hundrai over. "Let's take a look at the map."

Bebe released herself from her seat-belt and stretched her limbs while he donned his reading glasses and opened the book on his lap. "Are you starting to think we should have called ahead?" she suggested.

"Should I be? I thought the plan was to stop wherever we liked the look of and find ourselves a room."

"So long as we don't end up sleeping in the van."

"Once we wouldn't have minded that, would we? Not when we were Gail's age, not on a night like this is fixing to be." He leaned over, ignoring a pang at the base of his spine from having sat for hours, and kissed her soft wrinkled cheek. "Trust me, I'll find somewhere fit for us."

"Try not to be on the road too much longer. You know I like to look around wherever we end up before it gets dark."

"An hour from now we'll be somewhere we didn't know we'd be, and that's a promise," he said, peering at the map.

The double page was scattered with names that might have

been designed to underline how bleak the Scottish landscape with its bared crags had become: Castleweary, Cauldclench Head, Maiden Paps, Bellybought Hill, Foulmire Heights, Meggethead, Black Law . . . The road was pinched between two sheer slopes bristling with fir trees. While it had followed a river for miles it had seemed altogether more attractive than the motorway, but now it was clear that the road would take considerably longer to reach anywhere like a town than the map had encouraged him to think. He ran a fingernail along the yellow line that twisted across the blue-veined map, and glanced up as an oncoming car executed a deft U-turn and swung into the space in front of the van. "This could be help," he said.

He was making to climb out when the other driver did. His face was dominated by spectacles heavier than Paul's and a shock of blonde hair. As Paul lowered the window he sauntered up to the van. "Are you lost?" he said, or rather "Air ye loast?"

"We aren't too located," Bebe said.

"Where are you looking to be?"

"A good hotel not too far from here," Paul hoped aloud. "With a view would be ideal."

"That's what you're used to at home, am I right?"

"We've tried to earn ourselves a good life," Bebe said.

"Far away from it now though, eh?"

"We're touring your fine country. Is that gorgeous accent from round here?"

"That's where I picked it up, sure enough," the man said, and leaned his head in. "Show me where you think you're bound."

Paul used his thumb to prod the first block of grey that denoted a settlement on the yellow thread of a road. "Is this the kind of thing we'd like?"

"You deserve more than that," the man said, reaching down to turn the book on Paul's lap towards the window. "Have you no family to see the sights with you?"

"Our daughter lives over here," Paul said, and felt suddenly compelled to give Bebe the assurance she wanted. "We'll be seeing her again before we go home."

"Just the daughter, is there? No wee bairns?"

"She's married and they've presented us with a grandson," Bebe said.

"That's what I like to hear."

"So maybe you could direct us," Paul said, "Mr.—"

"Call me Dean." The driver closed the book on Paul's lap and rested his hand on the cover. "Forget that. You won't need it any longer. I'll do more than direct you, I'll take you."

"That's very kind, but we wouldn't want to take you out of your way," Bebe said.

"You won't. We'll be going to a view I want to see," the man called back, striding to his Vauxhall Cavalier.

"If it's straight along this road—" Paul shouted after him.

"It's not. I'll be taking you a short cut that's not on your map," the man responded, and slammed his door.

Bebe stowed the book and watched the car as it crept forward, twitching its turn signal. "Do you like him?"

"Well enough. Why, don't you?"

"There's something about him . . . I don't know."

"I guess that's true of everyone you've met apart from me," Paul said, and left his mouth open.

"You and your jokes when I'm trying to be serious."

"Are you telling me we shouldn't follow him?"

"I don't suppose. It would be rude when he was kind enough to turn back to help us."

"I didn't realise he had."

"He went by just as you parked."

Paul dropped his spectacles into the case clipped inside his breast pocket. "I'd better do without these and try to keep more of my wits about me, do you think?"

"You've still a few left. Don't encourage me too much, I'm sure he's harmless. I expect he's the way Scottish people are. The worst he can do is take us to his family's place."

"Where they eat travellers, you mean, or just rob and murder them?"

"I was thinking more of a hotel. We'd best move if we're following. He must be wondering what we're saying about him."

Indeed, the man might have been attempting to overhear. He'd wound his window down, and was resting his hand on the outside of the door, stroking it rhythmically with his fingertips. Paul started the Hundrai and tapped the horn, and the car pulled out ahead of him.

By the time Paul reached the first bend overshadowed by trees the car was several hundred yards away at the next. "Have some thought for us oldsters," Paul murmured and took the second bend as fast as he thought safe, a manoeuvre that carried the Hundrai across the grey hump of the roadway. The car was a quarter of a mile along the sunless road. "Don't let him rush you," Bebe counselled as if Paul hadn't already slowed the van in the hope that his startled heartbeat would slow down too. He braked again well in advance of the next bend, so sharp that the far end of its crash barrier was hidden by the knife-edged barren outcrop around which the road had to angle itself. He wouldn't have been surprised if the car had been out of sight, but it was halted half a minute's drive ahead.

"Here come the slowpokes," Paul muttered, and the car moved at once. It swung into a side road that was indicated by a pointer— would have been identified if the pointer hadn't been obscured by several dangling branches of a shrub that left only a letter Q visible. "Q for a question," Paul said to Bebe, which gained a response that fell short of a laugh.

The side road was worse than the one he was leaving—half the width and even more devious, little better than a track. Only a settling flurry of dust between the jagged grey almost vertical slopes to which a few undernourished trees clung with exposed roots showed where the car had passed, and when the Hundrai caught up with the dust Paul saw another flurry beckoning him to the next blind turn. "He must know where he's going," he declared.

"I wish we did."

Paul took that as a reason to speed up wherever the road was straight enough. In five minutes the sheer towering walls were bare of trees. If it hadn't been for the occasional stretch of wire netting that prevented the stone from collapsing into the road, he might have thought the route had been abandoned. He was no longer being met by raised dust; the other vehicle had to be too far ahead. When yet another tortuous bend showed him no car, he leaned on the horn. The walls threw its flattened blare into the van, and Bebe jumped. "What was that for?"

"To stop him so we can have a word."

"If we see a better road before we find him, Paul—"

She shrugged or gave a start, he wasn't sure which. The van had rounded another unfriendly bend, two hundred yards beyond which the car was waiting in the middle of the road. Paul thought the horn had made its point until he saw that the way was blocked. The blonde man's hand emerged from the window and jabbed a finger at the wooden barrier, then pointed over the roof of the car. The hand vanished, and the car swerved into an opening Paul hadn't realised was there. "Good heavens," Bebe protested, "where does he think he's going now?"

"Looks like we have to find out," Paul said, and drove to the barrier, which was no more than a log on sawhorse legs, not even the width of the roadway. It looked so temporary and so inadequate that he was tempted to move it rather than follow the car down the obscure track narrowed by dusty bushes. That would be absurd, irresponsible, dangerous—no doubt there was a rock fall out of sight around the curve beyond the barrier—but he wished the other driver had waited so that they could talk.

The track sloped downwards at once. It was scattered with unavoidable chunks of rock that made the van waver and lurch. To the left, over a tangle of bushes, Paul saw nothingness, hundreds of yards of it gaping between the track and a rock face. Only a heap of rubble at the top of the track had prevented him from seeing this from the road. Bebe laid a hand on his wrist, then let go in case it interfered with his driving. "This is nuts," he said. "Maybe he can use this route, but he isn't driving a van." He was about to sound the horn—sound it for as long as it took to provoke some response—when the Hundrai wobbled around a steep curve, and he saw the car had stopped.

It was parked on the inner edge of the next bend, below which Paul could see where the track led—to a disused quarry. "He's realised his mistake," he said angrily to Bebe. "He didn't know where this went after all." He trod on the brake and felt a chunk of rock

crunch under a wheel. Bebe clutched his wrist, and he sensed she
was imagining how he would have to reverse up the uneven track,
to steer backwards around the curve above a drop of a hundred feet
or more—and then he saw why she was close to panic. The blonde
man had stuck out a hand, inviting them to overtake.

"Not at my age, or half of it either." Paul kept his foot on the
brake and flashed the headlamps. The man's hand lit up like a plastic toy and dimmed, and beckoned impatiently. "You're fooling,"
Paul muttered. "Even I don't think that's much of a joke." He let
loose an echoing blast of the horn and lowered his window to raise
his own hand in refusal. "We're backing up," he shouted. "This is
as far—"

The revving of the car engine blotted out his voice. Did the
man intend to give Paul space to turn? That course seemed even
more perilous than backing the van all the way to the road. He
moved the gear shift, as gradually as he meant to inch the Hundrai
up the slope. He hadn't raised his foot from the brake when the car
reversed towards him.

It was coming far too fast—so fast that Bebe dug her nails into
his wrist. "Slow down, you maniac," Paul gasped, and tried to ward
the car off with both the horn and the headlamps. "There's no
room to—" The car didn't falter, though it was heading straight
for the front of the Hundrai. His limbs crippled by panic, he jerked
the van into reverse and sent it as fast as he dared up the slope.

He saw the curve speeding towards him in the mirror. The car
was gaining on him. He swung the rear of the van towards the inside of the bend. He'd known the bend was steep, but now he
found it tilted sharply inwards. He felt the van begin to topple, out
of control—he saw the wall of rock lurching towards it. He
dragged at the steering to compensate, only to compensate. The
left rear wheel snapped a branch, and another, and for a dreadful
moment he couldn't think which way to steer so as to bring the
wheel back from the edge. Just as he did, he heard and felt the support that was no more than a bush give way, and the corner of the
van tilted over the brink.

"Paul," Bebe said. It wasn't a cry, hardly even a protest—more
her way of reminding him she was there. She snatched her hand

away from damaging his wrist and covered her eyes. He blared the horn to shift the car, which had stopped no more than six feet ahead. He would crash into it if he had to, assuming that he could get the van moving, or should he persuade Bebe to climb out first? He took hold of her wrist as he clung one-handed to the steering, and had just uncovered her eyes, sending a solitary tear down her cheek, when the car's reversing lights glared white. Before he could react, the car was shoving at the front of the van.

The impact was unexpectedly gentle, but it was enough. As Paul stamped on the brake so hard his knee ached, the right rear wheel slewed over the edge. "Oh," said Bebe, a tiny despairing groan that was all that she couldn't keep to herself. Paul felt the front wheels holding the road, and released the brake as he floored the accelerator. The wheels lost their grip, and the van plunged backwards.

He found Bebe's hand and squeezed it, and held on. When he tried to speak he felt as if his innards from his throat to his groin had been wrenched out of him. "Brace yourself. Your head," he pleaded, pressing his own against the head-rest, sensing the collision that was rushing at it from behind. He was straining his eyes towards their corners, to see whether she understood, when the van struck bottom.

The rear window shattered in the midst of a crunch of metal and rock. The glove box sprang open, flinging its contents at Paul's chest. The book of maps smashed his glasses in their case, bruising his chest, and for an instant he was able to believe that might be the worst of his injuries. The van teetered vertically, then slammed down onto its wheels. Every one of Paul's joints felt dislocated by the first impact, and he had no way of protecting himself from the second. His head jerked forward, wrenching his neck. He clung to Bebe's hand, squeezed harder, but there was no response. Her eyes were closed, her face was lolling away from him.

"Beebs. Bebe, honey." He could barely hear himself; his ears were stuffed with a huge raw echo of the crash. As he stroked her hand as if it was a talisman that could bring her back to him, he heard fragments of glass falling into the rear of the van, and a duller sound, growing louder. Perhaps his hearing was returning to

him, but besides that, the sound was approaching. The car was
coming down the track.

When it coasted onto the stretch of rock between the Hundrai
and the bared lead of the wall, there was very little Paul could do.
His emotions seemed to have been pounded flat by the fall, and he
wasn't sure he could move. He saw the driver climb out of the car
and stand with his hands, now gloved, on his hips. He took some
moments to scrutinise the smashed vehicle like an artist consider-
ing his own work in progress. His expression didn't change as his
gaze passed over Paul and Bebe. Then he met Paul's eyes, and
strolled over to speak to him, no longer bothering to sound Scottish. "Give me a message for Geoffrey," he said.

twenty-nine

Geoff nearly believed in Ben at the funeral, and it seemed everyone else did. When they returned to the kennel house, out of the rain that had muddied the graveyard on the hill below the church that had failed to snag the rushing black sky with its grey spire, all the old ladies who helped Geoff's grandmother pour large glasses of sherry and empty them almost as fast had nothing but praise for both boys. "What perfect little gentlemen," declared the lady who appeared to be entitled to all the superlatives on offer—oldest, slowest, heaviest, most thoroughly dressed in black. "They're a credit, Thora, to you and poor Rod and your daughter." Presumably she and her friends were approving of the boys for offering around the platefuls of sandwiches, minute triangles of bread so thinly filled with ham or tinned salmon or cheese that the recipients had to lift a corner to discover which. Even Geoff's parents were impressed, not to say surprised, by how self-effacing Ben had grown, how unobtrusively sociable—for the moment as discreet as the kind of waiter he was playing—and Geoff could only think they were so worn out by their problems at home that they had no energy left to turn against Ben, to continue to be suspicious of him. The sherry helped the women sniffle as they talked about his grandfather, Geoff observed, and didn't know where to look—certainly not at Ben. It was Geoff's father who rescued him and audibly himself as well. "I'd better be getting them home, then," he said.

"Go on, you leave us women to our waterworks," said the boys' grandmother, dabbing all four corners of her eyes one after the other.

"Get your goodbyes said," Geoff's father told the boys.

Geoff couldn't help suspecting this was yet another trick. Apart from his mother, who contented herself with a kiss from him, all the women insisted on having a hug. Trying to give each of them a quick embrace only made them hug him harder—as hard as he saw Ben hugging them. At last he was done with being enfolded in scent and having tears dripped on him, and he and Ben were in the hall. Even more incredibly, so was Ben's suitcase. Instead of running to it, Ben turned to the depths of the house. "I'm off now, Lady," he called to a frenzy of barking.

Rain and barking urged them to the van, where Ben joined Geoff on the front seat. As Geoff's father started the engine he scowled across his son at Ben. "This family's good enough for you now, is it?"

Geoff shrank inside himself. It was over a year since Ben had invented a family to tell his schoolmates about, but this was the first time Geoff's father had confronted him with it. Ben only smiled. "It always was, dad."

Geoff's father gave his attention to the road at once, and didn't say another word for the eventually less rainy hour and sunny half it took him to drive home. As they came in sight of the house Mrs. Slough peered over the shared hedge, then stooped out of view. "We're back all right," Geoff's father said, and Geoff thought he might even be including Ben. "Should have helped us get our compensation if you wanted rid of us."

As he opened the gates the dog started barking in the house, and Ben gazed eagerly up the path. "What did you call him?"

"Rex," said Geoff, overwhelmed by the relief he'd spent most of the day holding back.

"What's that mean?"

"Means a king," Geoff's father said. "Should have thought you'd know that. Not as clever as you wanted us to think after all, are you? Only middle of your class at school."

He'd hardly unlocked the house when Rex dashed out, all yelps and tongue, to greet Geoff. "It's just like Lady," Ben said, more delighted than Geoff would have dared hope.

"Go to the chippy if you're starved," Geoff's father told them. "I've got sums to do about this place."

Geoff had heard him complain too often recently about their finances to take the bait. "We can just have a sandwich."

"Make it yourselves," his father said ungratefully, and shut himself in his office.

Ben patted the dog's head, earning a friendly bark. "Don't disturb our dad while he's working," he murmured, and to Geoff "I'll make friends while you do dinner."

Geoff buttered some sliced bread before quartering the lump a tin of corned beef expelled onto a plate. Ben joined him in the kitchen, Rex trotting after him, and poured two glasses of milk. Having served himself half the corned beef, he cut off a piece and fed it to Rex, his fingertips brushing against the dog's teeth. "You're not afraid at all, are you?" Geoff blurted.

Ben's eyes took their time about finding him. They seemed to have grown paler in the years he'd been away—pale as eyes in a photograph that had faded or not yet developed. "I'm never going to be afraid again," he said.

"What was it like while you were away?"

"I'll let you know sometime."

It must have been too bad to talk about so soon, Geoff thought. "Sorry," he mumbled, and felt shy of speaking until Ben did, which meant there was no more talk while they finished eating and washed up, at which point Ben said "You're tired."

"I know. I'm going to bed." Geoff let Rex into the back garden, where the dog's ears pricked up at the sound of the motorway, and chained him in the kennel where Geoff's parents made him sleep. "Be good," he murmured, ruffling the fur on the nape of Rex's neck, and stumbled to his room.

He was asleep so quickly he didn't remember climbing into bed. Now that Ben was back the house felt like a home—no longer so weighed down by the burden it was to his father. He wakened once with the impression that Rex had barked, and then there was another stretch of sleep before the sun was glaring into his eyes and he heard voices raised downstairs. His father had turned on Ben. "You can tell him what happened. Tell him what you did."

Geoff ran downstairs, a cold smell of stale vegetables catching in his throat. His father and Ben were in the hall, and neither of them looked at him. "What is it?" he cried, stopping short of "What's he done?"

His father jerked his calloused upturned hands at Ben, who let his head sag and blinked at Geoff. His eyes were cloudy enough for tears. "I was just telling dad, the dog. I woke up early and then I couldn't sleep, so I thought I'd . . ."

"What, Ben? What?"

"I just took him out for a walk, that's all."

Geoff felt as though he had to drag himself forward through layers of words to reach the truth. "So?" he pleaded.

"There was a motorbike that came when we were crossing at the lights. They were red."

"He's never—" Until now Geoff had thought only people in films trailed off like that. "Where is he?" he had to ask.

"That's it. I don't know, Geoffrey. The bike scared him coming at him, and he ran off."

"Couldn't you have held onto him?"

"Don't you think I tried?" Ben displayed the reddened palm of his right hand. "Look what his lead did."

"He'll be back, I reckon. We all come back round here," Geoff's father said with little enthusiasm. "Watch out for yourselves if you go looking for him. I'm off to the site now to make some cash for him to gobble up."

"When are you back?" Ben asked.

"When I am. I've got to fit in the solicitor. I'd like to fit him in the ground for all the use he's been, the lot of them, damn bloody—" His voice was sinking into him, but then he remembered something. "While you're out see if one of you can get a tube of superglue. Your mother keeps it in the kitchen, but I can't find where she's put it. She can't have used it up."

Geoff sprinted upstairs, trying not to hate Ben for having lost the dog. He pulled on yesterday's clothes, which felt as if they were beginning to sweat in anticipation of the chase, and ran down to the hall. Ben was gazing at an object in his hand. It couldn't be remotely as important as finding Rex, and Geoff demanded "What have you—"

Ben moved his hand away from his face. He was holding a small mirror of the kind their mother always carried with her. He slipped it into a pocket as he turned to Geoff. For the briefest instant his eyes looked as tearful as before, then they were dry as stone, and as expressionless. "Fooled him," he said.

"You mean dad? About Rex? You're saying he's all right?"

"That's him. Mr. Davenport. The man everyone's cleverer than. And you're his son, so you believed me too."

"I know," Geoff said, which didn't soften Ben's stony gaze. "Where is he, though? Where's Rex?"

"Remember when I used to hide things and draw you a clue? I've been looking forward to playing that again all the time you left me with the dogs."

"I didn't leave you, Ben. I couldn't stop the grownups, could I? When I tried to say anything they shut me up." Geoff heard himself begging, but it had no visible effect on Ben, who reached in his pocket for a folded scrap of paper—a page torn from a school exercise book. He unfolded the page and held it up.

It was a picture of the path that led behind the house. A curved line under a straight one with a sketch of a train on top, and another with a car, showed where it passed beneath the railway and the motorway. A stick-figure was running along it with hands like gloves pressed to its swollen panicky balloon of a head. The figure was supposed to be himself, Geoff saw, because it was running towards a pair of words hovering above the far end of the path: WOOF WOOF. "Why?" he wanted to plead, but could think of far too many answers. When his stiff shivery lips managed to open he said "What did you do to him?"

"You'll have to find out." Ben's eyes were bright and dancing, but no more alive. "Better not waste time. Shouldn't think there's much left," he said, and slipped the sketch into the pocket with the mirror.

Geoff's sense of almost understanding sent him racing to the gate, where he discovered that Ben had shut the front door and followed unobserved behind him. As Geoff ran around the outside of the garden to the grassy slope that descended to the path, however, Ben crossed to the opposite pavement. "Aren't you coming?" called Geoff, who had hoped Ben's face might betray when they were near wherever he must have tied Rex up.

"I'll be watching you. I'm going to the shops."

"Why? What's the point of that now?"

"You heard what he said. Got to replace the glue."

The playfulness that entered his voice for the last few words dismayed Geoff beyond thinking, and he slithered down to the path. The morning roar of the motorway sank with him and filled the air between the grassy banks three times as tall as he was. "Rex," he shouted, and was answered only by his echo, squashed small as a toddler's voice by the noise of traffic. He dashed under the railway arch and stood where it would act as a megaphone. "Rex. I'm coming, Rex."

The barking started at once. Geoff had to move out from beneath the weight of the traffic noise into the heavy sunlight before he could be sure that the dog wasn't Rex—that it was guarding a house above the right-hand bank. He hurried down the rough path, which snaked between nettles as high as his waist. "Rex," he kept calling as his voice grew parched. Once he heard a rustling in a clump of nettles to his left, but whatever was in the undergrowth, which was so thick he couldn't see through it, didn't bark. Once some children in the garden of a house with an organ-pipe chimney, its three pots growing progressively lower, imitated Geoff's shouts before they settled for laughing at them, and he saw a girl of about his age soar in a swing above the hedge as if she was acting as his lookout. When he shouted up to her to ask whether she could see a dog she only giggled as she continued to reappear and vanish.

She and her friends had gone when at last Geoff trudged back along the path. He'd found a fallen branch with which to poke and slash at the weeds, but all it achieved was to sting his hand with sweat where it gripped the scaly bark. Was Ben spying on him? If he could have found the other boy he might have attacked him with the stick to force him to say where Rex was—except that he knew it would take more than he dared imagine to affect Ben now. The rumble of the motorway gathered in his ears, compressing his thoughts and muffling his senses, so that he might have walked past the place where he'd heard the rustling in the nettles. But he saw a feeble movement beneath them.

He cut down a swathe of nettles so as to step off the path. There was fur in the depths of the weeds, and he slashed at the leaves above the supine body to clear his view. Then his mouth wrenched itself open, but he felt as if he was incapable of uttering enough of a cry, of making any sound at all—

"Geoff. Geoff."

The sunlight went out as his eyes jerked open, and darkness pressed down on them. He was lying on his back in bed. Gail was holding onto his arm, and in not too many seconds he distinguished her face above him. "You were having a bad dream," she murmured.

"That's all, you're right. Just a dream."

"Do you want to talk about it?"

"Better not. I'll sleep now. I've a long way to go in the morning."

Gail lingered over giving his forehead a stroke and a kiss and pulling his arm around her as she lay down with her back to him. Eventually he felt her reluctance to sleep without having talked yield to sleep, and wished he could follow her. He'd dreamed only at the very end; everything else had been memories that had resurrected themselves as he'd tried to doze. But the nightmare was closer now, its pitiless light finding all the darkest shadows in his mind and laying his emotions bare, and there was no point in telling himself it was only a nightmare—not when he knew the truth.

thirty

Gail slept until Geoff whispered in her ear "I'll see you as soon as I can."

"Are you heading off now?" She rolled over to face him, leaving sleep behind. "Why didn't you waken me?"

"I just did," he said, and keeping his voice low "Paul's still dead to the world."

She eased her legs over the edge of the bed and succeeded in coaxing the floor to keep most of its creaks to itself as she followed Geoff to the stairs. Paul's hands were clasped together above his head as if he was celebrating victory in a dream. Once he was out of sight she murmured after Geoff "Did you manage to get enough sleep when you're driving so far?"

"I managed to catch up with myself."

"Rest on the road if you need to," she said down the next flight of stairs. "Don't feel you have to hurry back to us if you'd be driving while you're tired."

"I'll want to be back. Maybe I'll give you a ring if I've anything to tell." He opened the front door, and seemed arrested by the muttering of a train on the track that bridged the river. He turned and delivered a kiss and a hug, fierce but so quick she felt as though he was already on his way before he'd finished. "I can't imagine I won't be home tonight," he called over his shoulder.

"Just be sure to let us know if you won't be," Gail responded as he hurried into the faintly misted shadow of the bridge. She wasn't dressed for the morning chill; she rubbed her bare arms as she retreated into the house. She'd seen her husband off to work, and now it was time to get ready for hers. But she knew they'd both just faked a scene neither of them wanted to admit was faked, and she might have said so if he hadn't been about to drive so far.

She shouldn't be surprised if he was dismayed by the thought of children being maltreated. She could understand that he might find his feelings difficult to talk about, especially when it had taken him so long to admit to her that he had a brother—when it had apparently needed their investigation of the children's home to jar him into admitting even that much. That he found his feelings so hard to talk about struck her as proving he should, and if not to her, to whom? They were going to talk when he came home, she vowed to herself. It seemed to her that for weeks they had only pretended to talk.

She took a mug of coffee with her to the shower and left the bathroom door open, and heard Paul stirring as she dried herself. As she climbed into the bedroom he wobbled to his feet only to bang his elbow on the rail around the cot, and she cuddled his small body warm as sleep to help him decide against crying. "Ow," she said on his behalf, and carried him down to the bathroom, where she loitered while he pulled off his sleepsuit and used the toilet and washed himself before walking rather than clambering upstairs to get more or less dressed. "Let mommy just do this for you," she said, tucking the tags of his T-shirt and denim overalls inside their collars and tightening his left sandal a notch. Then came breakfast—a bowl each of cereal so much healthier than she'd eaten at his age that she felt a little guilty for robbing him of tastes she could still remember—after which she called Twenty-four Hour Knights to send a cab.

The Greek driver was listening to the news and weather. Storms were sweeping down the country from the north. "I hope your dad isn't driving into that," she said to Paul, "it doesn't sound like much of a day for grandma and granddad either," and imagined their joints beginning to twinge with cold and damp.

From Hammersmith she took the Underground, and more of it from Notting Hill Gate. Paul's hand in hers was clammy with travelling by the time they climbed into the deafening sunlight at Marble Arch. The security guard at Metropolitan Television was handing a visitor's pass to someone who was either an actress or an impassioned spokeswoman for a cause, but he spared Paul a grin as Gail trotted him past to the crèche beyond the elevators.

She had to knock and be identified through the window in the door by the slim young nurse in her pink overall. By now there were nine toddlers—more than Gail recognised—in the room full of toys and games as bright as their advertising and books with cardboard pages, not to mention all the materials the nurse would have to clean up at the end of the day. "New friends, Paul," Gail said, but he was busy leading the nurse away by the hand.

Gail took the elevator up to the fourth floor, where she found Angharad working on a crossword in the *Telegraph* and fiddling with the comb in her red hair while she waited for her colleagues to help solve a clue. "Clambered," Bella offered, and Anna proposed "Chastised." All of them looked behind Gail as she closed the office door. "Only half of you?" Angharad said.

"The better half," said Bella, never one to let a good phrase die.

"Where's our token male?" Anna said, and to Angharad "Childhood?"

"Didn't he call you back last night, Angharad? We were asleep on our feet, but that's not like Geoff. He's meeting a contact. There's children or anyway a child in danger, he's sure of that much."

"That's you and Geoff both, then," said Angharad, laying the newspaper aside.

"I'm sorry, I don't . . ."

"We've a contact for you too. The one who got scared has spoken to someone who isn't."

"The wife of a Frugo ex-manager who started hating the whole setup," said Anna. "She seems pretty set on him talking to us."

Gail read the notepad page Anna gave her. Mrs. Catherine or maybe Katherine Mason lived in Portsmouth, and here was her number. "Impressions?"

"Round about middle-aged and determined not to be nervous."

The number Gail dialled was instantly seized. "Who is it?" a woman said, so urgently her Cornish accent could hardly keep up with her voice, beyond which Gail heard the harsh repeated squeal of an alarm.

"Am I speaking to Mrs. Catherine Mason?"

"We'll see about that. Who are you?"

"It's Gail Davenport calling from *The Goods*, Mrs. Mason."

"I don't know you, do I?"

"You spoke to my colleague Anna Wren before. I'm the one who's paid to do the research, but you can speak to her now if you'd rather."

"You'll serve. I don't want to do you out of a job," the woman said, her accent slowing her voice down. "Only it isn't me you're after, it's my Ken."

"Is that a problem?" Gail said, having heard that it was.

"He's gone out to see what they've done to the car."

"That's the alarm I'm hearing. Did someone . . ."

"They gave it a knock. We didn't see who, but we've a good idea. They'll have to do worse than that to shut us up."

"Let's hope they don't, Mrs. Mason. Shall I hold on?"

"They won't dare once it's public. He can call you back."

"I'm entirely happy to hold on."

"He'll be a few minutes. Doesn't get about too fast any more. Have you got your own number? Give me that and I'll make sure he calls."

As soon as Gail had read out her desk number the alarm fell silent, but only because Mrs. Mason had cut her off. She hung up and leaned back in her chair, and the phone shrilled at once. She grabbed the receiver and crouched forward, ready—she thought—for anything. "Mrs. Davenport?" the receptionist said. "Call for you."

"I'm expecting one already. If it's for *The Goods* can you put it through to someone else here?"

"It's personal." For a moment Gail wondered why the receptionist had paused: of course, she'd thought that would be enough. When Gail didn't respond she said "It's your father."

thirty-one

He should have spoken up, Geoff thought as he came to the end of the motorway. He should have, but he couldn't. The words had never left him.

He was back yet again, and he didn't want to be recognised—couldn't afford the time that would take. At the outsize crossroads bristling with traffic lights he swung the car away from the route that led to his old home. Another left turn took him off the dual carriageway into a street where parked cars basked under trees outside pairs of stocky houses standing shoulder to shoulder. One more left and then a right led him into a short narrow street with a sign at its dead end. When he halted by the sign he saw that it did indeed point the way down to the path behind the houses, which was now a cycle path.

He switched off the engine and unbent onto the choppy pavement, and all at once he was barely able to stand up. He used a knee to slam the door as he leaned his forearms and his aching fists on the hot dusty roof. He'd been driving for close to five hours without a break, but there were other reasons why he felt glassy and nauseous. He'd come to the end of the trail, he was certain.

The envelope he'd found in the ruins of his grandparents' house had contained Ben's sketch of the path—of Geoff's childhood self with its balloon head and big scared eyes running towards the barking in the air.

He had never been able to find Rex. Months later, someone else's dog had led them to a corpse in the nettles by the path. It had been little more than a skeleton, with nothing except its contorted position, its legs pressed inseparably together in pairs, to suggest how it might have died. On hearing about the discovery from a schoolmate who lived nearby Geoff had known at once it was Rex, but when he'd made himself venture to look it had gone, leaving a cleared patch and a trail through the weeds. He never learned who had found the body or how it had been disposed of—and since he'd heard no more, he'd known that only he and Ben realised how the dog had been prevented from struggling to his feet while he had suffocated to death.

Geoff hadn't told his father about the game Ben had made him play. His father had been blaming more and more people for his failure to get the compensation he wanted or to sell the house for even half the price he believed was fair, and whatever Geoff might have felt Ben deserved, he'd been afraid his father would do far worse to him. Once the boys' mother returned from looking after their grandmother and confined her regrets about Rex to a grudging sentence, the grownups had quickly forgotten the dog—since he'd ceased to be a puppy they had barely tolerated him and the expense of him. But when Geoff had heard that the corpse had been found he'd set out to tell them the truth.

He'd tried that night at dinner. He'd met Ben's eyes across the table, he'd seen Ben realise what he meant to do, and then he'd turned to his father, to wait until his complaint about the day was finished. "What?" his father had demanded at last, though not before Geoff's mother had indicated the boy might want to speak. "What are you after?" But it hadn't been the roughness that had paralysed Geoff's tongue—had made the unspeakable words gather into an immovable mass, a mouthful he could neither spit out nor swallow. The more he'd fought to speak, the bigger the insubstantial gag grew, until his father had turned away with a contempt he'd previously reserved for his stepson. Hardly knowing where to look, and no longer wanting to be seen, Geoff had found his gaze straying to Ben. With no more than a stony blink Ben's eyes had told him he knew Geoff could never tell.

Geoff shoved himself away from the car. He might have been too young then, but he wasn't now. He'd never been at ease with Ben after that—had tried never to be alone with him, had been alert for hints that he was planning some further revenge—until Ben had vanished on his eighteenth birthday, when Geoff had come to believe that freedom would be enough for Ben: that he could achieve freedom. Now, as Geoff hurried down to the path, he felt neither of them had.

A stick was lying in the weeds to the right of the way down from the road, a branch some four feet long, its splintered end gleaming white as bone. He couldn't help wondering as he picked it up whether it had been snapped off a tree to point his route. Since his childhood the trees had grown higher than the grassy banks, but he knew where he was going. In a minute he saw the organ-pipe chimney pots above him, and within the bend of the path ahead was an expanse of undergrowth where the dead dog had been found. Before he reached the bend he spied the corner of an object almost hidden by the weeds.

It was white, it was rectangular. It seized his heartbeat as he ran to the bend. He had to swipe the knee-high nettles flat before he could see that his prize was an empty packet of condoms. He began to poke the fat green stalks aside, and then to cut them down, flinging them across the path. In a few minutes he'd cleared a patch larger than a man could hide in, and he was able to see all the way to the grassy bank, but there was no sign of an envelope.

He wiped his forehead with the back of one hand and leaned on the stick, which creaked. Might someone else have found what-ever had been left for him, or could the childhood sketch now mean that he had to search the whole length, mile upon mile of it, of the path? He made himself straighten up before the weight of the thought broke the stick, and a white object revealed itself at the edge of his vision. It was a butterfly so basic it didn't even run to colour, and he had to restrain himself from lashing out at it; he dealt the weeds in front of him another dull scything instead. Stumps of nettles snapped and squelched and flew in all directions, and the tip of the branch frayed on a surface harder than earth.

He poked soil and fallen weeds aside, exposing a flat stone an arm's length from the edge of the path. The stone was as wide as his face, and the colour of dried blood. As he levered it up with the stick he saw moist pinkish segments withdrawing into the earth. Then the stone tipped onto its back with a thud, uncovering the envelope.

He trod on the flattened weeds and stooped to it so fast the smell of mingled growth and decay surged up at him. A sting found his thumb as he snatched the envelope. The pain wasn't worth cursing under the circumstances, and he retreated to the path, tearing at the flap of the envelope with his thumbnail. The stick fell into the nettles with a wet thud as he took hold of the photograph. Two words were written on the back in wrong-handed capitals: NEVER TELL. "I told you I wouldn't," he muttered, and turned the photograph face up.

The mumble of the motorway lurched at him out of the trees. All at once his surroundings were a lurid image of themselves, the greenery glaring like lightning that refused to be extinguished. The photograph began to distort itself before his eyes, to curl towards him as though his panic was drawing it closer, until he managed to relax his cramped hand.

He was looking at a small figure photographed as it walked away from a zoom lens. The person whose hand it was holding was cut off by the right edge of the frame, but he didn't need to see more to know that she was Gail's mother and the green blur to the left was a shrubbery beside a path at Kew. The photographer's subject, as unaware of being followed as the rest of the party had been, was Paul.

thirty-two

Gail had crouched towards the phone, but she sat up with the receiver before saying "Dad?"

"Daughter."

"Are you all right? You sound . . ."

"Uh huh?"

"I don't know. You just sound a bit strange."

"Maybe it's all the driving we've been doing. Or maybe I'm catching a cold from your limey weather. Could be this pay phone doesn't work too well. Go figure."

"Strained, that's how you sound."

"Through a sieve, I shouldn't wonder, which is what this old phone looks to have for a mouthpiece."

"I don't suppose you can be that bad if your jokes are. Where are you calling from?"

"That's why I'm calling, to let you know me and Bebe are back."

"Back in . . ."

"Here in London. The rain chased us down."

"Well, good. Great." Whatever undefined doubts she'd been

experiencing gave way to relief. "You'll stay with us tonight, won't you?"

"She'll think she's on her way to heaven, your mother. Another night or even several in Barnes sounds good to me too. We'll see how your patience holds up, shall we?"

"The only thing I'd lose it with is too many jokes like that. I'll be home, let's see, I should be there by six at the latest. If by any chance I'm not I'll find you in the pub by the river. Make my apologies to mom, will you? Tell her we'll have a marathon talk, all the stuff we hadn't time for, only right now I'm expecting an important call."

"You don't want me to tell her we aren't so important."

"A research call, dad. Business. Professional. I shouldn't think you'd want me or Geoff letting personal matters take precedence if we came to work for you."

"Consider me chastened. Pardon the ravings of a grandfather. Speaking of which . . ."

"I can hear you're having fun, but I really do need—"

"Can you spare me just this moment? Your momma would ask, only she's in the powder room, and you say we haven't time to wait. She was wondering if we could take our grandson somewhere for the afternoon. I know he's in the crèche there right now."

"When did I tell you and mom about that?"

"Maybe you only told her. I found out from your switchboard lady when I asked if he was with you. How about it? Bebe would be so pleased, and you needn't ask how I'd feel."

"You don't have to work so hard to persuade me. Where are you planning to take him?"

"Where does he like? I mean, where does he like best?"

"The zoo's one of his favourites if you want a place to stroll around. You won't be driving there, will you? Not when you've driven so far."

"Don't worry, there'll be a pro behind the wheel. I'll arrange a taxi. If you're going to be busy on the phone, shall one of us come in and collect our spoils?"

"That might be best. Taxis can't wait long round here."

"Look for us later, then. We'll see if we can't give him more of a surprise than the zoo." The static that had persisted throughout the call—a sound so regular it suggested that a piece of material was being drawn back and forth across the mouthpiece—intensified, then diminished. "Say goodbye to Geoffrey. We nearly forgot him, didn't we?" he said.

For the duration of the call, she had. That would explain why she'd been troubled by a nagging sense of something unidentified: while her parents were staying she would have to postpone her talk with Geoff. She was about to take her leave of her father when the abrasive static swelled up and was swallowed by the dial tone. While she had the receiver in her hand she phoned downstairs.

The extension had begun to seem content simply to ring when it let her hear a silence so profound she said "Is that the crèche?"

"That's us, Mrs. Davenport. We're just having story time."

"Sorry to interrupt. I can hear the suspense. I hope it won't be another interruption, but my parents want to pick Paul up for the afternoon."

"I'd better make sure he finds out the end of the story."

"Sure, and could you let me know when my parents arrive?" Having been assured of that, Gail replaced the receiver and stood up to stretch before moving to the window. Taxis were swarming around the junction at Marble Arch, but none seemed bound for Metropolitan. She was watching an airliner thread the lacy hem of a white cushion of cloud when a phone went off behind her. "Yours, Gail," Anna said.

Gail sat and spun her chair towards the phone and used her legs under the desk to halt herself. "Gail Davenport."

"Cath Mason. You buzzed us before."

"Thanks for calling back so soon. Is Mr. Mason there now?"

"He's here. Take it, Ken. Do what you said you'd do."

This sounded less promising than her last conversation with Gail had, and so did her husband's voice, which was slower and heavier than hers. "Someone Davenport, is it?" he demanded, so distantly that Gail was unaware of being spoken to until he said "Is that who you are?"

"Gail Davenport, that's me. I'm—"

"Isn't Davenport the feller who runs the show?"

"Runs, well, he fronts it. We're a team. Not just him and me, but I'm the researcher. I'm his wife."

"There's one of them behind a lot of us."

"Beside rather than behind, it sounds like in your case."

"She's a good old sort, true enough. So she's been telling you our troubles."

"It wasn't me she spoke to first, but she left the telling to you. What would you like to be public?"

"All of it. The whole damned sly business."

Gail heard him using stronger language than he ordinarily would. "That's the spirit, Mr. Mason. So to be specific . . ."

"I'm not a sneak. I never was when I was a kiddie. You wouldn't have wanted to be one at our school."

"Got you," said Gail, though she wasn't sure if he was praising or bemoaning the school. "But you wouldn't call it sneaking on a firm that put you out of a job."

"They didn't put me out. I put myself."

"Because you didn't like their methods, I believe Mrs. Mason said."

"Did she?" There was a silence in which she could imagine he was looking at his wife, and Gail was about to try to regain whatever ground she'd lost when he said "She'd be right. I told one of the local rags about it, but they weren't that interested. My guess is they can't afford to be."

"We are," Gail assured him as Anna's phone rang. "The bigger the game the better we like it."

"For you it's a game, is it?"

"Game as in quarry. As in what we trap, you know, hunt down, flush out, bring into the open. That's what you want, isn't it, Mr. Mason?" Gail said, and with her hand over the mouthpiece "What is it, Anna?"

"It's the crèche. Someone's here for Paul."

"Tell her to let them take him, would you? I was going to go down, but you see I can't now. Sorry, Mr. Mason. Say again?"

"I said I don't mind playing if it helps bring them to book. It's my old staff that need protecting, not us."

"They're still working for the firm, or not?" Gail said, and had to cover the mouthpiece again while she strained both ears. "I can't talk to her now, Anna. Doesn't Paul want to go?"

"The shop's still got its claws in them," Ken Mason said. "I'm only doing this for them."

"He's happy to, Gail, only your parents have sent their driver in to fetch him."

"Then there's no problem," Gail said, and bared the mouthpiece. "They must have been lucky to have you for a boss, Mr. Mason, and now they've got you for an advocate."

"More than that if you want."

"We want as much as you're willing to give, so tell me what that might be."

"You use some kind of spy video, don't you? You put one on the girl who worked at the children's home."

"We can surely do that if you think you can get anything on Frugo," Gail said, relaxing a little as she saw Anna relinquish the phone. "Where do you think they'd let you in?"

"How high do you want me to go?"

"As high as you feel safe with, Mr. Mason," said Gail as Anna's phone shrilled again. "We aren't in the business of putting our informants at risk."

"They won't dare do anything to us when I've finished."

"So long as you're sure," Gail said, and heard Anna say "Geoff."

"Don't you fret on our behalf. I know who's got the biggest mouths. I'll be asking them to leave us alone, stop trying to scare us dumb, and you'll have what they say to stick on your show."

"It's worth trying," Gail said, and waved away the other phone as Anna mouthed Geoff's name.

"I can put you onto somebody who still works there as well."

"They'll talk, you think, or wear a camera?"

"Both. She's only a few months to run, and she's just waiting to get out so she can speak up."

"I believe he's with his grandparents," Gail heard Anna say, and focused her attention on Ken Mason, who was saying "I'll introduce you somewhere we won't be spotted."

"Any idea where? Do you want to tell me her name?"

"She's on her line, Geoff. That's why you were put through to me."

"I'll tell you when I introduce you. I'll fix up with her where to meet. You won't mind coming down here, will you?"

"She's talking to a source. I don't know how long."

"Not at all, Mr. Mason. Wherever's best for you and her. Do you have a sense of when?"

"You're in a call-box, are you, Geoff? Try again in a few minutes."

"I'll see her at the weekend. I'll have a word with her over a pie in the pub and give you a buzz back."

"I'll be waiting to hear from you, Mr. Mason. If there's nobody here you can always leave a message, even if you just say you called. Thanks for all you've done so far. If it weren't for people like you we wouldn't be able to broadcast the truth," Gail said, and saw Anna still on the phone. She laid the Masons' call to rest and swung herself out of her chair. "I'll take it now, Anna. What on earth is his problem?"

Anna gave her a baffled shrug along with the receiver. "Tell me about it, Geoff," Gail said.

"About what?"

"About whatever was so urgent. Did you make your contact? I just did, a solid one, I think. I wouldn't be the Frugo people when we're through with them."

"There was nobody here. Forget that story. What's this I was hearing about Paul? Anna seemed to think he was with your parents."

"He is. They're back in town, I'm glad to say for all sorts of reasons."

"I understand, but where? I mean, where have they, where's Paul now?"

"With them. Isn't that enough? You've seen how they take care of him, even more than they did of me."

"I know they will, but what's their itinerary? That isn't much to ask."

"I don't know."

"You haven't, you're saying you've no idea at all?"

"I suggested the zoo, but now I think about it, mom never liked seeing anything caged, so I wouldn't think they've gone there. You can ask where they went when they bring him home."

"When?"

"I told them six, and if I'm not there—"

"I will be."

"I didn't say that, no. You'd need to drive all the way back without a break, wouldn't you? I said they should wait in Paul's favourite pub by the river."

"They'll be tired by then, won't they? They must have driven further than me. I'll make sure I'm home in case you aren't."

"You're right, they ought to be able to get in for a rest. I'll make certain I'm there when they arrive, so you needn't—"

"We both will. I'm on my way," said Geoff, and was.

thirty-three

Glue, thought Paul, and tried to move away from the smell of it. He'd forgotten that hurt so much. Every inch of him had pain in store for him, and the more he shifted the worse it grew. Best to keep still with his arms around Bebe and his lips pressed against hers until his head stopped swimming with the smell and he could think well enough to plan. Best to loll there on the front seat of the van in the unfocused dimness that was almost dark, and hope that he and Bebe would be found and taken care of before he had to discover for himself how badly injured he was. At least Bebe was unconscious, though she'd stirred in response to him—she'd followed his numb lips with hers. "Rest," he would have whispered if he had been able to operate his lips, and so he thought it instead. "Save your strength until . . ."

He wasn't sure what he was proposing: perhaps just the hope that she wouldn't regain consciousness before the ambulance came. Very little was clear to him except that both of them must have been made to sniff glue by their guide who had proved not to be one at all. Perhaps he sniffed glue himself—that would go some way towards explaining his behaviour if the practice affected his mind as it was affecting Paul's. All his dull sensations and his memories were melting together into a shapeless mass that was himself, and he didn't know how much that he seemed to remember had actually taken place.

Did the driver of the Cavalier prowl the back roads in search of lonely travellers to lure away and perhaps to rob? He'd moved the barrier that had closed off the abandoned quarry, Paul had deduced, but how often did he play that trick? Was the quarry hiding other wrecked vehicles besides the van? The thought dragged his senses outwards, and he seemed to hear, through the rain that was hammering the metal roof and thumping the windshield and splashing in the shattered rear windows, the sound of rusty vehicles creaking with the downpour—seemed to grow aware of corpses in them, a stillness composed of abandoned flesh, a heavy absence pressing closer to him. His innards flinched from it, his consciousness swayed like a boat wrenched from its moorings by the storm, and then he was able to think again, to fend off the gluey hallucination, because the reality was terrible enough. Though what was it exactly? What was meant to happen to Bebe and him? How could he judge that when he couldn't even grasp the last words the man had said to him?

"Give me the rest of your—" "Gonna make a mess of your—" He couldn't have said "Geoffrey"—Paul must have been desperate to hear something familiar in the midst of his shock. The man had stared at him as if he was prepared to wait as long as it took Paul to understand; then his eyes had brightened with loathing, and he'd hauled the door open and punched Paul quite lightly, even deftly, on the chin.

The memory of that—of his own inability to protect Bebe—swayed Paul's consciousness afloat again on the gathering darkness. Surely the man hadn't felt the need to do anything to Bebe, who had already been unconscious; indeed, Paul had thought she was dead. She was still insensible, and might be hurt worse than him—why wasn't he trying to go for help? Nobody was coming for them; the man would have replaced the barrier, and they were by no means visible from the road. However much pain and dizziness he might experience wouldn't have to matter. The worst part would be leaving Bebe in the van, since he didn't dare risk moving her when he had no idea how badly she was injured. As long as he could struggle to the road, he'd wait until a car chanced along— soon enough for Bebe, it would have to be, must be. He tried to flex his fingers, which were clasped together behind her back so tightly his hands felt like a single lump of bony meat, and opened his mouth to tell her what he had to do.

As his lips, which felt swollen and somehow weighed down, parted so did Bebe's. Even if she wasn't conscious, she was giving him a drowsy kiss. He responded with a gentle pressure and made to pull away and speak. Her head rose too, her lips stayed fastened to his, pulling them away from his teeth. Without thinking he sucked in a breath that tasted of glue and felt himself sucking it out of her. He gasped, and her lips clung to his as the air was expelled back into her mouth. Then the pounding of rain clamped itself to his ears, and the smell of glue tried to float his mind away from ac- knowledging at last what had been done to Bebe and himself. Now he knew why her hands were fastened together behind his back as inexorably as his were behind her—knew when he tried to force his clasped hands apart, to move even a finger. He had to part them, however much he damaged them, or he would be useless. Once he had his arms free he would be able to slip out from under Bebe's, he told himself desperately—but he didn't want even to begin to consider how he would have to separate their glued- together mouths.

thirty-four

By half past four Geoff was in London, just a few miles from home. He'd raced down the North Circular Road onto Hanger Lane when several cars ahead of him switched on their hazard lights, and the traffic crawled to a stop. For twenty minutes he could only inch the car forward next to a ghetto blaster in the shape of a Jamaican's Jaguar, and he felt as though the pounding bass was embedding itself in his skull. When he tried to listen to a local station, to concentrate his mind away from the uproar and to gain some explanation of the delay, he began to dread what else he might hear. But there was no news flash about an American couple and their grandson, and no traffic news either.

In sight of Ealing Common the traffic picked up speed, and by the time the main road changed its identity yet again, becoming Gunnersbury Avenue, Geoff was driving half as fast as the signs said he could. There was no sign of any reason for the holdup, but he did his best not to feel it had been contrived expressly to delay him, any more than all the traffic lights by Gunnersbury Park and beyond it turned red because they sensed his approach.

It was twenty past five when he reached Kew Bridge. As he

passed the botanical gardens his hands gripped the wheel so hard his palms stung. He was remembering the back view of a figure crouching with a camera over a flower beside the path, or rather not remembering it except for the notion of it, not a solitary detail. He should have been suspicious of a photographer, he thought: of anybody loitering anywhere near his family or doing anything that let them look innocent . . . He wasn't too late, he would be home to meet Gail's parents with Paul, and then he was going to have to tell Gail everything about Ben, despite the warning on the back of the last photograph. Maybe the presence of her parents might even help him tell.

He drove down through Richmond and swung towards the Thames at Mortlake. In five minutes he was abreast of the side road where he and Gail parked. Nobody was waiting outside their house beyond the bridge. A bus flashed its headlamps to usher him across its path, and he swerved into the side road, accelerated past his space, reversed fast into it, lurched out of the car and used slamming the door to send himself onward. It was only a quarter to six, but there might be a message at home.

He heard the phone as he ran under the bridge. By the time he shoved the key into the front door it had stopped. He was hushing the alarm when the answering machine emitted a click that indicated the tape had finished inviting the caller to speak. A silence gaped out of the speaker, then even that was cut off.

The display already showed four calls. Geoff elbowed the door shut and hurried to rewind the tape. It hadn't started to run forward when he knew it had no voice. Each call held its breath for a few seconds before giving way to the next, and he was sure there had only been one caller. As the fifth silence made itself heard he twisted the knob to send the tape back to the beginning. It was on its way when the phone rang.

He grabbed the receiver before it could repeat itself. "Hello?"

"Mr. Davenport?"

The man's voice was light and efficient and quick. "Yes?" Geoff said as fast.

"Would the G be for Geoffrey, Mr. Davenport?"

"It's for Geoff these days. If you're selling something—"

"Forgive me, Mr. Davenport, but you sound like the television personality. Is that you?"

"Whoever I am, this is my home number. Can you just—"

"Have you a son, Mr. Davenport?"

Geoff leaned hard against the banister. "Yes," he said, and not quite as firmly "Why?"

"About three years old, will he be? Blonde hair, grey eyes, and wearing a blue overall and a white T-shirt and sandals?"

"Coming up to three, yes, and as you say, except I don't know what he's wearing. Could you—"

"You don't know, Mr. Davenport? Is there some trouble in your family? Some breakdown of communication between you and your wife?"

"Of course not. I've been away, that's all. What's this about our son? Who am I speaking to?"

"Does he answer to the name of Paul?"

"That's his name. Is he there with you? Where—"

"Calm down, Mr. Davenport. No need to persuade me you're concerned. He's secure. He's in our hands now."

"Whose hands? Are you the police? Was somebody trying to take Paul away?"

"Who might that have been, Mr. Davenport?"

"I don't know. If someone's been arrested, you tell me."

"You must see that's an odd assumption for you to make if there's no more to it than you're saying."

"I'll explain once I have Paul safe with me. Now please just tell me where—"

"I regret that's not allowed, Mr. Davenport."

"What the hell do you mean, not allowed? Then you bring him here to us."

"That isn't the arrangement either, I'm afraid. Do I take it your wife's with you?"

"Not yet. Soon." Geoff felt that the receiver was about to splinter in his fist, and managed to relax his grip. "You tell me what this is about. I want my son, and if he comes to any harm—"

"I told you once. He's in our hands. Yours and mine," Ben said, resuming his own voice.

Geoff's free hand groped for the banister and steered him around it so that he could sink into a crouch on the stairs. The edge of a tread dug into his spine, but he no longer knew how to remedy that. "What have you done?" he said.

"Ask yourself that, Geoffrey."

"What have *I* done?" Geoff's head felt thin as china. "Everything you asked for. I'm the one you want, so leave my son alone. You don't need—"

"You told."

"No I didn't. I don't know where you got that idea, Ben, but you're completely wrong for once. You didn't have to remind me never to tell, because I already—"

"Why, Mr. Davenport." The official voice was back. "I thought you said there was no breakdown of communication in your family. Which story do you want me to believe?"

"Not the way I thought you meant it there hasn't been, no, but I swear I haven't said a word about you to my wife or anybody else. If that's why you—"

"Don't try and tell me you keep secrets from each other. That isn't how a perfect family operates."

"Who said it was perfect, Ben? I'm not. I didn't realise how much I'm not till I started hearing from you." Geoff heard a car door slam, and was near to panic. "Look, my wife may be home any moment. That doesn't sound as if I've told her, does it? Tell me where you are and I'll come now, just me, wherever you are. You haven't really got Paul, have you? You're only trying to scare me, but believe me you don't need to. If you'd got him you would have let me hear him by now."

There was silence, or at least no answer. Geoff strained his ears for any background noise that might suggest the kind of place Ben was calling from, but it was so soundless he could only assume Ben was covering the mouthpiece. All at once Ben said "You can find me. This is your last call. You know enough."

"I don't, Ben, truly. I haven't the least idea where to look. Give me some help if you want me to find you as much as I know you do."

Ben's voice seemed only to be playing at sounding playful. "How's this for help?"

Geoff pressed the receiver against his cheekbone as though to squeeze whatever he was meant to hear out of the unresponsive plastic. He had time to start consciously taking a breath before, audibly proud of being able to get the word right, Paul said "Help."

"That was helpful, Geoffrey, am I right? It always helps my mind, a bit of danger. It used to be a bit of fear. Don't keep us waiting long, will you? Just you, all by yourself. And keep that mouth of yours shut, or I'll have to give your little pet more than a kiss."

"If you—" Geoff began, so tightly he felt he was choking. He heard a clatter, and footsteps moving away. Ben had left the phone off the hook. As soon as Geoff dared he began to shout, praying that someone at the other end would hear. "Hello? Anybody there? Hello?"

He must have been shouting for at least a minute when, with no prior sound to warn him, he was answered by a clatter. "Don't hang up," he yelled. "Speak to me. Hello? Will you speak?"

"You've come through to a pay phone, old boy."

"Did you see who was on it just now? Can you still see them? They can't have gone far."

"I'd have to tell you I can't spy a soul."

"Where are you, then? Where is that?"

"Can't help you there either, old chap."

"Of course you can. Where are you speaking from? What's the address? Where is it near, for God's sake?"

"It's nearer me than you were hoping, Geoffrey," said Ben in his own voice, and hung up.

Geoff slumped as though only the connection had been supporting him. He poked the digits that would identify the number from which the call had been placed, but of course it had been withheld. He hauled himself upright with the banister so as to drop the receiver into place, and heard across the room a key probing the lock. The front door opened, and Gail came in.

thirty-five

He was emerging from the phone booth in the alcove off the hall when Mrs. Minken accosted him. She lowered her square head, giving him even more of a view of her permed auburn hair foaming over it like beer out of a tankard, to gaze expectantly at him. "Is your wife missing the family, Mr. Reaper?"

"Call me Ted, won't you? She's hoping she can join us later in the week."

"That would be happiest, wouldn't it? What did you say she did?"

"She's a carer. Some people won't be happy till everyone has one."

"She ought to be given her break when she booked it, all the same. Can't someone take over for her while she comes away?"

"Some of these cases get to know the person they're assigned and won't have anyone else."

"They oughtn't to be let expect so much, should they? I'll say no more, I see you're keeping your thoughts in. Is the little soldier missing his mam?"

"I'm doing my best to make sure he doesn't."

"You could have a handicap at that and still come out the winner. He's a credit to you. A little credit, aren't you? A credit to
your dad."

"Mrs. Minken is saying you're a good boy, Ben."

"Ben."

"Ben, that's right. That's your name."

"Isn't he a treasure. Doesn't say much, but when he does it's as
clear as the news on the telly. I wish all the kiddies we've had staying were like him. Put you off your Sunday roast, it would, some
of the language we've heard and the mess we've had to clear up
after them. Does he speak up for himself more when he's in the
mood?"

"He's learning at his own pace. I'm teaching him all the time.
As you say, we wouldn't want him coming out with things we don't
want to hear."

"I didn't mean a word against him or you either. Is he a bit tired
as well? Is that part of why he's so quiet?"

"I think you could be on to something, Mrs. Minken."

"And I hope you won't mind me opening my mouth a bit further, but you look as though you could do with some sleep too."

"I've been driving quite a way of late. That's my business, long-
distance transport. I'm hoping to catch up on my rest before I
have to get going again."

"What must you think I'm thinking of? Don't let me keep either of you from your beds." She stooped to tickle the toddler
under the chin. "You're the image of your father," she said.

"Thank you for reminding me, Mrs. Minken." As the hotel
landlady vanished into the basement kitchen he used the club attached to the room-key to prod the toddler onto the stairs beneath the teardrop chandelier too large for the hall. "Up you
scrabble," he murmured. "Nobody's making you do anything you
don't want to do, are they? Can you hear the television? You can
watch mine when we're in the room."

On the middle floor the child tramped straight to the room at
the front of the building. It was furnished with a double bed and,
closer to the floor, a single truckle. A chair beside a wardrobe faced
a shrunken television on a ledge, next to which a frosted-glass en-

closure somewhat larger than a cupboard managed to contain a toilet and a shower booth. Outside the window, above which the hotel cocked a satellite dish at the evening sky, a cordon of white three-storey hotels did for most of the view, but the toddler wasn't bothering with that. He waddled to the truckle and sat facing the television. "Want to watch, do you?" his guardian said. "Call me pa, then. Remember how we practised on the way. Say pa and you get the control. Pa, that's better than dad."

"Dad," said the toddler, and his face searched for an expression.

"Never mind him. He doesn't mind anyone he can't make into a film. Not going to start howling, are you? Boys aren't supposed to do that. Boys who don't act like men get to stay in a room with something nasty in it and a dog outside. Here, look at your picture you like."

He slipped the American passport out of his pocket and found the photograph, and the toddler's face cleared. "Randad."

"Randad! That's a good name for them. None of them ran fast enough, though, randad or randma. Nothing grand about them either when I'd finished with them." He closed his fist around the passport, just not tightly enough to bend it out of shape. "You call me what you have to call me and you can see him again later. Pa. Say pa."

"Pa."

"That's it. That's what you say when you need anything. You've nobody else you can ask," he said, and thrust the passport into his pocket. "Here, I said you could watch."

He snatched the remote control from on top of the television and brandished it in front of the small intent face. "Push this to switch on, look. And this button with an arrow on it changes channels. You try now," he directed, and dropped the control on the truckle bed.

As the boy started to play with the channels, Reaper eased his legs onto his own bed with hardly a sound. Now he could observe the chained door, the boy he need only lean sideways to reach, the ash of the twilight gathering on the dull red roofs beyond the window. He'd set the volume of the television so that he would hear any noises on the stairs well before anyone came close to his room.

Here was a United Nations meeting, a bombed street full of dust and gunfire and some corpses, policemen digging up the garden of a council house, men in turbans picketing a women's refuge. "Slow down a bit," Reaper said, beginning to grow restless. "Find something to put you to sleep."

A game show host zooming about in a wheelchair. A man playing two miniature piccolos stuck up his nostrils. A chimpanzee with electrodes on its skull and using its food to construct a barrier within its cage. *The Arranged Marriages Show*. A man with a toy rocket emerging from his fly to the sound of laughter and cheering and applause. . . . Reaper was making to put on his gloves when the parade snagged on a cartoon, and the toddler let the control drop.

An old woman and a canary were avenging themselves on a cat. Whatever was done to their victim, it regained its shape in the next scene so as to come back for more. "Dogs don't do that," Reaper commented. "Grannies and their husbands don't either." He was close to the state in which he was intensely but calmly aware of everything around him, and nothing could threaten him, because it was all a part of him—he was close, but not there. He must be failing to achieve it because he had to share his room. "Not for long," he said, quieter than the cartoon. "Better than sleeping three to a cell, I can tell you."

He wasn't really speaking to the boy; the very fact that the boy wasn't listening, and would surely not understand if he did, helped Reaper talk. "The only place to get a real education, all the same. Harder to get into than you might think. I had to go for someone's face with an army knife before the judge thought I was fit to be let in. Can't even remember whose face it was. Less of a face than it used to be, I'll promise you that." His reminiscent smile was floating out of him, hovering invisibly in the dim flickering air. "The system tracked my mother down, her and her hero who stuck Geoffrey in her, but they didn't want to know. Don't know if they told Geoffrey, and I'll let you guess if I care. I almost feel like thanking them for helping me become myself. Is Geoffrey going to come for you when he never bothered finding me? Do you think that's fair?"

But the toddler was saying even less than usual, because he was asleep. Except for the glow of the screen, on which a hairy man was staring at a footprint on a supposedly deserted beach, the room was dark. Time could pass like sleep for Reaper when there was no immediate reason to be alert; his surroundings turned into a dream from which he could instantly waken. He switched on the light and pulled the sheets over the toddler, then tucked them beneath the mattress of the truckle bed to pin him down. Once he'd given the room a slow thorough survey he switched the radio between the beds into its intercom mode. "Don't bother trying to hear me," he mouthed at it, and having locked the toddler in, went soundlessly down to knock on the door marked PRIVATE. "You said you'd listen out for him when I'm not there, Mrs. Minken. I'm just off for my constitutional."

"That's what our air's for." Nevertheless the landlady's face, which the doorway extruded gargoyle-like, bore a concerned look. "Have you and your little prize not had any dinner?"

"We ate just before we got here. Someone couldn't wait. I can see you're thinking I ought to be firmer with him."

"I was only thinking I hope he won't be hungry if he wakes up. If you see the light under this door you can always ask me to make him a sandwich."

"Thank you, Mrs. Minken. That's thoughtful of you." Reaper was out of the hotel before adding "Better not think too much about us." That was meant to give him back his sense of power, but instead it confused him—made him feel close to being pushed beyond the point where he could choose, as he liked to push himself when the times came. "Just another old bitch," he muttered, strolling away from the hotel. Once he was out of sight from it he veered deeper into the town.

Very soon the pale houses gave up having notices in their front windows and grew thinner to make room for more satellite dishes. The gleam of the streetlamps clung like frost to the net curtains, contradicting the mugginess of the night. As he crossed narrow intersection after intersection he felt compelled by events to move faster than he liked, but it would be no faster than he could cope with. There was the pub on a corner ahead.

It was called the Game Dog, and it was no larger than any of the houses in either of the streets onto which its opaque windows faced. The houses seemed to be ignoring it, preoccupied as they were with elaborating themselves: front doors were attended by pairs of antique carriage lamps, and one bore a knocker with the face of a Greek god; there were doors carved of mahogany, porches composed of oak or stained glass. Two dead streetlamps framed the mouth of an alley that led back where he came from. Having established this in case of need, he went into the pub.

Beyond the door, the upper third of which contained four panes that had been painted black, was a single room. Some cigarette smoke made its escape as he entered, but there was still far too much for the size of the interior. Nevertheless it was criminality more than smoke he smelled, and so he knew he'd come to the right place.

A bar whose front was upholstered in leather and studded with brass slanted across the corner farthest from the door. The rest of the room was occupied by six round black iron tables and twice as many stools hard with leather. Quite a few of the men poised on the stools had rendered themselves bald as the day they were born, and they weren't the only ones bearing tattoos to show they had form. Those who were facing the door were watching the newcomer, while the rest seemed more interested in the rugby game on the television above the bar, which meant they were waiting for him to walk past them. None of them knew how much worse he'd done than they could imagine, and that excited him as he moved through the undergrowth of muttered conversation to the bar.

The barman was perched on a staircase behind it. His thin bare arms wired with veins were the colour and texture of leather, his sharp face looked as though it was being tugged against the bones by his greying pony-tail. He let his reddened gaze stray over the other patrons before acknowledging his customer. "After something, chum?"

"A drink if it's not too much trouble."

"There's never trouble here," the barman said, and used an unenthusiastic thumb to indicate the shelves beside him and the pumps behind the bar. "If you see it you can have it."

"I'll have a Coke."

"Suit yourself." The barman came fast to the bar as if to startle him, but Reaper only observed him while the machine between them stuttered out the drink; then he dropped a note beside the mat the barman slipped beneath the glass. "Don't let me drink on my own."

"Drop it in there," the barman advised him, having produced his change from an old brass till, and nodded at the Care for a Child tin on the bar. "Or are you asking me to fix you up with someone, love?"

Reaper left the change where it was and rested his gaze on the barman's eyes. "Barney," he said, only just raising his voice.

"Not much of a name to give me."

"The word is it's all I need."

"What makes you so special?"

Reaper was letting his eyes suggest that when a voice behind him demanded "Who said ask for Barney?"

He didn't turn. He waited until she appeared alongside him and he could judge how he'd managed to overlook the presence of a woman. Her bullet head was shaved grey; the tops of her breasts, now that she was close enough for him to see into the meagre cleavage framed by her camouflage waistcoat, were as elaborately tattooed as her muscular arms. "Wal in Soho. Old Compton Street," he said.

"You're famous," the barman told her, not that it sounded much like praise.

At a look from her he unbolted the flap of the bar and jerked his head to signify that Reaper should climb after her. Years of smoke from the bar seemed to cling to the bare yellow bulb over the narrow stairs, and to stain the walls brown as nicotine. The woman's trousered buttocks kept thrusting towards his face like a pair of giant gloved fists warning him how she treated anyone unwelcome. She stumped left at the top of the staircase and switched on the light in a room.

The unshaded bulb glared at the windowless walls, at the frayed carpet on which two folding chairs faced each other across a rickety card-table, at the dusty glass of three framed photographs leaning against the wall, photographs of boxers dressed in thigh-length shorts and squaring up to each other. The woman dropped herself in the chair with its back to the door and kicked the legs of the table wider open as Reaper sat opposite with his drink. "What's Wal up to these days?" she said.

"Passports."

"That's why you went to him, is it?"

"I got one from him, and now I need another."

"Why couldn't he do it?"

"I didn't have time to see him again."

She planted her fists on the table, backs upwards. Having scrutinised him for a few moments, she turned her right fist on its side and curled its stubby forefinger. "Got a photo?"

Reaper passed her a quarter of the strip of photographs a booth had taken for him. Once she'd swivelled it the right way up she said "How old is he?"

"He's working on being three in October," Reaper said, and held out his empty hands to suggest how his innocence had allowed him to be robbed. "When his mother grabbed him so I had to steal him back she took his passport."

"I didn't ask, did I? Anyone can see he's yours. Got his details?"

Reaper gave her the folded sheet bearing the information he'd written with his left hand: name, date and place of birth, nationality, gender . . . "Benjamin, do you want him to be?" she said, and a whistle shrilled below them.

Reaper let a smile play with his lips. When the muffled roar of the rugby crowd recommenced underfoot he said "You're right, he's got to be Benjamin. How long will it take?"

"How good do you want his passport?"

"How good does it need to be?"

"Depends where you're taking it and if you want a visa in it."

"I'll know tomorrow when I've booked the flight. How much longer do your visas take?"

"I'll tell you when I know where it's for. Lots of countries don't need them. Turkey, you slip them a fiver in the passport and they give you the visa right there."

"Without a visa, how long?"

She rolled her eyes upwards as though she was running out of patience, but she must have been going behind her eyelids to think. "Day after tomorrow, same time here."

"No chance of tomorrow?"

"Maybe for an extra hundred. Don't know what Wal charges these days, but here it's three plus the extra for the rush. That's for a passport nobody's going to look at twice in Europe, and once you've got that far, nowhere else either."

"That's as far as I'll need to go," Reaper said, pushing his knife deeper into his pocket while he dug out the wad of notes. "Here's half," he said, and pocketing the rest, stood up.

The woman stuffed the notes into her breast pocket, exposing another coil of a snake nestling in her cleavage. "Where can I find you if I have to?"

"You won't." Reaper picked up his glass to empty it. "I'll find you, no fear," he said, and wiped his fingerprints off the glass with his sleeve as he skipped downstairs. He slid the glass off his palm onto the bar and sauntered to the door. Outside the Game Dog he walked away from the direction he'd come from, and only when he was several streets away and certain that he hadn't been followed did he set about doubling back.

He was as sure of himself as he could be, but not having been for even a moment made the inside of his flesh feel exposed. He ought to have noticed a woman in the bar—he'd spent his life learning to be aware of everything around him and letting nobody realise he was. "It's you, Geoffrey," he said to the deserted locked-up curtained street. "You rushed me, not keeping your mouth shut. You'll be sorry."

The thoughts this aroused sent him hurrying back to the hotel. The left-hand window on the middle floor—his window—was dark and silent as a switched-off television. Nobody but Geoffrey would have dared remove the toddler, and Geoffrey could never have found him so soon. Reaper let himself in, an average father who had needed an hour's babysitting to give him time for a stroll at his own pace, and padded upstairs to unlock his door. At the sight of the toddler gift-wrapped by the sheets of the low bed, he experienced a smile that almost involved his eyes. "It isn't just a dog this time, Geoffrey," he whispered as he eased the door shut. "You haven't long left to care."

thirty-six

When Gail let herself into the house and saw Geoff she felt as much exasperation as relief. She'd raced to be sure she was home in time for her parents and Paul, and she needn't have bothered. She'd thought the Underground would be quicker in the rush hour than a taxi, and so she'd run for a train at Marble Arch and another at Notting Hill Gate, only to find that train was branching off to Wimbledon. When at last she'd arrived at Hammersmith on a Richmond train she had to catch a bus, and standing on it all the way home had used up the little moisture in her mouth. She made for the kitchen with barely a glance and a pursed smile at Geoff as he put the phone down. "That wasn't them, was it?" she said.

"Who?"

Gail fed herself a palmful of water before filling a glass and turning impatiently to him. "Who do you think? My parents, of course."

"No."

She didn't understand his tone—even less so when, after a pause, he repeated the word. "What is it, Geoff?"

He stared at the phone as though it was dragging at his eyes, then he raised them to her. "Come and sit down."

"I can't just yet. I need to fix dinner for more of us than I was expecting tonight. Mom and dad won't want to dine out when they've been on the road for so long. Talk to me while I dig stuff out of the freezer."

"Leave it." He clenched his fist and thumped himself on the heart before adding more gently "Please."

"Geoff, what's the matter with you? What's been the matter these last weeks? Is this more of it?"

"Yes."

He was staying by the stairs, his opened fist held out to her. For a moment she was only mad at him for persisting in trying to lure her away from her task, and then she saw him appealing mutely for help. "Geoff, if you have to tell me something, just say it. I can't cope with this."

"It's Ben."

"Your brother? Half, I mean? What about him?"

"He's . . . he's been . . . calling me." Without warning Geoff backed away from her and sat down on the couch. "Please come here, Gail. I need to tell you all this fast, and then we can—then we'll have to . . ."

Frustration that felt poised to become something worse sent her to perch on the edge of the chair opposite him. "I'm here. So tell me and stop thinking you can't, however bad it is. Since when has he been calling?"

"Since the night I was in Edinburgh."

"All these weeks, that's what it's been? Oh, Geoff, why didn't you—"

"Gail."

"No, listen. I know you must have found it hard to talk about after keeping it to yourself for so long, but once you'd told me he existed—"

"I promised I wouldn't tell anyone about him. I promised, but I ought to have realised he would end up not believing me. He thinks I told you everything. I should have, I know. I can't expect you to forgive me."

"Geoff, don't be stupid. What could be so bad—"

"These couples we've been hearing about, found murdered. An old couple in Surrey just the other week, just after he first called me."

"Geoff, you aren't saying— You are."

"It's him."

"Geoff." She felt she was using his name to prove he hadn't changed. "How can you be certain?"

"Because he told me just enough that nobody except the person responsible would know."

"Don't tell me, not yet anyway. Let me think. If he only told you—"

"He wanted me to find him. He still does, only me. I've been trying, following his clues. That's why I went . . . back home the second time."

"I really wish you'd told me sooner. Of course I forgive you, I can imagine how hard it must have been for you. Jesus, no, I don't believe I can. It hasn't caught up with me yet. Finding out that the last of your family—" The question she was amazed she hadn't thought to ask finally occurred to her. "Was that him on the phone just now?"

"Yes."

"What did he—"

"Gail, listen."

"I am. I have been. It's a lot for me to take in all at once, you know."

"I appreciate that. You're being great. Nobody else could— Only—"

"If there's more, Geoff— There is, isn't there? Tell me. You're going to have to," Gail said, her throat suddenly dryer than before.

"I've been trying to tell you as much as I can as fast as I can so that you'll—so that you won't—" He raised his hands and stared at the nothingness between them. "Gail, try not to panic when I tell you this. It's just another way to keep me quiet and make me go after him. He's—it seems as if he's taken Paul."

At that moment all the fears Gail hadn't dared admit were conceived in the deepest part of her. She sat forward so violently she might have been about to hurl herself at Geoff. "You mean he says he has. He can't have really."

"Gail, that's what I—"

"We'd have heard if he'd taken Paul away from my parents. They haven't called, have they? They didn't leave a message."

"No, but Gail—"

"Then don't *you* panic. Never mind telling me not to. They'll be here with Paul any minute, and as soon as they are I'm calling the police. We'll make sure your half a brother can't . . ." Her voice trailed off, because his eyes had filled with sympathy that seemed too close to helplessness. "Why are you looking like that?" she cried.

"Because I spoke to him just before you came in. To Paul."

Her having missed that chance—to speak to Paul, and to do she didn't know what else—made the situation piercingly real. It possessed her mind like a nightmare, but it was as big as the world around her. "What did he say?" she pleaded, not bothering to control her voice.

"He said hello." Geoff lingered over the syllables of the last word as though she was supposed to find it reassuring. "He sounded fine. Ben hasn't harmed him, and I'm sure he won't. He must know he doesn't need to for me to go all out to find him."

"Then do it. Forget me. Ignore me. What are you waiting for?"

"I need to think. I've got to try and work out where—"

"No, you haven't. What you have to do, and if you don't I will, is call the police."

"Gail, please don't even consider that. It's the only way Paul would be at risk, if anyone but me turns up."

"How can you say that? How can you expect me to believe that when this bastard, this secret you shouldn't have kept from me and look what keeping him secret did, when he took Paul away from— Wait." She clutched at her temples with her fingernails as if the sharp ache might send her thoughts the way they should go. "I still don't understand why if he took Paul my parents haven't been in touch."

"How did they seem when you saw them?"

"I don't understand what you're asking me," she said savagely. "Anyway, I didn't see them. We talked."

"You must have seen them when they picked him up."

"I didn't, no. He was down in the crèche. And they didn't come in, they sent their driver."

"Their what, Gail?"

"What's wrong with that? They were tired from driving, so they left the van—I don't know where they left it, but what's so strange if they decided it was safer to take a cab?"

"And sent the driver in for Paul rather than get him themselves. You don't think—"

"What was I supposed to think? I was talking to a source, Anna said someone was there for Paul and he was happy to go with them. If you'd told me I needed to watch out for someone—if you'd told me when you called up while he may still have been in the building—dear God, Geoff, if you're saying that was him and you didn't give me a chance to realise—"

"I don't know, do I?" Geoff held out his empty hands and let them drop. "If your parents were going to have Paul picked up, wouldn't they have told you in advance?"

"What difference is that supposed—"

"Which of them did you speak to?"

"My father. Why should that— Oh God. Oh Jesus Christ almighty."

"What, Gail?"

"Shut up. Now *I* have to think." She'd noticed how her father's voice had sounded on the phone—strained, and further blurred by the static that could have been the dragging of a handkerchief across the mouthpiece—but now she realised there had been more to notice. He'd called her "daughter" when he never did, nor had he ever referred to Bebe as her momma. She'd thought those were two of his deadpan jokes, but now— Her mouth opened as if to mime the stupidity of which she had just convicted herself. "It wasn't him."

"Are you sure? What makes you—"

"He nearly got it right, but he used words daddy wouldn't say. How did he know what to sound like? If you've let my parents come to harm—"

"Gail . . . Sorry. I won't touch you if you don't want me to. Just don't hate me too much yet. We haven't time for that now. We need to support each other until they're all found."

"Found how? Found like all the other couples were found?"

"Gail, listen. Try and hold onto this. He doesn't kill them, he leaves them to die. I'm calling the police right now."

"You just got through saying we can't tell anyone."

"This is separate. It'll have to be."

He was already making for the phone. As he passed Gail he ventured to rest a hand on her shoulder, and she reached automatically to place a hand over his. For just that moment she was able to believe their life was, or would be, as it had been. Then he was phoning the police, and she stiffened on her chair, ready to jump up and intervene if she disagreed with anything he said. He identified himself and told them that he and Gail had been waiting to hear from her parents since last night, that they'd promised faithfully to call and would have done so unless something was very wrong. He gave the registration number of the van, the area of Britain where he'd been led to expect it would be, a description of Gail's father and one of her mother . . . By now every one of Gail's nerves was working to send her to her feet, to grab the receiver and tell the police about Paul. She was clutching her knees, not knowing whether she meant to keep herself seated or shove herself out of the chair, when Geoff put the phone down and stared at it once more. "You're a good liar," she heard herself say.

"Not to you, never again," he said, and risked lifting his gaze. "If it's not too late."

Gail didn't know, and preferred not to speak. He saw that, and had clearly expected no better. "We've got one advantage," he said, and waited for the question to glimmer in her eyes. "We know someone who knows what Ben looks like."

thirty-seven

Now it was dark—as dark, Paul thought, as the inside of a block of coal: so dark his eyes might as well have been transformed into the substance. He'd always believed that being unable to see your hand in front of your face was one of those exaggerations people substituted for imagining how a situation would really appear, but now he saw how accurately it summed up the experience, even supposing he'd been able to separate his hands in order to confirm the invisibility of either of them, even if there had been room for one between Bebe's face and his. It was so dark he kept fancying he could see her face that was pressed against his own.

He didn't know how long it had been since her face had flickered with a last hint of dimness before going out—didn't know when his being barely able to see her had turned into remembering. He mustn't let that distract him, mustn't let it lure him into the dark of his mind. He needed to know only that Bebe was alive. All he had to do was summon help while she could still be saved.

She'd relapsed into unconsciousness. At least they wouldn't be struggling to move without either of them knowing what the other meant to do—without being able to see in order to communicate.

But he'd seen her eyes flutter open and manage to focus on his in the instant when the darkness took her face. He couldn't have dreamed that, any more than he was dreaming the almost imperceptible throb of her heart against his chest, and either would have been enough to rouse him. He and Bebe weren't finished yet. They only had to make it to the road.

He couldn't just lean over to the door behind her. He might bang her head against the window, which could be ready to shatter at a touch. He lifted her awkwardly with his forearms under her armpits, edged himself across the seat he was sharing with her, let her down onto it as gently as he could, drew a shaky breath through his raw nostrils, lifted her again and moved another fraction of an inch. Lifting her body, which had seemed to sail into the air like a bird taking flight when he'd carried her across the threshold of their first apartment, sent shivers and piercing aches up his arms to penetrate the rest of him, which felt as though it needed just one wrong movement to reveal how damaged it was. None of his suffering could be allowed to matter. Not being able to see helped him focus his other senses, so that he knew he was about to touch the door just as his knuckles rapped against the chilly metal.

A dizziness that smelled of glue rose to meet him as he groped for the handle. The fingertips of his right hand bruised themselves against it, and he thrust them under the metal plate and tugged. The handle lifted, but the door didn't budge.

He expelled what was left of the aching breath he'd drawn to give him more strength, and felt a gentle answering breath on his upper lip. It was a sign from Bebe—it couldn't be his own breath returning to mock him. He mumbled an undefined syllable twice into her mouth, the best he could do towards speaking her name, and dug his right elbow into the seat so as to lever himself up. The gluey dizziness slopped back and forth in his head as he threw all his weight and Bebe's on his fingertips. The handle gave with a creak, but the door didn't shift, and he heard stone grinding against metal.

He heaved himself up on his elbow, he shoved his toecaps against the floor and his fingers deeper beneath the handle, and wrenched at it with more force than he would have dared believe himself capable of exerting. This time he not only heard the edge of the door grind against the obstruction, he sensed how immovably wedged the piece or pieces of stone must be—driven so hard between the door and its frame that he knew the blockage was deliberate.

The thought made his body flare with rage, and he thought he saw the blackness turn red. He was quickly chilled by the nightwind through the smashed rear windows, and he lowered Bebe against the seat, trapping his right arm, before sagging there himself. He swallowed dryly, appalled by the thought of retching while his lips were fastened to Bebe's, and tried to breathe slowly and lightly to recapture some control. He was struggling to think what more he could do—imagining his vain attempts to reach his door, his clumsy efforts to lift Bebe past the steering wheel—when he heard a sound, faint but increasingly definite. It was a car, and it was approaching.

It wasn't the blonde man's car. The instant Paul was sure of that, he lifted Bebe off the seat and lurched for the steering wheel. She felt lighter, surely because of the way he was lifting her, not because some part of her had gone away. He jabbed his left elbow at the dark where he knew the horn to be. But his movements had confused him. He toppled against the dashboard, his shoulder colliding with a bank of switches, and the hazard lights flashed on.

There was no use hoping they would be enough. His shoulder was throbbing all the way to the bone, his head felt as though he and Bebe were continuing to fall, but the lights weren't visible from the road. He strained his head back, taking Bebe's with it, and managed as pain impaled his spine to find the steering wheel, a curved blur that appeared and vanished in the pulsating glow from the dashboard switch. He jammed a heel against the floor and hitched up his body and the almost immovable burden that was his wife's, and shoved at the horn with his left temple. He shoved until the skin and fragile bone felt close to giving way, but the horn didn't utter so much as a croak.

It had been either damaged by the crash or disabled on purpose. Not only that almost made him give up. All of his weight and Bebe's seemed to be resting on his neck, which was extending its agony down to the base of his spine, and he caught himself wishing to pass out. But the car was still coming, and he couldn't deny Bebe the chance it represented. He straightened his crippled legs and thrust at the floor, and managed to heave himself far enough to rest his flinching shoulder against the wheel: then, with a last shuddering effort, his elbow. He shoved with it, and all at once was toppling towards the seat almost as fast as the inside of his head was falling. He twisted himself around just in time for Bebe to fall on top of him. His ribs cracked, the smell of glue sloshed through his head as though she'd gasped it into his face, but he held her just as firmly as he dared, and she settled on top of him as she often had while they were courting. He could have wept at that, and his vision blurred as he stretched out his legs on either side of hers. He strained upwards until his toes encountered metal beyond the dashboard, and set about kicking the front of the van with all his remaining strength.

Not just the front but the entire vehicle began to resound like a drum. Each kick appeared to rouse the orange flicker of the hazard lights. He held his feet in mid-air for a few seconds, painful though that was, while he tried to judge whether the noise he was making had had any effect on the progress of the car. He couldn't tell, and so he went on kicking, each kick more of an ache. He desisted only when the aches became unbearable, and heard the car. This time there was no question that it was receding.

For a dreadful moment he imagined tearing his face free of Bebe's in order to yell for help—found himself trying to decide in the trapped dark of his mind whether any injury he might do her, any disfigurement she would suffer, mustn't be preferable to letting her die before help reached them. A moan of distress so profound he wouldn't have been able to put it into words released itself into her mouth. The car engine shrank into the night and turned into a humming that had no existence outside his ears. It was gone. It had been the only car since he'd regained consciousness. Perhaps it was the last he would ever hear.

The notion brought with it a resignation calmer than despair, and he seemed to be looking down on himself and Bebe, a pair of lovers still together after all the years whose end was now, an end they could never have prepared for. At least they were in each other's arms, and perhaps in whatever dream she was having Bebe knew they were. He let his legs sink and laid them protectively against hers. He mustn't close his eyes yet, in case he drifted away—in case she came to herself only to discover he'd abandoned her. The flashing of the hazard lights would help him maintain his vigil, however distant they seemed—the ticking of the mechanism would, even if the glow seemed to be fading, unless his awareness of it was. He only had to stir for any number of aches, so monotonous they were almost soporific, to sharpen and jar him back to awareness.

Then something else did: a sound advancing out of the blackness. He had to hold back from straining his ears, because their throbbing deafened him. It was a vehicle, no doubt of that, but suddenly he wasn't sure that he wanted its driver to find him and Bebe. He hugged her body closer as he realised that the sound beyond the feeble flicker of the hazard lights was descending into the quarry—was coming to find them as only someone could who already knew they were there.

thirty-eight

All at once Geoff knew where Ben was. In some ways it was the least likely place, and that was why it was obvious—so obvious that he wondered how long it would take Gail to think of it too. Could that be another twist of Ben's game—that Geoff had to get there before she did?

She was sitting opposite him with a mug of the coffee she'd made for them both. Her hands were cupped around the mug as if to drive out of them some of the chill that, if she was feeling like him, had spread through her body from the deepest part of it. She was staring into the stagnant drink she'd hardly sipped from, and he didn't like to think what she might be seeing—perhaps only the photograph of Paul at Kew he'd given her, because she hadn't spoken since. He'd meant it to prove somehow that he was near to finding Paul, but now that he knew he was, how much could he tell her? She was bound to hate him more fiercely for withholding information she yearned to know, but he couldn't let that deter him if it was the price of saving Paul. "Gail," he said, already on his way to standing up so that she would have less of an opportunity to detain him, and the phone rang.

Before Gail could put down her mug Geoff had launched himself from his chair and claimed the receiver. "Davenport," he gasped.

"Am I speaking to Mr. Geoffrey Davenport?"

Even without the lengthening of the name, the man's accent—thickly Scottish as a haggis—would have made Geoff suspicious. "Could be," he said. "Who's asking?"

"Inspector MacBeith of Lockerbie Constabulary."

"That's going to be you, is it? How do you spell the bit after the Mac?"

"With an I, Mr. Davenport. I'm calling with news for yourself and your wife."

One word jerked out before Geoff was able to contain it. "Good?"

"The people you reported missing have been found."

"My wife's parents, you mean."

Gail stood so quickly she almost spilled her coffee. She set down her mug and strode at Geoff, who waved an urgent finger in front of his lips. "My wife's parents, is that right?" he demanded.

"I was checking, Mr. Davenport. If I can just confirm with you the registration number of their vehicle."

"That's theirs," Geoff had to say when the number was read to him. "So are they . . . You're saying . . ."

"They're on their way to our hospital."

"Are you speaking from Lockerbie police station?"

"That's where, yes."

"It's my wife you should be talking to. I'll get her. We'll call you back," Geoff said, and broke the connection at once.

The hand Gail had extended for the receiver closed on nothing. "What are you doing?" she cried. "What did you do?"

"We have to be certain, Gail. It wouldn't be the first time Ben has caught me out by pretending to be someone else."

"Then don't waste time explaining. Call him back." She watched him dial Directory Enquiries before she let herself say "Mom and dad, if it's true, they're . . ."

"Being taken to hospital," Geoff said, and was grateful to be interrupted. "Lockerbie police station in Scotland," he responded, and the female voice was replaced by one less human put together from a jigsaw of syllables and digits. He barely gave the dialling tone a chance before he poked the keys. "Lockerbie police station," said the voice they found, and put him through to MacBeith, who no longer sounded like a disguise. He handed Gail the receiver, but their hands didn't touch.

"Gail Davenport," she said with a steadiness that made Geoff yearn to support it. "You called about my parents."

It seemed there was little for Geoff to do except loiter. He sat on the stairs and listened to her questions. Her face was refusing to give way to her feelings, and as she ended the call her determined expression grew stiffer. "They've been in an accident. A helicopter found them. He won't say how bad . . . They haven't been able to say what happened. I should go to them."

"You must. They've only got you." Geoff let that reach her before he said "I was about to tell you when he rang, I've figured out where I have to go."

"Tell me."

"Let's leave it at that, Gail, just in case . . ." In case he was mistaken, or she would try to follow or to have him followed? He didn't know himself. "I'll keep in touch. I'll call you as soon as there's anything, before that if you like."

Her face wasn't relenting. She only said "Who's taking the car?"

"You take it if you're happy, I mean, feel fit to drive. I'll hire one."

"So you've a way to go."

"I'd rather not say, Gail, really. If I do I'll worry about having done it. It'll be on top of everything else."

Her face couldn't have grown sterner, but her eyes did, and held his. "Do what you have to, Geoff. Just be sure it brings Paul back safe. If it didn't I'd never forgive you."

"I wouldn't expect— You won't have to."

He tried to look as though he hadn't let the uncompleted sentence slip. As he moved off the stairs so that she could go up he risked a faint smile, but it changed nothing. He wondered why she took so long to fetch her coat, and then knew she was gazing at Paul's empty bed. He was on the point of following her when she reappeared, and he could almost believe her face hadn't wavered. As he followed her to the front door he was searching for words that might reassure her. "I know what I'm doing," he said, which earned him a pleading glance almost too big for her eyes. Then she was striding towards the car, and he shut the door. He had to get going himself.

He thought it would be simple to hire a car, but it took him nearly an hour. Some firms didn't answer, some answered with machines. By the time he'd located a suitable vehicle on the far side of the river and reserved it with his Visa, the phone felt as soft as his fingers had grown hard. He had one more call to make, and then he would be on his way to find Paul.

He wouldn't be calling the crèche nurse yet, nor the MetV security guard. He wanted to be closer to finding Ben before he asked one of them what he'd looked like—he didn't want either of them to suspect anything wrong until he was about to right it. He picked up Gail's mug and fed himself a mouthful of cold coffee before using the phone yet again. He'd scarcely finished dialling when the receiver announced "Twenty-four Hour Knights. Jess speaking."

"Can I have a cab for Davenport to go from the Terrace in Barnes?"

"Of course you can, Mr. Davenport. How are you?"

"In a hurry."

"We're on our way. It's Geoff Davenport, Muhammed. You know the address."

"I'm sorry if I was short just now," Geoff said. "I'm a bit, things are . . ."

"I'd forgotten it already. We're here to be quick. Another time I'll have to send you your biggest fan."

Now that the taxi was on its way, Geoff found he preferred not to wait alone with his thoughts. "Who's that?"

"Pete. I've never sent him, have I?"

"Not to my knowledge. What does he look like?"

"Black curly hair, and usually he has a beard. He had last time I saw him."

"Not somebody I know."

"Strange now I think about it. He let another of the boys come to you once when he could have. Make that twice. Maybe he's shy, except I'd say he was anything but."

"Maybe he doesn't want to meet me in case I'm a disappointment. How much of a fan are you saying he is?"

"Only this much. The one time I went to his flat he was watching a tape of one of your shows, and I couldn't see another tape in the place."

Geoff became aware that the edge of the receiver was biting into his cheek. He relaxed his hand, though that made it shake, and said "You wouldn't remember which programme it was."

"I do, Mr. Davenport. The one about the children's home. I thought at the time it might mean something special to him. Sorry?"

Whatever Geoff had muttered was for himself alone. "Tell me his name again," he said.

"Pete Denton. I thought you said it didn't ring a bell."

"It's new to me." Of course it was new, he thought, but the name from which it had borrowed all its letters couldn't be more familiar. "I ought to meet him. Where does he live?"

"You won't find him there now. He's gone away to his parents."

"He's the family sort, is he?" Geoff said through his teeth.

"Must be. He called to say he had to go, didn't even say where they are or when we can expect him back. Mr. Adrian wasn't too pleased, I can promise you. So if you don't mind waiting, I can put you in touch when Pete comes back."

"You're a help. What else is he like? What are his eyes like if they spend so much time watching me?"

"They're grey if they're anything. Mr. Davenport, is there something about him I should know?"

"No more than you do," Geoff told her, and was wondering how he could extract more of that when she said "I'll have to say goodbye. Someone's waiting."

For a moment Geoff was uneasy for her, and then he knew he was squandering his nervousness. Ben couldn't be anywhere near her; indeed, she had confirmed Geoff's idea of his whereabouts. Geoff replaced the phone and switched off the lights and set the alarm before letting himself out to wait on the pavement. A wind as chill as the river tightened the skin of his face and made him feel all the more driven. If Ben was so anxious to be found, he was about to have his wish. Geoff knew not only where to find him but what he looked like.

thirty-nine

Ted Reaper slapped aftershave on his smooth pink cheeks and chin and ducked his head at the mirror to peer over the clear lenses of his spectacles at the hint of stubble on his scalp. "Time to find a barber," he declared, and took his face that was stinging with readiness for anything into the bedroom. "Want some breakfast, Ben? Want some of that English breakfast you can smell? Better make the most of it. Give me that condolence card and we'll go down."

The toddler was sitting on his low bed, the control of the television in one hand, his grandfather's passport in the other. When he'd started whining in the night Reaper had stood the passport on the windowsill above the truckle bed. The sight of his grandfather's face glowing like an image on a tiny television beside the street-lamp had quieted the boy, and soon Reaper had been able to resume his watchful trance. Perhaps he'd underestimated how comforting he had allowed the picture to become. As he stooped to retrieve it, the boy pressed it against his chest and bowed forward as though to make it harder to reach.

Reaper snatched his gloves from under his pillow and pulled

them on before taking hold of the boy's face. He felt the eyes trem-
ble against his palm and the mouth deliver something like a kiss,
but he pushed no harder than he felt he needed to. As the child
opened out of his crouch, Reaper peeled the startled fingers away
from the passport and slid it into his hip pocket. "Don't start howling," he said as he returned the gloves to their den. "Nobody cares.
Kids are expected to sound like that, so nobody's even going to notice. You can have him back when we're by ourselves if you can't
stand being alone with me."

Little Ben blinked moistly at him. His mouth worked as if he
was just starting to taste his grief, but he had apparently been persuaded not to make a row. "Randad," he pleaded.

"More than he could say last time I saw him. Mm-mm would
be the best he could do. Mm-mm."

The boy giggled at that, more loudly when it was repeated.
"Mm-mm," Reaper said, protruding his lips that were keeping in
most of the noise. Abruptly he tired of the stupidity of it, the waste
of himself. "Go and do whatever you do in the bathroom."

"Bath."

"Not a bath, no. You can do without them. I'm not giving you
one," Reaper said, and wiped on his trousers the memory of feeling the child's mouth. "Use the toilet."

"Toy."

"That's it, use your toy, and I hope you aren't expecting any
help. Always kept mine to myself, so you can. Don't want un-
dressing, do you? Get on with it, then, and make damn sure you
don't wet yourself."

At the first sound of pouring beyond the frosted glass Reaper
turned up the volume of the cartoon. None of the figures, which
appeared to require so much energy to move their mouths that the
rest of their anatomy had to stay still, could utter more than half a
dozen words at a time, and left too many silences that were filled
with the noise from the cubicle. Reaper dragged the sash up and
stuck his head into the fresh air until he heard the toilet flush.
"Hope you can clean yourself up when you need it," he muttered.
"I stopped wiping up muck a long time ago."

He slammed the window as the boy trotted back into the room.

His hair looked like an old cartoon of madness, his clothes as if he'd slept in them, which he had. No wonder the landlady swooped at him as he reached the downstairs hall. "What can your dad be thinking of," she cried. "Let's give you a comb."

Reaper was gratified to see him flinch and sit down hard. She must seem more of a stranger to him than his new guardian did. "He got away before I could groom him," Reaper said.

"You shouldn't ever let them get away from you, not at his age." She was parting his hair with a comb she'd produced from beneath her striped plastic apron. Perhaps the comb scratched his scalp, or perhaps he was echoing her use of the name when he protested "Dad."

"You've confused him. We call me pa, don't we, Ben? Who's pa?"

"I'll have to keep remembering you're old-fashioned." The landlady patted little Ben's combed head. "Now nobody will say he needs his mater. Should he get changed before you go out, do you think? It's already hotter than yesterday."

"I'll fix him. Don't give it another thought." Reaper had begun to wonder what else the pressure of events might have hurried him past noticing. "I'd better see to his feed first," he said.

The dining-room was large and bright and almost full. The table farthest from the door and by the wide bay window was un-occupied. Between the window and a small subdued television el-evated on a pedestal, a serving hatch allowed whoever might be in the kitchen to spy on the room. Just two of the seated adults looked as if they could be or act like police, and they were close enough together that a fork in the eye would take both of them by surprise. Reaper didn't think that would be necessary, not least since his seat in the corner enabled him to watch both the room and the street, but he enjoyed imagining the shock, the chaos, his escape with Ben in the midst of it. "Is it two big breakfasts for two big men?" the landlady said in a tone that brooked no disagreement, and hardly waited for her answer.

Reaper surveyed the street, where a slow march of old people was loading itself onto a coach, before he fixed his gaze on the toddler as he supposed a father should. Or were you meant to play games if you had a child? He took hold of his knife and fork, and was thinking how to use them to make the toddler laugh when his neighbour said "None of us know if we're safe any more, do we?"

He gave her and the rest of her red-headed family a harder appraisal. She wore a loose white dress printed with brown spots like enlargements of the swarm of freckles it was doing its best to hide. Her plump children were more lightly sprinkled, and her stout husband had escaped the contagion, though he spoiled his fresh-faced appearance with a moustache so rectangular it might have been attached to an adhesive strip. Nobody who looked so fake, or their associates, could be anything but what they seemed, Reaper decided, but his voice still came out sharp. "Who doesn't know?"

"Well, do you? He can't any more than the rest of us, can he, Arthur?"

Her husband lingered over chewing his mouthful of breakfast before he reluctantly swallowed. "So you say."

"I do, because it's so. That's his way of agreeing with me. Haven't you heard the news this morning, Mr. Forgive Me?"

"Reaper. Ted Reaper." He'd missed the early news because he had been keeping the toddler happy with cartoons. He laid his hands flat beside his knife and fork, exactly close enough just to feel the edges of the metal, to remind himself how much control he had. "Which news?" he said.

"He should always keep his eye on it, shouldn't he, Arthur? We're religious about it since we've had these two. You're not even safe when you're older, not with this thing on the news."

Her husband poised a fork piled with toast and black pudding and egg in front of his open mouth. "He doesn't know which thing, Doris."

"It'll be on again in a minute," she said, brusquely enough to make him load his mouth. As though she had only been waiting for him to be quiet she added "Here it comes."

Reaper turned to the screen and saw a tousled man grinning as he pointed at the weather map behind him, which showed suns multiplying and driving black clouds armed with lightning north-wards. Reaper thought she was trying to trick him until he grasped that she was referring to the trayful of breakfast in the hatch. The landlady's top half bustled away to bring the rest of itself into the room and carry the tray over. She had just arrived at Reaper's table when a newsreader appeared on the screen with photographs of Geoffrey's in-laws at his shoulder.

"They're for Mr. Reaper," the landlady said, setting down his overloaded plate and a coffee-pot in front of him. As she blocked his view he lurched sideways to watch the screen, and little Ben turned to see where he was looking. "Randad," he announced at the top of his voice.

Reaper moved so fast to prod the small arm out of the space between the utensils that only the boy could have been aware he'd used not his fingertips but the prongs of the fork. "You're right," he said, "the old gentleman getting on the coach does look a bit like grandad."

At least he'd made the boy forget the television, but his eyes had tears in store, and what might Reaper have to do about them? Then the landlady deposited a smaller plate in front of the boy, and he decided against crying. "Careful. Hot plate," the landlady said. "Can he see to himself?"

"If he can't I'm not his pa."

When the boy dug his spoon into the heap of scrambled egg the landlady sighed her approval and moved away, clearing Reaper's view just too late for him to be sure if he'd seen Geoffrey's face vanish from behind the newscaster. The bumble of conversation and the mechanics of breakfasting drowned out the man's voice as if the more Reaper strained to hear, the more some substance clogged the mouth. "What did he say?" he demanded as an image of two juggernauts sprawled one on top of the other manifested itself behind the newsreader.

"Just that they haven't been able to talk about it," the freckled woman said.

Reaper picked up his knife and fork before saying as little as possible. "Who?"

"Only some relatives of that investigator who showed the children's home there was all the fuss about on television. Let's hope this creature's taken on more than he bargained for this time. He'll have all the media after him now."

Reaper copied her grimace of anticipation as he began to cut at the food on his plate. "Which creature is that?"

"The one who's—" She shuffled her chair away from her children to face him. "Who's been leaving all these old couples God knows how, God forgive him."

"How do you know he's a he?" her husband objected.

"Because a woman wouldn't do such things, would she, Mr. Reaper?"

"I'm sure that—" Just in time he saw the trap. "How can I say when I don't know what they are?"

"You know he kills old folk. Isn't that enough?"

"Do I?" Reaper said, beginning to enjoy the game. "Didn't you tell me they were supposed to be going to talk?"

"These are. He must have been in too much of a hurry this time. He left them for dead, but they aren't, neither of them."

"Neither."

"Either, then. Whichever you like. I don't know why you men are so bothered about what people say instead of what they mean," she said with a reproachful pout at her husband. "All I care about is what this creature's done, and I know what I'd like to see done to him."

"What would you see?"

"Whatever he does, twice over. What would *you* do, Mr. Reaper?"

"To someone who has to do that to old people?" He felt his knife slicing through the fleshy bacon and scraping the plate. "I'd beat him like a dog until he couldn't stand, and then I'd lock him in a cage no bigger than a dog's cage and let him starve to death, except that's too good for him."

She was nodding and screwing her eyes up and shaking her head, and he saw he'd impressed her. "Your heart's in the right place, that's for sure," she said.

He was enjoying holding her eyes with his forthright gaze so much he couldn't look away. "I'd feed him dog food. I'd force-feed him with it and never let him out. Or maybe I'd let him out when he was so crippled he couldn't stand up like a man. Then you could take him for walks on a lead for everyone to jeer at, and after that he'd have to go back in his cage without even being cleaned up. And something else we could do—"

"Mr. Reaper." She was only shaking her head now, jerking it sideways. "Big ears."

"I just wanted you to know I'm one of you."

"You ought to hear Arthur when he gets started." Nevertheless she seemed wary enough of Reaper to place her chair between them as she stood up. "Come along, you three. Time to walk off our spread."

As Reaper saw how like a procession of overgrown toddlers the family looked while they waddled out of the room their ability to threaten him lessened enough that he could dismiss them to the back of his mind. He set about eating some of his fragments of breakfast to pass the time before he could watch the news in his room. As soon as little Ben had finished strewing around his plate the bits of egg he hadn't managed to put in or near his mouth, Reaper laid his knife and fork together and tipped the boy out of his chair. They were nearly at the door when the landlady blocked their way, and Reaper almost went for the knife in his pocket. "Stop there," she said, reaching for a paper serviette to mop the child's face.

"Men," Reaper said to her, and knew he should have let her say it. Once she wasn't watching he used the attachment of the key to prod the boy none too gently up the stairs. "Mine," he snarled when the boy made to pick up the remote control in the bedroom, and snatched at the channels until he found a news summary. Geoffrey's in-laws had indeed been rescued, and there was no indication that either of them was dead.

"This is what I call a game," he said. "The closer it gets the better it is." Could the media be trying to convince him they were alive so that he would betray himself? "It'll take more than that," he muttered. Time was shrinking, but he mustn't let the urgency distract him. Having someone with him was enough of a distraction to deal with; it had already interfered with his concentration too often. He held out the control to bring the boy to him. "You're doing it," he said. "You're your father."

forty

When Geoff saw the downstairs hall light up he stepped out of the dark beneath the arch. He'd arrived before dawn and had parked out of sight beyond the bridge, and then he'd crept around the hotel to confirm there was no escape route at the back: the hedges were far too high and thick. He'd had to wait until there were signs of activity within the building so that he could gain entry without risking awakening too many people—without giving Ben the chance to sneak away in the midst of any confusion. Waiting had felt like being paralysed by a nightmare that his eyes parched for sleep kept reminding him was real—paralysed both by the need to wait and by thoughts of what might go wrong.

Except that nothing would, he reassured himself. Ben had wanted to be found, and now he was. Paul had served his purpose, and so there was no reason for Ben to harm him. Since Ben wanted only Geoff to find him, he couldn't draw attention to himself, couldn't object if Geoff had the landlady take care of Paul while the men confronted each other at last, wherever they might do it, whatever conclusion they might reach. The landlady could call Gail and let Paul speak to her. As Geoff thought all this he was striding towards the hotel, his legs no longer wobbly with lack of sleep, his eyes burning with determination as well as wakefulness. He had unlatched the gate and was swinging it away from him when a man's silhouette loomed on the frosted glass of the front door.

Its head expanded, the outline fraying, as it leaned forward to peer at Geoff with its disintegrating blobs of eyes, and then it reached a ragged hand for the latch. In a moment Geoff saw a man in a dilapidated grey suit and a shirt buttoned to its tieless collar. The toes of his boots were almost as bald as the suntanned mound of his scalp above the sample of yellowish hair that led behind his skull from ear to ear. He was carrying a large empty wicker basket, and raised one end of it at Geoff. "Can I—" he said, and less uninvitingly "Aren't you—"

Geoff shook a finger at his own lips as he went quickly up the slope. When he was close enough to murmur he said "Do you mind if I come in? I wouldn't want to disturb anyone."

The man rubbed the skin above his eyes as if to tug them more awake. "You're not expected, are you?"

"Who by? I mean," Geoff said, and then only "By whom?"

"My wife and me. Who else?" Before Geoff could decide how to answer that the man said "If you think you are I'm afraid there's been a mistake."

"No, not really. Let me explain, but do you think it'd be best if we—"

The man rubbed his forehead harder. "I don't understand why you're here. I can't believe you're supposed to be."

"I think you'll find I am," Geoff said, gazing past him. There was no sign that they were being overheard, but every moment increased the risk. "Is your wife about?" he whispered.

"She can't do any more for you than I can. She'll only wonder why you're here instead of with your wife's people that we heard about on the news."

"Good God, is that already—" If the radio in the hired car hadn't been faulty he would have known. How might the publicity affect Ben? Geoff felt as if he was being hauled towards the confrontation by his nerves. "I didn't realise that was public knowledge, didn't know it was what was bothering you, rather. My wife's gone to them. There's something I have to do here first."

"I won't ask what. Sorry we can't accommodate you," the man with the basket said, stepping out of the house, and made to close the door.

"Don't—" Geoff blurted, and grabbed the man's arm. "Excuse me. I meant here. There's someone staying with you I have to meet."

"First I've heard of it," the man said, freeing his arm and splaying his fingers at Geoff.

"Don't think me rude, but would you necessarily expect to?"

"This early, believe me."

"Yes, I see. I do understand. He'll be looking for me as soon as I can get here, that's all, only I couldn't name a time. The sooner I finish with him the sooner I can be with my wife."

"What's the name?"

"He hasn't told me that yet, but I know how to recognise him. He'll be with a toddler, a boy about three years old."

The man reached for the door again. "Not here."

"You surely can't— You don't ban children, do you? The impression I had of your wife . . ."

"She's all for them. We've none of that age with us now, that's what I'm telling you. Nobody younger than ten."

"He must be here by himself, then," Geoff pleaded, not daring even to begin to imagine what that implied. "Some kind of a change of plan. If I could glance at your visitors' book I ought to be able to spot him."

But the balding man had turned towards the sound of footsteps on the concealed stairs. Geoff's eyes began to sting as they urged the newcomer to step into view. It was the landlady. "Who—" she said, and then "Mr. Davenport. Invite Mr. Davenport in, Desmond, make him feel at home. Mr. Davenport, how are your poor wife's poor parents? Is it true what they said on the news?"

That set off a flare of panic in Geoff's head. "Who said? Are you saying they've been speaking?"

"I'm saying they were on the news. They've said nothing that I've heard."

"I'm on my way up to them. I just had to make this detour on another matter, and if I can glance at your visitors' book . . ."

"Someone told him they'd be staying who isn't, Martha."

"You see for yourself, Mr. Davenport," the landlady said, and passed him the book. "Will you have a cup of tea? I'm just making one."

"That's very kind. Do you mind if we leave it until . . ." Geoff heard his voice become irrelevant. All the signatures on the right-hand page were in Japanese, and the latest before them was almost a week old. For a moment the column of Oriental characters seemed to be a message it was crucial for him to decipher. "Have you anyone who hasn't signed?" he hoped aloud.

"We'd never allow that. We're professionals too, you know. This week has been booked up for weeks."

Until that moment Geoff hadn't realised how completely he had been taking for granted that he was about to find Paul. He was holding himself straight, though he felt as though the setback was dragging him down into a hollow at the core of himself, when the landlady said "I know who you're looking for."

Geoff's hot dry eyes rose to her, and then his stiff face did. "Who?"

"I didn't get his name, but the chap who rang day before yesterday. You weren't here, Desmond."

"Then I won't be much use, will I? I ought to be at the allotments."

"Off you toddle," she advised as he wagged his basket at Geoff in some kind of adieu or farewell. Geoff was struggling not to lose control of his impatience when she said "A man and his son. Does that sound like your people?"

"How young? The boy, that is."

"His dad didn't say. Under five, though, because he wanted them sharing a room, and they could have for nothing if we'd had one."

Geoff imagined Ben and Paul together in a room, but his mind refused to go into any further detail. "So you've no idea where they went," he said dully.

"I have. That's why I mentioned it."

"You know—" Geoff had to swallow. "You can tell me where they are?"

"Not quite, but I can tell you where I recommended. He was after somewhere not too close to town. I looked some up in the hotel guide for him. I'll show you."

She disappeared into the office for less than a minute, but to Geoff it seemed unconscionably longer. She came out waving a glossy brochure, which she opened to the most dog-eared of its pages. "I told him to try there, and there, and this one. And was there another? Yes, that."

Geoff was copying down the last address when she said "Have you time for that cup of tea? And a sit down for a few minutes. I should."

"Thanks again. Next time, I promise. I'd better be . . ." He'd revealed enough, he thought—more than he wished he had to. "You know, my wife and her parents," he said.

The landlady was silent as far as the front door. As she opened it for him she said "Should we watch for it on television, whatever you're off to follow up now?"

"I'd rather not say yet. I hope you understand. I need to keep it quiet for now. Thanks for being so much help." That drew a smile from her that looked, thank God, like a promise not to talk, and Geoff felt it speeding him towards his goal. So did the clang of the gates behind him as he hurried to the car. "Don't think I'm not coming," he said fiercely. "I'm nearly there."

forty-one

When Gail reached the Scottish hospital at last the windows of the field of cars in front of the building were crimson with the dawn. She spent five minutes driving up and down the ranks of unresponsive vehicles before a Mini whose driver must have been in it all the time pulled out of a space twice its size. Gail backed the Rover into the white sketch of a box and raised herself stiffly into the sharp chill air. She felt as though she was still driving, her hands numbed by the wheel, her body swaying back and forth with the curves of the road, as she stumbled at a run across the car park.

Beyond the wide glass doors of Accident & Emergency the reception area was lit like the inside of a glacier yet relentlessly warm as a hothouse. A few bruised people were slumped among the rows of chairs as though enacting the way Gail hadn't time to feel. She hurried to the enquiry desk, behind which a young woman whose face looked scrubbed awake had already sat forward to await her. "I'm here for my parents," Gail said. "They were in an accident. Paul and Bebe Henderson."

The receptionist's eyes shifted as if she might have liked to glance away. "And you'll be . . ."

"I'm their daughter. Gail Davenport, if you need to write it down. What's wrong?"

"They aren't—" This time the receptionist did glance aside, and Gail was almost certain she glimpsed relief in her eyes. "Dr. McKechnie? This lady wants to see her parents, the Americans, you know. You're bound that way, aren't you? She thought she had to come to Accident."

Gail turned and saw a youngish doctor in a not entirely tidy white coat. The black circumflexes of his eyebrows gave him a surprised expression that the rest of his broad face seemed designed to contradict. "Where are they, then?" Gail said in a voice she had to steady.

"They're in Intensive Care. They're stable, let me say. Do please come." He pushed open a pair of doors, releasing a disinfectant smell that would have seemed cool if the heat had let it. "It's a good bit walk."

"I can use it," Gail said, but wasn't expecting him to set off so fast down the long white corridor, almost as if he preferred to outdistance any questions she had. As she caught up with him, the heat laid hold of her. "Why," she said, and waited until that slowed him enough for her to talk as well as breathe. "Why was I in the wrong place?"

He didn't quite look at her. "Who told you what happened, Mrs., now it won't be Henderson, will it?"

"Davenport. The police told me all I know, which isn't much."

"I think they might rather I left it to them."

"How far am I supposed to go without knowing what's happened to my parents?" She was being unfair to him, making him feel not merely responsible but also younger than he was, but she cared far more about her question. "I want to be ready, don't you understand? I want to know what to expect when I see them."

Gail saw him glancing about for somewhere private, but there were only wards and glassed-in offices with people in them off this corridor. "Talk to me," she urged him. "I've had a night of not knowing."

A nurse hurried by, his eyes reminiscing about sleep, and then the excuse he gave the doctor not to speak was gone. McKechnie turned his bedside face to Gail, who could almost have imagined he was about to offer her some comfort until he spoke. "The best guess is they were enticed to one of our old quarries."

Perhaps it was a Scottish trait, or only his, to be as blunt as possible once he'd undertaken to talk. "You mean it couldn't have been accidental?" Gail demanded.

"No reason they would have been out there at night by accident. Seems they were driven off the road and over the edge, and then—well, at least he must have been in some kind of a hurry, so they were lucky there. None of the others he caught were found alive."

"Who are we talking about?" Gail heard a small voice say—her own.

"The one who—he doesn't just kill old couples, doesn't just leave them for dead."

It was Ben. Gail was scarcely aware of having halted until the doctor hesitated and came back to her. "Pardon me, Mrs. Davenport. I should say he did do what he does."

"To my parents. He did it to them." She could hardly speak for her loathing of Ben, of the man who was no longer a child—who was this—but she had to say "What?"

"He—sticks them together. Glues their mouths. We've separated them, but there's bound to be scarring, and then there are the injuries from the crash."

She felt as though all she had been told was crushing her, preventing her from moving. She lurched at the next pair of doors and bruised her knuckles against them to reveal yet another corridor. "How much farther?" she protested, too much like a child.

"A bit way yet," he said, and nothing more until they were halfway down the hollow disinfected corridor. "They're in the best hands," he offered her as some kind of an answer to the plea she had kept to herself.

"I'm sure," she responded, but she was thinking of Geoff. If he'd told her sooner then her parents might be safe, and so might Paul, and she found she had hatred to spare for him. She followed the doctor through one more set of doors, to be confronted by an arrow pointing left to Intensive Care. "Will they knew I'm here?" she said.

"I shouldn't expect too much."

But she was, and her sense of being confined to her own head was intervening between her and everything else. She watched herself turning the corner into a stubby side corridor, at the end of which the windows of a pair of doors showed her an indoor camp, a row of screens pitched along either side of an aisle in which deserted chairs sat back to back. The doors were guarded by a busty sister whose uniform buttons were only just taking the strain, and who sailed out of her office without abandoning the frown she'd been training on a stack of forms. "Sister, here's Mr. and Mrs. Henderson's daughter," the doctor said.

The sister blinked her frown away as she appraised Gail. "You'll have come a good distance, will you?"

"Drove all night," Gail said.

"You'd best go through. I'll show you to them. Only see about not making much of a noise, would you? We mustn't have people disturbed."

She eased the left-hand door past a faint creak and held it until Gail ventured into the stagnant heat of the ward. A chorus of electronic bleeping seemed to raise all its voices to greet her. She was staring at the uncommunicative screens and listening for even a hint of which might hide her parents when the sister gripped her elbow momentarily to steer her leftward and inched back the nearest screen, and Gail saw them.

How could she be shown to them when their eyes were shut in their masked faces? Then she grasped how the sister had meant the phrase, and her mind had no more ruses to distract her from the sight in front of her. Only her parents' heads and shoulders and arms were visible above two lumpy stretches of white sheet that lay altogether too still; even her mother's slim elegant neck had vanished within a fat off-white ruff. Their mouths were blanked out by white bandages that shrouded them from just beneath their nostrils to their chins, and their hands were gloved with bandages. A feeding tube was taped to her mother's upper left arm, another to her father's right. Beside each of them a monitor bleeped in time with a green blip that might have been in search of a sing-along tune to illustrate. Their beds were close enough for them to have reached across the gap, and the sheets beneath the hands they would have used were crumpled, so that Gail could imagine they were yearning to find each other. "Can I touch them?" she whispered. "Can I hold their hands?"

"Gently. Here, let me bring you a chair." The sister moved the nearest into the space between the beds. "I'll leave you, then. I'll be out of the doors if I'm needed," she said, and drew the screens together.

Gail lowered herself onto the chair, which emitted a slow breath, and took her parents' bandaged hands. "I'm here," she murmured. "Can you feel me? I'm holding both of you. We're all together."

No response. The hands in hers felt lighter than they should, hardly there. The upturned faces, as much of them as was exposed, looked smoother than when she'd last seen them, as if they were in the process of transferring their wrinkles to the pillows. "Don't go away. Stay with me," she pleaded, and hardened her whisper. "I know who did this to you. He's going to be caught, only you need to tell the police what he looks like."

Did the fingers she was clasping almost flex themselves at that, or was she feeling only her own pulse? "You don't have to talk. You can write, or you can draw. Anything that helps to track him down. We have to catch him."

No movement—not the slightest flicker of an eyelid. She wasn't meant to be disturbing anyone, she thought; suppose she was reminding her parents as they lay helpless, at the mercy of their dreams, what had been done to them? It couldn't help for her to talk about it now—it couldn't help Paul. She had to believe that Geoff was close to finding him, perhaps on the very point of it. Her job was to coax her parents back to the surface of themselves when they were ready to come.

The moment she wondered why she was thinking of it in those terms she knew. She had been five years old and just learning to swim. She'd seen a schoolmate at the far edge of the pool, and she'd run to greet her—had almost caught her when she'd felt the tiles slide away, flinging her into the water, no longer the friend she'd made of it. It had given way beneath her and dragged her down, it had piled on top of her, shoving her face deep into itself and itself deep into her nose and mouth. It had filled her brain until there seemed to be no room for her, so that she'd floated out of herself into a depth where not even light could reach.

She'd never known how much time had passed before she'd grown aware of her body again. It had felt so much like water that the struggle to regain it had hardly seemed worthwhile. Only her hands had felt solid, because each of them had been clasped by one of her parents, whose resolute grip had succeeded in dredging her up from wherever she'd gone. As her watery eyes had focused she'd become aware that they were both stroking her forehead, drawing her towards the light of their faces. She'd forgotten that as a cough had spewed water out of her lungs, jerking all her sensations back to life—the unyielding tiles beneath her back, the shouts and splashes in the pool, the taste of chlorine filling her throat—but she remembered now. A white glow was gathering within the enclosure of the screens as the sun raised itself above the mountains, and to her sleepless eyes it appeared that the light was transforming the two faces on the pillows into itself. That had to mean what she remembered it as meaning—she would make sure it did. She bent her head to kiss each of the hands in hers. Surely there was more than a trace of warmth in them. "You brought me back, and now it's my turn," she whispered. "You were the only ones who could, and now I am."

forty-two

As Ted Reaper stepped out of the barber's, his shaved scalp tingling, a little girl of about his boy's age trotted by at the end of a lead. One end of it was handcuffed to her wrist, the other to her father's. "Here, boy," said Reaper. "You don't need one of those to remind you to do as you're told, do you? You know at your age you're the same as a dog."

He felt playful again, in control of the game, still on the winning streak his life had been since he'd left the home that had always been Geoffrey's, never his. Geoffrey's in-laws were providing him with additional excitement, the will to play harder, to do whatever was necessary to protect himself. Just because the grandparents hadn't spoken yet, that didn't mean they ever would. He didn't think he could have left them much in the way of mouths, not once they were pried apart or however the doctors would have to separate them, and they were bound to be on so much medication to keep the pain away that it would surely be another reason why they couldn't talk. If they were remembering him they might think he was only a nightmare, in which case he hoped it went on for the rest of their lives. Serve them right for being who they were. He'd reached all these conclusions in the hotel room, luckily for the boy—lucky for him that Reaper's monologue had proved to be one he could giggle at rather than needing to fear it. "Giggle as much as you like," Reaper said, though he thought the sound might grow irritating with too much repetition, "let everyone see how happy you are with your pa," and pointed at the luminous green cartoon that was bleeping to summon them across the busy road.

"Cross."

"I'm supposed to say that, am I?" said Reaper with a smile straight into the face of a woman with a poodle struggling in her arms. "Cross it is, and don't be shy of telling me any other words I ought to know. Your pa has to know all the commands or he can't be your pa."

The boy stayed alongside him as he crossed to a department store and pushed open the door nearest a security guard. It was always best to head straight for anyone who might suspect you. "Boys' togs?" Reaper said.

"First floor, sir," the guard told him, hardly glancing at the boy before she turned to bar a group of noisy children.

Reaper lifted the boy onto the third step of an escalator by the scruff of his overalls and stood one step behind him. At the top the boy stumbled onto the floor but didn't fall, and Reaper only had to stroll towards the children's empty clothes to make him follow. As Reaper expected, loitering as if he didn't quite know where he was brought him yet another of the women who liked to play mother if they saw a father with a child. "Do you need any help, sir?"

"Clothes for him. You say which you like, Ben. You won't believe this," Reaper told the assistant. "Our suitcase was stolen outside the hotel. All the stuff his mother packed for him."

The assistant took a breath that swelled her generous bosom, and shook her head while she exhaled. "You don't need to tell me what it's like. Anyone could be a criminal these days."

"I couldn't have put it better myself," Reaper said, and gave her his broadest smile.

"Let's see what a big boy you are," she said, pulling up the tag at the back of the toddler's overalls. "What sort of thing are we looking for?"

"Whatever boys like him are supposed to be wearing."

"These will be cool for him," she said, indicating a carousel of T-shirts. "And they're all wearing these shorts. Will he need something warmer as well? You'll find there's a chill to our evenings."

"He'll have been put down by then."

"Don't forget undies," she said, and waited while Reaper unhooked a bag of underpants from the stand. "Shoes and socks are downstairs."

He thanked her and said no more until he was behind the toddler on the escalator, where he leaned forward to mutter "You won't need those where you're going." He used the tag of the overalls to swing the boy off the lowest tread and kept a finger through the tag all the way to the cash-desk. He was slipping a credit card out of his wallet when the faintly moustached young woman at the till said "I'm sorry, sir, we don't take cards."

"Then here's the real thing." But most of it was to buy the passport, and as Reaper peeled the topmost note from the wad of twenties in his pocket he was leaving himself only just enough. The assistant had bagged his purchases and dropped far less than a handful of change into his hand before it occurred to him that he could have outfitted the boy more cheaply at the charity shop he'd just noticed on the far side of the road. "Thanks," he said with a smile that stretched his cheeks to aching and pressed against the inside of his eyeballs, and led the boy out by his tag.

Next door was a travel agency—too close, his instincts told him. A quick walk through a pedestrian precinct, past any number of children lipsticking themselves with ice cream, brought him to another window full of cards offering last-minute holidays abroad. The earliest date was next week. He restrained himself from yanking at the tag as he sent the boy ahead of him into the shop, towards a young man whose badge proclaimed him as a Travel Operative. "Seen something you like, sir?" he said.

"Sit up there, Ben," Reaper ordered, steadying a chair while the boy clambered off it to perch like a mascot on the edge of the counter. "Have you nothing sooner?"

The clerk raised his eyebrows, sending wrinkles up his forehead almost to his receding hair. "How soon would you like?"

"Can we get away tomorrow?"

"We're talking abroad, are we? Today, if you've got your passports and you're packed."

"You're joking," Reaper said, remembering to smile as he bared his teeth.

"I wouldn't waste your time, sir. There are nearly always some that haven't gone."

"Keep those legs still, Ben." If he'd got the boy's passport sooner the day could have seen them where Geoffrey would never find them—where the boy might even prove to be the best disguise he'd ever had. "So tomorrow's possible, is it?"

"At least that, if you'd like to give me an idea of your plans."

"Turkey's popular, isn't it?"

"It is, but I'll bet we can sneak you in somewhere."

"Turkey sounds like the place for us, doesn't it, Ben?"

"Urkey."

"I expect he thinks it's Christmas," the clerk said, rapidly typing on his computer as a drop of sweat broke cover from his hairline. "Nothing there," he said in a tone that suggested he was delighting in the chase, and mopped his forehead. "Let's try somewhere else."

The clacking of the plastic keys might have annoyed Reaper less if the boy hadn't been enacting his impatience. "Sit. Sit still," he said as the clerk eventually announced "Now here's a room. Are you after just the one with another bed for him in it?"

"I'd have nothing else. Where have you found to send us?"

"Kusadasi, that's the biggest tourist town. A hotel smack in the middle. I can show you in the brochure if you like."

"Do," Reaper said, having realised not to tell him not to bother, and looked suitably impressed by the photograph on the glossy page: blue sky, blue pool, white balcony. "How long are you giving us?"

"Thirteen days on the ground. Fly tomorrow night and be there by dawn. Shall I go ahead?"

"Sounds a perfect place to lose ourselves, doesn't it, Ben? Let's make it definite."

"Brilliant. I'll just take your details. You'll have passports or one for you both, obviously."

"You don't need to see them."

"Just checking you have them. Can I take your last name first? Not so grim, eh? And your first initial."

"T. I told you to keep still, Ben. That's E, I should say, for Edward. That's how it is on the passport."

"Fantastic. And he's a little B, is that right? Now then, your address?"

"That's—" As Reaper suppressed the name of the hotel he realised that he hadn't armed himself with a local address. The only residential one he could bring to mind was the street he'd followed to the Game Dog. "Cod Street," he said. "Number one."

"Wonderful. I don't need to ask your nationality, do I? Date of birth? You don't look it. How about him? That's a pity. Sorry for that."

"Legs, Ben. That's the last time I'm saying it." The boy had already distracted him enough—had prevented him from noticing which way the numbers of the houses in Cod Street ran. "Why?" he said, so calmly his voice felt like a grip on his throat, to the clerk.

"Just he's too old to travel free."

"Don't worry about him. I've taken him into account."

"Terrific. So how will you be paying, Mr. Reaper?"

"Visa, like your sign says."

"Will you be wanting our insurance?"

"No need," Reaper said, and saw that wouldn't do. "I've a company I always deal with."

"There won't be a discount then, I'm afraid. It's the amount here on the screen," the clerk said, and having tried a grin to see if it fitted, dabbed at his forehead. "Less than a thousand, not bad for a fortnight for two."

"My card won't even feel it."

Reaper watched the clerk slide the card along the slot and wait in a silence broken only by the subdued drumming of the toddler's heels against the counter. "It takes a while sometimes," the clerk explained, just as a strip of paper buzzed up from the printer. "Will you sign that for me?"

"Nothing simpler." Saying so gave Reaper time to recall he was T on the card, not E—it had only been for the passport that he'd felt obliged to formalise his name. "How's that?" he said, signing with a flourish.

"Perfect," the clerk said despite having yet to reclaim the form and compare the signature with the one cramped into the rectangle on the card. "Fine," he enthused once he had. "I'll print you your itinerary."

"And you'll be giving me my tickets."

"They'll be waiting for you at the airport, Mr. Reaper."

Reaper saw him head off another trickle of sweat, as if he'd betrayed more than he had meant to—that he was sending Reaper into a trap. Reaper knew at once what had distracted him into imagining such nonsense: the drumming on the counter. He felt as though the small heels were kicking the inside of his head. "I told you," he said, and used the fat brochure to deal the tops of the boy's thighs a slap so satisfying that he wondered why he hadn't tried it sooner.

The child bowed forward—would have fallen off the counter if Reaper hadn't dug the corner of the brochure into the heaving chest. "Don't start," he said as he'd heard quite a few parents say in the open. "Nobody wants to hear you yell."

He thought the warning had found a home until, as the computer began to issue a page, the toddler unleashed the howl he'd been storing up. "Keep that up and you'll get another," Reaper responded as he'd observed parents did. That had no effect on the volume, and though the boy kept hiccuping that only punctuated the howl. Reaper did his best to ignore it as everyone else in the shop was doing, but when the clerk passed him the itinerary the words and numbers composed of grey dots meant nothing. He stuffed the folded page into his pocket and swung the boy off the counter by his tag, which he was using to propel the child streetwards when the clerk said "Any Turkish money, Mr. Reaper? Travellers' cheques?"

The shock of his feet on the hard floor had silenced the child, but he must have been deciding how his reddened legs felt, because he set about howling even louder as he hobbled towards the door. "Later," Reaper told the clerk, giving him a wink as he jerked his head in the direction of the problem.

Out on the street was a crowd to pretend to be part of, and nobody looked as if they thought a howling child was in any way special. The noise bothered Reaper, though; he couldn't think for it. He was tempted to present the boy with another slap or several—a mother was demonstrating how to do that to a little girl not a hundred yards away, and shaking her into the bargain—but that would only aggravate the racket. "You're not that hurt," he said, something else parents were supposed to say. "Nobody wants to know." Quite a few of the crowd were amused by the chorus of the howling boy and the screaming girl, but that didn't stop the row. Something had to, because Reaper needed to think, to be sure he'd overlooked nothing—and then he saw where the girl was being dragged away from. It was a cinema into which families with children were streaming.

Reaper almost lifted the boy by his tag to the level of his face before he thought to stoop. "Do you want to see a film? Will that shut you up?" he muttered, slitting his eyes against the sight of the trembling upper lip gluey with snot. "Stop your yowling and I'll take you. Stop it now, scumface."

The boy took a few seconds to gulp himself silent, and Reaper wasn't sure if he'd understood or was simply cowed. He led the snuffling toddler up the marble steps into the foyer, where he was relieved to find he could use his credit card. He snatched a serviette from the refreshment counter and rubbed the boy's upper lip red, and shied the loathsome wad into a bin. The boy's face had begun to quiver as he stared at the ranks of confectionery purchasable only with cash. "No sweets for you," said Reaper, feeling more than ever like a parent. "Think yourself lucky you're seeing a film. Open your mouth and we're going straight out again."

An usherette halved his tickets and showed him into the large auditorium, which was moderately full. The lights were just starting to dim. Children fled back to their seats amid an uproar of stamping and cheering that grew louder as the curtains bared the screen and the film announced itself with a Parental Guidance certificate. As the usherette raised her flashlight beam along a row of empty seats, Reaper saw a tub of popcorn lying on its side in the middle of the row. Once the usherette had padded away and the audience was intent on the screen he scooped the spilled popcorn into the tub, which he handed to the toddler. "Here, cram yourself with that if it'll gum you up."

Though he'd whimpered as he sat down, the boy was soon busy feeding himself and gazing at the screen, not even asking idiotic questions as nearby children were. Perhaps he was identifying with the boy who'd been left by himself in an apartment at Christmas while two burglars tried to outwit him. Before long Reaper was watching too, having laid out his schedule in his mind: buy foreign money after the film, collect the child's passport after dark, drive to the airport tomorrow afternoon, and then goodbye to the police and equally useless Geoffrey, and onward to an even bigger game than Reaper's life so far had been. He could imagine that the taller and clumsier burglar was Geoffrey—Geoffrey falling over himself in pitiful attempts to save the boy. He had no chance, because he'd brought a partner when he'd been told not to, and Reaper had already hidden the boy and ensured he couldn't move or speak, or breathe for much longer. Geoffrey and his partner couldn't see Reaper, didn't suspect they were being watched and filmed by him. He was sinking deeper into the comfort the spectacle of their helplessness afforded him when he started so violently he felt his skull grate against his spine. The boy had nudged him in the ribs. "All right," he snarled. "Keep still. Just—"

But it wasn't the boy, it was the usherette. "It's over, sir," she said, repressing half her grin. "Didn't you see the end?" The lights were blazing, the ranks of seats were gaping emptily at the shrouded screen. Next to Reaper a tub containing a solitary spat-out piece of charred popcorn stood on the littered carpet. There was no other sign of Geoffrey's son.

forty-three

When Geoff reached the first of the hotels on his list an actor was descending the front steps. The creases of his long pale face were so deep that Geoff imagined decades of makeup had been dug out of them. "Not a mattress to be had, old dear," he mourned as his white mane fluttered in a summer breeze. "Not even the foot of a bed. Theatricals stacked high in every room, nay, every cupboard." He looked extravagantly hurt when his performance failed to deter Geoff from ringing the heroic brass doorbell. Not only was there no room, the landlady informed him, but she'd nobody except regulars staying and never took children, so that Geoff had to wonder how much use the list might be.

It must be able to lead him to Ben. He was the second man who'd recently assumed a child would be welcome at this hotel, which surely meant that Ben would have tried another on the list. Geoff couldn't know which, only try them all.

By the time he arrived at the hotel overlooking Sefton Park, the suburbs were humming with the race to beat the rush hour. Through the wide bay window next to a front door crested with a stained-glass fan the breakfast room might have belonged to an old folks' home, and the landlady told him she would have preferred not to take the man with a small son even if she'd had a vacancy. "The least thing can give my residents a headache," she said, jangling the bangles on her thick tanned arms as if to demonstrate.

Geoff hurried back to the car, though its hot heavy smell of having travelled such a distance with scarcely a break was starting to sicken him, and drove down to the river. When the road had had enough of being a promenade it bricked up the view with warehouses opposite which, on the edge of the city, several new hotels had been built. The one he'd been directed to, however, was no more than a house on the corner of a nondescript gardenless street. Except for the Rooms To Let placard leaning back against the grimy net curtains of a downstairs window, he wouldn't have guessed that the plastic sign with a chunk out of it had once said HOTEL.

A Mercedes was parked outside, and a businessman with a briefcase rendered lumpy by its contents was following a girl whose hair was dyed almost as red as her tight buttock-length dress into the twilit hall. As Geoff stopped his car just short of the Mercedes, the man who had admitted the couple stepped onto the pavement to confront him.

His small suspicious face looked rubbery, the skin stretched pale over the angles of bone. As he gripped the door-frame and levelled his face at Geoff, his enlarged reddened nostrils appeared to be scenting him. He stared at Geoff for some seconds, and favoured him with a sour whiff from the pits under his singleted arms, before demanding "What's it about?"

It was clear he knew more than the other hoteliers had. He must have been told to expect Geoff, who had to restrain himself from flinging him aside and lurching into the deserted dingy hall. "About what we both know," he parried instead.

"You've come to the wrong place, la. I know buggery, and that's a fact."

"Now that isn't the way I read you at all. No point in underrating yourself. I'd lay money there's nothing goes on round here you don't know about."

"You watch who you're telling that."

"I'm telling you. I'm not saying you're involved, just that you're the one to ask for information. I can see you're the type that wouldn't let anything slip past him."

"Nothing worth your kitty, la."

"We'll see," Geoff said, clenching his fist once it was in his pocket. "So long as it's worth both our whiles."

"What do you reckon you're buying?"

"I don't suppose you'll have a visitors' book, will you? How about the number of a room?"

"We've none of them."

"Then just direct me to it. What's the price of that?"

"Here's the deal, la," the manager said, leaning forward to bring his face within inches of Geoff's. "Seeing it's you, I'll tell you where to go for free if you can't guess."

It was only the way the wallet bulged Geoff's fist, making it difficult for him to wrench his hand out of his pocket, that gave him time to realise how unproductive violence would be. He had to draw on all his experience of the frustrations of interviewing to help him contain himself. "Then we'll both be none the better off, won't we?" he said as lightly as the throbbing of his head permitted. "I can't believe you're the kind to miss a chance."

The manager straightened up, leaving his stale breath in Geoff's face, and stared with renewed distrust at him. "Come ahead then, let's hear what you reckon you're after. Bit small for you, that's what I'm thinking before you open your trap."

Any possible interpretation of that seemed capable of enraging Geoff beyond control. "Tell me they're in there at least," he blurted. "Tell me I'm not wasting my time."

"Who?"

Geoff dragged both his fist and the wallet into the open. "Let's respect each other's intelligence. What's the asking price?"

"A bunch of those when I know what you're sniffing after."

"It looked to me as if you knew before I got out of the car."

"You want to try being a bit less sure of yourself, la. I know your game, so don't tell me about intelligence."

"How do you know?"

The manager sniffed with such disdain it appeared to suck his upper lip towards his nostrils. "Even round here we're clever enough to turn on a telly, Mr. Goods."

"I'm sorry. Don't imagine I was meaning to suggest—" It wasn't only his own time he'd wasted, it was Paul's. "I'm trying to make contact with someone who I understand was given your address. He'd have checked in last night. A man with a boy about three years old."

"Oh, them."

"Yes." That was a gasp as much as a word. "Are they here?"

"What's it worth?"

Only a sense that he might have to negotiate further deterred Geoff from handing over all the cash he had. "Enough?" he said, and when the twenty was met with silence, doubled it. "I hope that does it for you."

"No," said the manager, closing his fist on the notes.

"No what? What do you mean, no?"

"They aren't here."

Geoff could have floored him, had it not been for the hint of an informed gleam in the man's eyes. "But you know where they are," Geoff said.

"Sounds like you'd pay to hear."

"I'll pay. Better watch you don't price yourself out of my pocket."

The manager used two fingers to extract his previous fee from the back pocket of his shabby jeans, and having doubled it, eased the wad out of sight. "I sent them downtown to my cousin's place," he said then. "I wouldn't have a kid here."

"You're going to tell me the address, are you?"

"You reckon."

Geoff pulled a twenty from his thinning wallet, and two tens. The manager only stared at them. "This is all I have," Geoff almost pleaded, showing him the twenty that remained.

"It'll do." The manager withdrew it from Geoff's wallet with the deftness of a conjuror and used it to pinch the other notes. "You listening? I'm not writing it down."

Geoff tensed himself to be alert for any hint of deception, but the address sounded likely enough. The manager ended it with a sharp nod as if to butt Geoff on his way; then his eyes owned up to a speculative gleam. "Is he a peedy? Is that what you're after this time?"

"Maybe something like that. Wait and see." Though Geoff sensed that the man wanted the information to sell if he could, his fury at the notion didn't prevent him from thinking. "Nothing your cousin will need to deal with," he said. "I give you my word you don't need to call ahead. Please don't do that or I might lose the trail."

"You'll see if you have when you get there, I reckon."

Geoff didn't know if that was intended as a demand for more money, or an expression of indifference, or even a grisly attempt at a joke. He stepped close to the manager and exhaled so hard it drove back the man's stale breath. "No more games. Don't play with a child's life," he said. He could have vowed to have the place closed down if he found Ben had been scared off, he could have promised to hunt the manager down too, but he thought he'd conveyed what he was capable of. He turned and strode, not quite running, to the car.

forty-four

For some seconds that felt like the rest of his life Reaper couldn't move for disbelief. They'd taken the solitary advantage of him they could find: himself. They'd made him fall asleep. Geoffrey had by rushing him, by discussing him while pretending he never would, but most of all the boy had prevented him by sharing his room from resting enough. Could Geoffrey have sneaked the child away before the film was over? If Reaper turned, would he see the police sneaking up on him? He might have lost the child, but he still had the usherette and his knife. Was she as amused as she looked by having had to waken him, or was she doing her best to hide her nervousness? Just in time he disentangled his thoughts. He could still play, it was still a game, and he hadn't lost yet. "Where . . ." he said.

"It's like I say, it's finished. Everyone's out in the sunshine but us. We've got to clean up before the next mob piles in."

She wasn't hiding anything. She didn't know he'd had a child with him, or his question would have meant that to her. Should he seek her help in tracking down the child and the bag of clothes he must have taken with him? Reaper only had an instant to decide, and then it was too late: if he asked now the delay would seem too odd—might be remembered later. He stood up, automatically placing a hand on the seat to hush its creak, and turned away from the usherette to confirm that nobody was behind him except one of her scavenging colleagues. He was making for the left-hand exit by the screen when the usherette said "Could you go out through the lobby? We keep those exits locked till after the last show so the scallies can't bunk in."

"Thanks," he said, and thought of another way she could help him. "How long has the film been over?"

"Not that long. Five minutes if it's that."

The boy had been too engrossed in the film to leave before the end. Reaper was wide awake now—his eyes and the mind they concealed felt brighter than the relentless lights of the auditorium. A few swift silent paces took him into the lobby, which was a mass of children, quite a few of them blonde, none of them tagged by the blue overall. He wasn't alone in watching the crowd: a uniformed manager almost entirely reduced to monochrome and with something of the demeanour of a children's entertainer hoping not to be asked to perform was standing near him. "Excuse me," Reaper said over the uproar. "Have you seen a little boy on his own?"

"What age are we talking about, sir?"

"You'd think he was three. He'll be lucky. Comes up to here," said Reaper, dangling his fingers in front of his crotch. "And of course he looks like me."

"I can't say I've noticed him." Without warning the manager began to shout so loud it quelled the hubbub. "Brian? Tina? Anybody taken charge of this gentleman's three-year-old boy?"

All the staff in the box office and behind the refreshment counter shook their heads as if they had only the two names between them. "I'm sorry, sir," the manager said. "It doesn't look—"

"Don't give it another thought. He'll be with his grandparents. My fault if I gave you the impression he was at any risk."

"As long as you're sure. You don't want me to call—"

"Please forget I bothered you. You've enough to cope with.

They're more trouble than they're worth, his grandparents. I know where they are, that's the main thing. They won't be messing me about again, I can promise you."

"I expect that's best," the manager said, and Reaper saw he'd played his role exactly right: a frustrated parent, righteous and ready to be vengeful. He strode the sticky smeary crowd aside all the way to the front exit, and groped for an object to drop. Not his passport, not his credit cards—his keys. As son as he emerged into the sunlight that felt like his alertness intensified he let them fall. They hadn't struck the marble steps when he was going down on all fours.

He wanted to see as little Ben would have seen, and he did. He saw the elephantine legs of adults tramping past, the buildings that hoisted the sky as impossibly high as the sun, the hordes of unknown children towering over him. Even the noises packed into the street seemed gigantic, and the swarming of so much garish reddened flesh dressed up in clothes as bright as wrapping paper took his words away. This was how he used to feel, pressed smaller and smaller by his own insignificance once Geoffrey was born. But he'd found a way to reclaim himself from that, and now he had a new one, because he was no longer little Ben. Little Ben was separate from him now, somewhere in or beyond the crowd. As if the thought had taken hold of the chaos in front of him and forced it to make sense, a gap in the crowd let him see what little Ben's attention would have fastened on—the toy store on the far side of the pedestrianised street. He snatched up his keys and sprang from his crouch and didn't give himself time to breathe until he was inside the shop.

Five aisles walled in by shelves heaped with toys and games led away from the doors. There were even more colours in the shop than outside, but only two that he wanted to see, and at once he saw them—blond hair and blue denim vanishing around the end of the right-hand aisle. A giggle accompanied them, and he realised the child was playing with him. "You won't like the way the game ends," he heard himself saying, though not aloud. When the child didn't reappear he paced down the next aisle to head him off.

He'd almost reached the end when he heard another giggle

from halfway along the shelves. He dodged into the right-hand aisle, but the child was faster: none of the children being told to leave the contents of the shelves alone was Reaper's quarry or anything like him. Reaper sidled deftly past a wheezing grandmother bundled into a floral dress barely able to contain her, and darted around the streetward end of the shelves. Little Ben wasn't in the next aisle, but from the one beside it he heard a snort imitating a pig.

"That's not the only noise they make," he muttered. "Little pigs have to squeal." When he veered around the shelves there was no sign of the child, yet the noise hadn't moved. He must fancy he could hide among the toys—he'd trapped himself. Reaper crept along the aisle and lurched at the source of the noise, only to find a soft pink pig with a ring in its back for producing its voice. He planted a hand on its face and squeezed until he felt its mouth and eyes cave in, and heard a giggle from the aisle he'd first used, as if he was crushing the sound out of hiding. He could still feel the small face collapsing in his grip as he sprinted on tiptoe, a father playing with his child until he caught him, back to the end that faced the street. "That's enough of this game," he announced, and threw out a hand that could have seized the toddler's blonde hair but restrained itself to grabbing the collar. He was opening his mouth to thank the wheezing grandmother for cutting off the child's escape when she cried "What are you doing to her?"

"Good heavens. I'm so sorry." Before the woman had finished speaking, her last word no more than a wheeze that fell short of the final consonant, Reaper saw his mistake. He let go at once. "What a blunder. I thought—"

"Are you all right, love? Did the nasty rough man hurt your poor little neck?"

She was a grandmother, Reaper thought, and took a moment to visualise her mouth gummed shut, her throat clogged with glue, her eyes bulging so desperately they stretched the skin around them. His apologetic smile failed to persuade her to tone down her performance, which now attracted the manager. "What's the situation here?" he demanded, holding out his unnecessarily large hands as if to display how capable he thought they were of holding Reaper. "What seems to be the trouble, madam?"

"It's entirely my fault," Reaper said, ignoring the hands in case his expression hinted how he could see himself bending back all the fingers until—pop, pop, pop—the joints gave way. "My little delight's given me the slip. Likes to be chased, and I thought he'd run in here, but you see how wrong I was."

"We don't allow unaccompanied youngsters in this establishment."

"Very sensible. Highly commendable. How's your neck now, little girl? All better? I didn't hurt it, did I? This is to buy a treat with all the same in case I scared you." He dropped a pound coin into her greedy hand and marched across the front of the shop for a last survey of the aisles. "Just checking," he told the manager, who had no reason not to take him for a concerned parent, and gazed at him to be certain of that before hurrying into the street again. The moment he was free of the shop he heard a burst of sounds across the pavement: gunfire, bombs, the grunts of the punched, the screams of the wounded. It was an amusement arcade, and he made for it as fast as he was sure little Ben had.

An introverted chatter of fruit machines greeted him. Pensioners were hauling on the handles as though to prove they still had strength. These machines wouldn't have appealed to little Ben, and so Reaper headed for the depths of the arcade. Teenagers were pressing their crotches against the pinball machines they were assaulting, others were drawing cartoon blood from combatants on screens, while most of the crowd of younger children had to wait and watch. None of these was little Ben, and so Reaper dropped to all fours, but his prey wasn't crouching under any of the machines. He stood up and almost butted in the face a youth with a leather pouch of change at his waist. "Lost something?" the youth said, narrowing his eyes in imitation of his slit of a mouth.

Reaper knew him instantly for someone who watched out for crimes with all the self-righteousness of a criminal, and not a reformed one either. "My little boy," Reaper said.

"You'd not be the first we've had creeping round in here after

a kid." The youth let that linger in case Reaper wanted to raise an
objection that could be an excuse for a fight. When Reaper only
looked puzzled while he imagined using the handle of a fruit machine to knock out the youth's teeth a few at a time, his interroga-
tor demanded "How old's he supposed to be?"

"Coming up to three."

"Brought him in here, did you?"

"No, I mislaid him outside. I thought he might have—"

The left side of the youth's mouth jerked, perhaps only acci-
dentally indicating the notice on the doors. "Can't you read?"

"I can indeed. You too. Isn't education wonderful. Children
under sixteen have to be with an adult, I see that. I thought he
might have tagged along with some of these older customers of
yours."

"You're after a kid that goes with anyone, are you?" When
even this didn't provoke Reaper, the youth grimaced. "Take a look.
I'll be behind you."

"Be wherever you like," said Reaper, and went swiftly through
the arcade. He should have sought out the attendant to begin with
and asked for his help, as a father would. The pressure Geoffrey
and his son would like to exert on him had distracted him. If he saw
any police on the street he would go to them—even if Geoffrey
had dared to betray him, it was the last thing anyone who thought
they knew about Reaper would expect him to do. "Thanks," he
said, having seen that Ben was nowhere in the arcade, and gave the
attendant an uncontrived smile to interpret however he liked. He
stepped out of the clangour of the arcade to look for the police,
and saw a sight that halted him.

Until that moment the crowd hadn't let him see the newsstand
a hundred yards away. An old man with hair not much less thread-
bare than his ancient jacket was hunched silently on a folding chair
behind a box stacked with newspapers. A poster caged with wire on
the front of the box said GLUE MANIAC'S VICTIMS CRITI-
CAL. Couldn't they have found a less banal name for him? It was
blotted out by the crowd as it deserved to be, and Reaper turned
away from it, only to see the guard from the department store

striding towards him. She was gesturing the attendant in the arcade to detain him.

So this was how it felt to have people think they'd trapped him. If Geoffrey had sent them or caused them to be sent, so much the worse for him and the people he loved. Reaper only had to lose himself in the crowd and steal back to his car without returning to the hotel, and then he would find Geoffrey before Geoffrey found him. Geoffrey was bound to take the boy up to the hospital in Scotland, and this time when Reaper got hold of the child he would show Geoffrey all the skills he'd learned since the messy business with the dog. He had taken a step forward when the guard he was miming not having seen called to him. "Sir? Gentleman with the little boy? Hello?"

He could keep walking—she could scarcely appear to mean him when he had no little boy with him—but then a cordon made up of at least two families blocked his way. "Ey up, chum," the broader of the fathers said with heavy joviality. "Lady wants you. Must be your lucky day."

As Reaper turned to the guard he was seeing how the father's face would look while a tube of glue was squirted into his astonished mouth. "Aren't you out of your territory?" Reaper said.

"Do you think you may have forgotten something?"

Her expression was so clearly withholding most of itself that Reaper had to search for an answer he could safely give. "I believe you're right," he said.

"Would you like him back?"

"There's nothing I'd like more."

"Better come along with me, then."

Her playing at arresting him could hardly mean that she intended to do so in reality. That was a trick he might have played, but he was special. By the time the store came in sight he was making her keep up with him. He held the door open for her while he assured himself that none of the several people whom he'd easily identified as store detectives was alert for him. The game was his again, and he had to remember to keep his smile inside him as she led him into a passage beyond the changing cubicles and pushed open the door of a staff room. "Here's your dad," she said.

Little Ben was sitting at a table, his lips smeared with milk. He'd been drinking from a glass, but it seemed to Reaper that any of the three women who were fussing over him could have had him on a breast. Reaper hadn't time to let the notion sicken him, because the boy had met him with a bewildered look not far short of disappointment. "I'm his pa," he said. "That's right, isn't it, Ben? What do you call me?"

"Isn't he your dad, son?" said the guard.

Reaper struck his chest as he would have liked to punch her in the breast. "Who am I?"

"Pa."

The women sighed with delight, which made the boy giggle and abandon his bewilderment, all that Reaper needed. "Drink up and we'll be on our way. We've bothered these kind ladies enough," he said, and thought what a father should ask. "Where was he?"

"I happened to see him outside with some boys I'd had to chase," the guard said. "I knew he was supposed to be with you. How did they get hold of him?"

"They must have been in the cinema, were they, Ben? I took him to a film and then I nodded off. What kind of a father has he got, I know you're thinking."

The women shook their heads and chorused their denial. When that was over, the oldest and most buxom of them said "So long as you don't let him stray again."

"This is the last time he ever gets away from me. Finished, Ben? Say goodbye."

As soon as the boy set his glass down the buxom woman produced a handkerchief from her sleeve and dabbed at his mouth. "Bye," she said, leading the chorus, which turned to sighs again as the toddler said "Bye" and waved. Reaper thanked all the women and followed him out of the room. They were nearly at the door into the shop when at least two of the women shouted "Hold on!"

Reaper grabbed the boy's tag. It would take only a second to fling the door open and steer the child through it, and outside were any number of clothes racks on wheels to be used to block off pursuit. He felt as if he was already enacting all this as he glanced over his shoulder. The guard was striding after him. "Don't you want these?" she said.

"Look at that, Ben. Look what you nearly made me forget." Reaper took the bag of clothes from her and left her with a final thanks. In less than a minute the man and his boy were one more family lost in the crowd on the street, and Reaper saw he needn't delay speaking to the boy until they were alone; after all, he would be acting like a father. He hauled on the tag and made the boy stumble on tiptoe while Reaper spoke into his face. "That was your last chance," he said.

forty-five

Geoff reversed into the space between two cars in a single sinuous manoeuvre. He slid the window up and cut the engine and without a pause ducked out of the car. He took a breath that helped him straighten up as he strode across the pavement and up the three white railed-in steps to the open door. As though Geoff's urgency had brought him forth, a man came along the hall to meet him. "Just seeing who this is, dear," he called, and having patted the knot of his wide silk tie, brushed at the shoulders of his dress suit with one fleshy hand. "Looking for a room, sir? I've a nice top floor single that's free for the weekend."

No more than a hint of a resemblance to his cousin was discernible within the plumpness of his face, and Geoff deduced he would prefer to be as unlike his relative as possible, which must be a good omen. "I'm looking for a couple you have staying," Geoff said.

"Be my guest if you won't be my guest. Any special pair?"

"Very." It was clear to Geoff that the manager hadn't been forewarned about him. "Only I hope you won't think this is too odd, but I can't tell you their names."

"I've heard odder in this job. Seen it too. We had a student we thought was with his mother, but it turned out—" He summed up the punch line by coughing with all the discretion of a butler. "I can see you haven't time for what my wife calls my rovings when she doesn't put an a in it instead. Let's see if we can't pin these folk of yours down."

"They'll be a man a bit older than I am and a boy no more than three."

"Well, of course. The little chap my wife took a fancy to."

Geoff stiffened to keep in a gasp of relief. "They're here?"

"Were."

The word seemed to snatch his life out from beneath him. "When?" he demanded. "How long ago?"

"Half an hour or so. Thirty minutes, not much more. Were they expecting you?"

Had Paul been? The question was another layer of distress. "I was expected. I know I was."

"Then I'm sure they'll be back before you know it. Would you like to wait in the lounge?"

"What makes you say, why do you think they'll be back?"

"They've a room for the week for a start. Besides, they won't have gone far. I heard your friend saying to his son they were off to shop, and the car's still there."

"Where? Which one?"

"Over the road there, just behind the skip."

Geoff had already noticed the hulk of an empty skip outside a building under renovation. The car parked close behind it was a nondescript black Vauxhall that, he saw, only needed to have a name and phone number perched on its roof to do duty as a taxi. Ben would surely have taken it unless he meant to return. "So will you be in the lounge?" the manager prompted.

"That's the best plan," Geoff said, and was moving farther into the concealment of the hall when the manager put up a pudgy hand. "I don't think you'd be wise to leave your car there."

"Why, what will it—what do you—"

"Just our local warden's a miserable little tyke. Only happy when he's writing you a ticket."

"I'd rather not go far in case I miss my people again. I should be all right, do you think, if I keep an eye out and move over the road when there's space?"

"I can't guarantee it. I wouldn't want you to be sorry later."

Geoff felt as if his own doubts were being expressed by the manager, but however Ben might react to the sight of Geoff's car, he couldn't see it any sooner than Geoff would see him from the lounge. Besides, wasn't the whole point supposed to be for Geoff to find him? The worst possibility—so bad that Geoff didn't want to consider it—was that Ben himself mightn't be sure what game he was playing. "I'll be responsible," he said.

"Will you have a cup of something while you wait?"

"I'd appreciate a coffee," Geoff said, and halted in the doorway of the lounge. The tropical mops of potted plants that stood in every angle of the room weren't the only occupants. A small boy was sprawled in the largest armchair to watch a cartoon on television with the sound turned down. "You don't mind if the nephew sees his programmes, do you?" said the manager. "There'll be no peace otherwise."

"Not at all," Geoff said, making for the chair nearest the bay window. Like all the chairs except the one with the boy in, its top was draped with lace not unlike a handkerchief keeping the sun off a head. Geoff was moving the chair to command the view from the window when the boy said "Don't you want to see *Crime Smashers?*" and lifted his face as if to catch the answer on it.

"I've got to watch out for something else."

"Haven't you see them? They rid the world of crime every week."

"So I've heard," Geoff said, having recognised the slogan, and sat towards the street. "I did have a look at them once."

"Have you got some children?"

Though Geoff saw how the question followed, he wished it hadn't been asked. "Just one," he said.

"Are they like me?"

"He isn't half your age," Geoff said and crouched away from him. That didn't bring Paul into view, nor Ben either, and so only the arrival of the manager with a tray bearing a coffee-pot and its accessories helped Geoff control his thoughts. "Say if he's bothering you," the manager advised.

"Not at all," Geoff felt bound to assure him. "Nothing wrong with a child speaking up for himself."

Suppose Paul said something that gave Ben away or that Ben imagined had done so? Surely it would send them back to the hotel or to the car. Geoff poured himself a drink, only to have the jittery cup spill black coffee over the saucer and onto his crotch. He was mopping at the stain that looked altogether too much like evidence of panic when he became aware of activity across the road. The car behind the Vauxhall was about to move off.

Geoff was behind his own wheel in seconds. By the time he'd started his engine and remembered to strap himself in, the other driver was still waiting for the traffic to let him loose. The moment the other car swung out, Geoff executed a U-turn that smelled of charred rubber and drove into the space, then crept forward until his bumper touched the Vauxhall's. "Get out of that," he muttered as he dashed back to the hotel.

He fed himself coffee as he waited for his trap to work. At first he wasn't sure if the caffeine or the wait was affecting his senses, and then he grasped that the sound of the cartoon was indeed, if almost imperceptibly, growing louder. The boy was teasing it with the remote control while he provided the action with a voice-over, whether for his own benefit or Geoff's wasn't clear. "He'll stop him soon. He won't let him do anything really bad. He isn't dead, he's pretending. He'll get there in time."

Geoff had glimpsed enough of the cartoon at home to be reminded agonisingly of Paul, and as he sat forward over his replenished cup of coffee he didn't know if he was trying to keep more of a watch or distance himself from the encroaching sounds. Nobody who looked at all familiar had appeared in the street when the manager returned. "Any other way we can take care of you?" he said.

"Is there a phone I could use?"

"The pay one's waiting for the engineer. Life or death, is it, your call?"

However little of a joke that was meant to be, it felt like less of one to Geoff. "I said I'd call my wife."

"Like I said, life and death. Your life won't be worth living if you let her down, not if she's anything like mine. I'll watch out for your friend while you use the phone in our office."

"That's very kind of you," Geoff said, feeling as though he had to wrench Gail and himself apart when they had almost been together. "Don't think me ungrateful, but I'd better stay here just to make certain I don't miss them again."

"I don't see why— Turn that down a touch, would you, Sylvester?" The manager bent his upper half towards the boy until he obeyed. "I don't see why you can't have our phone in here for a few minutes. You won't be too long, will you?"

"I'll be as quick as I can. Thanks again."

A plastic clatter and a muffled bell heralded the return of the manager, who plugged the phone into a wall socket before handing Geoff the instrument. "Shall I send him out?" he murmured.

"Don't disturb him," Geoff said, trying to remember the number for the operator to call. It came to him as she responded, and then she made way for a succession of sounds, each of them closer to him: a clicking, a ringing, a woman's voice that, once he'd asked to speak to Gail, wanted to know who he was. "I'm her husband," he said with less conviction than he might have liked to have.

"Do you know which ward?"

"I'm afraid I don't. Don't you?"

She was silent for a few seconds, at least towards him. He wasn't sure if he heard a muffled dialogue beyond the mouthpiece before she said "I'll have a word with sister."

"You might just tell me which ward—" But she'd gone, and all Geoff could hear were the sounds of the television creeping up on him again, and the boy's commentary: "He's never really dead." Then another female voice, uninviting despite its words, said in Geoff's ear "Yes, can I help you?"

"Is that where Gail Davenport and her parents are?"

"It may be. Who's enquiring?"

"I'm Geoff Davenport. I'm her husband."

"Are you that. Don't fly at me, but can you prove you are?"

"Prove it? How am I supposed— Just what exactly is the problem?"

"There's been a few reporters trying tricks to get at her. You'll have an idea how they operate, these media people."

"I promise you I'm her husband. I don't know how else to convince you."

"Isn't there something I can tell her only you and she would know?"

Geoff felt his memories of Gail withdraw from him as though he'd ceased to deserve them. For an aching moment he thought he had no answer to the question, no way of reaching Gail, but he was almost as dismayed by thinking of one. "Tell her she's waiting for an update on my brother."

"Will he mean a whole lot to her just now, do you think?"

"How much does he have to mean?"

"A fair bit at the moment, I'm afraid," the woman said, and for some seconds nothing more. It seemed her silence meant she was deciding whether to trust him, because she broke it by saying "Her mother died an hour ago."

"The bastard. The fucking bastard." Geoff only mouthed the words, which didn't begin to sum up his feelings about Ben, but he turned to see if the boy across the lounge had witnessed him. When the information that the boy was busy pointing the control at the loud bright violence reached his brain, he sat back in the chair to keep his voice from straying past it. "Then for God's sake let me speak to her," he said.

"Hold on while I see how she is."

He lurched forward to peer both ways along the street—a large selection of adults, but not a solitary child—and stayed alert until he heard footsteps approaching the distant phone, two pairs of footsteps. As he sat back he might have been trying to hide from them. "I'll stay by your father until you're done," he heard the ward sister say, and the closing of her office door. He heard the receiver scrape a desk, and the creak of plastic in a fist. "Gail," he said, "I'm so—"

"Have you got him?"

He couldn't blame her for sounding as cold and sharp as a knife; he blamed himself. "I'm where they are. I just have to wait. But Gail, let me—"

"Wait for what?"

"For them to come back. They have to. The car's here." And whatever luggage Ben had surely must be, he thought, or the manager would have observed its removal. "I know what I'm doing. I wouldn't have called you otherwise," he said. "I just wish—"

"Like you did last time?"

"Like I . . . I'm sorry, love, I don't quite . . ."

"Like you knew what you were doing when you left him at large?"

"Gail, I was wrong. I was trying to do what I thought was best for us and maybe even for him, but I—Christ, you don't need to remind me what I did. That's why I can't be wrong now. I won't ask you to forgive me for everything that's happened, but I hope you know I—"

"Don't, Geoff." The sharpness had gone from her voice, leaving no emotion, just weariness. "I know what you want to say, but it doesn't mean anything now. Maybe later it will. Maybe not."

"I'm sorry."

"Never mind. There isn't time. Just do one thing for me."

"Anything. You still know that, I hope."

"Don't speak to me again until you've got Paul safe."

"All right. That's a promise." Geoff yearned to hear more hope in her voice—wondered if her mother's death might seem to presage a further loss. "If I only ever get one thing right for the rest of my life—"

"I mean it, Geoff. Don't speak to me. I have to go now and be with my father."

"Yes, you must." There was so much more that Geoff wanted to say, but he didn't feel entitled to have spoken even those words. He heard Gail replace the phone quite gently, and wished he could think the gentleness was intended for him. When the operator had told him the cost of the call he unplugged the phone and counted out the money once he'd hurried back to the window to watch while he awaited the manager. The shrill jagged pounding theme music of the cartoon series announced that the episode was over, and the boy turned down the sound. "Thank you," Geoff said, not looking at him in case that invited conversation.

His gratitude seemed to have done so, because the boy said "Hey, mister?"

Geoff sighed only inwardly. "Yes?"

"Did you say to my uncle you wanted the little kid and his dad?"

"Yes." Geoff gave the street a look so searching it stung his eyes and glanced at the boy. "Yes, I did," he said more urgently, and when that brought him no response "Why?"

"They came while you were on the phone," the boy said.

forty-six

There wasn't a second to be lost in asking questions, and yet so much to learn. Geoff was hardly aware of crossing the room to lean over the boy. "Did they see me?"

The boy appeared to think that was some kind of joke. "No," he said, more like a question.

"When were they here?"

"When he was tying him up."

Geoff took only a moment to understand, but that was too long. "You mean the end of the cartoon."

"Nearly. He pulls his arms out like string, and then—"

"I get the idea. Did you see which way they went, the people?"

"Up."

Geoff almost clapped a hand over his mouth as if that could take back how loudly he'd been speaking. "Are you saying they're still here?"

The boy was seeing another joke. "Haven't come down," he said.

Geoff stepped into the hall. Neither it nor the equally deserted stairs offered him more than silence. "Come here a second," he murmured, and when the boy ambled over, clutching the remote control: "Can you show me which room they're in? Don't make a noise. I want to surprise them."

The boy emitted a snort of mirth and a sample of the contents of his nose. "Never mind showing me," Geoff whispered, resisting the urge to push him back into the lounge. "Just tell me which room."

The boy rubbed the back of his hand across his face and then on his trousers. "First one on the middle floor."

"By first you mean—"

"When you get up the stairs."

"I'll be facing it when I reach the top," Geoff persisted, and saw the boy nod. "Look, another cartoon's starting," Geoff added to get rid of him. At that moment he heard the secretive creak of a door somewhere above him.

He was at the foot of the stairs before he had time for a breath. Ten steps took him high enough to see that the door of the room at the top of the stairs was shut. Had Ben overheard him, despite the thick carpet that might have been designed to muffle Geoff's tread, and dodged back into the room? Was he skulking beyond the door with his hand over Paul's mouth? Geoff strained his ears, and in a moment he heard furtive footsteps. They were hollow and metallic, and they were moving away from him.

He crept fast up the last few stairs and heard the clank of an unguarded footstep. It came from the end of a short corridor that led to the back of the house—from beyond a fire exit someone had left ajar for fear of drawing Geoff's attention to it sooner. He dashed along the corridor and shoved the door open with both fists, and toppled out onto the fire escape.

It led down to a stone-flagged yard in which the hotel kitchen left room for nothing much. On the far side of the yard a door was being dragged shut. Through the doorway that gave onto an alley he glimpsed the back of a man wearing a baseball cap and hauling a suitcase out of the way of the door. Resting on his shoulder, and nodding with his movements as though to encourage them, was a small blonde head.

"Wait," Geoff shouted. "What's the point? Why are you—"

The yard door slammed, and he saw the baseball cap begin to race along the alley towards the street that met the road onto which the hotel faced. The cap faltered, then rushed onward, spurred by the scattering crash of an overturned waste-bin. The perspective let Geoff see the blonde scalp of the boy who was clutched against the man's chest. For Geoff almost the worst part was that he hadn't managed to see Paul's face—that he didn't know how Paul had reacted to his voice.

The fire escape shook as he ran down it two steps at a time, it tolled like a rusty bell. Before he reached the gate he heard another bin fall, and another. He threw the gate open just in time to see the man use his suitcase to knock over the last of the bins as he dodged out of the alley with the small blonde head pressed against his cheek.

"Not this time," Geoff said through teeth that felt as if they were about to splinter, and launched himself into the alley. He jumped over the spillage from the first bin, he pressed both hands against the brick walls of the alley as he vaulted over a bin that was jammed between them, and saw a black taxi cruise along the street at the end. No sooner had it passed from view than he heard it stop.

It could have been halted by the lights at the crossroads, he thought as he tried to leap over all the strewn contents of the next bin—and then he heard the passenger door slam. His foot snagged a bin-bag and sank into mush, and he nearly sprawled on his face. The walls scraped his palms as he caught at his balance. He hauled the last bin aside with his stinging hands and threw himself out of the alley. The taxi was indicating to turn right and downhill at the crossroads. Just visible above the back seat was the top of a small blonde head.

"Stop," Geoff yelled, and ran so fast that when he tried to repeat the word it was driven back into his mouth. He was a hundred yards short of the taxi when an oncoming car flashed its headlamps to urge it to turn. He waved his arms to catch the attention of the taxi driver, he pointed frantically at him for the benefit of a Jamaican who was standing by the cab. The taxi turned right and sped downhill, and the Jamaican reached the corner of the pavement just as Geoff sprinted to it. "It was taken, man," the Jamaican told him.

A traffic light turned red above Geoff's skull like a cartoon of rage. It wasn't safe for him to dash to his car, but he did, between vehicles that screeched and blared at him. He shoved the key into the door and twisted it so hastily he felt it start to bend, he rammed the second key into the ignition as he flung himself into his seat and yanked the belt across his chest. He shouldn't have trapped Ben's car, he realised now; he'd alerted Ben. Beyond it and the skip he saw the taxi panting fumes as it waited at a further set of traffic lights. He backed up fast and nosed the car into the traffic, then had to stamp on the brake as a Cortina racing to beat the amber brayed at him. The lights beyond the taxi counted down to green, and the taxi vanished left without indicating.

A bus gave Geoff the benefit of its headlamps in his mirror, and he swerved out of the trap. The traffic lights had just turned red. "No time," he snarled, and skidded left into the street parallel to the route the taxi must be following. He sped to the end as much faster than the speed limit as he dared, in time to see the taxi swing downhill at the lower intersection. It was heading for the river.

Whenever he began to close the gap, another red light delayed him. He was further off than ever when the taxi swung onto the riverside road, but he glimpsed a small blonde head rising next to the baseball cap to look at the jittering ripples. The taxi sped past the hotel where Geoff had seen the businessman accompanied by a girl in a token dress, and all at once he guessed where it was bound: the airport, miles ahead.

A police helicopter was hovering above the river, so that Geoff couldn't chance exceeding the limit, even though the blonde head had disappeared. The thought of Ben's hands on Paul, pushing him down out of sight, made Geoff's do their best to choke the wheel. Then the road curved inland to meet a dual carriageway where traffic lights pointed an arrow in the direction of the airport. The arrow brightened as the taxi approached, but went out as Geoff followed. The green light remained steady, and he swung right at speed, just as an oncoming juggernaut did.

Geoff wrenched the wheel all the way to the right and trod on the brake so hard his leg throbbed. The monstrous boxy head swung towards him for the kill and then, with three huge pneumatic gasps, halted just short of his car and the metal barrier that divided the road. He was drawing a breath he would use for a shuddery sigh of relief when he saw he wasn't merely cut off but trapped.

It took the driver less than two minutes to back the lorry far enough into the blocked side street for Geoff's car to have room to pass the cab, but by then the taxi was long gone. Geoff waved something like thanks and accelerated as much past forty as he dared. Miles of houses beside the road opened out at last to reveal the airport in the distance, but the taxi was nowhere to be seen. He was on the dual carriageway that curved towards the airport when he saw the taxi coming back.

The driver either hadn't noticed him before or was pretending not to do so now, but Geoff couldn't mistake the last three letters of the registration number: END. He backhanded sweat from his forehead to keep his eyes clear, and saw the malicious glint of an airliner dwindling above the river. Ben and Paul surely hadn't been in time to board that plane, but when was the flight beyond the low elongated terminal due to take off? "Not yet," he pleaded, ignoring the speedometer as he accelerated towards the car park.

He snatched a ticket from the machine to make it lift its arm out of his way, and sped across the fish-bone pattern of dozens of unoccupied spaces to an empty oblong less than two hundred yards from the terminal entrance. In seconds he was sprinting down a brick path between the cars, and at the automatic doors so fast they almost didn't slide aside in time.

The voice of a giantess was announcing a flight to Belfast. There was no sign of Ben or Paul, not on the seats that divided the long white hall, not at any of the airline counters nor among the queue of passengers progressing slowly into the departure lounge. Geoff hurried past the queue to a young woman in uniform with a fistful of boarding cards. "Excuse me, have a man and a little boy gone through?"

He hadn't finished speaking when a security guard appeared beside her. "Will you wait in line, please, sir?"

"Don't anyone think I'm trying to jump the queue. Just finding out where some people are."

"What are their names, sir?" the guard said.

"They're a man around my age and a little blonde boy about three," Geoff told the young woman, and saw recognition in her eyes. "It's extremely urgent. Look, send someone with me. If I can just—"

The guard held up a hand level with Geoff's face, and several wiry hairs sprang free of his shirt cuff. "We need names. Move aside, please, sir, and we'll discuss it when you're out of the way of these people waiting to board."

There was no question that he would respond to nothing until Geoff did as he was told. Geoff was about to back off so as to argue his way into the departure lounge, though the prospect of retreating from Paul clutched at his guts, when he froze. Beyond the security equipment a family had finished being searched, and as they moved apart he saw the small blonde head vanishing through the doorway to the lounge. The sight robbed him of all control. "Paul," he shouted.

The small head was snatched out of sight at once. The guard turned to look, and the young woman leafed through the documents in her hand. "That isn't the name," she said.

Geoff dodged the guard and ran through the electronic arch, which began to bleep. Both of the guards who were conducting body searches abandoned the travellers they were patting and came at him. He didn't punch them, he only shoved each of them with a fist, but the one who was a woman staggered against the wall, thumping it with her shoulder. He would apologise once he'd claimed Paul—he would be able to show her why he'd had to fight her off. He rushed into the lounge half full of passengers and saw the man in the baseball cap steering the boy between the seats to the far side of the room. There was no way they could elude Geoff now, and everything he'd undergone to track Ben down drove his words out of his mouth. "Ben," he called. "You know I'm here. Paul, here I am."

Everybody who was seated in the lounge stared at him. He didn't care how absurd he seemed to them, he only wanted Paul to acknowledge him. What was Ben doing to the boy that was preventing him from acknowledging his father? What had Ben said to him? Geoff started in a fury across the room, and saw the man push the boy towards an empty seat and sit beside him. Their faces were visible at last, and for some moments Geoff forgot how to breathe as he realised he had never seen either of them before in his life.

When two uniformed men grabbed his arms he could almost have thought they were supporting him, dizzy as the revelation had left him. Then they hauled his arms behind his back. "I thought it was my son," he gasped.

"You'll have to do better than that, sir," said the man he'd fought outside the lounge, and peered into his face. "Well, well. We know you, don't we? You did a television show about how bad some of us are supposed to be. What are you up to this time? Come with us and we'll have a nice long talk."

forty-seven

Everything all right, Mr. Reaper? You look as if you've caught a prisoner."

"That's what he is, Mrs. Minken. He tried to run away."

"You mustn't do that, Ben, it's naughty. Why would you want to run away from your father? Doesn't he look after you? You know he does." The landlady had squatted in front of the boy, and Reaper let the tag go slack in case she thought it was choking him, but the boy didn't speak. "Your pa, I mean," she remembered. "You mustn't get yourself lost in these crowds. Someone might take you away."

"Pa."

"That's it. Just you never forget he's your pa." She stood up and hushed her voice. "I'm right though, aren't I, Mr. Reaper? You can't be too careful with the sort of people that are about."

"You can't. If you'll excuse me I'll take the miscreant up to his cell. He won't be coming out of there again today."

"Not even for dee eye double en ee ar?"

"After what I just said? Do you think it's fair to break your word to a child?"

"I don't indeed, Mr. Reaper, but I wouldn't want to think the little scamp was starving."

"That'll take a few days. Will you leave me to deal with him now?"

"You won't be too hard on him, will you, now you've got him back?"

"No harder than I have to be to keep him," Reaper said, and gave the tag a gentle yank. The boy climbed the stairs so enthusiastically that Reaper congratulated himself on training him. As he followed he sensed the landlady's concern like a cobweb on the back of his neck. He shrugged off the sensation and overtook the toddler. As soon as the child had ambled into the room, Reaper shut the door. "Trying to get me into more trouble, were you?"

The boy raised his small face. He looked trusting, and ready to emit his giggle if he was offered an excuse. For a moment Reaper didn't know how to respond to such trust—felt suspended in a place within himself he didn't recognise—and then he saw how dangerous that was. He'd almost let himself be rendered vulnerable by little Ben's vulnerability, and he focused on it all the contempt his life had gathered in him. "Can't you take me seriously?" he said, closing the curtains. "See if this helps."

Though he was smiling so tightly it squeezed his lips dry, the toddler didn't flinch. He looked ready for a game when Reaper lifted him by the tag and fitted it over the hook on the back of the door. The collar of his overalls dug under his chin, and his face started to redden, his eyes to blink and leak. When his small fists began to thump the door while his heels drummed against the lower panel, Reaper roused himself from a trance of watching, of enjoying the new spectacle even more than he'd anticipated, and lifted him down.

Little Ben's heels struck the carpet, jarring more moisture out of his eyes. As he gulped red-faced and opened his shaky lips, Reaper thrust his face so close to the boy's he thought he saw himself loom within a swelling tear. "Don't make too much noise. We don't want anyone to think you're getting worse than you deserve, do we? That wouldn't be fair to your pa."

He saw the boy decide against howling, as if Reaper's closeness had forced the outburst back into his mouth, which appeared to be struggling to find some way to placate him. "Papa," it stammered, spitting the consonants straight into Reaper's face.

Reaper felt the alien spittle on his lips. All he did, because otherwise he couldn't have predicted where he might have stopped, was wipe them fiercely on his sleeve and inch back from the toddler. "Get those off and put on some of the stuff I've had to buy," he said, pointing at the overalls. "We'll keep those for if I need to hang you again. And while you're out of them, do what you do in the toilet. I don't want to have to clean you up."

Once the garment fell around the boy's ankles, taking the underpants with it, Reaper trod on a trouser cuff to urge him to step out of the clothes. "Toilet," he repeated, and kicked them into a corner as the small bare pink figure waddled into the cubicle containing the toilet and the shower.

The noises that ensued were a problem. Reaper made sounds like that himself—had to live with them—but the presence of somebody else's was nearly unbearable: they seemed to be located inside his own skull. "Better not be too much longer. Better not be disgusting when you come out," he warned, staring at the intercom to confirm he'd switched it back into its radio mode when he'd returned last night from the Game Dog. "Can't hear me, can you?" he said to it. "Not still listening in case he cries? If I thought you were you wouldn't need that to hear him scream. Come on if you're listening or it'll be too late for him."

The toilet roll rumbled on its spindle, and then the toilet flushed. As the boy slid open the cubicle door Reaper pulled on a glove. He planted the heel of his hand on the small forehead and shoved it back, not looking at the pink stump sprouting from the junction of the legs. "Get in the shower," he ordered, treading on the sandals to force the boy to step out of them. "Let's make sure you're clean. There's nothing dirtier than a whelp."

"Help," the boy seemed to imagine he'd said, and stepped into the shower.

Reaper pinched the child's scalp between a gloved finger and thumb to turn him away. "Face the wall. We're going to hose you down," he said, and unhooked the hose before addressing the intercom. "How hot do we want it? They used to have it scalding in the prison, but they never made Ben scream. Maybe this would."

As the jet of water struck the boy he arched his back like a bow and jerked his trembling fists high. Reaper was close to believing himself to have done as he'd threatened until he realised the child was only reacting to the impact—or could he understand more of Reaper's words than he admitted and have tried to trick him? Reaper held him still by gripping the top of his head and directed the water at his lower half, and didn't relent when, having found that squirming failed to impress his captor, the boy started to wail. "That'll do," Reaper said at last, meaning both the shower and the boy's protests, and dropped a towel on him. "Dry yourself and get dressed. Nobody wants to look at you or listen to you."

The boy stood in the shower to rub the towel up and down his front, and Reaper was beginning to think he was afraid to emerge until he padded to the bag of clothes on the truckle bed, printing the carpet with wet tracks as he went. "Wait," Reaper ordered, and held the towel taut between his hands so as to drag it back and forth over the boy's spine and buttocks and legs. "Stop whining. Put something on and lie down till it's dark."

He watched the boy sit on the bed to drag on underpants and shorts and a T-shirt with a television hero flattened on it. He stared at him until the boy withdrew further onto the bed. He saw the small face build up to giggling at his stare and subside instead, he saw the mouth begin to loosen as though the stare was a weight that was pressing it open in preparation for a burst of wailing. Only a whimper emerged, and the boy looked scared to have released even that. Reaper watched with hardly a blink as the small face sagged, as the eyes dulled, as the boy forgot his feelings in the process of retreating inside himself. Before long the cowed eyes pulled their lids down, and he was asleep.

Reaper continued to watch as if the face might have some revelation in store for him. In time it grew bruised with twilight. The gathering darkness shrivelled the features, so that he seemed to be watching the face decay, an idea that made him feel peaceful. His calm couldn't rob him of awareness, however. He heard the slow careful footsteps before they began to ascend the stairs.

They were alone, and so he waited until they arrived at his door. He heard a muted thump, a jumble of sounds that belonged to the dining-room, a key sneaking into the door, a knuckly rap on a panel. The boy awoke and rolled over to blink at the door. "Dad?" he said, indistinctly but loud.

"May I come in, Mr. Reaper?" said the landlady's voice.

"Not while the bolt's on you can't," he said, and for her to hear "Give me a moment." He took longer than that to lean his face so close to the boy's he felt as if his own indrawn breaths were sucking the child's attempts to breathe out of him. "Pa," he reminded him, "pa," and went to the door.

Beyond the lens of the spyhole the landlady appeared to have served up her swollen head on a tray. All it needed, he thought, was a fruit to gag its mouth. In fact she was bearing two plates of lamb chops and potatoes and peas, not to mention a cruet and utensils. "Since you've paid full board and you aren't coming down," she said, "I thought I'd bring your dinners up to you."

"Look how kind your friend is, Ben. She must have thought you wouldn't last the night."

The landlady stood the tray between the beds on the legs it proved to have. "They need looking after at his age."

"Do you think I may be failing as a parent?"

She hesitated just long enough to let him know she had. "I'm sure you wouldn't do anything except the best for him, you and your wife. Maybe he's missing her and that's why he strayed off."

"That would certainly explain it," Reaper said, moving to the door so as to coax her out of the room.

Hadn't he satisfied her? Was she unsure about something? Her reluctance as she followed him was obvious. She had nearly reached the door when she stopped and looked towards the child, and Reaper experienced the tingle he only ever remembered when he felt it—the delight of knowing that a situation had gone too far, that somebody was beyond surviving it. Then she said "I've given you nothing to drink."

"We'll get something when we go out for a walk." He didn't know if he felt relieved not to have to deal with her, or let down, or both. "Thanks from the bottom. I don't know what we'd do without you," he said, and shut her out of the room.

He wasn't just being sarcastic. By trying to admit herself she'd reminded him that she could reach the boy if he was left alone. "Feed yourself," Reaper said as he heard her plod downstairs, and wasted some patience on watching the boy struggle to cut meat off the bone in imitation of him. "Gnaw it," he said, picking up one of his own chops to demonstrate.

He finished before the boy did, and had to watch. He thought of putting the plate on the floor so that the boy would have to go down on all fours, but instead he spied on the street and the reflection of the boy until he saw him fork the last potato like a lollipop into his mouth. "Time to go out. Put your sandals on, and don't you even think of running. I know everything you think. I'll hang you up again," he said, and was pleased to see the child flinch when Reaper took a step towards him.

He left the tray in the downstairs hall. Outside the night was ideal: warm and dark. As soon as the hotel was out of sight he removed his necktie—the tag of the T-shirt was too short for him to hold without having to touch the child. He knotted the narrower end of the tie around the boy's wrist, tightly enough to draw a whimper from him, and held onto the other end. An old couple out for a stroll looked as if it was the kind of thing they expected to see or approved of. Otherwise the houses on the way to the Game Dog were keeping their occupants to themselves.

Only the barman was in the bar. His head rose as though it was being forced back by the hair, the pony-tail tugging his eyes narrow. "Not in here," he said.

"I see that," said Reaper, glancing up at a collision of footballers on television as he pulled the boy after him. "Where is everyone?"

"Which are you, deaf or stupid? I said not in here. No kids in here."

"I need to wait for Barney. What do you want me to do, tie him up outside?"

"She's on her way. I don't care what you do with him so long as it isn't in here."

Reaper had meant to exaggerate, but it occurred to him that there was very little he could do in public to the boy that wouldn't make him seem more like a parent, not less. He led him to the headless streetlamp a few yards from the pub door and tied the free end of the necktie around the rusty shaft. "Stay," he said into the boy's face, and returned to the bar. "There, I hope that cheers you up."

"Depends if he starts making a row," the barman said, more lugubriously than ever.

"Better give me something to keep him quiet, then, and the same for me," Reaper said, and took one glass of Coke outside. "Drink this and don't drop it and don't cut yourself. I'll be watching you all the time."

Though the pub windows had been painted black, other customers before him had needed to watch the street. Several patches no bigger than his thumbnail had been scraped clear, and from his seat at a table by the door he had a view of the boy's head. In the secretive glow from the pub it looked metallic, a mechanical object that kept dipping to the glass of Coke. He'd begun to imagine how the blackness around it would swallow up the small head, fill the mouth and extinguish the eyes, when he saw Barney approaching the pub.

She wore heavy boots and outsize Boy Scout shorts and a short-sleeved ribbed sweater that appeared to have been woven of grey string. She marched into the bar and addressed herself to the room in general. "Who tied up that poor little tyke out there?"

"You know the rules," the barman said. "Can't have—"

"There's rules about how you treat kids all right. Laws about it too."

"Don't use language like that in here, Barney. The last thing either of us wants to get mixed up with—"

"Is giving kids the kind of time I had when I was one. Watch out I don't take my business somewhere else."

"No skin off my dick if you do, lass."

They seemed to have forgotten Reaper, who gave a dry stuttery cough of the kind the person he was meant to be might have emitted. "I know I shouldn't have brought him, but it was either that or risk having my wife find him."

"Could have taken him for a walk till I came, couldn't you? Maybe she ought to have him if that's the way you treat him."

"She's not the one who's paying you."

"There's some things I won't do for money, so don't you go thinking it. Any reason why she wants to keep you and him apart, is there?"

"She's a bitch. She'd do worse to him than leaving him outside a pub if she got her hands on him again, believe me."

"I don't know if I do."

The barman swung round from pretending to watch a slow-motion replay. "Take it upstairs."

"I'm going nowhere I can't see my son."

That apparently convinced her. "Let him bring him, Frank. Don't be more of a sod than you have to be. I want him up there too."

The barman raised his hands as if flinging two missiles high in the air and turned up the volume of the football crowd. Barney lounged in the doorway to watch Reaper unpicking the knot on the lamppost. "Keep still," he whispered fiercely as the child appeared to toy with the notion of backing away—of making the woman suspicious. Reaper almost split a fingernail before he managed to coax the knot loose. He sent the boy towards the pub and flapped the free end of the tie to demonstrate how comical it was. "Couldn't find one of those leads for children in any of the shops, they're so popular."

Barney unbolted the flap in the bar and slapped it with a hand that sounded like a large steak while Reaper followed the boy through. She led them onto the stairway that smelled as grey as it looked, and into the bare glaring room. "You park your bum, Benjamin. You've done enough standing around."

The boy only gazed about as if she didn't mean him. For longer than a moment Reaper didn't know why, and all he could think of was the knife. His hand was straying to his pocket when he understood. "Here, Ben, have the seat the lady's offering. You don't answer to Benjamin, do you, Ben? Sit, boy, sit."

When the boy perched on the chair Barney pushed it close to the table, then stood where she could watch Reaper and the child.

"Comfortable now, are you, Ben? Looking forward to going away with your dad?"

The boy's face lit up. "Dad," he said eagerly.

"He mostly calls me pa, don't you, Ben? But you see how much he's looking forward to it. Good job we won't be letting him down."

He'd said too much, Reaper saw. He ought to have let the boy's enthusiasm speak unaided. Barney's stare said as much before it sought the child. "And what do you call your ma, Ben? Ma?"

"He doesn't call her what she deserves to be called. I don't use words like that in front of him."

"Let him talk for himself. Mummy, is it, Ben? Mum?"

"This isn't why we're here," Reaper said, and reached in his pocket. "It's time to—"

"Mum."

The boy's face had brightened again. Perhaps it had only cleared of puzzlement, but Barney stared harder at him. "Tell me the truth, Ben. Don't let anyone stop you. Is it your mum you want to be with?"

The glare of the room seemed to lurch at Reaper, to penetrate his eyes and set his brain ablaze. He'd had enough. Words hadn't worked—the boy was making him lose control of them—and so it was time to back them up. "See what you made me do," he could already hear himself saying to the boy as they left the room with Barney and the barman in it. His fingers pushed the wad of notes aside and closed around the knife, and he spoke another line of his role to distract the woman. "Are you leaving me out of the question?"

For a moment it seemed she wouldn't admit to having heard him. She didn't look away from little Ben before saying "Or your dad."

"Dad."

"You want to go away with him? Is that what you're saying?"

"Go dad," the boy pleaded, gazing at Reaper.

Reaper trapped the woman's stare with his. "Are you sure yet? Anything else you need? Maybe my birth certificate to prove I'm his father?"

"Nobody's going to give you an argument about that. I just don't like doing anything that puts a kid at risk."

"Which are you, a crook or a social worker?" What Reaper said aloud, not smiling as he kept his gaze as steady as a church, was "Do I look as if I would?"

She didn't move until his eyes began to smart and the skin of her face glared like the light bulb. Then she lowered her head and pulled out a passport and laid it on the table with a loud snap that the walls applauded. "Look, Ben, that's you," said Reaper. "That'll be you on a plane tomorrow."

"Play."

"That's the word," Reaper agreed, and took his hand out of his pocket. He'd hardly dropped the wad of notes on the table when they were hidden in Barney's fist. At that moment he remembered that he hadn't yet bought foreign money for the trip. He would do that in the morning. The world was his game, and he was the winner. "Thank the lady, Ben," he said. "Say ta. Say it twice."

Barney didn't wait for that. She patted the boy on the head with an awkwardness that suggested she was having to remind herself not to be rough. Reaper led the boy downstairs and past the barman's back, and was opening the door when Barney called to him. "What do you think you look like?"

"A father who's determined not to lose his son," he said, and wagged the end of the tie at her as he guided the boy out of the door. Its metal elbow pulled it shut with a weary creak that made him glance up, and he saw the number. It was the first building in Cod Street—the address he'd given to the travel agent.

It surely couldn't matter. The credit card he'd used was valid, and so there would be no reason for the agent to check anything else. Nevertheless, once again the boy had succeeded in confusing him, and that couldn't be allowed. As he urged the boy downhill towards the hotel, the roofs cut off a glimpse of lights on the horizon—of Liverpool, fifty miles away. Their disappearance felt to him as though he had stopped being watched. "Nobody knows we're here. Geoffrey's not so clever," he said. "When we're back in the room I'll show you a trick with a knife."

forty-eight

The press conference was held in a disused ward of the hospital. As Gail followed the officer in charge of the case down the long white room, which the dozens of reporters seated on folding chairs didn't begin to fill, everyone grew silent, so that all she could hear were extra footsteps failing to keep up with hers—ghostly footsteps that were nothing but her own echoes. She felt how empty her hands were, and her face stiffened at the thought, her mouth worked at becoming unmanageable. She rubbed her lips hard with the back of one hand as she reached the small bare table decorated with a single blotch of ink like a miniature painting of a black sun with outstretched rays. By the time she took her seat next to the policeman she was as calm as she could be—calm as ice, and just as brittle.

He inclined his massive forehead-heavy head in her direction, bestowing on her a cold sharp almost metallic scent of aftershave, to study her before he spoke. "Mrs. Davenport wanted to be present at this conference, but will you please address questions to me."

He was wrong: Gail didn't want to be there—she only had to

be, to hear what was said. The day sister on the ward where Gail's father was lying unconscious had promised to let her know the instant anything changed, but Gail's hands ached to be holding his and refusing to let go. She gripped the wooden seat as if doing so could stop her wishing the conference was over—stop her imagining that her father would regain consciousness while she was away and have to ask someone else where her mother was—stop her rushing back to him precisely because she couldn't avoid knowing she might even be relieved if someone else told him.

The policeman was speaking. Quite a few of the reporters kept glancing at her in admiration of her visible effort to control herself. She didn't want them to think she was being brave; she was simply living the situation because there was no alternative. They couldn't know she was gripping the seat with all her strength so as to hold herself back from blurting out the truth.

No positive leads as yet . . . liaising with other police forces . . . at least seven similar cases in as many years . . . psychological profile drawn up by forensic psychologist . . . The monologue was reaching her in fragments, every one of which made her body clench with a sense of helplessness. Except she wasn't helpless: she couldn't bear to be. If Geoff hadn't kept his secret from her she might still have a mother. She'd been powerless then, she'd had no chance to save her, and her only way of dealing with that knowledge was not to miss the slightest opportunity of saving Paul.

When the policeman started answering questions she felt her hands relinquish their grip on the seat. They rose not very steadily into view, and she used one to muffle a loud harsh cough dried up by the heat of the hospital. Then her fist struck the table, and she folded her other hand around it so hard its knuckles bruised her palm. "I've changed my mind," she said. "I want to talk."

The policeman turned his upper half to her and laid a hand palm down next to hers, whether for companionship or as an admonition she didn't know. At least a dozen reporters waved to signal questions, and several mouths opened to utter theirs first. "I don't want to answer any questions," Gail said. "I just want to say what I have to say."

The policeman folded his arms and sat forward, thrusting his face at the press until their hands sank. "Please do, Mrs. Davenport."

"I want . . ." She wanted her mother back, and almost said so except for knowing that would lead to useless tears. "I want to send a message."

She saw pens being poised over notebooks, and microphones rising to catch her words. The sight drove her words out before she was sure what she meant to say. "Tell everyone my father's nearly ready to talk. They'll be taking the bandages off soon, and then he will. He'll be able to describe this guy, this thing who did that to him and my mother. Tell the guy he may as well give up. He should turn himself in to the police before everyone knows what to look for. And tell him—" On the edge of saying too much, she did her best to draw back. "Tell him if he harms anyone else I'll find him and I'll fix him. That's what my life's worth now."

Several heads nodded, and she heard murmurs of understanding. Then any number of mouths opened, putting her in mind of fish eager for another helping of food. When hands began to compete at waving she said "I want to be quiet now. I've nothing more to say."

The questions swerved to the policeman. Of course they had to ask how the investigation was progressing, but his guarded answers frustrated Gail, left her alone with her nervous doubts over having said so much. At last he declared "Thank you, ladies and gentlemen, that's all" and ushered Gail away so swiftly that the press were out of sight as soon as she turned the first corner. "Thanks for looking after me," she said. "I can find my way now."

"I'd like a word before I leave, Mrs. Davenport."

"I need to get back to my father."

"I'll speak to you there then, if you don't mind."

His voice had grown heavier—its weight had laid itself on her, not unlike a hand on her shoulder. "You'll have to," she said, and didn't even glance at him as she strode to the ward.

Her father might not have moved since she'd left him. His bandaged face was upturned on a pillow not much paler than his skin, his arms lay limp on the coverlet as if they'd abandoned searching for a hand to hold. His chest was as still as his closed eyes, and Gail was unable to go forward until she saw the top edge of the coverlet rise feebly and sink. She sat by the bed and took hold of his hands, and ignored the policeman as he placed a chair opposite her and drew the screen shut behind him. When he sat forward so that his knees touched the bed she glanced up sharply. "What did you want to say?"

"Don't take this wrong, Mrs. Davenport. Don't mistake my meaning, but you seemed very sure of yourself in there."

"Maybe I know how to deal with the media because I work for one," Gail said, stroking and stroking the hands in hers through the bandages.

"There would be that, only I was thinking more of how you felt you could speak for your father."

"I don't know anyone who's better qualified, do you?"

He raised his face so that he appeared to be sighting along his nose at her. "What I'm getting at, Mrs. Davenport, is how you could be certain your father can describe the attacker."

"He must have seen him, mustn't he?"

"Must he? We'd hope so, but I don't think we can assume it yet, or even if he'll be able to remember. Or is your thought that the attacker was personally known to Mr. Henderson?"

"Of course not. Obviously not."

"You're very definite. What makes you so positive?"

"My parents had never been to this country before," Gail said, and had to restrain herself from gripping her father's hands. "Their only time, and see what happened to them."

"It's a dreadful business. Worse than tragic." After a pause he said "So would it be fair to say you'd do anything to see this man brought to justice?"

"Anything I can, you bet. Such as . . ."

"Such as making him believe a description is about to be circulated."

"If it scares him into the open," Gail said, trying not to imagine how that could go wrong. "You don't blame me, do you?"

"I'd let that go, I think. By itself I would. Only there's another point that bothers me."

"About what I said? I didn't say much."

"That's rather it. It's what you didn't say. You weren't cut short, were you? You didn't mean to go on?"

Gail felt as though he was tempting her to blurt out everything she wasn't even certain she ought to keep to herself. "Like how?"

"I'm thinking of, I suppose the word would be the threat you made. Not that I or anybody else has the right to object if that's how you feel."

"Why on earth wouldn't I?"

"I don't know if you recall exactly what you said. You wanted him told he'd have you to reckon with if he harmed anyone else." The policeman inclined his face towards her father without removing his gaze from her. "You'll excuse the trespass, but I don't see why you'd need anyone besides your parents to make you feel that way. You don't give me the impression that you would."

"I don't."

"So you were simply trying to head off another tragedy, as we all are."

"What else could I have been up to?"

"You didn't have anyone specific you didn't want to come to harm."

"Who?" Gail demanded, and tried to take refuge in gazing at her father. "What do you want me to say?" she heard herself protesting. "I know who that, who he is? I know where to find him?"

"If any of that is the case, Mrs. Davenport, yes."

She imagined how she would feel if she saw another face in the state of her father's, or worse still her mother's, the eyes closed forever—Paul's face on a pillow, his injuries tastefully masked, the horrors he'd had to suffer locked into him. She'd been manoeuvring herself towards a point where she would be unable to keep quiet about him, she realised. She held onto her father and met the policeman's patient gaze. "He said he'd kill our son if we told anyone," she began, "but I know where my husband's gone to find him."

forty-nine

Perhaps the man in charge of airport security that day was thorough or just slow, or perhaps he'd taken a dislike to Geoff. In a windowless room behind the scenes with nothing in it other than a table and four chairs so basic they resembled early stages in the production of themselves, he had each of the guards give a detailed version of events before he would entertain so much as a word from Geoff. He listened to the accounts with his downcast eyes nearly shut, then raised the lids as gradually as his red hefty face. "Well, Mr. Davenport. Is that how you normally conduct your research?"

"I thought—"

"I'm aware some of the media these days seem to be competing to see who can behave worst, but I understood you were supposed to have a reputation to maintain, at least in public."

"I was trying—"

"Besides which I'd have assumed a show like yours needed you to be discreet."

Geoff felt as if the interruptions were a series of ponderous burdens being heaped on top of his speech. He was desperate to be out of the airport, to be left alone so that he could try and think where Ben could have taken Paul. "It wasn't—"

"Yes, Mr. Davenport? I'm listening."

Geoff had almost blurted out that the incident had nothing to do with his work. "It wasn't the man I have to interview. He was trying to take the boy somewhere his wife can't regain custody, wasn't he?" he appealed to the guards. "That's how it sounded from what he tried to stop the boy saying."

"We've had no notification of that," said the man in charge. "As far as we're concerned there's no reason to hold him. You're the one who caused the trouble, and it won't help you to blame him."

"I'm not blaming anyone. I just meant that was why he was running away, and I had to get close enough to see his face before I knew he wasn't my man."

"And why were you after whoever you thought he was?"

"I can't reveal that, not even to you. You'll see why when the story breaks."

"That's a considerable distance from being anything like good enough."

"You know who I am and what. Won't that do?" Geoff twisted in his chair to face the female guard. "I'm sorry I hurt you. I really didn't mean to. I just thought if he'd got on that plane I might have lost him for good. I lost my head, and that's the truth."

She frowned like a mother forgiving a child. "Not much damage done. I'll survive."

"Thank you. Really, thanks. I promise you won't regret it when you understand what was involved. So if that's settled, will it be all right if I—"

"Nothing's right and nothing's settled," said the man in charge. "You put security at risk and assaulted a member of my staff."

"I did apologise for that, and since this lady doesn't want to make an issue of it—"

"You're wasting your time, Mr. Davenport," the man in charge said. "I've already called the police. They don't like threats to security any more than I do."

The door wasn't locked. Could Geoff simply jump up and run?

Might that be so unexpected it would give him time to reach his car, even to pay to leave the car park? He was realising how helplessly cornered he was to consider such a scheme when he heard footsteps marching towards the room. The door was opened to an officious knock, and two policemen came in. "Ready for us?" the stockier and more thoroughly bald of them said, not to Geoff.

"Whenever you want him."

"We'll have him now," said the second policeman, who was cropped and moustached like an army sergeant. "Be in touch."

Geoff stood up quickly, and the other policeman grasped his arm. He let go once they were clear of the room, but now Geoff had a policeman on either side of him, and could only walk and return the stares of everyone who saw him. "Well, Mr. Davenport," the stocky policeman said, "we hear you made quite a scene."

"I told them why. I thought someone I was chasing was getting away, only it turned out I'd been after the wrong man. That's all I can say at the moment. I know you expect me to explain myself better, I really do want to cooperate, but—"

"We understand why you did it."

"You do? How—I mean, what—"

"Your wife told them up in Scotland."

The automatic doors drew back, and Geoff felt as if the outer air, summery though it was, had frozen his face. "Told them what?"

"About your son and who's got him."

As the air grew heavy with the rumble of a descending plane, Geoff had the impression that the noise was taking the place of his thoughts. "She couldn't," he muttered, and didn't even know whether that was an unfinished sentence.

"Don't worry, Mr. Davenport," the moustached policeman said, "we're as keen not to take any risks with him as you are. We've people who are experienced in these situations. Which is your car?"

"I thought he might recognise it. It's parked in town. I followed him, except as you know it wasn't him, followed him in a cab."

Too late he saw that the security cameras would have recorded his arrival in the car park. The stocky policeman swung a hand towards him, but only to point at a police car ignoring double yellow lines. "We'll drive you to the station," he said.

No sooner had Geoff strapped himself in than the police car took off, flashing its urgency lights as it screeched into the road. It retraced his route considerably faster than he'd dared to follow the taxi. In less than fifteen minutes it was speeding past the riverside hotel, which dragged at his mind with a sense of how much time he'd wasted. Five minutes later the car was swerving across the dock road and into a grey concrete yard behind a police station built of much the same material.

The stocky policeman let Geoff out of the car while his colleague typed the combination of the metal door at the rear of the building. Beyond it was a concrete corridor barely relieved by six featureless doors, the furthest left-hand one of which Geoff's stocky guide pushed open. "Take a seat in here," he said.

Two chairs, one table, no window. Geoff sat facing the doorway and propped his elbows on the table while he pressed his fingertips against his temples. He had to work backwards to where he'd gone wrong—had to identify the clue Ben apparently thought he was able to follow. Only the noises resounding down the corridor—thick blurred shouts that sounded like a prelude to violence—were distracting him, and so was his need to remember before someone else's questions prevented him. He was rubbing his forehead in a fierce attempt to wake its contents up when a tall man in a suit as grey as his curly hair tramped into the room. He gave Geoff's hand a solitary shake as he sat opposite him. "Ware, Mr. Davenport," he said.

"Hello."

The policeman's greyish eyes in his broad face were calm in a way that seemed not far short of weariness at having seen too much. "May I start by being personal?" he said.

"I don't see how I can stop you."

"I want to ask you not to blame your wife, that's if you do."

"Blame her, no. Wish she hadn't brought you into it, I can't help that."

"I understand, but I'd ask you to believe it's my experience of these cases that it isn't our involvement that can lead to problems."

"Cases like what? He doesn't want money, he just wants me to stop him, only me. He's wanted it since we were kids."

"Perhaps we can arrange for that to happen. He needn't see us unless it becomes absolutely necessary."

That struck Geoff as very little of a promise. "Are you looking for them now? What are you looking for?"

"Your wife gave us a photograph of your son and a description of the man she got from a nurse in the crèche at your workplace. And of course your wife informed us you were searching Liverpool. If you'll tell me what leads you've been following that will be helpful."

Geoff couldn't see how a refusal or a lie would help Paul, and so he spread the contents of a pocket across the table. "He made me follow a trail. This one's the cycle track under the start of the M62."

"I know it. I often bike it with my children."

"Do you?" Geoff felt a parental smile tug at his lips and lose its hold. "And this is the one I found there. It's my son. It's meant to show how close my, he's not my brother and never was, how close he came to us without anybody noticing."

"I see that." Ware separated the pictures Geoff had dealt him, lined them up with a fingernail against the edge of each. "But how did they lead you to the man you followed today?"

"I'm supposed to guess where Ben would go. The house we used to live in is a hotel now. They told me there they'd given a man with a boy about my son's age some addresses, and I tracked him down."

"You did well." The policeman seemed engrossed in the photograph of Paul. The beginnings of a frown poised themselves above his eyes as he looked up. "Where did you find this? In the undergrowth by the track?"

"Hidden so I almost didn't find it."

"Can you think of any reason why it should have been left there in particular?"

"To remind me what he did. To make me have to remember. He left my dog there to die when we were kids. Glued up his nose and mouth and his legs together, he must have. I never told anyone, and if I had Ben mightn't have gone on the way he has. He must have wanted me to remember that too."

"That's a good deal of reason." The policeman still appeared to be about to frown, or hopeful that he needn't. "You don't think there could be even more to it."

"Tell me what."

"Could he have put it there to indicate where you should look for your son?"

"You mean like—" The words Geoff had to utter tasted like bile. "Like my dog. Christ, I don't know. Christ, the bastard. If he—"

"We won't waste time speculating," Ware said and stood up, his frown disappearing as if, Geoff thought, it was no longer enough. "I'll have a search begun at once."

"I want to be there," said Geoff, stumbling to his feet, and wondered whether that might prove to be the worst lie he would ever tell.

fifty

Reaper touched the eyeball with the dull edge of the blade and felt the eye flinch shut. "No you don't," he said. He held down the lower eyelid with his thumb and raised the upper lid with his forefinger until it couldn't twitch however much it struggled to, then he rested the flat of the blade against the bared eyeball. "This is good, isn't it?" he said through his teeth. "I ought to thank you. I'd started forgetting what danger was like. Just watch and I'll show you. It's time you knew."

The boy squirmed, but he wasn't moving, not even in his sleep. Only the moisture trying to protect Reaper's eyeball from the knife made him appear to stir. He'd crawled into the truckle bed as soon as they were in the room, and had instantly fallen asleep. Reaper held the eye helplessly wide and drew the blade over it until the point was stinging the thin tissue at the pupil. He felt metal penetrate him, and saw blindness swelling to take the eye. A convulsion nearly wrenched the lids shut, and the hand with the knife jerked so violently that he didn't know how deep the point had sliced. But the hand had snatched the knife away, and the piercing sting was only from the touch of metal. "Ah," he gasped as his sight returned, sharper than ever, and moved to stand over the boy. "Your turn," he said.

The small face ignored him. It stayed trustfully upturned on the pillow, miming a conviction that nothing could befall it while it was asleep. Reaper poised the knife above it, pinched the handle between finger and thumb and swung the blade like a pendulum over the eyes. Now it was only a foot away from them, and he let the handle slide out of his slackening grip. He saw one eye spring open to receive the blade, but instead he caught the point on the palm of his free hand. "Not yet," he muttered, wiping away on his trousers the trace of the boy's breath on the back of his hand as he retreated to his bed. "You may still be some use."

He closed his eye while the stinging faded. Seen with the remaining eye the boy seemed robbed of presence, even less real than before. Reaper sat back on the bed, his spine against the padded headboard, and rested the knife against his crotch, point upwards. "You don't know what danger is, do you?" he said. "If you don't you may as well not know anything. I'll help you find out. I owe you that, don't I?"

"Please tell me what the world is like, pa."

"I'll tell you a story, shall I? That's what fathers are supposed to do. A bedtime story, except for that you'd have to be awake." He stared at the boy's face trapped by the glow of the streetlamp and thought of rousing him, but was too close to a trance of his own. "Who do you want to hear about? The old woman who puckered up her mouth to help her lipstick be put on? Maybe she was dreaming she was looking at herself in a mirror, but I can promise you she never saw herself again. What about the old man who kept licking his lipstick off and had to have his tongue poked back in with that knife? Like playing with a snail. A bloody snail. And there were the old couple who started snuffling when they'd had their kiss. Sounded just like dogs. Dogs stuck together."

"Won't you tell me a story with magic in it?"

"Do you want to hear about the boy who was never afraid again?"

"Yes please, pa. That sounds like the best one."

"Pity Geoffrey won't be able to hear it. Might have amused

him. It could have been his reward for chasing after me. Hope our game was as much fun for him as it was for me, don't you? I've been having fun ever since the time I'm going to tell you about, all sorts of fun."

"Fun."

"Who said that? Was that you or me? Thought you were awake for a moment there. I don't suppose it matters if you're awake or asleep, you'll understand as much. You're the best kind of audience, the kind that can't say what it heard. Can't say anything unless I make it talk. Maybe I should have been a ventriloquist, there are so many dummies about."

"Aren't you going to tell me the story?"

"Don't worry, I never disappoint anyone. Once there was a boy. He could have been like you, except he was older than I think you're going to be. He started off living with his parents, but then the wicked father had the boy's father sent away and made another boy to take the boy's place. After that nobody cared about him, and the worst of them was the boy who pretended he did so he could make things worse for him."

"Did they all live long ago in a faraway place?"

"Of course they did. They lived by a track the metal beasts ran along all day and all night. And the wicked father couldn't keep the beasts away, so he blamed the boy for them. And one day he told the boy he was going to stay in a magic land by the sea, but instead he took him to an old man and woman who kept beasts and lived like them. And the beasts were the one thing the boy was scared of, and he had to live with them for years."

"How did he live?"

"I just told you, like they did. He slept in a bed like a heap of old rags, and he ate food the beasts ate when he couldn't stomach any more of it. And whenever he wasn't at school he had to tend to the beasts. Had to feed them and clean them out and hear them trying to get to him. And the only walks the old man and woman ever let him take were with them and the beasts."

"What did he do? Did he kill all the beasts?"

"He only killed one, and that was the old man. He didn't even know he could at first, he just kept dreaming about it all the time.

Only he made up a family for himself so he could tell the boys at school about them, and then the old man found out and nearly had a heart attack." He demonstrated by holding his breath and clutching his chest and kicking his legs while he wheezed desperately, and the knife performed a jerky dance against his crotch. "So then the boy wondered if he could make him have a better one. He only wanted to kill him to see if he could, and then he'd be able to wait until he grew up."

"Did he kill him? How did he do it? Tell."

"Maybe his fairy godmother helped him. A woman in a big shiny silver car did, anyway. She brought the most expensive beast they'd ever had to care for, and the fastest too. It was so precious that the old man wouldn't let the boy near it. He fed it and cleaned its cage and took it for its walks himself. And all the boy had to do was fix its door so the old man would think he'd shut it when he hadn't quite. The beast got out, and the old man chased it until his heart blew up. Then he lay in the dirt coughing up pints of blood, and when the ambulance came it was too late. That's when the boy found out he could even cry if he needed people to see him doing it. He could look like anything he had to. So there's some magic in the story, isn't there?"

"Was that when he found out he needn't be afraid of anything?"

"No." He stared at the boy's peaceful face laid out for the streetlamp to beam upon. He felt as though the interrogation had caught him out—felt compelled to teach the toddler not to want to know so much about him—and then he relented. "You're right, I ought to finish with that. That's the best part."

"Did the precious dog ever come back?"

"Who cares? Who wants to know? Never mind asking questions like that or I'll think you don't care about the parts that matter. It did, since you're so worried about it, and the woman who owned it went to the old man's funeral, silly bitch. That was after the part you're supposed to be interested in, when the boy had to kiss the lump of meat out of the freezer."

"Why did he?"

"Because that was what the magic had turned the old man's face into, and the old woman said he had to put his lips on it. He wasn't scared of that, he just thought he'd be sick on it if he did. He tried to look as if he was kissing it, but that wasn't enough for the old woman," he said, and raised his voice to a shrill croak. "Give your poor grandfather a kiss after all he did for you. You never showed him any affection or respect while he was alive, show him some now he's been taken from us. He's looking down on you, did you but know. He wants to see the boy he tried to make you into. You stay in here till you've made your peace with him."

"She never shut him in with the old man's body, did she?"

"That's what she did, and that's not all. Maybe she didn't mean the rest, but she could have. She'd been drinking all day and shouting at the old man. She went off to get herself another bottle, and maybe on the way she fell against a door. And she let out the dog that used to chase the boy."

"Didn't she know?"

"Are you missing your master, poor old girl? *You'd* kiss him given half the chance, wouldn't you? You'd show that ungrateful boy how to behave." He lowered his voice from the croak. "She knew all right, but she didn't care, and then she drank herself to sleep. So the boy had to stay in there with Old Man Meat starting to go off, and the dog snarling and scratching at the door if he went anywhere near it. He had to shove the only chair in the room under the doorknob, and every time the dog tried to get in the chair would dance."

"What happened? What did the boy have to do to escape?"

"How do you think the story ought to end? The boy found a place inside himself that was like being asleep and watching and waiting, is that enough? I should think if anyone had seen him standing by the bed all night and not moving in case he made the dog knock the chair down they'd have said he was a soldier, don't you? A soldier who'd learned how to kill, and now he had all night to dream of better ways to do it. He thought of a good one, and he decided to try it out on a dog to stop it yapping. And after that it gets better and better."

He let his mind sail through the scenes his words had just evoked. At last, or rather for the moment, there were no more, and it came to rest on the sight of the boy's slack upturned face, unresponsive as a photograph of itself. "You don't seem to like that ending very much," Reaper said. "Haven't you been listening? Don't you know what I've been telling you?" He hadn't long to wait now, he mustn't let the boy weaken his patience. "I'll tell you what," he said, and gave in to a smile that felt like a part of the dark. "You can be the boy in the story. You can wait until daylight, the way he had to, and then you'll find out how it ends."

fifty-one

The sun was going down by the time they were sure no small body was hidden in the undergrowth beside the path. Geoff watched lorry after lorry drag its shadow along the edge of the motorway and wished he could feel more relieved. He and the police had spent hours searching, and all that was nothing but time during which Paul had still not been found. His thoughts felt crushed beneath the notion that he would only understand what clue Ben had given him once he was left alone to think.

Three boys on bicycles sped by, evidently more anxious to be out of sight of the police than to learn what the situation was, as Ware came up to Geoff. "I believe we can assume your son was never here," the policeman said.

"It wouldn't make sense for Ben to have harmed him," Geoff said, trying to convince himself. "He needs to keep Paul safe until I find him."

"We're taking that into account. We won't move on any sightings without you. Perhaps you should try and catch up on your sleep if you can. We'll contact you the moment there's any news. Would you be best booking into a hotel?"

"If there are any with room."

Geoff trudged after the police under the motorway, on the far side of which they climbed to a street he knew all too well. "That might do for you," Ware said.

He was indicating Geoff's childhood home, outside which a man was carrying suitcases down to a hatchback while his wife strapped in their two children. The landlady was waving them off, and saw first the police, then Geoff. "Why, has it been you all the time, Mr. Davenport?" she said, nodding at the line of parked police cars. "We wondered what on earth was going on."

"It's over," Geoff heard himself say as if to mock his own hopes. "It was a false trail."

"You look tired out. We've rooms tonight if you need one."

All at once Geoff seemed to lack the strength to disagree with the consensus on how he should proceed—and then he saw a problem. "How will the police be able to contact me if you and your husband are asleep?"

"We've a cellphone you can have. A salesman who was staying gave us it to try, but we've never found much use for it."

Once Ware took his leave, having copied down the number of the phone, Geoff insisted on paying for his night's stay in advance. "We've finished dinner," the landlady said, "but I could throw something together for you. How does bangers and mash sound?"

To Geoff it sounded unnervingly as though he was being coaxed into reliving his childhood, much as the house was affecting him. "You're very kind. I'm sure they would go down a treat."

He grew less sure as he awaited them—had time to wonder when Paul had last eaten and what, how much if any care Ben was taking of him, how much longer Ben could be expected to wait for Geoff to interpret the clue Ben was apparently convinced he'd laid . . . When the meal arrived, however, he was ashamed to discover he was ravenous. "Sleep well," the landlady said with a maternal smile at his cleared plate. "Sweet dreams. Pleasant memories."

She'd given him the room he'd led her to believe had once been his. He hurried out to the nearest late-night shop for a toothbrush and razor and the rest of the items his brain had become almost too dull to remember. The first thing he saw as he let himself into the room was the letter carved into the skirting-board, an initial forever undecided which letter it meant to be. He brushed his teeth and showered and shaved his vagrant's face, none of which enlivened his thoughts. He felt as if his brain was pressing against the inside of his skull, and his being alone was only making it worse. He had to speak to Gail, whatever she'd said last time.

"Geoff Davenport. Can I speak to my wife?"

"I'll see, Mr. Davenport."

Perhaps the sister only meant that Gail might be asleep, but the longer he waited, the likelier it seemed that Gail wouldn't want to talk to him. At last he heard the receiver scrape a desk. He was struggling to think of a message to leave for Gail when she said "Yes, Geoff."

"I just wanted to say I needed you to tell the police. I don't think I ever could have."

"Have they—"

"Not quite yet. I've been given a cellphone, so they can tell me the instant they know where I have to be, and then they'll be there if I want them. They've got their special knowledge, and I—well, I must have."

"What about the clues you were supposed to be following?"

"I thought I was right, but I went wrong somewhere. I know there's something I should know if I can only think. If you like I'll call you when it comes to me and then we can decide together if I should involve the police or go alone."

"Call me when you need to."

So much besides distance had intervened between them that Geoff was unsure how to take her words. "You too, whenever you want," he said.

Her silence gave him time to regret having presumed she would, but then she said "You'd better tell me the number."

Geoff did before his tired brain produced a question he should already have asked. "How's—" he began, only to find that speaking Paul's name would bring far too many associations with it. "Your father, how is he?"

"He's still unconscious. He doesn't know yet."

"Have you been able to get any sleep?"

"What do you think?"

"Me neither."

He hadn't finished uttering the phrase when he winced at its crassness. The last thing he would have dared expect to hear Gail say was "You should try."

"You think so?"

"You'll need to have rested, won't you?"

"That's true enough. I'll say goodnight then, shall I? Remember I'm here."

"Where?"

"The last place you'd think. My old home that's been turned into a hotel."

"You're right, it never would have occurred to me." He was wondering if she'd had some further thought when she murmured "Good night then."

"Good night," Geoff said, and "I—" He'd paused too long, and was speaking to the drone of the hundreds of miles between them.

He hoped she felt less alone, as he did. If his mind wasn't clear yet, it wasn't quite as burdened; he might even be able to think. He kicked off his shoes and lay back on the bed with the telephone beside him, and tried to relax. His eyes yearned to close, but he mustn't let them, certainly not for more than an instant. The instant felt like sleep, and then it was.

A light in his eyes wakened him. He'd been dreaming about nothing at all, and so as he tried to blink away the glare he took his surroundings for a dream—wasn't sure if Ben or his father had found him in the room where he wasn't meant to be, didn't know which of them was probing his eyes with the beam. Then he thought to move aside, having seen it was the dawn through a gap between the curtains. At once he was fully awake, and knew not only where he was and why but where Ben must be.

Of course Ben wouldn't have expected him to think he was in their old house. By saying her colleague had gone to his parents, the telephonist at the taxi firm had confirmed Geoff in his mistake, but Ben would have gone to the only hotel where Geoff should have known he had reason to go—the one he'd been promised and then denied as a child. "Got you at last," Geoff cried, shoving the phone into his pocket as he leapt off the bed. He had to think as he moved now, he'd no more time to waste. He would know his destination when he saw it, he vowed to himself. After so many years, and with no reason to remember it, he'd forgotten the name of the hotel.

fifty-two

Reaper roused the boy by switching on the television news. A revelation about a member of the royal family, a bomb defused on an Intercity train, six men executed for last year's war crimes, a five-year-old boy chained up for months in a shed on his parents' farm . . . The toddler blinked at the screen as though in search of his companion, and Reaper thought he should—grew more resentful with every news item that was apparently regarded as more significant than himself. "See, nobody cares," he said to the toddler, "not even me," just as the grandparents' faces appeared, more like a cliché, he thought, than news. "Police are still waiting to question Paul Henderson, whose wife died yesterday," the newsreader said. "At a press conference Mr. and Mrs. Henderson's daughter made an emotional appeal to the killer to give himself up."

"Shouldn't have bothered, should she? I don't use emotions. Only how do they know it's a man they're after? If somebody's been talking— What's the matter with you?"

The boy was gazing wistfully at the screen, which showed a map of Britain breaking out in suns. "Gran."

"Gone. You didn't see her, you were dreaming. Get up and you can have breakfast. That's better than an old woman who can't do you any good, isn't it? Better than all your family that are just as much use as her."

The boy held out his hand for the control. "See."

"You can downstairs if you really have to. Don't you know you don't need to watch when you're one of the stars?" Reaper switched off the television and laid the control on top of it, out of the boy's reach. "You're starting to take after Geoffrey, living other people's lives for them. Watch out or you won't notice you had one of your own until it's too late."

"See."

Reaper rolled off the bed and stood up with hardly a sound, and stooped so close that he felt his own breath driving the boy's timid exhalations back into him. "Here's the last thing you'll see and the last thing you'll hear. Come and eat so you won't be whining about food, and we'll be off. Today's your big adventure."

For a moment he wanted to crush the boy's fluttering breath as though it was the insect it felt like, and then he knew he could wait. "Toilet," he urged, stepping back, and had the satisfaction of watching the boy scurry into the cubicle to release what sounded like a flood of panic.

The smells of breakfast seemed to distract him from uttering any further complaint. Reaper thought it best to seat him with his back to the dining-room, however. "Watch the street," he told the boy, preparing to do so himself.

The boy twisted round to stare across the room. "See gran."

"Is his granny coming to see him?" the fat freckled mother at the next table said.

"They'll be together just as soon as I can arrange it."

Before long Mrs. Minken arrived with breakfast and a question. "Going somewhere nice today?"

"Somewhere he's never been."

"Shall I say where you've gone if anyone calls?"

"Who are you thinking might do that?"

"Why, your wife."

"Who else." No sooner had his sense of danger flared up than it faded, rather to his disappointment: there ought to be more excitement so close to the end of this stage of the game—the boy hadn't proved to be nearly as much of a stimulus as Reaper had anticipated. "Your mum," he said in case that livened things up.

"Mum," said the boy, but most of his enthusiasm was directed at his food.

"I expect you're wondering why I never seem to call her."

"I'm sure I wouldn't dream of wondering about a guest's private affairs." When Reaper met her gaze with one so blank it could mean anything she murmured "Why, is there . . . has there been . . ."

"Do you think I may have done something bad? Don't be shy. What sort of thing?"

"Mr. Reaper, please."

"Bad enough to be on the news, do you think it could be?"

"I sincerely hope not, and if it is this is hardly the place . . ."

The only danger he was inviting was boredom. "I've a mobile," he said, "that's why I don't use your phone," and remembered she had seen him doing so.

"I knew it must be something like that. Now if you'll excuse me I must be seeing to my other guests," she said, and left him with a reproachful look.

There was no fun to be had in the hotel, it seemed. As soon as the toddler had managed to lodge most of his last mouthful in his mouth, Reaper finished sawing through a piece of gristle and dropped the knife on the plate. "Let's get this done with," he said.

The sunlight fitted itself to his skull as he stepped out of the hotel. A mile away along the seafront a roller coaster hoisted squeals above the roofs. A pink spade rattled in a pink bucket as a little girl ran by, and for an instant Reaper was able to imagine himself as one of the holiday crowd, a father who'd brought his son to experience the treats he himself had been denied—experience them on his behalf. The truth was that the place was absolutely barren of the magic he'd dreamed as a child it must contain. It was vulgar and garish and mindless and stale, and the only aspect of it

capable of quickening his interest was the spectacle of old couples
herding their grandchildren about the streets. "I haven't time for
you now," he muttered. "Lucky you."

Five minutes, during which he led the toddler by the tag of
today's T-shirt past at least a dozen old couples—some of their
number enticingly immobilised in wheelchairs—brought him to
streets that lay in the shadow of a building modelled on the Eiffel
Tower. Among the shops festooned with seaside hats and snorkels
and puffed-up rubber animals he saw a travel agency. It wasn't the
one he'd previously used, but then there was no need for him to be
recognised anywhere he didn't have to be. He steered the boy into
the long thin shop and up to the exchange counter.

A young woman smiled at him through the reinforced glass
above a trough. "How may I help?"

Reaper leaned over the boy. "Just some money."

"The more exotic the better. Try me for anything."

"Turkish."

"That's getting popular. Still lots of space if you want to stay
away from people, though. How much?"

"Say two hundred pounds' worth. I can always change more
once we're there."

"When would you like your cash?"

Reaper selected his credit card. Soon he would bid farewell to
that name. "Right away," he said.

"Ah, I can't quite do that. Can you give me a little time?"

"So long as it's this morning."

"A little more than that. I'm awfully sorry. Two days is usual,
but I could do my best to have it for you by tomorrow."

"That's no use to me. We're flying this afternoon, me and my
son. It's his first holiday abroad. He's been looking forward to it for
how long have you, Ben? Weeks?"

"As I say, I'm awfully sorry. Did you book your holiday
with us?"

"I didn't as it happens. Is that supposed to make a difference?"

"I was wondering if whoever you dealt with offered to get you
the money."

"Of course they did. I remember now," Reaper said, swinging the boy around by his tag. "Come along, Ben. If it wasn't for you I wouldn't have forgotten."

A trio of fat women like tents with heads were scrutinising all the offers in the window, and took their time about retreating arm in arm to let him steer the toddler out of the shop. He dodged around a pedlar with squeaky prancing puppets on a tray and through the maze of slow flesh to the travel agent's he'd visited yesterday. The Travel Operative who had served him was clattering the keys of his computer, and didn't glance up until Reaper was seated, the boy trapped between but not touching his splayed legs. "Remember us?" said Reaper.

The clerk typed a last symbol before he raised his head. Below his pale hair his high forehead looked more exposed than ever. "I certainly do. No problem, is there? No last-minute hitch?"

"There shouldn't be, should there? You were going to give me some Turkish money."

"That's right, but then you had to leave."

"I'm here now. I hope my money is."

The clerk dabbed at his hairline, where a bead of sweat had ventured out of hiding. "Excuse me, but I don't think you asked me to get you any, did you?"

"You didn't say I needed to, did you?" Reaper said with a smile that made his lips ache and his eyes smart. "Let's not waste time arguing. I'll buy whatever you've got up to a couple of hundred pounds' worth."

"I wish I could help you, sir. There's not a lira in the place, at least only the Italian kind, and you aren't going there, are you? When are you travelling again?"

This must be a trick, Reaper thought—a trick the clerk feared was obvious, which was why another bead of sweat was preparing to make a break. "This afternoon," Reaper said.

"Lord." The clerk's hand flew to his forehead as if he intended to dot a cross on himself. "Do you want me to issue some travellers' cheques, or would you rather try elsewhere for your cash and get your cheques there to save time?"

It wasn't a trick after all. If it had been, surely he would be trying to delay Reaper on behalf of whoever wanted him detained. Reaper had almost tricked himself. "Such as where?" he said.

"Another agent's, or maybe a bank. It's always possible someone may have just sold some Turkish money they didn't spend. Would you like me to ring round to see if anyone has some?"

"That won't be necessary. I'll see to it myself."

"If all else fails you could try at the airport."

"It isn't your fault," Reaper said, knowing whose it was. He took hold of the chair with the hands that could have helped his knee snap the boy's spine before anyone could intervene, and stood up. "Come along, Ben. I want more than a word with you."

"Satisfied now?" he demanded once he'd dragged the boy out of the shop. "If you hadn't distracted me when we were here yesterday—if you hadn't gone off with that gang—" He didn't care that he was raising his voice; he could see the crowd was on his side—he almost felt like one of them. It amused him to pretend he'd regressed to their state, and they were helping him dismay the boy, whose face appeared to be about to try to crumple itself smaller. "Let's see how much trouble you've made for me," Reaper said. He swung the boy away from the travel agency and came face to face with a policeman.

It was clear from the man's stolid gaze that he'd been listening, but that was as much as Reaper could tell. "Here's a wrongdoer for you," he said, gruff as a father. The man's gaze lowered itself to the boy, lingered momentarily, returned to the boy's captor. It was neutral, all but indifferent, and at once Reaper saw that the policeman was pretending not to have recognised the toddler.

So Geoffrey had indeed been unable to keep his mouth shut; he simply hadn't come himself—hadn't even cared enough to do that. Reaper felt less betrayed than enlivened: at least something was finally happening. He took a step back, dragging the boy with one hand while he found the knife in his pocket with the other. The knife felt heavy and dense, eager to open and be about its work. Another step back, and still the policeman only watched. "Looks as if you aren't going to be locked up today," Reaper told the boy, and walked fast with him into the crowd.

Geoffrey must be on his way after all—must have persuaded the police not to get involved, only to alert him. When Reaper glanced back from within the sluggish enveloping crowd he saw that the policeman had stayed by the travel agent's to speak into a portable phone. Reaper had to make it to his car before he was cut off, and once he'd shaken off pursuit he could decide where to drive—hardly to the airport when the police would be bound to question the travel agent. He ducked to mutter in the boy's ear as he marched him round a corner. "This is what I call a game. Enjoy it while you can."

Once past the corner he straightened up. No more than two hundred yards away was an entrance to the car park. He began to weave between the strolling families, all of whom might have undertaken to delay him. Only a hundred yards now, but he felt as if he was slowing himself down by holding the boy at arm's length like a device to ward off the crowd. "Come here," he growled, mostly to convince himself that he could bear the closeness for a few seconds, and lifting the boy around the waist, hugged him. Then the crowd parted to reveal two policemen between him and the car park, and the boy's head nodded towards his. Before Reaper could thrust him away, the boy's mouth touched his cheek.

He felt the fat moist strips of flesh press against him. He hadn't had to suffer that experience since his grandfather's wake, but now it seemed he'd spent the years imagining how loathsome a repetition would be. It was. For a moment he didn't know what he was about to do—had absolutely no control of himself. He saw the policemen identify him and the boy and understand where he was heading. He flung the boy and his sticky squirming lips away, only just catching him by the tag, and veered aside as though he'd never had any intention of making for the car park. At once one of the policemen positioned himself in front of the entrance and spoke into his phone while his colleague started after Reaper. He might have reached his car if he'd kept on, but now he never would. The boy's kiss had trapped him.

He felt as if the town had lured him back to catch him, to distract him and ensnare him with the omnipresent smell of hot fat, the squeals of artificial terror from the fairground, the amplified

Bingo voices nicknaming numbers, the toys and souvenirs so cheap and uniform they caricatured themselves and their own appeal, the children burying their faces in pink fluff on sticks, the mob dressed like revellers at a drunken party larger than he could see beyond . . . He walked the boy at arm's length away from the pursuer, and saw the policeman he'd encountered outside the travel agent's pacing him. He heard a music-hall audience in a fish and chip cafe singing "How Much Is That Doggie in the Window," and even when he realised it was a tape his surroundings seemed poised to turn into a parody of his childhood. That was seizing him, trying to transform him into itself—or rather, into his own self that had been lurking within him all these years, waiting for him to lost control of the self he'd devoted so much time to becoming. He was in danger of feeling as small as the toddler while everything grew larger than him, overwhelmed him. "I'm not you," he said through his teeth. "That isn't me."

The toddler gazed at him with a mixture of trust and incomprehension, and Reaper felt tall again, yet to be beaten. He stared about, not bothering to acknowledge the policemen so long as he knew where they were. At the end of the street a family emerged from a doorway, the mother comforting a little girl for whom the adventure had been too intense, and Reaper knew instantly that was where he would bring the game to an end. "Look up," he told the boy. "Look all the way up. It'll be better than a roller coaster. I'll give us both a thrill if I never do anything else."

fifty-three

The Royal," said Geoff, and overtook a lorry that was over-taking a coach. "The Royal or the Palace."

He was almost there, and almost sure where he was going. Nobody had hindered him, and nobody appeared to have followed him. The landlady had even insisted that he take the mobile phone with him. At the airport a taxi had deposited him beneath the eye of the security camera, but the sound he'd heard rushing towards him had been only the wake of an airliner. Once he'd paid the attendant in his hut and the barrier had deferred to him, more than half an hour of suburbs had tethered him to forty miles an hour until at last a motorway had released him. Dozens of caravans were swaying towards the Lake District, and at times the traffic moved no faster than the suburbs had allowed. But now, an hour later, he was about to leave the motorway, and he knew the name of the hotel where Ben had been led to believe he was going to stay with the rest of the family had something to do with the crown. The Kings, with or without an apostrophe, or the Queens? He would know it when he saw it—he would if he remembered where to look.

His speed was halved by a roundabout, beyond which a slow road stretched above miles of streets. Ahead on the horizon he saw the dinosaur curves of a roller coaster, and a Big Wheel turning as though to scoop up the glittering sea, and dwarfing the fairground from half a mile away the tower, five hundred feet or more of it. They were separated by the promenade to which—he was sure of this at least—the street containing the hotel led. When he saw a sign for the promenade he swung the car into the side road.

It conveyed him to the fairground end, where it became apparent that the holidaymakers thought their numbers were enough to daunt the traffic. They strayed across the dual carriageway whenever the fancy took them, they stepped into the road without warning, they weren't averse to strolling ahead of vehicles for a laugh, especially if that made the horns blare at them. Groups of them were riding in carriages drawn by horses, others were patting animals at stands or jumping extravagantly clear of the production of manure, and all these were reasons why the traffic kept slowing to the pace of the train that was hauling itself up a slope of the roller coaster. At least the lack of speed let Geoff survey the side streets. It had been a long walk from the hotel to the fairground, he recalled now, and it had seemed just as far to the tower. Was that the street on the far side of the dual carriageway, beyond a fortune-teller's kiosk, or was it the next street, which was just as full of white hotels? When he saw a gap being held in the traffic by the lights of a pedestrian crossing, he swerved the car across the road.

A man stout enough to be hiding a barrel beneath his flowered shirt mimed not being able to cross the intersection in time, then not knowing which way to get out of Geoff's path. Geoff braked, braked again, and again—not this time for the man, who'd hopped with a parody of nimbleness onto the pavement, but at the sight of a hotel halfway along the right side. Wasn't that the one—the Crown? He'd driven up to it and was searching for somewhere to park before he noticed that it sported a small garden beside its front steps. All the hotels in the street did, and it took them to remind him that the place where he'd stayed hadn't had one.

He had to be close. He swung into the road that paralleled the promenade, and in a few hundred yards turned left again. The

Friendly, the Cardigan, the Princess—no, that wasn't it—the Bed-
sock, the Trencher . . . the Royal. The white facade seemed to
blaze brighter than its neighbours, and he groaned aloud, a sound
both of triumph and of frustration at not being able to see anywhere to park. There had been on the street he'd just turned out
of. He reversed at speed and swerved backwards round the corner
into the space he could only hope was far enough from the intersection to be legal. He snatched the keys and ducked out of the car,
barely remembering to lock it. He dashed along the hot white
street and grabbed the railing of the front steps, and was running
up them when he stopped as if a weight had fallen on him. Every
time he'd left or entered the hotel he had counted the steps, eight
of them: child-sized steps, he thought now. These steps were
higher, and there were only six.

Could they have been rebuilt? Even if the hall beyond the front
door didn't look familiar, would it after all these years? The door
would have to have been replaced, since the one he remembered
had contained no glass. He was wavering halfway up the steps—
he was trying to fend off the sudden dreadful thought that Ben
might have been even less able to recall the name and could be in
any of the hundreds of hotels—when a man in shirtsleeves and
baggy trousers held up by braces, altogether more like a seaside co-
median than a hotelier, waddled into the hall and saw him.

He protruded his lips in a sad grimace and shook his large
blunt head. When the mime didn't shift Geoff, he laboured to the
door and panted at hauling it open. "Can't do a thing for you at the
present, old boy," he wheezed. "Haven't so much as a mouse-hole
to offer you."

"I'm not looking for a room. I thought I stayed here once."

"I hope you had a fine time if you did."

"I don't think I did. Stay here, I mean. Not with these steps."

"They're as old as me at least. When do you think you were
here?"

"As a child. More than thirty years ago. I know the place is
round here. I was sure it was called the Royal."

"Well, now." The man stretched his braces with his thumbs as
though poising himself to joke. "Maybe it almost was."

"Don't think me rude, but this is urgent. If you can tell me anything—"

"You wouldn't by any chance have the Royalty in mind, would you?"

"Christ, that's it," Geoff all but shouted, and saw the man's head jerk back from the profanity. "Sorry. Where is it, do you know?"

"The next street but one towards the tower."

"Thanks." Geoff was already running down the steps. "Thanks," he said again from the pavement, and sprinted along the street. A phone was ringing somewhere, ringing louder as he ran. It was in the road where his car was parked. It was in his car.

He thrust the key into the lock and threw the door open and flung himself across the driver's seat to grab the phone from the floor. It shrilled twice before he was able to switch it on, and brought it to his face as he crouched awkwardly over the seat, the car roof bruising the back of his head. "Geoff Davenport," he gasped.

"Ware here, Mr. Davenport. We've located them."

Geoff tried to speak without taking the breath he needed. "Is my son all right?" he just about finished.

"I'm assured he is. I fear there's a time factor in getting you to them, though. They're in Blackpool."

"So am I. I figured out that was where they had to be."

"In that case I wish you'd told us."

That sounded less reproving than regretful, and Geoff was afraid to learn why. "What's he done?" he made himself say.

The policeman's voice was so neutral he might almost have been describing a holiday treat. "He's taken your son up the tower."

fifty-four

It took Geoff five minutes to drive to the entrance to the tower—far too much time for him to have to keep reflecting that five hundred feet was more insanely high than anybody had a right to build. Each reappearance of the tower above the roofs was taller. He saw how the massive ironwork rose from a five-storey building and tapered for hundreds of feet until it swelled into the iron cage of a viewing platform, around the outside of which lights were pursuing one another in an endless mindless dance. Surely the platform must be safer than it looked. Surely—although there were few things he was less anxious to imagine—the tower must have seen accidents or even deliberate falls during its lifetime, and would have been made safe because of them.

He braked as yet another surge of holidaymakers dared him not to stop for them, and saw three police cars bunched in front of the tower entrance. Passers-by were glancing at them, but a crowd had yet to gather. He jerked his car to a halt behind the nearest police vehicle, and a young policeman strode over. "You can't—" he said, then his expression withdrew into itself. "It's Mr. Davenport, isn't it? Leave your car there and I'll take you to the officer in charge."

It seemed a long time since Geoff had been recognised, and there was no pleasure or reassurance in it now. Several pedestrians stopped to watch as he followed the policeman into the building. A woman peered out of the box-office at him, so that he had a grotesque sense of being given free admission to a show. He followed the policeman through twin doors, past which the man's shirt collar glowed white as ghost-train bones and a huge grim face bumped against glass to bare its many teeth. In the black light fish with faces like masks carved to represent indifferent cruelty turned as if to watch Geoff. Beyond the aquarium, the heroes of video games talked to themselves beside a fortune-teller's empty booth. Geoff found himself wishing he could foretell just the next few hours, surely not even so much of his future, but was that because he was afraid to live it? The metal walls of a lift exhibited his anxious face wherever he looked as it raised him five storeys to a corridor. A sign pointed to the Tower Ride, but when he followed it he came out on a balcony above a ballroom in which, beneath a ceiling painted with figures borne up by gilded clouds, couples waltzed across a tiled floor to music from a stage. For a yearning moment Geoff felt as if he'd stepped into the past—into a past where Paul was in no danger, where such things never happened— and then the electronic keyboard ceased being an orchestra and fell silent with a rattle of percussion, and several policemen set about ushering the bewildered dancers off the floor. "They're the last of the public in the building," Geoff's escort confided.

At the far end of the balcony a short corridor led to the lifts up the tower. Three policemen were distributed around a maze of railings intended to train the public back and forth across the carpet to the lifts. One, a broad-shouldered man with a wide face and a chin no less square than his crew cut hairline, came to Geoff at once and gave him a strong succinct handshake. "Mace, Mr. Davenport. I'm in charge. Are you ready to go up?"

"Can you tell me—"

"Of course. I was about to. I've men on the lowest level, and Davenport is on the next one."

"And my son? How's my son?"

"He's unharmed. We're keeping an eye on that with the security cameras. Davenport says he'll do no harm so long as nobody but you goes up."

Geoff thought of asking to see what the cameras showed, but he was already making for the lift the young policeman had opened on his behalf. "You've agreed to that with him," he said.

"For the moment, Mr. Davenport. Once you—"

"What do you mean? What are you planning to do? If he says it has to be just me—"

"I assure you we'll do nothing that we think may put your son at risk. I was going to say that once you're able to distract your brother, I propose to send men up the outside."

"You don't think that's a risk?"

"Less of one than leaving the drop unprotected."

"You're telling me it isn't safe up there?"

"Not entirely, Mr. Davenport. There are ways a motivated person could overcome the safety measures that are in place. I appreciate we might have been able to detain your brother before he got this far."

That only made Geoff feel helplessly guilty for having persuaded them to hold back. "It mightn't have been advisable."

"I believe that's all then if you're ready."

"Let's do it," Geoff said as if sounding like someone in a film might help, and stepped into the lift to send it upwards.

An emptiness that would have held several dozen people accompanied him. Through the windows on the two long sides he saw massive iron lattices falling away. In seconds they and the glass were all that stood between him and the town that was plummeting below him. Catwalks sailed past him, each of them exposing a wider view of the toys the town and its contents were becoming, cars he could pick up in handfuls, people so minute that any attempt to catch hold of them would crush them. He knew these thoughts were ploys on the part of his mind to fend off a sense of how high the lift had already taken him. A sea as wide as the horizon tugged again and again with its glittering ripples at the beach, an insistence that reminded Geoff of a child's bid for attention, a

small hand pulling at a large one. His own hands flexed themselves at the memory and found nothing but air to hold. Then the
lift glided to a halt, and the doors let in a wind as chill as winter.

He felt the sweat grow icy on his palms as he stepped into a
wooden shelter that opened onto a platform surrounding this level
of the tower. Above the chest-high railing of the platform, spikes
curved outwards higher than his head. A heavy net enclosed the
railings and the spikes and stretched overhead to within a foot of
the outside of the shelter. That gap robbed Geoff of any sense of
safety, and so did several holes torn in the net—holes no larger
than a child's fist, but evidence that the fabric could be damaged.
Two policemen were standing at the foot of a narrow spiral staircase beside a sign that said UP ONLY. "Mr. Davenport," one murmured, and the other whispered "They're at the top."

"The top?"

"Of these stairs," the first policeman clarified.

So it wasn't as bad as it might be, Geoff tried to reassure himself. He gave the policemen a nod that was intended to convince
them he was in control but didn't work for him. "Don't follow me.
Wait here," he said, taking hold of the spiral banister, which wasn't
much less cold than ice. He planted a foot on the lowest step with
a faint clank, and a voice came down to meet him. "Geoffrey, don't
say that's you at last."

"It's me all right," Geoff called—he didn't know how loud.

"We're waiting just for you."

Geoff let go of the banister and ran up the twisting stairs. A
blue sky draped with white clouds spun around him, the metal
treads clanged and shook beneath him, and he found his mind filling with clichés from old crime films. "Don't shoot, you'll hit the
kid." "Don't be a fool." "Don't hurt him. I'll do anything." Perhaps
the last one wasn't from a film, because now Geoff was at the top
of the stairs and could see the reality.

A man was standing on a platform outside a shelter like the one
below, with Paul perched on his shoulders. The man's face and
scalp were shaved smooth, and he wore rectangular metal spectacles. He began to smile at the sight of Geoff but stopped short of

halfway, as if the expression was intended solely for himself. In that moment Geoff recognised him—saw traces of his own face within the other man's, pinched thin and almost hidden. "Ben," he said.

Ben seemed not to think that worthy of a response, but Paul did. He'd beamed at seeing his father, so that Geoff had to restrain himself from running to lift him off Ben's shoulders. Now the boy looked bewildered, and made a sound that was close to the name. "Do you think he's talking to you, Ben?" the man who was holding both of his hands said.

Dismay at this jerked Geoff forward a step. "What have you done to him?"

"No closer, Geoffrey. That isn't the way these things are done. Didn't your friends in the police tell you that? Didn't they give you any advice how to take me off guard?" Ben moved back, placing a window between himself and Geoff, and glanced up at the gap between the safety netting and the shelter. "Shall we show Geoffrey a climbing game, Ben?"

It was only a threat, Geoff told himself, and then he saw that if Paul stood on his captor's shoulders he would be able to catch hold of the edge of the netting and haul himself onto it. "Don't," he pleaded. "Stay as you are, Paul. You wouldn't do that, Ben. There's no reason."

He saw Paul identify with his name as Ben's smile grew broader and more introverted. "I've got to have a reason, have I, Geoffrey? What have my reasons been all along, then?"

"The things that were done to you. The ways you were treated that I couldn't stop. I know that's what you meant the first time you called me. I understand." Geoff wanted to leave it at that for Paul's sake, but Ben's eyes were observing that he hadn't finished, telling him that wasn't enough. "Only none of that is an excuse for what you've been doing," he said. "Is that what you want me to say?"

"You think you know me, do you, Geoffrey? You think you know everything that's happened to me."

"If I don't, you tell me," Geoff said, advancing to the doorway of the shelter, only a few yards away from Ben, all that distance.

"Let's have that window out of the way. I'm sick of having to talk to you through one thing or another."

"Don't you think it's a bit late for us to get together after all that's happened to us both?"

"If it is, you tell me why I'm here," Geoff said, and saw Ben glance upwards and smile to himself. The wind, which was even stronger on this second level, was snatching at Paul's hair as if to demonstrate how it would play with him once he was on the net overhead. Geoff had to swallow before he could say "Tell me if there's something I don't know that you want me to know."

He was trying to judge how fast he would need to move so as to grab Paul before his captor could place him out of reach. Perhaps his thoughts showed in the way he was keeping his face under control, because Ben said "Don't play for time, Geoffrey. Don't waste mine."

"I'm not trying to. If you want me—"

"I've already told it once. I'm not repeating myself."

Absurdly, Geoff felt rebuffed. "Who've you told?"

"Who else but little Ben here. You don't mind if I call him that for old times' sake, do you?" Ben jogged the boy on his shoulders and turned his eyes towards him. "You remember our talk in the night, don't you, Ben? You were my best listener."

Geoff hadn't taken the step that would launch him at Paul while Ben's attention was on the boy when the eyes levelled themselves at him, and the smile grew stretched and bloodless. "No, no, Geoffrey. Stay right there. Try that again and you won't sleep for years. You'll lie awake thinking what you should have done, how you should have waited and then you might still have him."

Geoff swayed as a gust of wind like an exhalation from a walk-in freezer caught his face. He grabbed the edge of the doorway to steady himself. Paul giggled at the thump of his hand on the wood or the spectacle of his unsteadiness, and Ben cocked his head but not his eyes towards the boy. "What's that? Do you want to tell Geoffrey the secret I told you?"

After years of urging Paul to speak, Geoff was suddenly afraid he would say too much—would say something Ben might react against. "He won't tell. He can't. If you aren't going to, Ben," he said, digging his nails into the weathered timber, "why did you want me to find you at all?"

"He's asking why he's here."

Geoff had a panicky sense of being about to be shown rather than told. Ben had let go of Paul's right hand. Instead of lifting the boy, however, he gestured as though offering himself to Geoff. "Maybe I just wanted you to see me."

"I have. I do. So . . ."

"So describe me to myself. Presentation's your job, isn't it? Tell me what you see."

Geoff gazed at him. He had no idea what his own expression was; as far as he was concerned now, it could only tell the truth. "My brother," he said.

"Good try, Geoffrey. Terse and meaningful, but just a shade late. Very professional, though. Isn't he, Ben?"

"I'm not trying to trick you. I never have."

"Never?" Ben said, and raised Paul until the boy's knees were resting on his shoulders. "Careful, Geoffrey. Don't tell me things I know are wrong. I've never been your brother, and we both know it. That's what never means. Now we've rid ourselves of that misunderstanding, what do you really see?"

"Someone terribly sad."

"Sad."

That was Paul, and Ben cocked his head again. "Someone agrees with you. I thought him and me were getting on together, but now it turns out he's all yours."

"He doesn't understand. He's just repeating what he hears. Don't hold that against him."

Ben ducked away from the weight of the child. "You'd say anything, wouldn't you, Geoffrey?"

"What else would you expect when you're threatening him? Give him to me and I promise I'll stay up here with you. I won't let anyone else near till we've talked. We'll really talk."

Ben freed one hand to point at the security camera above the shelter. Paul wobbled on his shoulders and made a grab at the air—at the net, for the moment out of reach. "And how long do you think they'll wait because you say so?" Ben said.

"I don't know, but I'll speak up for you. I'll make sure they know everything that's happened to you, everything I know, and whatever the rest was if you tell me."

"Why, Geoffrey, I thought you said I couldn't use it as an excuse."

"You shouldn't, but maybe other people will. They ought to know what was behind all you've done."

He no longer knew how convinced or convincing he sounded, and Ben's face wasn't telling him. Geoff was gazing at Paul, and doing his best to smile at him to persuade both the boy and himself that everything was under control, when he heard Ben say "Can I trust you, Geoffrey?"

Geoff's gaze sank to meet his. "Who else can you?"

"Who indeed," Ben said, and glanced up at Paul without lifting his face, so that he appeared to be peering inside his own skull. "Then will you do something for me? You wouldn't want me doing it and risking him."

"Anything," Geoff was almost desperate enough to say. "What?" he said.

"Look over the edge and tell me if anyone's on their way up."

Geoff strode to the railings and stared down. Hundreds of feet beneath him, several uniformed figures were hurrying along the next to lowest catwalk. For a moment he didn't know what to say; he was losing his balance, and with it his ability to think. "There's nobody," he said, and swung round. Ben was nowhere to be seen.

The sky blazed like lightning around Geoff, the blinding sea tried to pluck his sight from him. He dashed to the corner of the shelter. The stretch of platform beyond it was deserted, but he heard a sound that terrified him: Paul's giggle. The wind was playing with it somewhere beyond the railings. The shock forced all the breath out of him. As he struggled to refill his lungs, Ben's voice came to him. "You can't stop it, Geoffrey."

It was above him, on the highest level. Geoff looked up so quickly that pain impaled his neck, but he couldn't see Paul or his captor through the net, which seemed all at once flimsy and narrow and utterly inadequate. He slithered and nearly fell on the slippery boards as he ran into the shelter. A policeman's face was

inching above the lower stairway, and one of his colleagues was audibly following him. "Go down," Geoff cried for Ben to hear.

"Down," Paul said in the wind.

"Down," Ben agreed with him.

There was more to his tone than agreement. There was en-
couragement, and Geoff was meant to hear it. He flailed his hands
to drive the policeman back—he had to restrain himself from kicking out at him. As the man's head retreated downwards, Geoff ran
to the stairs that led to the highest platform. "I'm coming up,
Ben," he shouted. "Nobody else, I swear."

"That's right, Geoffrey. This game is just for us."

Geoff had a dreadful sense of knowing which game that might
be. He flung himself up the clanking stairs, which shivered on his
behalf. The wind did its best to throw him backwards as he hauled
himself onto the top platform, but it wasn't only the wind that
made him feel suddenly trapped in ice.

The platform was half the size of the one below it, and had neither a shelter nor railings. A wall no higher than his chest surrounded it. Above the wall, safety netting twice as high bellied and
shook with the wind. A hole had been cut in the netting. Ben had
cut it with the knife he'd laid on top of the wall. The hole was big
enough for Paul to pass through—to have done so. He was clinging to the outside of the net below it, level with Ben's head.

He looked unsure of himself: a little proud, a little unhappy. He
was wriggling his fingers as if the mesh had begun to dig into
them. Geoff lurched towards him, but Ben held up a hand without
bothering to glance at Geoff. "Don't move too fast, Geoffrey.
Don't make him jump."

"Get hold of him, then. Bring him back in. I've sent the police
down. I hadn't told them to come up."

"I believe you." Ben turned to him, unsmiling, hardly even interested. "You needn't have sent them away. We've finished our
talk. I know what I wanted to know."

A wind flapped Paul's shirt and dragged him outwards. The
wire creaked as though the hole was preparing to tear itself bigger,
dropping the section of net to which Paul was clinging. Geoff took
a step across the ten feet that separated them, and Ben flattened a

hand in the air inches short of Paul's chest. "Stay there, Geoffrey. All he wants is a push."

"You wouldn't, Ben. Not to a child. Not to him."

"You think you know me that well, do you, Geoffrey?"

"I know I do. There'd be no point. Whatever you've done to adults, there's no reason for you to harm a child."

Ben blinked at him as though Geoff had caught his interest. "Especially yours, is that what you're arguing?"

"You said you'd been able to talk to him. You've some feeling for him, I can tell. He's your nephew, you know. Anyone could see that when you were holding him. You wouldn't—"

"I did well, didn't I? I always do."

That was when Paul took his left hand off the net to flex his fingers. He was dangling backwards from a solitary hand five hundred feet up, and didn't seem to care or even know. He began to kick at the netting as his face threatened to crumple with the pain of holding on. Geoff stumbled forward and saw Ben's palm jerk towards the boy's chest. Then Paul clutched at the mesh and was holding on with both hands. "You didn't answer my question, Geoffrey," Ben said. "Don't you have some praise for me? Aren't you impressed?"

"By—I don't—"

"By how I handled him. Haven't you understood yet? You thought I looked happy to be holding him, did you?"

"You did, so please for his sake—"

"I did. Well done, you should be telling me. Maybe even a round of applause. My last performance and my best. Do you know what the worst part always is?"

"Tell me when he's safe. Let me—"

"Listen to me. See me clear for once." Ben's playful smile did away with itself, leaving a weariness not far removed from boredom. "The worst part is touching anyone. Every time I have to do it it gets worse," he said, and grimaced as he planted his hand on Paul's chest and shoved.

Paul's eyes and mouth gaped with surprise, but he looked determined to hang onto the netting. Geoff sprinted across the platform to grab his hands, to hug him through the net, to— He

hadn't halved the distance between himself and Paul when the
boy's fingers lost their grip. He sailed backwards, and then there
was only the empty mesh fluttering in the chill wind.

All Geoff's breath left him. All his body ached with waiting for
the terrible protracted silence to be brought to an end by a thud
far below. He collided with the wall of the platform, scraping his
knees, and saw Ben pick up the knife to fend him off. Ben's face was
so unafraid that it was clear he wasn't guarding himself against an
attack, he was simply warding off the possibility of being touched.
Geoff seized the cold hard edge of the metal wall and made himself lean out. He'd scarcely begun to inch forward when, as if the
wind was playing a last cruel ghostly trick, he heard Paul's giggle
beneath him.

He lurched across the wall, pressing his face into the mesh.
Paul was lying on his back on top of the netting above the middle
platform—lying so close to the edge that his right hand was hanging over it. The enormous bright sea surged towards it and withdrew, leaving it to the wind to take him by the hand and pull him
over the edge. "Paul," Geoff called, and sucked in a breath to fight
the wind that wasn't letting his voice reach the toddler. "Paul, don't
move. Stay absolutely still."

The police must surely be able to see Paul through one of the
security cameras. Now that he was out of Ben's reach they had no
reason not to save him—every reason to—but there was no sign
of them. "Wait for me, Paul," Geoff shouted as the boy saw him
and grinned up at him. "Wait there just like that. I'm coming
down."

He thought he could do that—he thought Ben had finished
his game and wouldn't try to harm Paul further—until Ben called
out too. "Don't just lie there, Ben. Look down and you'll see
you've got an audience. They want to watch you fly. Show Geoffrey you can."

Upturned faces were indeed gathering on the promenade,
dozens of faces like grains of sand. "Don't look," Geoff cried. "Stay
still."

Perhaps the wind let only his second word reach Paul, unless
it was the gust flapping the net that made Paul move. He rolled

onto his right side and was no more than half his arm's length from the edge. Geoff heard him gasp at the sight of the drop, then start to whimper. "Roll over," he yelled, cupping his hands around his mouth, feeling as if he was trying to send his innards through the megaphone of them. "Roll away from the edge. Roll onto your left side. Just turn over."

The toddler had frozen—was as still as Geoff had wanted him to stay before. His left hand was gripping the net above his head so hard it looked capable of snapping the mesh. "Don't turn away now," Ben called down. "Just let go and you'll fly. Look, I'll show you. See these fly. I don't need them any more."

He hadn't finished speaking when an object hurtled down at Paul. Geoff thought Ben had flung the knife, and then he saw he'd dropped the spectacles. They sailed past Paul's outstretched hand, and Geoff saw the boy lean out to catch them—saw this only in his imagination, but that was dreadful enough. The spectacles vanished from sight, and seconds later Geoff heard a minute click as they hit the roof of the building that housed the base of the tower. Still grasping the net, Paul turned his face up to see where the missile had come from. "That's it, Paul," Geoff shouted. "Keep on turning. Just—"

"Just feel the wind between your fingers, Ben. That's how it'll feel when you fly. Stretch your hand out further and then—"

It was unclear which shout Paul heard: perhaps part of both. His right hand waved in the air as if feeling for the drop beyond the net, and then his left hand relinquished its hold on the mesh. Tentatively, almost lazily, his right foot strayed over the edge.

"Hold on," Geoff yelled in a voice that felt like sand in his throat. "Get hold. Turn the other way. Look at me, Paul. Turn like this."

"Catch the wind, Ben. Give it a kick." Ben was pointing the knife at Geoff's eyes in case Geoff lunged at him to silence him. "That's my boy," he called. "Show Geoffrey something to re-member after he's come all this way to see you. That's it, you're nearly there, it'll be like nothing you've ever felt, just—"

Both of Paul's feet swung out over the drop. Neither of his hands was holding on. The left hand made a convulsive grab for support. His finger and thumb closed around a single strand of the mesh. It must have been weakened. It snapped with a sound the wind bore away from the tower. Caught by the gust, his legs slewed into space.

"Hold," Geoff cried, too late—too late for Paul to obey him, far too late for Geoff to reach him. Then a policewoman darted into sight beneath the net. She seized the railings under Paul and heaved herself up with one hand. She stretched the other high and was just able to touch him with her fingertips—nowhere near enough. With a final effort she hauled herself inches further, her knees shivering as she gripped the railing between them, and shoved her knuckles against his hip-bone. The shove sent him rolling across the net to within inches of the gap alongside the top of the shelter.

Geoff closed his eyes for an instant of prayer too profound to be encompassed in words and then raced for the stairs. Five seconds took him down them and out of the shelter. He held out his arms beneath the gap as Paul, having seen him, risked a shaky smile. "Let yourself drop, Paul. I'm here to catch you."

The boy crawled to the edge of the gap and stared down. He looked as frightened as he might have been above the outer drop—frightened enough to retreat towards it without realising he was. "I've got you, Paul," Geoff insisted, cupping his hands towards him. Still the boy didn't move: not until the policewoman let herself down onto the platform with a thud. He must have been afraid she was going to poke him again, because without further ado he rolled over the edge and fell into Geoff's arms.

He weighed less than Geoff remembered. He was tousled and clammy and not very washed, and above everything else he was Paul. Geoff hugged the boy to him, and had to restrain himself from squeezing the breath out of him. He saw several policemen run up the stairs, but their activity no longer meant anything to him—not until he heard Ben's voice overhead. "Aren't you going to save me too, Geoffrey?"

"Would you expect me to now?" Geoff said, and looked up. Ben had enlarged the hole enough to climb out himself, and was standing on top of the wall of the highest platform, gazing across the sea to the horizon. Perhaps it was only the flapping of his trousers in the wind that made his legs appear to be trembling. He glanced down at Geoff with a smile that might have been playful or wistful or reminiscent or a last indication that he proposed to keep the secret that was himself. "You're right, I'm not worth it. I never was," he said, and sprang off his perch.

As he fell past Geoff he folded his arms and shut his eyes. For a moment he appeared to be reclining on the air. The seascape glittered around him. Then he vanished, leaving Geoff to stare at the miles of sunlit waves that immediately set about erasing where he'd been. The thump Geoff heard was so minute he thought it couldn't have been made by the fall of the smallest child. It was greeted by a chorus of microscopic screams. He'd hidden Paul's face against his chest at the sight of Ben on the wall, and he kept the boy there as he leaned between the railings to press his forehead against the net. Paul's rapid little heartbeats seemed infinitely more real than the view down the length of the tower of a doll sprawled face down on the roof, until he saw that part of it was moving. Around the head, extending so far that its size seemed almost miraculous, was a halo of shining crimson.

fifty-five

Since Geoff had left the mobile in the car, he was allowed to use the phone in an office off the ballroom. Signed photographs of stage and television personalities watched over him while he waited for the hospital to put him through to Gail. As soon as he heard her voice he said "I've got Paul. He's safe."

"Thank—" A thought must have interrupted her, because she said "Only safe?"

"He's fine," Geoff said as Paul twirled himself around in a swivel chair behind the broad old desk. "Thank God he's too young to understand."

"And Ben?"

"He's dead."

She greeted the information with a silence that felt like the emptiness the name produced in Geoff. After a pause she said "Are you bringing him?"

She meant Paul, of course. "I imagine so," he said, then realised he had absolutely no sense of what might be expected of him now. "Let me check."

He went to the door and cleared his throat. The policewoman

and a colleague were waltzing gravely to no music in the middle of the deserted ballroom. They parted and marched over to him, their faces turning professional at once. "Am I going to be able to take my son to his mother?" Geoff said.

The policewoman used the phone at her belt to bring Mace to him. "We'll find you if you need to ask you any questions, Mr. Davenport. Only forgive me, but you don't look fit to drive."

The notion that the family wouldn't be reunited until Geoff had slept was unbearable. "What am I going to do?"

"Under all the circumstances I think we can spare a driver to run you where exactly?"

"Scotland."

"Too far for you in your condition," Mace said as if the distance he was undertaking to convey the Davenports hadn't taken him aback. "I think we'd better get you moving before the press start gathering. Leave me the keys to your car and I'll have it taken care of."

Geoff explained it was a hired car that could be returned to the local branch, then he led Paul after their driver. "We're going to see mummy. We're going in a police car," he said as they emerged into the sunlight. While he dodged after the policeman through a crowd of people staring up at the tower and exchanging progressively inaccurate versions of events, he had a fleeting sense of Ben above him on the roof, or rather of the absence Ben had become. For just a moment he wanted to tell the crowd some kind of truth. Then the impulse was gone, and the driver was opening the rear door of the nearest police car.

Once Geoff's safety belt was secured he hugged Paul to him. The boy blinked at souvenir shops cruising past, and then he was asleep. Geoff interlocked his fingers and held Paul in the crook of his left arm, and let his awareness rest on the peaceful regular breaths of the small body in his care, every breath a reason to rejoice. His breathing settled down to pace Paul's, and soon he couldn't distinguish the boy's from his own.

Something like a cry wakened him. Though he hadn't been dreaming, he wasn't sure which of them had uttered it. They were

on the motorway, racing along the edge of a drop of a hundred feet
or more to a stream. Paul was staring through the window while
he tried to climb on Geoff's lap. "All right, son, he's there now,"
the driver said.

"Here I am, Paul. Snuggle close. What was he saying? Was it
for long?"

"He only just started. He was calling for you. For his pa."

"You've got him," Geoff assured him, and promised himself he
wouldn't fall asleep again. He kept his stare on the majestically
advancing landscape as it produced peak after peak. Then everything was still: the car, the driver gazing back at him, the trustful
arms around his neck. It was an hour later, and the car was in front
of a hospital.

"Any time you're ready, Mr. Davenport," the driver said
through the open door. Geoff thanked him, and having eased Paul
into the sunlight without wakening him, was making for the hospital entrance when the driver raised a thumb and mouthed "Good
luck."

Geoff had forgotten how much goodwill he might need. All he
knew was that he was bringing Paul back safe. He succeeded in
rousing his legs enough that they ceased stumbling as he approached the enquiry desk. The clerk was visibly less than charmed
by the unkempt tousled father who'd allowed his son to get into
the same state until Geoff named himself, at which she beamed
and indicated a corridor as a preamble to striking up an urgent
conversation with a nurse as soon as Geoff was on his way. Geoff
did his best to shoulder doors aside without jarring Paul awake, but
the toddler began to stir and practise opening his eyes. As Geoff
pushed open the door to the ward Paul's arms loosened around his
neck. "Mr. Davenport?" the sister said, emerging from her office.
"Your wife's with her father. He's just come round."

"That's good news, isn't it?" Geoff told Paul, and ventured into
the ward. He saw Gail and her father at once, beyond the open side
of a screen. She was murmuring to him and stroking his hands
while he did his best to focus on her. His lips were pink as a heal-
ing wound, and as wrinkled and uneven as one. Geoff winced and

hung back, painfully unsure of how Gail might react to his presence. Then Paul said "Mum" no more than conversationally, and
both Gail and her father turned to look.

She saw Paul first, and gave him a smile that couldn't begin to
express what she felt. She held it for some seconds before she
raised her eyes to Geoff. There was gratitude beyond words in
her eyes, and a kind of resignation. That was enough to let him go
to her and place Paul in her arms, but he hadn't touched her when
he stepped back.

"Thanks, Geoff," she said—perhaps only, he thought, for his
reticence. She held out a hand towards him, then grasped air with
her fist and wrapped her arms around Paul, burying her nose and
mouth in his hair. "When did you last have a wash or your hair
brushed?" she eventually said. "Just come and say hi to grandad
and then your father can take you and make you halfway to presentable."

Geoff couldn't have wished for more. He watched as Gail's father blinked slowly but determinedly at Paul. "Here he is. I feel
better already. Bottle him so I can take him with me," the old man
said with not too much difficulty as he attempted to smile, baring
the teeth at the corners of his stiffened lips. Then his gaze wavered
and turned aside, searching. "Where's Bebe gone?"

"Gone," said Paul, and giggled at the noise his mother was unable to suppress.

fifty-six

He was standing on the pavement opposite the house outside which two police cars were parked. The fringe of red hair poking out from his turned-around baseball cap looked artificial as a clown's wig. As the car wash on the corner of the street hissed at a vehicle, Geoff imagined for a moment that the man was emitting the sound. He barely glanced at the other before striding up the steps to the house. Whoever the man was, he didn't look like anyone Geoff would want to know. Geoff stretched out a hand and with just a second's hesitation—more than made any sense to him—rang Ben's doorbell.

He heard a window slide up overhead, and another. He retreated a step and stared upwards. Whoever had looked out of Ben's window had vanished. A woman was frowning at him from the flat below it, then she too disappeared with a slam of the sash and began talking in a high shrill voice that could only be addressed to a child. Geoff still felt watched, and was in a mood to confront the man on the pavement opposite when the front door was opened by a policewoman. "Mr. Davenport. Come up."

He followed her along the hall, whose walls were the glossy

white of a hospital or a morgue, and up the stairs. He'd just set foot
on the middle landing when the woman who had spied on him
from the window opened her door to watch him. She seemed to
decide against folding her arms, instead letting her hands rest protectively on the swollen midriff of her long loose black dress.
"You're Mr. Denton's brother, aren't you? Except he wasn't really
called that. He had your name."

"I won't deny it."

"We've seen your shows," the woman said, not necessarily expressing admiration. "Are you going to make one about him?"

"People keep asking me that. All I can say at this stage is I'm
not sure. At the moment we're busy with a supermarket I can't
name." If he had time before he went to work on the American
channel once Gail's father was well enough to travel back with
them—that was assuming they still both wanted Geoff with them,
whatever they were generous enough to say now. . . . "I do think
I'd be able to tell more of the truth about him than anyone else,"
he said.

"Who'd want to know?"

"Everyone who read a paper he was on the front page of, you
might think."

"That was because they cared about your little boy. They
weren't interested in your brother."

Geoff very much doubted that, but could see why she might
think so. "I suppose if I helped people understand, or made them
more alert—"

"People never are, not ordinary people. Don't you think I
should have noticed, living right under him?" She worked her
shoulders nervously and clasped her fingers over the egg of herself.
"He's best forgotten. He tried so hard not to draw attention to
himself, he should get his wish."

Geoff might have queried her assumption, but to what purpose? Besides, she had turned on the little girl who'd wandered
into sight behind her, swinging a doll by one floppy arm. "I said
stay in the big room, Valerie. We're just talking about Mr. Denton,
about the nasty things he did. It's not for you to hear."

"Maybe they were like dreams because he couldn't sleep," the little girl said.

"She has some strange ideas. I don't want them getting any stranger. We'll be moving once her dad comes back from the oil rig. Go and play with Squashy now, Valerie, when you're told. Remember you've a mummy and a daddy to see you're safe."

The woman turned back to Geoff before she'd finished speaking. She'd made him remember how sullen and resentful Paul kept seeming, as though he was missing someone. "My wife didn't know he existed till nearly the end," he said. "I let her think I was an only child."

"You must have wanted to be," the woman said, and closed her door. There was nowhere for Geoff to go except up to the flat where he could imagine she felt he belonged. He followed the policewoman, who had loitered discreetly, to the top floor. But once he stepped into Ben's flat he had no sense at all of Ben.

The walls of the corridor were the faded green of leaves about to brown, lit by sunlight through the four rooms. Several policemen were scattered through the flat, apparently at a loss for anything to examine. Perhaps they were helping the place to feel as if it had hardly been inhabited, despite all the suits in the wardrobe and other clothes in the chest of drawers that were the only bedroom furniture besides the single bed with a white pillow flattened by tight white sheets. All the furniture looked anonymous, secondhand though not shabby. In the bathroom, which smelled of the enamel bath if of anything, a white towel was draped over a rail, and some toiletries and dyes occupied a cupboard. They struck Geoff as being no more personal than the tins of food in the kitchen cupboards and the frozen dinners in the refrigerator a policeman was closing. Now only the main room was left—the living-room—and he braced himself to encounter signs of Ben's secret life. But on the green carpet was simply a chair facing a television and video recorder, and on the wall above the screen a mirror. He was trying to conjure up some sense of how Ben might have spent his time here when the doorbell rang.

At once he felt like an intruder—felt as if the tenant had returned to find his flat invaded. When the policewoman hauled the window up, he hurried to join her. A figure in a baseball cap was standing on the steps. "Can I help you?" the policewoman called. The peak of the cap tipped backwards, raising the face. Before Geoff had time to realise that the clenching of his innards meant he was irrationally afraid whom he might see, he saw it was the red-headed man who had been watching the house. The man flattened a hand where the front of the cap should be and squinted at Geoff. "I knew your brother."

Geoff gripped the sill with both hands. "Knew him when?"

"Do you want the street to hear this, or am I coming up?"

"No reason why he can't, is there?" Geoff said to the police. "He might be able to tell us something."

What appeared to be identities of Ben's from before the year he'd worked at Twenty-four Hour Knights had begun to surface. Geoff found himself growing uneasy as a policeman went downstairs and came back with his footsteps doubled. He saw the red-haired man enter Ben's corridor, still wearing the cap as he might have in his own home, and stroll towards him. His attention lingered in each of the rooms before coming to rest on Geoff. "That does it," he said. "That's what I expected. Seen what I wanted to see."

He looked anything but struck. More than one of the police would have questioned him if Geoff hadn't been faster. "Who are you exactly? Don't tell me you're press."

"That's your game, isn't it? Wouldn't want to be involved in it myself. I don't make up stories." When Geoff let that go the man said "Told you I knew him. He got between me and my girlfriend Jessy. She works for the last rank he worked for. You've spoken to her more than once."

That sounded like a challenge too, but Geoff only nodded. "He tried to scare me off, but he couldn't," the man said. "Took me for a ride in his cab, and then he found out who he was dealing with. Didn't dare touch me. Matter of fact, I think I scared him off."

"You didn't mention it to anyone."

"Didn't seem worth it at the time. We're a bit alike that way, aren't we, you and me? No way else, though."

"Maybe if you'd told someone there might be fewer dead now."

"I don't think so, mate. I think I'm looking straight at the geezer to blame for all that."

As Geoff lapsed into silence the most senior of the policemen said "Was there anything you felt we ought to know, Mr. . . . ?"

"I just wanted to see where our friend's brother lived. So arrest me if you can come up with a charge," he said, not looking away from Geoff. "He was nothing much, and this place shows it. He couldn't get what he wanted, so he took it out on other people. Didn't work with me, though."

"There was more to him than that," Geoff said.

"Less, you mean. Less than you media fellers are trying to build him up into. I'll tell you one thing, though. Nobody messes with me once they know I got the best of him," the man said, and laughed in Geoff's face.

Geoff was aware of several uniformed figures converging on him. He didn't know if they intended to shut the man up or prevent what Geoff was about to do to him. Then the moment was past, and Geoff opened his shaking fists. "I think you'd better leave, sir," the policewoman said.

"Since it's you and you're asking so nicely, love."

Geoff turned away before the man did. When he heard the downstairs door slam he crossed to the window and watched the man swagger away in search of the next confrontation. "It's never just the crime someone commits," the policewoman said beside Geoff. "It's the traces of themselves they leave in other people."

Geoff was wondering how that might apply to him when a policeman said across the room "Here's something. Mr. Davenport, it's you."

As Geoff twisted round, the television used his voice. "For most of us childhood is a place we had to leave, but for some it's a place they may never escape from . . ." It was the edition of *The Goods* about the children's home, and his introduction sounded insufferably glib to him. "You don't want to watch me, do you?" he pleaded. "Can we fast-forward to see if there's anything significant?"

The policeman who had switched it on handed him the remote control, and Geoff sped the tape past far too many images of himself among the blurred swaying nervous footage of the children's home and the accounts of victims who'd grown up. The end titles climbed the screen at last, taking Geoff's name with them, and then there was only teeming static. Since the counter had ceased to count, he knew the rest of the tape was blank. He switched off the static and lifted his gaze, and saw his own face.

Ben would have seen his face there whenever he watched television, he thought—and then he knew it wouldn't quite have been under these conditions. "Could you draw the curtains for a moment?"

The policewoman looked hard at him before she complied. At once his face in the mirror turned green as death. That was how Ben would have seen his—Ben's unreal face hovering above Geoff's as the latter talked about children who weren't Ben, as it exhorted the viewers to care about them; Ben's face elevated above the children and their suffering, but also excluded from their number. For an instant Geoff felt close to finally understanding Ben, felt he was sharing at least one of his secrets. In that moment, no longer than it took him to blink, he saw Ben's face look at him out of the mirror.

"That isn't it," he told the policewoman. "I don't know what I had in mind." He stood up as the uncurtained sunlight blazed into the room. "Thanks for letting me come," he said, "but I don't know if I should have." He saw himself turning away from the mirror, taking Ben's face with him inside his own. It had always been there, always would be, and he could only acknowledge it— must never deny it again, because doing so would give it power over him. He hurried downstairs, out of the shadow of the building, into the relentless spotlight of the sun. He wouldn't slow down until he was home, where there were people who might know him better than he felt he knew himself.